"No man challenges a woman to a duel!"

"You're wrong, Anya. Men and women challenge each other all the time."

"Not with sabers or pistols or—"

"Maybe not," Morgan interrupted. "But they use other, perhaps more lethal, weapons."

Anya tried to capture and make sense of his confusing statements, but her head spun. "For you, words are weapons."

"You're armed, too, Anya—with beckoning eyes, a gracefully beckoning body, and softly beckoning lips. *Are* you beckoning me?"

She stared at the strong fingers that gripped her sleeve. Standing so close to him, she felt the heat of his breath on her cheek, felt the heat from his hard body radiating toward her and felt an answering heat rise within her.

"What do you want?" she asked softly, tremulously.

"Satisfaction."

"In the form of a—a duel?"

"In the form of a kiss."

Dear Reader,

April brings us a new title from Lynda Trent, *Rachel*. In this Victorian love story, a young, impetuous woman falls for a mysterious man with more than a few skeletons in his closet.

With her book *The Garden Path*, we welcome Kristie Knight to Harlequin Historicals. When Thalia Freemont marries a handsome sea captain to escape her scheming brother, her new husband turns the tables on her.

A courtship that begins with a poker game soon blossoms into full-blown passion in Pat Tracy's *The Flaming*. A contemporary romance author, Pat's first historical is guaranteed to please.

Be sure not to miss *Dance with the Devil* from Pamela Litton. This sequel to her first book, *Stardust and Whirlwinds,* is the story of eastern-bred Libby Hawkins and Comanchero Mando Fierro.

We hope you enjoy all our titles this month, and we look forward to bringing you more romance and adventure in May.

Sincerely,
The Editors

The Flaming

Pat Tracy

Harlequin Books

TORONTO • NEW YORK • LONDON
AMSTERDAM • PARIS • SYDNEY • HAMBURG
STOCKHOLM • ATHENS • TOKYO • MILAN
MADRID • WARSAW • BUDAPEST • AUCKLAND

Harlequin Historicals first edition April 1992

ISBN 0-373-28721-6

THE FLAMING

PAT TRACY

lives with her young daughter in a farming community outside of Idaho Falls. Pat's love of historical romance began when she was thirteen and read *Gone With the Wind*. After reading Rhett and Scarlett's story, Pat immediately penned a hasty sequel wherein the couple lived happily ever after. According to Pat, there is a magic to be found in historical romances that can be found nowhere else, and she enjoys reading the many popular and talented writers who share that magic with their readers.

This book is dedicated in gratitude to
Kathleen E. Woodiwiss,
whom I regard with both awe and admiration.
Thank you, Kathleen, for all the wonderful,
breathless hours—mostly at 3:00 a.m.—
and for the unforgettable characters.
You've changed my life forever.

Acknowledgments

Special thanks to Jennifer Wise
for an Englishwoman's perspective upon
Anya Delangue and the period in which Anya lived.

Thanks to Maxine Metcalf and Sherry Roseberry,
two very talented writers, for their enduring
friendship and insightful critiques.
As always, I couldn't have done it without you.

And thanks, also, to Marsha Morgan,
gifted suspense writer, who knows how to take a
manuscript apart and put it back together—
better than it was.

Prologue

June, 1857
Bedfordshire, England
Late afternoon . . .

"You won't catch *me!*"

At the sound of her brother's voice, Anya pivoted.

The stables! She would intercept him at the south corner.

"George Herbert Delangue, I will catch you! And then we shall see what happens to little boys who put frogs in their governess's reticules."

She gathered her unwieldy skirts and moved stealthily through the open stable door.

"Dolly, be still," she instructed their plump mare.

Through a narrow window, she caught a blur of movement and smiled smugly. So her little brother thought he could outfox her? Running lightly to the window, she arrived in time to catch a glimpse of the rascal's blond head as he ducked into the stables. She had him where she wanted him. Walking straight toward her.

She darted behind a wide post. The rich aroma of horses, straw and hay hung in the air. George entered the mews, backing toward the very post that hid her. His gaze was pinned in the direction from whence he'd come.

Anya waited until he was only a foot away, then she pounced.

"Aha! I've got you now." It wasn't easy, but she wrestled the wiggling scamp to a straw-covered corner of the stable floor.

"Stop! Don't tickle," George cried. "I say, that isn't fair, Anya."

"Fair! You put an ugly frog in Smire's sewing bag."

"I—I'm s-sorry. I promise I—I am. J-just stop tickling me."

"You will apologize, then?" Anya granted her mischievous brother mercy and ceased her tickling.

"Of—of course. Now get off. You must weigh a hundred stone."

"Are you saying I'm fat?"

A giggle slipped past George's pursed lips. "No, dear sister. You are as light as a cloud."

Somewhat appeased, Anya sank back on her heels. Instantly her brother squirmed free.

"You're as light as a cloud because you're so s-k-i-n-n-y!"

"George!" Fighting her tangled skirts, she struggled to rise.

"And I already did apologize—to the frog!" He was gone in a flash.

"Don't you dare go to the tower by yourself," she called after him, rising and absently brushing the loose straw from her clothes. Oh, her George was a Tartar, he was. Against her will, she smiled at his cockiness. The smile faded quickly, and she sighed. Time and their somber older brother would soon take the starch from George's sails.

When Papa had died last fall, their brother, Edward, had been summoned home from his tour abroad. In the months since he'd assumed management of the family estate, Edward had become as sour as day-old milk. Anya supposed her brother was weighted down with the responsibilities of becoming the fifth Earl of Brimshaw, but did he have to be so...so stodgy?

She hastened her step along the pebbled lane that led to the manor, her thoughts turning to her older sister. Under the most fortunate of circumstances, Merrawynn's temperament was unpredictable.

Since she'd had to postpone her coming-out season for a year of mourning, however, Merrawynn's disposition had become even more fractious. Of course, now that she was engaged to the future lord and heir of Windham estates, Merrawynn's manner had brightened considerably.

Anya entered the manor house through the kitchens. The mouth-watering smells of roasting lamb, fresh-baked currant tarts and Cook's apricot pudding embraced her like an old friend. With a quick movement, born of frequent practice, she filched a tart.

"Miss Anya—"

Gone before Cook could lecture her, Anya took the back staircase to her room. If she expected to dine with Edward and Merrawynn, changing her gown was a necessity.

As she barreled down the hall, Anya popped the last of the tart into her mouth and began unfastening the buttons on her cuffs. When she passed the open doorway of Merrawynn's bedchamber, Anya's pace slowed. She found it impossible not to stop and admire the shoulder-length bridal veil that rested upon a hatmaker's head. An entire side of her sister's dressing table had been cleared to accommodate the elegant creation.

White netting as delicate as butterfly wings drew Anya closer. Beneath a silver tiara, fat pearls gleamed with opulent luster. Without conscious thought, she wiped her palms upon her skirts and stroked the veil's fragile netting. It was as soft as the fur of a newborn kitten.

Merrawynn would look like a princess wearing it. Slowly, Anya dropped her hand. It was difficult not to be jealous of her beautiful older sister. Of late, the suspicion had begun to grow within Anya that she would never wed. Why else would Edward and Merrawynn have promised to always keep a place for her within their households?

And why else did no one ever bring up the subject of her own coming-out season? When Merrawynn had been six and ten, the topic of her entrance to society had been the center of endless animated discussions. Now that Anya had reached that very same age, the subject of a London season for her hadn't once come up. Of course, she was well used to living in Merrawynn's shadow, but every now and then Anya resented it keenly.

She stared into the mirror that hung above her sister's dressing table and saw no blond curls, no rosebud mouth, no bright blue eyes. What she did see suggested that it *was* highly unlikely Anya would have a suitor—unless he were of a terribly forgiving nature.

She stuck her tongue out at her reflection.

Perhaps I don't want blond curls. Trying the thought on for size, she glared at the mirror's image. *And perhaps I like brown hair.* And...and why should blue eyes be more highly prized than brown? Both could see as well, couldn't they?

Anya frowned, deciding that she "saw" perhaps too clearly. If she and every man, woman and child in England had poorer vision, then no one would notice that her mouth was a trifle overlarge, her nose too bold and her eyebrows too pronounced.

Then, as she pictured her unfortunate countrymen running amok and bumping into sundry objects, she giggled. So that was why the Reverend Mr. Dingby preached so energetically against vanity. Look where it could lead—to national calamity.

She brought her fingertips to her cheek, sobering. Why did women desire pale skin that burned if the sun's rays should strike it? She preferred being outdoors. And even if Merrawynn did say it was unseemly, Anya also preferred riding astride. If a husband should come at the cost of giving up those pleasures, then...then who needed a husband?

She continued to study her unfashionably tanned face and raised her chin. She would simply be content without a suitor. Besides, Merrawynn had already won the handsomest man in all of England.

Again Anya's gaze fell to her sister's veil. Impulsively, she removed it from the hatmaker's head and eased the tiara over her coiled braid. In that instant she didn't appear a misfit at all. With the delicate folds softening her features, she almost seemed . . . beautiful?

Her sister's chamber door flew open, banging loudly against the wall. Merrawynn stormed into the room, her beautiful blue eyes red-rimmed, her flawless complexion smudged with angry splotches.

She swept across the bedchamber. "What do you think you're doing?" With a vicious burst of strength Merrawynn jerked the veil from Anya's head. "Give me that!"

Pinpricks of pain stabbed Anya's scalp as hapless strands of hair entangled in the tiara were pulled out by their roots.

"Ouch! Merrawynn, that hurt!"

"Brat, I've told you not to touch my things."

"I'm sorry—I didn't mean to—"

"It doesn't matter. My life is over. Everything is lost."

Merrawynn began to shred the fragile netting while Anya watched in horror.

"Merrawynn, what are you doing? Oh, stop!"

"He's dead," she wept. "Nigel's dead. He let some filthy highwayman shoot him. I shall never forgive him for this. Never!" She sank to her knees, still ripping the veil into jagged pieces.

"A—a highwayman?" Anya asked in disbelief, kneeling beside her sister.

"Probably the last in all of Britain, and Nigel let him find him, rob him and then . . . then kill him," Merrawynn sobbed.

Overwhelmed by a sense of helplessness, Anya patted her sister's arm. She must find Edward. He would know how to comfort Merrawynn.

"I cannot believe it. It isn't fair," Merrawynn wailed. "I did everything right. I said the correct words. I wore the correct clothes. I laughed at his endless jests. I permitted him to pursue me, kiss me. . . ."

Her heart breaking, Anya watched her sister's grief-stricken form rock back and forth.

"And it's all been wasted. All the hard work. Why couldn't he have been killed *after* the wedding? I would have had everything. The title. The wealth. The social position. Oh, why... Why did this have to happen to me?"

It took several moments for Merrawynn's words to sink in. "Merrawynn, what are you saying? You loved Nigel. He was so handsome, so full of life. And he loved you."

"Of course he loved me! I made him love me." Merrawynn raised her tear-swollen eyes. "You don't understand what it's been like for me. You're so plain that you have no conception of what it's like to be beautiful, yet poor."

"We are not poor," Anya protested.

"Of course we are. The estate isn't ours, it's Edward's. Our clothes are rags compared to what my London friends wear. My dowry is a pittance, and Edward refuses to combine yours with mine—even though it is obvious you shall never marry, and the dowry will go to waste."

At her sister's callous observation, Anya winced.

"And yet, despite all adversity," Merrawynn continued, "I was able to affix Nigel's affections upon me. And now the fool has gone and gotten himself killed."

"But, you *did* love him," Anya persisted, stunned by this shattering glimpse into Merrawynn's soul.

"Love! What has love to do with anything? Life is not fairy tales and romances. I liked Nigel well enough—he was handsome, rich and...fun. But he was still just a man. And men are different from women. They don't really fall in love, not like the poets tell us. They..."

"What do they do?"

"They *desire* women. And a wise woman uses that desire to further her position in life." Merrawynn laughed hollowly. "I don't know why I am telling you this. If ever there were a girl destined for spinsterhood, it is you, dear sister."

A shaft of anger pricked Anya. Even though her sister's words were spoken without malice, they hurt. She didn't appreciate hearing that no man would ever love her.

Merrawynn rose gracefully. "Oh well, there's no point in crying over spilt milk. Life must go on. I shall simply have to find another man worthy enough to sweep me off my feet."

Chapter One

England, Bristol Coast
Fall, 1865

Spawned by a storm-blackened sea, the north wind galloped landward, gaining momentum until it met and was resisted by the stone bulwarks of Hull Manor. Looking like recklessly flung drops of ink, icy beads of rain clung to the misted windowpane. Gusts of wind drove the droplets in jagged rivers toward the wooden sill.

On this endless night, it seemed to Anya there was no peace to be found anywhere. The nearby sea had become a raging beast, the land perilously vulnerable and the house itself forbidding. No, there could be no peace so long as the storm threatened, Merrawynn's husband, Richard, lay desperately ill, and her sister failed to return from London.

Anya rubbed her hands together, seeking both warmth and reassurance. Her growing concern for Merrawynn's husband clung to her like a clammy shroud of foreboding. If only Anya could see beyond the rain-splattered window...

She wiped the chilled glass with the palms of her hands, hoping to catch a clearer glimpse of the gravel drive winding toward the house. She could see nothing. Darkness without and darkness within. Darkness everywhere.

Her gaze went to Richard. Even though he slept, his breathing was labored. Anya suspected he only dozed. It had been a week since he'd been able to sleep through the night.

Merrawynn must return soon! Seven weeks had passed since she'd left for London on a shopping excursion intended to last a fortnight. Pressing her fingertips to her temples, Anya knew that under normal circumstances her sister's delay would not have worried her. Instead of weeks, Merrawynn's London visits often slipped into months.

If only this once her sister would hurry home. Merrawynn owed Richard that. He had been an exemplary husband—patient, generous, forebearing....

Anya's thoughts tumbled back eight years earlier to Merrawynn's wedding. Society had been scandalized by her sister marrying a scant three months after her fiancé's death. The fact that her bridegroom was forty years her senior and extremely wealthy had also fueled the gossip.

The ceremony had taken place at the village church. Anya remembered how distinguished and proud Richard had looked dressed in formal black for the occasion. Despite his age—to Anya, fifty-eight had seemed ancient—he had charmed her with his gentle manner.

She remembered Richard's smiling face, and her throat tightened. Merrawynn's youthful and slightly tipsy exuberance had amused him. Her sister had not been the least bit awed by her formidable groom. Instead, she had flirted outrageously with her new husband, looking much like a songbird flitting about a tranquil lion.

Richard groaned, pulling Anya's thoughts to the present. She moved to the side of his massive bed and tried to mask her dismay at his altered appearance. In the space of days he had become an old man.

"Richard, I am here." She touched his shoulder reassuringly, letting him know he wasn't alone.

"Merrawynn..."

His lips were cracked, his skin sallow and his jaw stubbled with gray. He seemed so fragile, so...mortal. Where was the robust man who'd taken the place of her lost father?

"Drink this," she instructed softly, helping him sit up. She pressed a half-filled glass of water to his mouth.

Not opening his eyes, he drank slowly. When he finished, she lowered his head against his pillows.

Gently, she smoothed his bed covers, drawing them to his shoulders. *Oh, Richard, we're losing you.*

In despair, she glanced about the darkened room, trying to ignore the acrid smell of medicinal vapors issuing from steaming pots. Why did death have to be so painful, so hurtful?

Unbidden came the sweet image of her brother, George. Tears streamed unchecked down her cheeks. His death more than seven years earlier had been painful, too. The breathing sickness, they'd called it.

Richard's eyes opened, focusing slowly. "Don't cry, Anya."

"I—I cannot seem to help myself."

"I need your strength. I do not have much of my own."

"I—I won't fail you, Richard."

"My faithful, little Anya... It isn't in you to fail."

She shivered at Richard's raspy endearment. He always called her his "little" Anya, even though she stood more than a half foot taller than Merrawynn.

"Anya—" A spasm of coughing seized him.

"Don't try to speak."

"I must... must tell you what I have done."

"Tell me on the morrow. You need to rest."

"My rest will come soon enough. I have done something many will think reprehensible. But you must know I did it for you, little Anya. And for my beloved Merrawynn."

Anya tried futilely to swallow the painful lump in her throat. "You could never do anything wrong."

"Others will disagree. Merrawynn most of all. But it was for her good—" Another paroxysm of coughing gripped him.

"Please don't try to say anything more. Save your strength."

His fingers bent like a hawk's talons, Richard clutched Anya's wrist. "Listen to me. You must not let me die. A man is coming. Papers must be signed."

Richard's agitation alarmed her. "Shh, you need to—"

"You know I love Merrawynn. But she is like a child. She thinks only of today, not tomorrow. You are the strong one, Anya. You must look after her. But there must be happiness for you, also. When Morgan comes, he will—" Richard could not continue past the ripping spasms that buffeted him.

Anya freed her hand from his desperate grip and reached for the silver cup that contained Richard's medication. The syrupy black liquid provided by Dr. Goodwin was the only thing that seemed to silence Richard's coughing.

Again she helped Richard up. Her arms about him, she felt every swallow he took as he drained the cup. When she eased him back onto his pillow, she noticed new lines of pain etching his mouth and forehead.

Anya smoothed his fevered brow and waited patiently until he rested before she picked up the amber bottle containing his medicine. It made her feel more secure to keep his bedside cup filled, ready for the next coughing bout. It took a moment for her to realize the bottle was empty.

She pulled the cord for Benson, Richard's servant. Minutes later the somber-faced man entered the chamber.

"Benson, we need another bottle of Dr. Goodwin's medicine."

"There is none, Miss Anya. The doctor said he would visit Lord Hull this morning and bring more."

"What could have delayed him? He knows how important Richard's medication is." Anya was sure that, without it, Richard would not survive the night.

"Perhaps he thought there was enough to last another day."

"Well, there isn't. Send for the groom and have him meet me in the library."

Tiredly, she descended the central staircase and wished for the thousandth time that Merrawynn would spend more time at Hull Manor. Anya was losing patience with her sister's refusal to live with her husband because his country home offered none of London's glittering amusements.

Anya loved the great old house with its high towers and breathtaking view of Bristol Channel on one side and farmlands on the other. Lord Hull's country estate was tucked in a sparsely populated region of southwest England, some fifty leagues from London. The main house sat atop a steep cliff that overlooked the farming community of Hobb's Corner.

Hull Manor had been Anya's home for seven years. After her younger brother's death, she could not bring herself to live where his memory seemed to pierce her heart daily. And even though Edward's new bride, Eunice, had been most cordial to her, Anya had accepted Merrawynn's offer to travel to Hull Manor.

As she stepped into the library, Anya shivered at the room's coldness. A sluggish fire burned in the hearth. Sighing, she reached for the poker and tried to ignore the dull throbbing in her temples and the sore scratchiness of her throat.

The woman who had served as Richard's housekeeper for the past thirty years was losing her battle with rheumatism. Of late, Mrs. Patterson had begun to turn over an increasing portion of her household duties to Anya. Instead of begrudging the demands of those duties, Anya saw them as proper recompense for the home and full life Richard had provided her.

"Miss Anya?" a nervous voice inquired from the doorway.

She turned and faced the rain-soaked junior groom. The lad looked cold and fearful. "Come in, Tom. Stand by the fire and warm yourself."

The boy remained in the doorway, and Anya bit her lip, impatient at his timidity. She'd forgotten that Merrawynn had taken the head groom with her to London.

"Come in," she repeated forcefully. "There's nothing to be frightened of. I merely need you to go to the village."

Tom's eyes bulged. "T-tonight? In—in this storm?" Clearly the prospect horrified him.

"You must go to Dr. Goodwin's cottage and secure more medicine for Lord Hull."

Tom's mouth fell open in terror. "Y-you want me to wa-walk to the village?"

"No, you goose, I want you to ride."

Immediately Anya regretted her sharpness. Usually she had better luck in curbing her tongue. But with her throat raw and her head pounding, she seemed to have used up her store of patience. She prayed that she wasn't coming down with the fever that had raced through the servants' quarters.

"B-but the storm?"

"The worst is over. Besides, if you get wet, you will surely dry."

The groom backed away. "I—I can't. The lightning would strike me dead."

If only Merrawynn hadn't taken the head groom with her! Harry Jarvis would have ridden through fire and plague to serve his master. Anya raked the trembling boy with a baleful glare, then bit her tongue lest she badger him further.

It wasn't his fault he had no courage. Two weeks earlier, Richard's stallion, Champion, had tossed Tom from the saddle. Since then the lad had been timid about exercising any of the horses. She couldn't bring herself to force the terrified boy to ride down Hull Cliff with a storm raging.

"Then I shall make the trip myself." She moved purposefully to the doorway. "Saddle Champion."

Her order given, Anya proceeded to her bedchamber and donned her riding boots and cloak. Minutes later, she was in the stable, watching Tom complete his task. Staring at the high-spirited horse, she clinched her hands into fists. This night she had need of Champion's speed and stamina. It was time the unpredictable brute earned his outrageous keep.

With a leg up from Tom, she mounted the black beast. Sitting astride, she gripped the reins, letting her skirts attend to their own modesty. Her booted heels dug into his grain-fed belly, causing the stallion to grunt as his powerful hooves assaulted the gravel drive. Grateful to escape the stifling atmosphere of the house, Anya melted against his back.

She needed this. Needed to feel the wind whipping at her hair and face. Her worry over Richard gave way to a mental numbness. Nothing existed beyond the road disappearing beneath her mount's thundering hooves.

As they traversed a flat stretch, she leaned forward, whispering encouragement to Champion. "Come on, let's win the race." Her words and the storm seemed to spur him.

Before long they came to the narrowest and steepest part of the road. By day, in good weather, it presented no hazard to a sober rider. But by night, ravaged by wind and rain, it was slippery and treacherous.

She tightened her grip on the wet reins and tried to slow the spirited beast. He had the bit firmly between his teeth, however, refusing to yield to her control.

"Slow down, boy!"

Tendrils of rain pierced her cloak, drenching her. Wind lashed at her unprotected face and hands. She could barely see beyond her rain-stung lashes.

Champion pounded onward, down the rocky path. Anya prayed they weren't racing toward their impending doom.

Chapter Two

Anya battled the runaway stallion, calling upon a well-spring of strength that astonished her. She tightened her grip upon the slippery reins.

"Whoa! Whoa, you infernal beast!"

She spat out a mouthful of wet mane. Arms aching, she refused to give up. At last she felt Champion's ungodly pace slacken. But there was no time to savor her victory, for when they rounded another sharp bend, she saw a coach drawn by four horses bearing down on her.

The driver shouted a warning. She turned Champion to the inside, trying desperately to give the coach berth enough to pass. A few yards from them a bolt of hot lightning speared the ground, causing both the air and her skin to vibrate with electricity.

The wind swallowed her scream. Through the blur of falling rain, she watched the clumsy coach roll toward the cliff's edge, where sea and jagged rocks awaited below. While the driver battled his fear-crazed horses, thunder roared. Absorbed by the drama of the coach teetering on the cliff's edge, Anya let Champion's reins slacken.

Another burst of lightning and an explosion of thunder ricocheted off the rock cliff. The stallion reared, ripping the reins from her hands. For a few dizzying seconds, she was airborne. The course of her flight ended when she hit the hard ground.

Dazed, she saw the door of the still-swaying coach being pushed open by a wide hand. Less than a foot from her nose, polished black boots struck the muddy earth. Through swimming senses, she thought she heard a deep-voiced oath. But then, she thought she heard the ringing of the village church bell inside her head, too.

For several moments she lay limp, pelted by the rain. Barely had she caught her breath before rough hands jerked her to unsteady feet.

"You damned fool, you almost killed us all!" The enraged man shook her by the shoulders, and her cloak fell back from her face. Another flash of lightning filled the clearing with a wash of brightness. His taut features registered first shock, then anger. "My God, you're a woman. Have you lost your senses? What are you doing out in the middle of a lightning storm?"

"I—I must get to the village." She had to shout to be heard above the wind and rain lashing out at them.

His hands moved from her shoulders to manacle her waist. "The village? You'll never make it alive. Better join me in the coach, and we'll count up how many bones you've broken."

No match for his superior strength, Anya realized that in order to gain her release, she was going to have to reason with her captor. "No! I need the doctor. A life hangs in the balance."

"There will be no catching your mount tonight. He's probably halfway back to his stall."

In desperation she twisted against the stranger's unyielding embrace. Then her gaze fell upon the horse tethered at the back of the man's carriage. "Then lend me yours."

"*What?*"

"Your horse. You're not using him."

Two more dazzling flashes of lightning highlighted the man's face. "You *are* mad."

"I ride on behalf of Lord Hull, the Marquess of Broderick." Even if the name meant nothing to the stranger, perhaps the title would. She felt the man's dark gaze bore into her, and Anya held her breath.

Morgan studied the woman who'd almost run him off the cliff. Her face was dominated by large, dark eyes. Beseeching eyes. He was tempted to simply thrust her into his coach and transport her to safety. But her mention of the marquess curbed his impulse.

If his uncle had sent this young woman into the heart of a storm, it wasn't Morgan's place to countermand his order. There had been too many times in the past four years when Morgan had been required to issue orders of his own, orders that had required the ultimate price from the men serving under his command.

"It doesn't matter for whom you ride when you're riding to disaster," he said, wondering if perhaps the woman could be dissuaded from her perilous mission with logic.

Anya brought her chin up defensively. "I am an excellent horsewoman."

He surveyed the mud and water running down her hair and clothing. "So I see."

If she'd had a pistol, Anya would have drawn it on the impossible man and demanded he give her the horse. "Please...."

It galled her to beg, but for Richard's welfare she would have crawled. An eternity seemed to pass while the stranger stared into her soul.

"Could I not dispatch the duty for you?" Even as he spoke, Morgan knew his offer was spurred by the code of Southern chivalry instilled in him by his father's second wife. Even so, the gesture amazed him. The South as he'd known it no longer existed.

She shook her head impatiently. "It would take too long to explain—just lend me the blasted horse."

Morgan turned. "Driver!"

"Here, sir."

"Prepare my mount for the lady."

"Yes, sir."

"You will have to ride astride," he pointed out.

"Of course." Anya waited impatiently for the driver to bring the man's horse. Visions of Richard being racked by violent spasms of coughing tormented her.

When at last she had the reins, Anya swung herself—with an unseemly but appreciated push against her lower person from the stranger—upon the steed's back. This time she took a commanding grip of the leather straps. "Do you journey to the high village?" she called down.

Morgan stepped back from the dancing hooves. "Yes."

"I shall return your horse in the morning. Thank you for the loan of him."

"You are wel—"

She was gone, swallowed up by the darkness, before his final words could reach her.

"Well, driver, it seems we're not the only ones out on this hellish night."

Morgan returned to the shelter of the coach and soon was on his way again to meet with the man who'd summoned him across an ocean. The voyage had been a healing time, Morgan supposed, leaning back against the seat. A time to distance himself from the seemingly endless series of battles, the relentless rounds of cannon fire and the agonizing screams of men dying in open meadows....

For the hundredth time Morgan wondered why, when so many had perished, he had been spared. He thought about his father, and a familiar sense of guilt welled up inside him. If Morgan had left his fledgling ranch in Texas and returned sooner to fight alongside his family and friends, would his father be alive today? Would the fact that his father had *two* sons wearing the gray have kept him from plunging recklessly into battle?

Old men and boys too young to shave—in the end, that's what it had come down to. Morgan couldn't forget that he had tried to sit out the war hundreds of miles away.... Was it guilt compelling him to consider his English uncle's amazing offer? Morgan scowled down at his newly purchased boots. He could feel the weight of the mud that caked them.

It hadn't been easy for him to part with the coins necessary to outfit himself in garments befitting a prospective bridegroom, but a man needed proper clothing if he planned on marrying an heiress.... Nor had it been easy to pack his comfortable denims, cotton work shirts and western-style boots inside the trunk strapped to the top of the coach.

His new boots felt stiff, as did the rest of his clothing. And the sensation of nakedness he experienced without his Remington at his side was damned unpleasant. But then, maybe getting an English heiress wasn't supposed to be easy.

Broodingly, he stared out the small coach window. There was nothing to see. His thoughts drifted to the family plantation, Taopath. Had he not considered it his duty to save Taopath for his late father's third wife, Lavinia, and her twin sons, he would have turned the coach around and headed straight for London, then America.

Morgan shifted, recalling the London attorney to whom he'd been directed and the documents he now carried inside his coat pocket. He found himself wondering about the uncle he'd never met. But most of all, he wondered just how homely and unappealing he was going to find Miss Anya Delangue, his future wife.

Anya tied the stranger's horse to the picket fence in front of Dr. Goodwin's cottage and raced across its flagstone walkway. She pounded on the weathered door. When the physician failed to appear, she continued beating her fist against the wet barrier. Finally a cautious opening of the door spared her hand further damage. Mrs. Goodwin poked her head through the exposed crack. The woman had been married to the village doctor for over forty years and was well acquainted with inopportune assaults upon her front door at all times of day or night and in all kinds of weather.

"Mrs. Goodwin, I must speak to your husband."

"But he's not here."

"Where is he?" Anya cried in despair.

"It be Sarah Percy's time—he's at the inn."

Without another word, Anya turned away. Leaving the meager protection of the porch, she again surrendered herself to the storm's tumult.

When she swung open the door to the inn and stepped inside, sudden quiet struck her. She was able to savor the respite from the raging elements for only a moment, however, before a scream shattered the silence. Anya pulled her sodden skirts above her muddied boots and took the stairs two at a time. The sight of Hume Percy pacing before a closed door spared her the need to ask the doctor's whereabouts.

She burst into the bedchamber. Seeing the aged physician bent over the innkeeper's young and clearly terrified wife stopped Anya in her tracks.

"Dr. Goodwin..." Tearing her gaze from the panting woman, Anya drew a steadying breath. "I need more medicine for Lord Hull."

The doctor raised his eyes from his patient. "Miss Anya, the medicine only prolongs his suffering. There is nothing more I can do for him. Can you not let him go in peace?"

Sarah Percy let out another bloodcurdling scream.

Goodwin turned his back to Anya, his attention refocused upon the birthing. "Push, Sarah. Push...."

Anya raised her hands in supplication. "But, Doctor, he needs—"

The physician's head snapped up. "He needs to die. His welfare is in God's hands, not mine—or yours."

"But you can't just let him die!"

"Don't you understand? There's nothing more I can do for him."

Once more, Goodwin turned his back on her, and Anya knew she had heard the doctor's final word.

Sarah Percy screamed again.

With the woman's shrill cry and Dr. Goodwin's harsh words ringing in her ears, Anya turned and fled the room. Blinded by tears, she left the inn and remounted the borrowed horse.

With each plop of her mount's hooves, Dr. Goodwin's pronouncement echoed in Anya's thoughts. *Had* she been selfish and cruel in trying to prolong Richard's life? The storm's fury subsided, and a quiet rain fell from skies that had once spewed fire.

Finally she reached the misted courtyard of Hull Manor and dismounted, her stiffened joints crying out in painful protest. She supposed she was beginning to feel the effects of her fall. Oh Lord, she hoped she wasn't coming down with the fever that for the past few weeks had ravaged the manor's staff. She needed her strength to care for Richard.

Dispiritedly, she walked the horse to the stables so Tom could unsaddle and care for it. Seeing Champion settled in his stall provided a measure of relief. She prayed that she would find Richard also safe.

Minutes later, Anya entered a side door to the manor. She sensed what news awaited her inside and her heart ached. With a deliberateness born of habit, she removed her wet cloak, then hung it on the coatrack. With detachment, she watched a dripping puddle form upon the polished floor. Benson would have to see to the mess. Tonight she would consider herself fortunate if she could make it up the staircase unassisted. Never had she felt so weary. And she still had to ask after Richard....

Through the muddled confusion of her mind, she thought she heard voices coming from the library. Instinctively, Anya moved toward those reassuring sounds. As she pushed open the library doors, she stopped. Benson stood beside Richard's desk, pouring a good-sized portion of brandy into a glass held by a man she did not immediately recognize. Both Benson and the stranger looked up at the same moment.

"Benson, how... how is Lord Hull?"

The servant set the decanter on the desk, then regarded her somberly. "I'm sorry, Miss Anya. He died less than an hour ago."

"I tried to bring Dr. Goodwin, but he couldn't come. He was attending Sarah Percy. He wouldn't give me any more medicine. I hurried. I did. I rode as fast as I could." Anya's throat closed over her unchecked stream of words. Unshed tears burned her eyes. "I failed him," she whispered in a choked voice. "I failed him, after all."

"No, Miss Anya. Lord Hull died peacefully." The faithful servant leveled a speaking glance at the stranger.

"I should have left sooner...."

Benson's companion shrugged. "It would have made no difference. He was ready to die."

At the stranger's coldhearted observation, Anya's head shot up. She finally recognized the voice of the man she'd almost run off the cliff. Meeting his narrowed gaze, she frowned.

"But *I* wasn't ready." How she resented that Richard had spent his last moments with this indifferent man.

"Don't cry, Miss Anya. Mr. Grayson is right. It was his lordship's time. You did everything you could for him. Without your care, the master wouldn't have lasted this long."

She pressed her fingers to her throbbing temples. "I pray you are right."

"Are you well, Miss Anya?" Concern laced Benson's voice.

Before she could reply, the stranger stepped toward her. "No, she's not well. Can't you see she's about to collapse? You'd best have her bed readied for her."

"I'm fine," Anya protested, wanting to contradict the annoying man.

"You're shaking like a leaf," he corrected quietly, moving her toward a chair when Benson left the library.

Mesmerized, Anya backed up. All she could focus upon was the steely force of the stranger's relentless stare. "But I'm—"

"Sit before you faint."

The backs of her legs hit the chair and—quite unceremoniously—she sat. Knowing her wet skirts were ruining the brocade upholstery, she decided then and there to bill the man for damages.

"Here." He held out the brandy snifter. "You need this more than I."

Anya eyed the half-full glass. She rarely consumed spirits. The man raised a dark eyebrow, as if to challenge her courage.

"Come now, don't be stubborn. This will warm you more thoroughly than a roaring fire." He stepped closer.

Anya looked at the large hand cupping the snifter, then beyond the outstretched arm, past wide shoulders, into determined dark eyes. She read their implicit threat—that she'd better take the drink before he poured it down her throat.

She reached for the glass. "Thank you," she managed through clenched teeth.

"You've hurt yourself." He captured the wrist of her right hand and examined her scraped knuckles. "Was it when you fell?"

Heat seemed to spill from his touch, and she jerked her hand away. It took her a moment to bring her injury into focus. "I'm not certain. I felt no pain until you mentioned it."

He extended the glass again, and Anya's fingers curled about it. She was trembling so hard, she feared she would spill the amber liquid. To avoid mishap, she downed the drink in one, swift swallow.

The bitter draught seared her throat and stole her breath. Tears fell freely. "Aaugh, this is vile."

He retrieved the empty glass and stood back to study her with undisguised interest. "One learns to appreciate it."

Anya knew she presented a pitiful sight and, at his continued scrutiny, anger stirred within her. Had the man never seen a wet woman before? She decided he was the most unconscionably rude person she'd ever met. How dare he focus his hard gaze upon her person when she looked and felt so...so wretched!

"Why are you staring?" she challenged finally, her voice surprising her with its hoarseness.

"I'm familiarizing myself with Richard's beloved little Anya."

She resented bitterly the sound of Richard's pet name emerging from the stranger's lips. Her eyes narrowed at the scarcely veiled sarcasm his deep voice conveyed. Then she remembered she'd almost driven him off the village road and had "borrowed" his horse. Feeling his anger might be slightly justified, she decided to overlook his rudeness.

"I am Anya. But it is my sister, Merrawynn, who was Richard's beloved."

"If you say so."

"Who are you?" She realized for the first time that they hadn't been introduced. But in her heart she had already guessed whom he must be. He was the visitor Richard had clung to life to see.

"Morgan Grayson," he said then paused. "Morgan *Hull* Grayson, Richard's nephew," he finished softly, before pouring himself more brandy and leaving her to ponder the enormity of his announcement.

Hull! Warning bells went off in Anya's head. Deaths invariably meant bequests and wills. Both she and Merrawynn had believed Richard to be without living family.

"He never spoke of you."

"No reason why he should have. He was my mother's brother, and my mother died before I turned two."

"You're not English," she accused, his unusual manner of drawing out his words becoming more noticeable as he continued to speak.

"I'm an American."

He might as well have said he was a pirate, Anya thought, studying the rugged, dark-haired man with undisguised curiosity. He was the first American she'd ever met, and he fit precisely her conception of one. He was a barbarian. Hadn't they just fought that horrible war? And, as if four years of chaos weren't bad enough, they'd assassinated their president.

"Did you have an opportunity to speak with Richard before he . . . he—"

"I did. He was lucid to the last."

"I shall miss him. He was a dear, dear man."

"Did his wife not know of his illness?"

"Merrawynn is in London. I've sent her a dozen messages, but there's been no response. I kept hoping she was on her way." Anya raised her eyes. "At least you arrived in time. He seemed determined to hang on until he had spoken with you."

"I would have been here sooner, but the train from London was delayed."

"I wonder what has kept M-Merrawynn," Anya said through chattering teeth. For reasons she didn't understand, she hated exposing this new vulnerability to Richard's offensive nephew.

"You're shivering again," he observed, frowning. "You need one of the maids to attend you."

When Anya tried to stand, she discovered her legs had turned to porridge. She giggled, then, eyes wide, she placed a hand over her mouth. *Porridge...?*

"Merrawynn took th-three maids with her to London. I ordered the two she left behind to b-bed with fevers. The housekeeper is visiting her daughter. And *I* am capable of attending to myself."

Pleased she was able to both state her mind and prevail over the wave of dizziness that swept through her, Anya stood. Her pride surged at that remarkable accomplishment.

"Better than you sit a horse, I trust. By the way, did my mount arrive intact?"

"Oh! I knew you were still angry about that. I'm truly sorry I nearly ran you off the cliff, but I scarcely expected to encounter another traveler upon so hideous a night."

"The storm didn't keep you from riding out."

"I—I had no choice," Anya replied, disconcerted to see the library walls begin to sway. She took a wobbly step toward the door. "I—I shall see you in the morning, Mr. Grayson."

"It is morning."

"So it is," she acknowledged in surprise, noticing for the first time that sunlight streamed through the library windows.

Another wave of dizziness washed through her. It seemed that one moment she was dismissing the impertinent Mr. Grayson, and the next she was firmly locked within his powerful embrace. Her last coherent thought was that his clothing was scarcely dryer than her own.

Hush, Anya wanted to say. Why was Merrawynn shouting? How could anyone be expected to sleep through such a commotion? Then Anya heard the sound of a man's angry voice raised in retaliation at her sister's shrieking invectives. Richard and Merrawynn must be quarreling.

No...

Whatever the provocation, Richard never raised his voice to Merrawynn. Anya frowned, trying to sort through the confusion. But she'd lost her ability to concentrate. She felt so weak. She couldn't even open her eyes. Her throat was dry and scratchy. She wished someone would offer her some water.

"I told you to stay out of her room!" Merrawynn cried. "You have no right to be here."

"I have more right than you," Morgan Grayson countered grimly.

"And how vulgar of you to remind us!"

"If I hadn't seen to your sister's needs, she probably would have died."

"That would have certainly suited your purposes, wouldn't it?"

"Please, I can't sleep with all this shouting."

Silence greeted Anya's raspy moan. Then, suddenly, she found herself clutched violently to Merrawynn's bosom. Anya's eyelids fluttered open, only to close against the assault of harsh daylight. When she tried to take a deep breath, she felt a dull pain in her chest. Both the pain and Merrawynn's wild embrace were overwhelming.

"You're smothering the woman." The man's voice was harsh. "Let her go."

Immediately Anya felt herself released. She fell back upon her pillow with a thump, and a cannon blast sounded in her head. She opened her eyes, saw Morgan Grayson towering above her sister and remembered everything.

"Oh, Merrawynn, Richard is dead!"

"I know. Oh well, it is for the best. He's been slipping for months."

"I—I tried to bring Dr. Goodwin."

"So I heard. Whatever were you thinking to ride out in such a storm?"

"She was 'thinking' of trying to help my uncle," Morgan observed. "Your sister doesn't need your questions now. Join me in the hall, Lady Hull. I will send for the nurse to take care of 'little Anya.'"

"Nurse?" Anya asked, bewildered by Morgan Grayson's apparent command of their lives.

"Minnie, the fountain of endless cheer. Mr. Grayson hired her to care for you," Merrawynn managed to announce before the American led her from the chamber.

While trying to make sense of the puzzling circumstances that had greeted her awakening, Anya was confronted with a short, plump woman who literally burst into her chamber.

"Well, now, missy, you've finally decided to wake up, have you? You've had us all fretting." Sparse brown hair sprinkled with gray and pulled into a tight bun showed beneath the white cap perched upon the middle-aged woman's head.

"I have?"

"Yes, indeed." The nurse smoothed the starched white apron she wore pinned over her gray gown before placing a work-worn hand against Anya's forehead. "Well, now, you've done it. You've gone and broken that nasty fever. Minnie's proud of you."

"You're Minnie," Anya ventured with a tentative smile.

"Of course I'm Minnie. Who else would I be?" She presented her broad back to Anya, then turned and proffered a glass filled with cloudy liquid. Using her free hand, the nurse leaned forward and slipped a sturdy arm between the pillow and Anya's back. "Here, now, have a drink of this."

"Thank you." As Anya quenched her deep thirst, she inhaled the oddly soothing scent of cloves. Surprised by the wave of emotion she experienced at the nurse's kindness, Anya blinked back sudden tears. It had been a long time since anyone had taken care of her.

When Anya had drunk her fill of the tart beverage, Minnie eased her gently back onto her pillow. Anya concentrated on lying very still, trusting that the painful throbbing in her head would soon diminish.

"Are you hungry?"

"Perhaps . . . I'm not sure."

"I have soup cooking downstairs. I'll fetch you some. That should perk up your appetite."

"Thank you," Anya murmured.

"Just rest yourself. I'll be back before you can say frisky kittens." She bustled from the room as Anya dozed.

"I see Minnie has taken charge."

Anya opened her eyes. Morgan Grayson stood watching her from the doorway of her sleeping chamber. She drew the bed covers to her chin, wanting to point out that it was he who seemed adept at taking charge.

"She appears eager to be of service."

"She's that, all right." The American boldly entered her bedchamber.

Anya's mouth fell open. Did the brash American have no concept of propriety? Did not he realize how highly improper it was for him to initiate a conversation with her while she lay in bed?

"I—I don't seem to recall her being from the village."

As if he had the right, Richard's nephew rested his shoulder against a column of her canopy bed. "She isn't. Dr. Goodwin recommended her."

"But why?" Anya tried mightily to ignore the strangeness of having a man in her bedchamber. The feat, however, proved beyond her.

The American's darkly riveting eyes, his rugged bearing, his... maleness overpowered the feminine trappings of her room. There he stood, tall and scowling, his black eyebrows, sharply hewn cheekbones and square jaw intimidating, indeed. His dark suit seemed a harsh invasion of the flowered prints that covered her walls and bedding.

"Because of the gross incompetence surrounding the running of Hull Manor, I felt I had no other choice."

Anya stopped conversing with the second brass button of his waistcoat and met his gaze head on. "'Tis a pity I haven't been well enough to attend to your needs, Mr. Grayson. I suppose Benson has not been up to your impeccable standards, either. How tiresome of him to insist upon feelings of grief when *you* required his undivided attention.

"And how inconsiderate of our housekeeper, Mrs. Patterson, not to have known in advance to postpone her visit to her daughter," Anya continued, gaining strength. "I suppose Cook's simple dishes displease you, too. And for the maids to be ill! Just poor planning on our part, I must admit."

"Enough," he protested, his dark eyes gleaming. "I have no complaints about my stay at Hull Manor. Even if I did, I would not direct them to you."

"Did you wish to address the queen?"

He laughed softly and, as she stared at him, the word *handsome* flitted through her thoughts for the first time. Handsome was as handsome did, however. The American interloper's irreverent amusement, when she'd just administered him a severe dressing down, set her teeth on edge.

"I was referring to the care available to *you*. But clearly your wits are razor sharp, and you are on the road to recovery."

"No doubt, I have you to thank for that," Anya snapped, thinking of the nurse he had hired to care for her. "I certainly had no intention of becoming your responsibility."

A strange half smile softened the man's bold features. "Think nothing of it. The truth is I've enjoyed my role in helping you regain your health. I have no complaints in that area. I don't recall doing anything in a long time that afforded me the pleasure helping you did, Anya."

The sound of her name emerging from his lips struck Anya as shockingly personal. Nor did the wicked grin he flashed or the alarming twinkle in his eyes do anything to dispel her uneasiness.

Before Anya could reflect further upon the matter, however, Minnie returned, bearing a silver tray. Forgetting completely the American's presence in her bedchamber, Anya focused her attention irrevocably upon the bowl's aromatic contents. Suddenly she was ravenous.

After waiting with ill-concealed impatience for Minnie to set the bowl before her, Anya addressed herself to the clear broth with a single-mindedness that made the American smile. He watched her dainty gluttony for several moments before quietly slipping from the room.

After having her fill of Minnie's delicious concoction, Anya fell back against the pillows and slept again. She did not reawaken until the following morning, at which time she was plagued by a rumbling stomach and a dozen questions. Minnie satisfactorily solved the matter of food with porridge and sweet muffins. Merrawynn, however, was less accommodating in supplying answers to Anya's questions.

"Merrawynn, why did it take you so long to return?"

Before responding, her newly widowed sister settled herself comfortably upon the pink chintz chair next to Anya's bedside. Anya took note of Merrawynn's elegant black velvet dress. With its low-cut bodice, the gown seemed more suitable for evening than day wear. Nevertheless, her sister was—as always—beautiful. Her pale blond hair fell in soft curls about her delicate face. Her bottom lip was thrust forward in an appealing pout.

"I know I should have returned sooner, but I was having such fun. And I had just arrived. Besides, your letters were confusing. It didn't seem possible Richard's health could have declined so quickly. You always were overprotective toward him. Anyway, I was only gone a fortnight or so.''

"You were gone almost two months." Anya corrected her with uncustomary sharpness.

"Perhaps. You know I never pay attention to the calendar." She smoothed the expensive folds of her gown. "Anyway, I had assumed you would take better care of dear Richard." A hint of reproach crept into Merrawynn's silken voice.

Anya flinched. "I did my best for him."

"Of course you did, dear—as did I. Now tell me, what do you think of Morgan Grayson?"

The question caught Anya by surprise. In truth she was embarrassed by her scathing remarks to the man. Usually she was more skillful at controlling her temper. Chagrined, she realized her retorts to him had bordered upon the childish.

"I really don't know him. He just arrived last night."

"Anya, you've been ill for more than a week—in some kind of delirium, according to the man. I only arrived yesterday."

"I had no idea so much time had passed. . . ."

"Yes, dear. You've been, well, quite alone with Morgan Grayson for all that time."

"He seems to have done a fair job of keeping me alive." Anya wondered at the intentness of her sister's stare. "Why is he still here?"

"Hull Manor is his now, Anya. Richard left it to him. It is we who are the intruders."

"Even so, I'm sure Richard left you comfortably settled, Merrawynn." But even as she tried to soften the blow to her sister, Anya remembered Richard's distress over something he'd done to affect Merrawynn's future, something he'd said her sister would not approve of.

"He provided for both of us indirectly, but it is that wretched Yankee who ends up with the bulk of the estate."

"I fear that was Richard's wish, Merrawynn."

"Morgan Grayson is utterly devoid of conscience. He intends on turning us out into the cold with nothing. *That* cannot have been Richard's intent."

Anya could think of no response.

"Morgan sent for a nurse because he wants to make certain you're well enough to travel," Merrawynn continued. "As soon as possible, he wants you gone from here."

"I will grant you that he does seem formidable, but I cannot believe he would turn you out of the home you've known for the past eight years. Surely, he has placed no restriction upon how long you may remain here. Besides, the law states quite clearly that—"

"It's not just me," Merrawynn interrupted sharply. "You, too, dear sister, are being evicted."

"But I have no claim to Richard's home in the first place. I've been a guest here these years."

"You've run the entire house! Supervised the meals, the maids and even the gardens. My goodness, you've given your life to Hull Manor. You deserve better than this."

Anya had to smile at Merrawynn's impassioned vehemence. In the past, her sister had always de-emphasized Anya's contributions to the running of the manor. "It won't be so bad for me. Our brother has often urged me to return home."

"Only because Eunice is seeking a glorified nanny for her brats."

"Actually, I was thinking of becoming a governess."

"You would work?" Merrawynn cried, clearly horrified. "I cannot believe you would sink so low."

Anya smiled again. During her years at Hull manor, she'd worked very hard. "I shall be fine."

"But what about *me?* Shall I be fine? Do you expect me to... to *work?*"

Anya's smile faded. "Certainly not. We must convince Mr. Grayson that you deserve assistance. Just what did Richard leave you, Merrawynn?"

Merrawynn hesitated. Instead of answering immediately, she cast her sister a penetrating stare. It had been years since she'd truly looked at the girl. Anya had always been destined for spinsterhood. Of that there was no debate. Now that she was four and twenty, her fate should have been sealed.

And yet, as Merrawynn studied Anya, she detected for the first time a hint of comeliness in the girl. *Why,* Merrawynn discovered in surprise, *Anya really wasn't homely.* Of course, her recent illness had bled the color from her cheeks, and her hair was a disaster. But notwithstanding those drawbacks, there was an earthy appeal to the chit. Her complexion was flawless, her lips soft and full. Thick lashes accented her wide, brown eyes.

As for Anya's figure...well, there was no arguing that she was a large woman. Then, as Merrawynn scanned her sister's shape beneath the blankets, she amended that opinion. Aside from Anya's tallness, she was daintily boned.

Merrawynn speculated on whether or not Morgan Grayson might have begun to fancy her sister. The girl certainly had no *secrets* from him. Blue eyes narrowed as they considered Anya's delicate proportions. In London she had learned that some men liked boyishly shaped women.

Lowering her gaze, Merrawynn began some hasty planning. How foolish Richard had been to think she would let a codicil keep her from inheriting his estate—all of it.

"My portion is a mere pittance. Before the solicitor left yesterday, he informed me that I am ... destitute."

Chapter Three

"I will speak to Mr. Grayson immediately upon your behalf, Merrawynn."

"No! You mustn't do that. He is a terrible man. I cannot repeat the unspeakable statements he has made to me. I hate him!"

Anya listened, somewhat surprised at her sister's vehemence. Usually Merrawynn reserved her passions for inanimate objects, such as the cut of a ball gown, the number of facets in a diamond or the length of her hair. People rarely provoked such a vigorous response. Mr. Grayson must have been offensive indeed. But then, the man had elicited the same kind of hostility from her, and Anya knew *she* was a most reasonable person.

"I'm very tired, Merrawynn. Could we discuss this later?"

"Of course, dear sister. You rest. You mustn't worry about me. Actually, it was the man's uncouth allusions to you that I found the most offensive."

Anya's eyes snapped open. "What did he say about me?"

"He...he stated you were unfit to be left in charge of Richard's welfare, and that you acted irresponsibly," Merrawynn said swiftly. "He also indicated that if someone else had assumed control of the situation, Richard would be alive today."

"But on the night we met, he said that I had done everything that could have been done for Richard."

"I'm certain he truly feels that way. But he plans to use anything he can to cancel any claims we might place upon the estate."

"He's a beast!"

"All he's concerned with is his portion of the estate," Merrawynn observed scornfully. "That's all Yankees ever think about—money. Why, he's even demanded the expenses incurred by Richard's interment in the family vault come from my small portion."

"How cruel!"

"Oh, yes, you'll soon discover the evil character of the man. Wait until he unleashes his disagreeable temper upon you. Then you shall see."

Anya closed her eyes, relieved from any earlier pangs of guilt she might have felt about her rudeness to Richard's nephew. The American deserved every unkind thing she'd said—and more! Though she felt no urge to hurry her next confrontation with Mr. Grayson, she decided then and there that when next they met, she would give as good as she got.

The morning of his tenth day at Hull Manor, Morgan rested his elbows upon a roughly hewn fence and stared at the ill-natured beast that had almost killed him, his driver and Anya Delangue.

"He's a handsome devil, I'll grant you that."

Harry Jarvis pushed back his cap. "Always been a mite too unpredictable for my tastes."

Morgan's jaw clenched. "Your mistress was willing to risk her life on his back."

"Miss Anya?" The bandy-legged groom nodded. "Aye, she would have."

"Someone should have stopped her."

"Tom ought to have made the trip for her—for the master."

"Why didn't he?"

"Last month Champion tossed him a good one."

"If he's lost his nerve, he's unfit for stable work."

"'Tis what I told him in the tongue-lashing I gave him."

"Doesn't Anya have her own mount?"

Jarvis nodded again. "Aye, she does. A fine little mare with more heart than some men I know."

Morgan turned and faced the groom. "Then why didn't she take the mare?"

"Lady Lore has the heart, but Champion has the speed. Miss Anya was riding for the master."

"So she chose for speed."

"When it comes to heart, Miss Anya has plenty of her own."

Impressed by the groom's assessment of his mistress, Morgan frowned reflectively. Not many words had been exchanged between himself and Anya Delangue, but his opinion of the Englishwoman had grown steadily in the week he'd been here.

"I'll wager she has more heart than most women," he observed thoughtfully, recalling her extraordinary attempt to save his uncle's life.

"That she does, sir. That she does."

Morgan's frown deepened. "I would have given Tom more than a tongue-lashing."

"Considered that, but he was a boy trying to do a man's job."

Immediately Morgan remembered the Southern and Northern boys who'd died trying to fight a man's war. His stomach twisted. Would the memory of those bloody scenes never fade?

"Nevertheless, you showed more restraint than I would have."

"'Tis the way Miss Anya would have handled it."

"Is it?"

"Aye."

Looking into Harry Jarvis's rheumy gray eyes, Morgan again sensed the man's respect for his mistress—the kind of respect money couldn't buy.

After his enlightening conversation with the groom, Morgan walked to the nearby churchyard cemetery and stared at the impressive Hull family crypt. Even though he was related to those interred within the stone edifice, Morgan felt no stirring of emotion.

He and his late uncle might share a distant blood bond of kinship, but Morgan's only real contact with the deceased man had been ten minutes of conversation and several jointly signed documents—the documents that had the power to alter irrevocably the direction of Morgan's life. Thinking about the papers signed with Richard's spidery scrawl, Morgan again pondered the peculiar fates that had delivered him to English soil.

His former fiancée, Collette, who'd jilted him to marry his half brother. His half brother, who in a few months intended calling due the loans that Morgan's stepmother, Lavinia, had borrowed from Collette's late father.

Morgan gazed at the bronze plaque that listed those for whom the crypt was a final resting place. Richard's name had not yet been added. It was the unexpected letter from his late uncle, promising a sizable legacy to Morgan should he travel to England and marry a woman named Anya Delangue, that had offered Morgan a way out of his financial woes—a way whereby he could finally return to the ranch waiting for him in Texas.

A series of totally unrelated facts were all converging to this one point in time....

Morgan ran his fingertips across the plaque's raised letters. For some reason he was reminded of a play he'd seen years ago. He couldn't remember its name, but he recalled how smoothly the actors had delivered their lines.

"Well, Uncle, you've certainly set the stage." Morgan turned his collar up against a sudden breeze. "Too bad you didn't see fit to provide us with our lines."

Restless, Morgan walked back toward the stables. He would work off his excess energy with a ride. Of course, he'd take the stallion. Hadn't he always preferred a challenge?

Champion didn't disappoint him. The first few minutes on the brute's back required total concentration. Even then, it was debatable which of them would win the battle of wills.

The stallion shied, sidestepped and pawed the air before settling into a gallop. Approving his mount's spirit, Morgan leaned forward to savor the ride.

Beautiful, untamed countryside flew by, and Anya Delangue's image sifted through Morgan's thoughts. His intended? If they *both* agreed to it.

Richard's codicil jointly bequeathed them Hull Manor, the farms, a coal mine and two hundred thousand pounds. Those astonishing assets were his and Anya's—if they married within six months. Merrawynn would inherit thirty thousand pounds per annum. Very generous, for a tart.

If no wedding took place, the estate would be divided into three even shares. Obviously it was in Merrawynn's interest that he and Anya consummate nothing more intimate than a handshake.

Champion's hooves pounded, and Morgan's thoughts traveled in a new direction. What was wrong with the men of England? Why hadn't one of them already taken Anya Delangue in marriage and plucked her maidenhood?

From Richard's letter, Morgan had expected Anya to be older, plainer and thoroughly undesirable. Since that was obviously not the case, he wondered if perhaps some tragedy had stolen a sweetheart from her. He could not believe the Englishwoman had never been courted.

When he'd first read his uncle's tantalizing proposal, it had mattered little what Anya Delangue looked like. She could have weighed two hundred pounds, been ugly as a toad and had the disposition of Merrawynn.

He would have married her in a minute for a share of Richard's estate—for the freedom to give an unencumbered Taopath to Lavinia and the twins, and for the freedom to put from his mind forever the war-torn South and return to the Rio Grande valley. To gain those freedoms, he would have saddled himself with an English wife, sight unseen.

Now that he had examined the documents, however, he realized that a third of Richard's bequest was sufficient to clear Justin's claim upon the family plantation. A bride was no longer a necessity.

Morgan noticed Champion's pace had begun to slow and pulled the horse to a canter for the return trip to the manor. In the past few days, he'd begun to consider marrying the Englishwoman on her own merits. She was young, comely and available. What more could he seek in a wife?

Collette intruded briefly in his thoughts and he scowled. Love was a delusion a wise man avoided. He was almost thirty. It was time he had a wife. Anya suited his needs admirably.

Clearly, she was a well-brought-up young lady, just what he required for the mother of the sons he intended to sire. She had spirit. And maybe a little vinegar? His scowl faded. He found spirit, grit, even vinegar preferable to the simpering young women matchmaking mothers had lately begun to foist upon him since his recent return to Taopath.

Anya Delangue in Texas... He liked the sound of her aristocratic English accent. She definitely would be a civilizing influence in the rugged land he now thought of as home. After the rawness of war, he was more than ready for the healing balm of female softness in his life.

He thought of the two-story white frame home he'd built with Collette in mind as its mistress. The house had a coldness he suspected Miss Delangue would thaw most satisfactorily.

The memory of Anya's supple body settled cozily into his thoughts. The night he'd removed her wet garments, he'd been astonished by her loveliness. The sweet swell of her pert breasts, the soft curve of her narrow waist, the silken nest of dark hair... Truly she was as beautiful as any woman he'd known.

Of course, he hadn't planned on enjoying the deed of removing her clothes quite so much, but he wasn't a monk, after all. He had managed to curb his baser instincts and behave like a gentleman, even if his thoughts had taken a few intriguing detours. A man might not need a woman's love, but it was a cold world without a woman's—

Morgan reined in Champion. Merrawynn stood on a gravel path less than four yards from him. It took him only seconds to size up her appearance. Her hair was precisely arranged, her cheeks delicately rouged and her lips moistly pouting. She wore a low-cut black gown that probably had cost as much as the stallion. Even in widow's weeds, Anya Delangue's sister projected an image of calculated brazenness that repelled Morgan. He wasn't the kind of man to be controlled by feminine wiles.

He dismounted.

A gambling man by nature, he would have bet his share of Richard's estate that Merrawynn Hull was about to offer herself to him. But she wouldn't come cheap, and Morgan had no intention of paying her asking price.

She smiled radiantly. "So Champion didn't throw you?"

"He wanted to run more than he wanted to fight," Morgan answered noncommittally. Taking a firm grip on the reins, he led the horse toward the stables. Merrawynn sidled up next to him and put a restraining hand on his arm.

"Run or fight?" In a sensuous gesture, the tip of her tongue remoistened her lips. "Isn't there a third possibility?"

"Not that I know of." Shaking off her hand, he lengthened his stride and left the woman behind. He wasn't about to stick his hand or anything else into a honey pot swarming with bees.

"But, Minnie, I cannot lie abed for the rest of my life." Anya opened the doors to her clothes cupboard. "Help me select something to wear. What kind of day is it?"

The plump nurse joined Anya at the closet. "The weather makes no difference to you, miss, because you aren't going outdoors."

"No?"

"No, indeed. There's a fierce nip in the air. Freeze the skin right off your bones!"

Anya smiled. Minnie was scheduled to leave the manor later that afternoon. Clearly, the woman was trying to put a good scare into her patient so Anya wouldn't suffer a relapse.

Anya chose a gown that seemed appropriate for both the climate and her mood. It was dark blue, of medium thickness with a high neckline and long sleeves. A white collar and cuffs were its only ornamentation. Though simple, it was one of her most costly gowns.

Despite Richard's generosity, Anya had never felt comfortable with him spending money for her wardrobe. Through her brother Edward's generosity, Anya had her own funds available to her. Still, Richard had insisted upon supporting his wife's sister. A lump formed in Anya's throat. He had been a good man, and she was going to miss him greatly.

The nurse peeked into the Englishwoman's closet and was truly shocked by its meager contents. The girl must be a poor relation to have such a miserly selection of gowns. Why, her own daughter had married naught but a carpenter and boasted more finery than this sweet girl. There was nothing bright and pretty in the whole cupboard, nothing that would set off her fine brown eyes and lovely golden skin.

"Will you prepare a bath for me, Minnie, and help me wash my hair?"

"'Tis against my better judgment, but I'll draw you a tub of hot water."

After her bath, Anya dressed, feeling newly invigorated. Since she didn't possess a black gown, she decided the dark blue would have to suffice. "How is this, Minnie? Do I pass inspection?"

"Aye, my lady. You look like a princess, you do." The nurse was startled at how well the simple gown became the young woman, showing off her tiny waist and trim figure.

Minnie brushed her patient's waist-length mane of dark hair, admiring both its healthy abundance and luster. When the young miss insisted upon binding the shining masses in a simple knot at the base of her slender neck, the nurse couldn't suppress a sigh of regret. Surely the good Lord meant for such natural beauty to be displayed.

Later, as Anya walked stiffly down the staircase, she paused briefly before the large arched windows that rose above the lower stairway. Minnie had not exaggerated the blustery conditions outside. The windows provided a clear view of overcast skies looming above the well-groomed gardens. Trees and shrubs bent toward the west, and the stone-lined garden paths glistened from a fine, misting rain. Despite the warmth of the open hall, Anya shivered.

From her vantage point midway on the stairs, she had an unimpeded view not only of the gardens, but also of the wide hall below. The doors to the parlor and dining room were closed, while the door to the library was ajar. No one was in sight. Her sister was a notorious late riser. Mr. Grayson might also still be abed, yet somehow Anya doubted it. The restless energy the American generated made it more likely that he was skulking about.

She reflected upon her sister's revelations about the deplorable character of Morgan Grayson as she tiptoed past the library door. Certainly, the man's presence boded no good for either Merrawynn or herself. She was better off avoiding another encounter with him.

Anya knew precisely where she would spend the morning. She and Richard had spent months designing the conservatory constructed on the south side of the manor. Immense windows, larger replicas of those above the staircase, formed the outside wall. The cost had been sinful, and Merrawynn had complained bitterly about the extravagance. But then, her sister had resented any expenditure for Hull Manor.

Richard had persisted in the endeavor, however, and their reward had been this glorious room where summer abounded year-round. Anya moved through the fragrant array of exotic blooming orchids and roses, remembering the dear man who had spent so many hours with her there. Those cherished times were the happiest she'd known. For even though she preferred the unrestrained beauty of the sea and woods, she did love this fragrant room. Especially when foul weather chased them indoors.

Richard *had* loved both her and Merrawynn. Had his impending death somehow altered those feelings? How could he have left Merrawynn destitute? It made no sense.

Anya bent forward to sample the delicate scent of a red rose. Of course, she and Merrawynn hadn't known of Richard's nephew, the American. No matter how distasteful he was, the man did have a claim to Richard's estate.

It would be difficult leaving Hobb's Corner. She would miss the open spaces and her times alone. Her brother, Edward, would not countenance her riding astride, and Eunice would probably be wary of her husband's maiden sister interfering with the running of the household. Anya suffered no delusions about her own disposition. She knew she tended to manage the people around her. Except, of course, for Merrawynn. *No one* managed her tempestuous sister.

When Anya reached the end of the section of roses, she turned to retrace her steps, then stopped. Morgan Grayson stood at the front of the narrow aisle, blocking her path. He was staring at her as intently as the first evening they had met. His dark eyes seemed to survey every aspect of her appearance.

Unused to such blatant perusal, Anya flushed. Didn't parents in America teach their children manners? She scowled at the too tall, too aggressive foreigner. He was probably assessing her state of health, deciding how soon he could evict her from Hull Manor.

"You seem to have recovered," he pronounced gruffly.

Just as she had thought! "I feel fit," she replied evenly. He approached her with a purposeful gait. She stood her ground.

By the clear light of morning, Anya could see he wasn't as old as she'd first thought him to be. Though his features held a look of determination, she guessed he wasn't yet thirty.

Her eyes were drawn to the firmly chiseled planes of his face. Yes, he was handsome. She'd grant him that. But she didn't care for the way his jaw thrust forward, as if he anticipated a quarrel. Denying him one would be a pleasure.

Anya raised her chin. "I should be ready to leave immediately."

A look of puzzlement crossed his features. Good. She'd stolen his thunder.

"Where are you planning on going?"

The deep timbre and honeyed drawl of his voice caught her by surprise. There were several things about him she'd failed to notice earlier—like the way his peculiar manner of speaking warmed her skin.

"I'm not certain," she answered honestly. Then she recalled how abominably the man had treated her sister. Bitterness stirred within her. "But I have no wish to be in your way."

"I have trouble imagining you being in the way—anywhere."

He smiled, and Anya noticed healthy, white teeth contrasting with his tanned skin. She was amazed at how his smile altered the severity of his appearance. Why, he looked almost . . . English.

She swallowed, clinging to her righteous anger as if it were a shield. "I was informed you wished my sister and I to depart from Hull Manor at once." Why should she be polite when the man had accused her of causing Richard's death?

"That is not entirely accurate."

He came closer.

Anya backed up one step, then another.

"Are you saying my sister spoke falsely?" Anya's voice quivered. It wasn't like her to vacillate, but this...this bully seemed to have the power to make her tremble.

"If your sister informed you I wished you gone, Anya, then yes. She lied."

Anya stiffened. Not only had he called Merrawynn a liar, but again he had addressed her by her given name when she hadn't given him leave to do so. The man was a barbarian! He had crowded her into a corner and there was no retreat, save climbing over a bower of orchids.

"Mr. Grayson," she began, bludgeoning him with his name. "My sister—"

Merrawynn's voice, high and shrill, cut through the conservatory. "Here you are, Anya, dear." She swept into the room, acknowledging Morgan Grayson's presence with a quick nod. "There is a messenger in the hall for you, Mr. Grayson," she informed him icily. "We shall excuse you."

"Thank you," he replied ironically.

His footsteps had scarcely faded when Merrawynn turned angrily. "What were you thinking? I told you to stay away from that man!"

"He joined me. I didn't seek his company."

"What did he say?" Merrawynn demanded.

"Not much," Anya mused. "Actually, he seemed solicitous of my health. He didn't insist I leave."

"Did he invite you to stay?"

"Not in so many words, but now that I reflect upon it, his manner was almost cordial. His only real rudeness was to address me by my given name, and that's hardly a hanging offense."

"Hanging's too good for him!"

"He did seem annoyed with you, but perhaps your unfriendly attitude has precipitated his hostility."

"How can I be friendly with a man who insists on keeping fifty paces between himself and me at all times?" Merrawynn demanded impatiently.

"Perhaps your grief has made you suspicious of him and thus raised his ire. He might be fair with you, after all. You could go to him and—"

"You fool!" Merrawynn grabbed her arm. "If he was kind to you, it was for a reason!"

Anya tried to free herself from her sister's hurtful grip. "What reason could he have for any deception?"

"You are the most innocent creature alive. You might as well have spent your life in a convent. You know nothing of the world."

"I do, too!"

"I'm talking about men, you ninny! What do you know of men? Nothing! If you did, you'd know what Morgan Grayson wanted from you."

"Yesterday, you said it was my immediate departure."

"Perhaps I was mistaken. Oh, I know he wants me gone, but he might not mind you remaining here alone with him."

"Whatever for?"

"To be his mistress!"

Anya gazed at her sister in disbelief, then threw back her head and laughed. It was several moments before she could continue. "Merrawynn, you've lost your senses. *You're* the pretty Delangue sister. *I'm* the homely one. Have you forgotten?"

Anya's question held no rancor. It had been a long and painful process, but she had finally resigned herself to her plainness. Merrawynn was Anya's standard of feminine beauty and, since they contrasted upon every visible point, it was inconceivable to Anya that a man might prefer her to Merrawynn. Merrawynn had the good fortune to resemble their mother, while Anya took after her father. No amount of wishing would ever alter that.

"Looks aren't everything. You do have a body."

"Merrawynn, I know you have just cause to despise Mr. Grayson, but what has the man done to give you the bizarre idea he has dishonorable intentions toward me?"

"You idiot! Do I have to explain everything to you? Who do you think undressed you and put you to bed the night Richard died? You were totally at his mercy. For days, he had you completely to himself. He's touched you, seen you naked without a stitch of clothing."

Merrawynn knew her sister's incredible modesty better than anyone. When they were growing up, the girl had been reluctant to change her clothing even in the presence of her own sister.

Anya's face paled dramatically, and Merrawynn feared she'd gone too far. "Don't swoon, for Lord's sake. I'm not saying he ravished you. I'm just saying he's had an opportunity to examine you thoroughly and, being a grossly vulgar man, he probably feels he's entitled to sample you further.

"If you remain here under those circumstances you are inviting him to do so," Merrawynn continued. "Are you prepared to have his hands all over your naked body again—this time when you're awake?"

Anya shuddered. The only men with whom she'd been acquainted were Richard, her brother Edward, the servants and the young tutor from the rectory. Now to know that Morgan Grayson had seen her, touched her...

Embarrassment turned to anger. Morgan Grayson's effrontery was an outrage! How dare he? Just who did he think he was, taking such a scandalous liberty with her person? The man had the scruples of... of a marauding cossack.

Without warning, Anya's virginal mind veered in another direction and a hot blush burned her skin. *Had* the American taken any undue liberties with her, beyond the actual removal of her clothing? A strange fluttering sensation uncurled within her. She swallowed convulsively. Had he... had he approved of what he'd seen?

"Anya!"

"Yes?" Oh, she was a wicked girl to entertain such improper thoughts, surely as wicked as the American himself for performing such a dastardly deed.

"You understand that you must leave immediately? It's for your own safety."

"Yes... yes, of course."

"I didn't wish to speak with you of this, but it is important that you are not misled by any surface charm Morgan Grayson might direct toward you."

"Thank you, Merrawynn. I know it was difficult for you to tell me this, and I appreciate your candor." Anya squared her shoulders. "Rest assured, I have not reached the advanced age of four and twenty without learning to fend for myself."

After instructing Benson to bring her trunk upstairs, Anya retired to her bedchamber. She would leave for Bedfordshire in the morning. The idea of facing Morgan Grayson again was so repellant, she had no intention of leaving the sanctuary of her room before her departure.

That evening, she ordered a dinner tray sent to her chamber. After the tray was taken away, she began to industriously gather up her belongings—until there was an authoritative knock at her bedchamber door.

"Miss Delangue, we missed your company at dinner."

Anya froze, clutching to her breast the delicate chemise she had been folding. It was he! She glanced at the closed door, grateful she'd had the foresight to push the bolt home. Who knew what the uncouth American might do next?

Instinctively, she shoved her undergarment beneath the feather comforter. When she realized what she'd done, Anya felt incredibly foolish and more than a little defiant. "I didn't feel up to coming downstairs. Cook prepared a tray for me."

"Would you mind opening the door? We need to talk."

All Anya could think about was that the man presently conversing with her through the locked door had seen her as naked as she'd been the day she was born. Her skin burned with embarrassment and, even though she knew the American couldn't see her, she fastened the top button of her sleeping gown.

"Anya, open the door."

A definite edge had crept into his deep voice. *Good!* "I think not, Mr. Grayson. My bedchamber is hardly the place for us to conduct a conversation."

Heavy silence greeted her words. Anya assumed the barbarous man had gone away. When he spoke again, she jumped.

"Then come downstairs to the library."

"I'm ready for bed, Mr. Grayson—" She broke off and bit her lip at her ill-chosen remark. She wasn't at all comfortable with him knowing she was dressed for bed. "It's late."

"Barely nine," he pointed out.

"Still, I am very tired."

"I understand Benson brought your trunk to you."

"He did."

"It's important we talk before you leave Hull Manor. We need to discuss several conditions of Richard's will. Put on a robe and come to the library. I'll sleep better after we've had this conversation."

You'll have to do better than that, Mr. Morgan Grayson. He must think her terribly dull-witted to believe such nonsense. Surely they had nothing to discuss regarding Richard's will. Any such conversations would be between him and Merrawynn. "It can wait until morning."

"All right then. Tomorrow it will be." Annoyance rolled off his terse words.

Clearly, Morgan Grayson was not accustomed to being thwarted. Anya did not release the breath she'd been holding until she heard his retreating footsteps.

Later, when she slipped into bed, she smiled smugly. Before the American arose in the morning, she would be on her way to Bedfordshire. She wished she could see his expression when he discovered she had outfoxed him.

Silly man to think he could get the best of her....

Chapter Four

The following morning Morgan sat at his uncle's desk, staring at the handful of papers that would save Taopath from his half brother Justin's clutches and allow Morgan to return to his ranch. He wondered what Anya would think of Texas. Would she—

The sound of a heavy thud on the stairs shattered his half-formed thought. He went to the library door, opened it, and was astounded to see Benson at the lower end of a heavy trunk that Anya was trying to push from above.

"Please, Miss Anya, don't help. I can manage."

Anya looked past Benson. At the sight that greeted her, her heart sank. There stood the tall American, his arms folded across his chest, his dark eyebrows drawn together into a glowering scowl.

"And what do we have here?" he inquired with a feigned patience that didn't fool her for a minute.

In waves, the man's barely checked fury lashed out at her. She trembled, keenly resenting that she wasn't made of better mettle. Then she thought of his despicable actions the night she'd fainted and blushed red-hot. She had no intention of answering his question. Nor did she meet his gaze. For good measure, she again resolved never to speak to him.

"I asked you a question."

Anya's chin came up. She had no intention of breaking her vow of silence.

"Miss Anya asked me to take her trunk downstairs," Benson finally answered.

"Well, Miss Delangue, have you lost your voice as well as your manners?"

That this . . . this *American* could impugn the decorum of an Englishwoman was more than she could tolerate. "Sir, you are hardly qualified to speak of manners."

A full twenty paces from him, she felt the brunt of his glare.

"When you know me better, Miss Delangue, you'll find that I speak about any damned thing I choose. Benson, return Miss Delangue's trunk to her room. She and I are going to have a chat."

Benson moved to obey the American, lumbering past Anya with the unwieldy trunk. She missed the satisfying barrier it had provided between herself and Richard's nephew.

"Shall we proceed to the library?"

His deliberate politeness made her want to slap his handsome face. When she reached the bottom of the stairs, however, she settled for ignoring his extended arm.

Walking stiffly into Richard's study, she told herself she would only survive this confrontation with the odious American by not thinking of the night he'd removed her garments. When, contrary to her resolve, her mind betrayed her with the clear image of Morgan Grayson doing just that, her cheeks burned.

She would never survive this encounter!

"Will you be seated?" He pulled forward a rosewood chair.

His politeness grated upon her nerves. "I prefer to stand, thank you." That way she would be able to make a quick escape, should he...should he... She tried to fathom what form an improper advance might take, and her mind promptly went blank. How frustrating to stand in peril, but have no idea from whence the danger might come.

Morgan Grayson stalked to Richard's chair, muttering something Anya suspected to be uncouth under his breath.

She remained standing by the door, ready to bolt. If the American tried *anything* with her, she'd make a run for it. Dignity be hanged.

"You haven't had an opportunity to read Richard's will for yourself."

He held out a handful of documents. When she refused to accept them, he dropped the papers onto the desk.

"There is no need for me to read his will. My sister has informed me of its contents."

"And what is your reaction?" he inquired, his dark eyes studying her with that familiar intensity she found so disturbing. And yet she couldn't deny that there was a strength and power to the American's bold features that made her pulse quicken. In fear?

"I—I think Richard's will is both vile and uncivilized."

The man's lips thinned. "Your mind is made up then?"

"Beyond a doubt. If Richard had not confessed his guilt concerning the will, I would have believed you manufactured those documents to cheat Merrawynn out of a just bequest."

He steepled his fingertips and studied her above them. "You don't seem to have a very high opinion of me, Anya."

"I did not give you leave to call me by my given name! And no, I do *not* have a high opinion of you." For the first time she allowed her gaze to boldly meet his.

"Damn your English manners!" He shoved back his chair and stood, towering above her. "They seem to apply only to foreigners, anyway. May I observe, *Miss* Delangue, that you are a singularly thorny young woman?"

Thorny? The insult stung. "Calling me names doesn't alter the fact that you are turning my sister out into the cold without a farthing to her name. Merrawynn is Richard's widow. She deserves more than poverty for her years of marriage to him."

"Your sister is a whore."

Anya's mouth fell open. She had only heard that shocking word spoken once before, from the pulpit. That the American should pronounce it in her presence—and in ref-

erence to her sister—scandalized her. He was far more
wicked than she had supposed.

Trembling in outrage, she turned toward the door. "I will
not listen to such filth."

Before she could step from the room, Morgan inter-
cepted her. His hands came about her shoulders, and he
forcibly ushered her to a chair, none too gently pushing her
into it. Then he kicked shut the library door and turned to
face her.

"You *will* listen to what I have to say. Your sister is not in
the dire poverty you seem to believe. Here, read this." He
thrust the document into her hands. "Or do you know how
to read?"

"As well as you, I daresay."

"Then do so."

At first, Anya had difficulty comprehending the oblique
phraseology of the words she read. But after rereading
Richard's will several times, she grasped its import. Her
sister had lied to her. . . .

It was that simple and that devastating.

Richard had left Merrawynn thirty thousand pounds per
annum. Various seals and official signatures attested to the
veracity and legality of the document.

Anya's hands shook. Merrawynn's deceit stung, and to be
proven wrong before this insensitive man was unendurable.

"What do you have to say now?"

"I was misinformed," Anya acknowledged simply, returning the papers to Richard's desk.

"Since you admit I am not the heartless monster your
sister portrayed me to be, Miss Delangue, does that alter
your reaction to the other aspect of Richard's will?"

She stared at him in confusion. "I'm afraid I don't—"

He interrupted her. "Have you thought the matter over
carefully? Your rejection could be based upon your belief
that I was robbing your sister."

"I don't know what you're talking about," she admitted
reluctantly.

He ran an impatient hand through his hair. "The codicil, of course."

"What does it say?"

"You mean your sister didn't tell you?" Disbelief swept his features.

"I'm afraid not. Merrawynn merely told me she had been left destitute and that you wanted to—" Anya broke off when she realized what she'd almost blurted out.

His eyes narrowed suspiciously. "She said I wanted to what?"

"It—it isn't worth repeating. I'm certain now that it was an untruth."

"Then it definitely bears repeating. What did Merrawynn say?"

Anya felt her face flame, and she knew that she was flushing brightly. Silently, she implored him to let the matter drop.

"It's best to have it in the open." He flattened his hands against the desktop, his face betraying not one iota of mercy.

Feeling the intensity of his will pulling at her, Anya wondered how it was possible that even with the massive desk separating them, he had the power to hold her with his glance. "Merrawynn said you wished for me to remain at Hull Manor as your... your..."

"My what?" he demanded.

"Your... mistress," she confessed starkly.

The silence that followed her announcement was deafening. Absolutely mortified by her admission, Anya felt a scalding blush tingle from her ears to her face, across every inch of her. Worse, she sensed the American was hard put not to laugh at her. She would never forgive Merrawynn for placing her in this humiliating position. Never!

"Other than the fact that I'm not English born, what made you believe such an allegation?"

"That, I cannot tell you," she whispered.

"Then your sister gave you cause to believe such a lie?"

Anya's breath locked in her throat. She was unable to breathe, let alone speak.

"Well, did she?"

Anya nodded miserably, her gaze dropping to the color-ful pattern of the Oriental rug. She wished desperately that she could slip between it and the floor.

"Then how can I clear myself of her charge? Out with it. What did she say I'd done?"

"She said you..."

"Yes?"

Anya groaned in surrender. "You dis-disrobed me the night of Richard's death," she said hoarsely, her pride se-verely trounced at repeating Merrawynn's lie to the now-vindicated American.

He met her gaze levelly. "I did."

"Oh!" She buried her face in her hands and, instead of wishing herself small enough to slip beneath the carpet, she wished herself to Bedfordshire.

"What did you expect me to do? Put you to sleep in wet clothing so you could die in full modesty? Or did you wish for Benson to perform the task?"

Morgan did have the decency to feel a flash of guilt at how much pleasure he'd derived from the deed, but he decided now was definitely not the time to admit that to Anya. Not quite comfortable with the surge of tenderness she stirred within him, he retreated behind a wall of studied calm. Per-haps he would use their tenth wedding anniversary as the occasion to confess her effect upon him.

More miserable by the minute, Anya realized that the American had merely performed an act of Christian kind-ness, and her own wicked thoughts had tainted his unsel-fish actions.

"Thank you, Mr. Grayson," she said quietly. "May I read the codicil now?"

"Of course." He handed her the two-page document. "And you can also begin calling me Morgan."

His steadfast gaze held her rivetted. "All—all right... Morgan."

"Does this mean I may call you by your Christian name?" A gentle smile played about his firm mouth.

Anya sighed. Since the American had no permanent place in her life, there was little harm in allowing him the familiarity—especially when one considered what had already transpired between them. "As you wish."

She began to read the codicil, and her astonishment increased with each passing word.

Simultaneously, Morgan's impatience grew when, after reading the papers through once, Anya flipped again to the first page and began rereading.

He studied her bent head, noticing how the morning light became her. Her dark brows were drawn together in concentration and her soft lips were pursed thoughtfully.

The gown she wore did little for the delectable body he knew it concealed. He found himself liking that about her. She might be soft and feminine, but she was also practical. Practical was what he needed in Texas. By day. By night he would be damned grateful for the softness.

He decided it was time to plead his case.

"Anya, I know we've gotten off to a poor start." Nothing like an understatement to begin a proposal of marriage, he thought wryly.

She looked up and stared at him. He read no emotion in her wide brown eyes, save polite attentiveness. He swore silently. Getting himself an English bride was more difficult than he'd originally anticipated.

"The point is," he continued resolutely, "there's a good life to be had in Texas if a person's willing to work."

He waited for her to say something. Anything. She continued to regard him mutely.

"I won't lie to you, Anya. The proceeds from Richard's estate mean a lot to me, but even a one-third portion would ease the situation back home."

"I see." She didn't, of course. She had no idea why Morgan Grayson was discussing his financial situation with her.

"I am thirty and in sound health. It's time I started a family. If you agree to marry me, I am prepared to increase Merrawynn's share of Richard's estate."

Why, he was proposing, Anya realized in astonishment. She gazed at him in absolute stupefaction. Unromantically, without the least bit of sentimentality, this stranger was actually asking her to honor Richard's will and…marry him.

She waited for the onrush of amusement she ought to feel. That her one and only proposal had come from this man was the cruelest of ironies.

He walked around the desk and knelt beside her, his eyes level with hers. "Consider carefully before you answer, Anya."

Bemused, she met his solemn gaze. "Why would you want to take a thorny woman to wife?"

Color stained his cheekbones. "Perhaps thorny was an overstatement."

She licked her lips. It was time to end this extraordinary interlude, before it went any further. Surely when she rejected him, Morgan Grayson would revert again to the obnoxious man who'd first invaded Hull Manor.

"B-but I cannot possibly marry you, Morgan." Not exactly a curt dismissal, she acknowledged. But to her surprise, she discovered she no longer wished to set down Richard's nephew.

The door to the library opened, and Merrawynn rushed into the room, wearing an elegant traveling gown of pale green. In addition to the anger she felt toward Merrawynn, Anya felt tears of sadness build. Poor Richard wasn't worth even a fortnight of mourning to her sister.

"Anya, our carriage is here. Are you ready to leave?"

"Accept my proposal, Anya, and I will settle an additional fifty thousand pounds upon your sister."

"Half that would be too much," Anya mused aloud.

"Anya, what are you doing?" Merrawynn cried, noticing the document Anya still held in her hands. "I would have told you myself about Richard's mad scheme to have you marry this creature, but I never for an instant thought you would accept him."

Her heart heavy, Anya stared at her beautiful sister. "Still, I had the right to hear his offer."

"You're a fool to consider marriage at your age, Anya. You've been a spinster for years. My God, you're four and twenty! You mean nothing to this man. He only requires you to get his greedy hands upon Richard's money."

Morgan rose. "That's enough."

Anya also stood, stepping between him and her sister. "Everything you say is true, Merrawynn. But Richard gave the choice to me."

"Fool! He'll take your money and abandon or abuse—"

"I said, enough," Morgan growled.

Merrawynn rounded on him. "I'll tell you when it's enough, you bloody upstart. My sister is too good for the likes of you, and furthermore—"

"Maybe she is," Morgan agreed, his voice low, lethal. "But as she said, the choice is hers."

Merrawynn's blue eyes glittered. "I won't allow her to—"

"Allow me?" Anya demanded incredulously, finally jumping into the fray. "I am fully capable of making my own decisions."

"But he's a...a *Yankee*," Merrawynn wailed, latching on to the man's most heinous flaw.

"He didn't choose to be born one," Anya snapped.

"Now just a damned minute," Morgan protested.

"You stay out of this," Merrawynn railed. "This discussion is between Anya and myself, and if you had the manners of a warthog, you would excuse yourself."

His lips thinned. "Not a chance, lady. I'm not letting Anya out of my sight."

Merrawynn's gaze narrowed. "Go to bloody hell."

"Stop treating me as if I'm a child who can't make up its own mind," Anya cried.

Merrawynn eyed her coldly. "This man is obviously a parasite. If you can't recognize that, then you're worse than a child. You're an imbecile, and not fit to manage your own affairs."

"That's it," Morgan said tersely. "You can leave willingly or I can toss you out. Take your pick."

"I imagine violence is not foreign to you," Merrawynn returned icily. "I shall see myself out. Anya, if you have any sense, you will leave here with me."

Neither Anya or Morgan responded.

Merrawynn swept regally to the doorway, then paused dramatically. "I'm waiting, Anya."

"I shall make my own way," Anya returned softly.

"But—"

"You said you were leaving," Morgan pointed out, his voice vibrating with barely leased fury.

Several moments passed in tense, angry silence, then Merrawynn, chin held high, marched from the room.

Morgan stepped to the window and watched the footman assist her into the carriage that he realized Anya must have ordered to be sent around for her own escape. He assumed Merrawynn would go directly to the railway station and from there travel to Richard's London house. According to the solicitor with whom he'd met in London, as Richard's widow, she was entitled to that property.

Anya joined Morgan at the window and together they watched as the coach sped from the courtyard in a flurry of flying gravel.

Morgan suspected that no words from him could ease Anya's outrage at her sister's high-handed intrusion into her life. No doubt Anya felt betrayed by Merrawynn's lies. Morgan knew about betrayal. His half brother had lied to him upon countless occasions. Only time and distance would put this memory into perspective for Anya.

"I never knew she hated me," she observed quietly.

"She probably doesn't. She just isn't the kind of woman to let anything or anyone stand in the way of what she wants."

At his cynical assessment of her sister, Anya shuddered. "I suppose I've always felt she was entitled to more, because she's so beautiful."

"Don't you realize that you, too, are beautiful?"

Anya became aware of how close Morgan stood to her. All at once there didn't seem to be enough air to breathe.

And when she took a deep breath, it was the essence of his unfamiliar scent she inhaled. "You needn't perjure your eternal soul to make me feel better."

"I suspect my soul already stands in jeopardy. Complimenting you will not blacken it further."

Morgan contemplated Anya's profile, appreciating her cleanly sculpted cheekbones and chin. Her skin was flawless, her nose straight. He stared at her soft mouth and a stab of desire shot through him, catching him off guard with its intensity.

His gaze dropped to her throat, where a pulse throbbed above the black piping of her collar, then lowered to the gentle swell of her bosom. He wanted her. All of her.

He told himself that his lust for her was acceptable. After all, he intended to make her his wife. As long as he kept his heart in check, she represented no threat to his peace of mind.

When his gaze returned to her face, he noticed the peach color staining her cheeks. "Aren't you going to take me to task for gawking?"

She turned from the window and faced him, her eyes wide. "I—I think I'm getting used to your American way of staring, though it is unsettling."

If Anya could read his mind, she'd be more than unsettled. "You'll find that we Americans like the direct approach. It saves a lot of wear and tear on the nerves."

"How . . . interesting." Anya stepped around him and moved to the center of the room. "Goodness, but it's warm in here. What could Benson have been thinking, to have stoked the fire so vigorously?"

Morgan looked at the pitiful flames sputtering in the library hearth and tamped down a grin. He was getting to her. Give him two weeks alone with the Englishwoman, and he'd have her eating out of his hand.

He'd wed her all right, and take her to his ranch, to his big brass bed. It would give him great pleasure to begin working on the next generation of Graysons. Of course, he would make sure Anya shared equally in the pleasure.

But first he had to get her to agree to the marriage.

"Do you have any gambling blood, Anya?"

Her eyebrows rose. "I beg your pardon?"

He reached inside his coat pocket for the deck of cards he always carried. "Back home, we play a little game called five-card stud. Are you familiar with it?"

Feeling the Englishwoman's curious gaze on the cards, Morgan was careful to keep his expression neutral.

"I never gamble."

"Never raced to the end of a lane, hmm?"

She stepped closer, watching the cards he shuffled as if they might disappear in a puff of sulfurous smoke.

"Of course I've raced to the end of the lane, but that's not really gambling."

"Do you like winning better than losing?"

"Everyone likes to win."

"Well, then, why don't we have ourselves a little game of chance and see how you like winning at five-card stud?"

Anya sensed the American was up to something. But, since he'd been so sympathetic in the face of Merrawynn's duplicity and had handled her own rejection of his proposal in such a gentlemanly fashion, she decided to humor him. What harm could there be in this game of stud?

"And can you guarantee that I shall win?"

Something hot and mysterious flashed in his dark eyes. "I'll do better than that. I'll guarantee that both of us win."

He placed two cards facedown on the desk, and Anya felt her attention drawn to the masculine symmetry of his tanned hand. She didn't understand why, but looking at his hand made her conscious of the flames flickering in the hearth.

Then she remembered that he had undressed and touched her with those hands....

Morgan laid a second card beside each of the first, this time face up, and her attention was pulled back to the game. His revealed card was a black seven, hers a scarlet woman wearing royal robes and a crown.

"See how lucky you are, Anya? You have my seven of spades beat with your queen of diamonds."

Anya nodded briskly, as if he had stated the obvious. "The queen of…diamonds is superior to the seven. I won?"

He chuckled softly. "It's too soon to tell, but you're doing very well." He gave each of them another card, also face up.

Anya stared in consternation at her red three. Because both her brother Edward and Richard had disapproved of gaming, she knew nothing about cards. Still, it was obvious from Morgan's words that the black monarch he'd placed beside his seven superceded her queen.

"You have won," she concluded.

"You're too impatient, Anya. The game is called *five-card stud*." He laid two more cards face up on the desk.

Anya smiled. "Now I have another monarch."

Morgan answered her smile with a grin. "That's a jack. He's under the queen and king—uh, the monarchs. But he does beat my ten."

She watched, fascinated, as Morgan laid down the next two cards. "Now I have a black seven and you have the letter *A*. Which is more valuable?"

"It's not an *A*. You're looking at an ace, Anya, the highest card in the deck."

She frowned, oddly deflated. "Then you did win?"

"Maybe."

"Maybe? This is a very silly game, if you don't know whether or not you've won!"

"Each of us still has cards that are facedown, Anya. We won't know who wins until both are turned over."

Immediately Anya reached for the first card. Morgan snagged her wrist. "Not so fast. We've played this hand without betting anything."

The pressure he exerted upon her wrist was firm, yet not hurtful. When she tried to tug free, however, he did not release her. "I told you I do not approve of gambling."

Beneath the sudden curving of his lips, even white teeth flashed. "It's too late to back out now."

"You—you expect me to—to present money?"

His gaze swept across her curiously. "Have you any on you?"

She flushed. "Mr. Grayson—"

"Morgan," he corrected gently.

"Morgan—"

"I don't want your money, Anya." His eyes held hers.

"Then . . . then what do you want?"

"The opportunity to spend a couple of days getting to know you, to see if we're . . . compatible."

She tugged once more against his unyielding grip. Nothing happened. "You have my hand," she pointed out, in case he hadn't noticed that his strong fingers bound her.

"So I do."

And what are you going to do about it? he seemed to ask, silently mocking her. Anya dropped her gaze to the ten cards laid neatly across Richard's desk. Morgan's *A,* or ace as he called it, was the highest card in the deck. It was senseless to wager. After all, the American had already won the game.

"Maybe I should explain that there are several ways to take the hand, Anya. For instance, a pair of any two cards will beat my ace."

Thoughtfully, she nibbled her bottom lip, amazed at how passionately she wanted to defeat the American. Glancing up at his face, she was struck again at how carefully he seemed to conceal his thoughts. Though, of course, from the ironic tone of voice, his amusement at her indecisiveness was obvious.

"And the wager you desire is that I remain at Hull Manor for two additional days?"

He nodded. "Where's your English pride? You're not going to let an *American* bluff you into folding, are you?"

Bluff? Fold? They were not everyday words to Anya, but she clearly read their import. Suddenly she realized she was going to do it, to take the wretched American up on his challenge. For England . . . She would do it for her country's honor.

She could feel her mouth widen into a smile. "I *never* fold. Your wager is accepted."

He released her wrist, and Anya rubbed her skin, bewildered that it continued to tingle even though he no longer touched her. Then, unable to curb her curiosity, she flipped over her first card.

"Another seven! Now I have two." She flashed a victorious grin at her opponent. "That means I—"

"Not so fast. Before you start gloating, let's see what Lady Luck has in store for me."

He turned over a second ace.

Anya's heart plummeted to her shoes. She'd lost!

"Don't look so sad. We can always play another hand—double or nothing."

"Double or nothing?"

"Four days. Or none. And, Anya, there's plenty of other ways to win that I haven't shown you yet."

She ignored the inner voice that advised her to run from the room and never again play this devilish game. After all, she couldn't just let him win. That would be cowardly, wouldn't it?

He finished shuffling the cards and again laid two facedown before placing two more cards next to them.

"You've got an ace showing, Anya."

Her gaze jerked to Morgan's disturbingly benign expression. "Do you offer your word as a gentleman, that you won't...er...cheat?"

Amusement gleamed in his eyes. "Absolutely."

Chapter Five

That evening Anya paced angrily back and forth across her bedchamber. A month! She'd wagered and lost a month of her life to Morgan Grayson. Ooh, what a fool she'd been to trust him! Despite his assurances to the contrary, he must have cheated. No one could be *that* lucky.

She stopped pacing. There was no way she could spend a month alone, unchaperoned, with a man. Why, her reputation would be destroyed.

She was simply going to have to explain to him, in a calm and rational manner, that—in her country, at least—a lady didn't move in with a gentleman. Surely he would understand her explanation and cancel the wager.

Moving to the small window beside her bureau, Anya parted the curtain. Dusk had settled across the gardens. What could she have been thinking to have spent an entire afternoon with Morgan Grayson playing his game of stud?

As she reflected back upon the episode in the library, she recalled that after losing the first hand, she had won the next. And the next. The flush of victory, along with Morgan's glowing descriptions of life on a Texas cattle ranch, had lulled her into forgetting the stakes for which they played.

Only when Benson had discreetly knocked at the library door to inform them that dinner would be served within the hour had the companionable spell of Morgan's nearness been broken. Then the American had tallied up the hands won and lost.

When he'd informed her that she owed him a full month of her life, she'd thought he was jesting. Then he'd handed her the score he'd kept, and she'd seen with her own eyes that she had indeed forfeited a total of thirty days.

Dazed, she'd retired to her bedchamber and dressed for dinner. But now that her initial shock was over, it seemed to her there was no way the American could have played an honest game and won so many hands. And surely honor didn't demand that she respect an agreement made with a . . . a scoundrel.

Feeling somewhat better, she surveyed her reflection in the standing beveled mirror. Again, she wore the dark blue gown, feeling it was her most appropriate garment for mourning. When she arrived at her brother's home in Bedfordshire, she would order up several dresses of black from the village seamstress. Until then, her gray and blue gowns would have to suffice.

Her fingertips went to the ruby brooch that Richard had presented to her on her twenty-first birthday. As she remembered his generosity both to herself and to Merrawynn, tears came. It seemed impossible that he was really gone from their lives. On the morrow she would visit the conservatory and clip a bouquet of flowers for him. Perhaps when she laid them at the family crypt, she would be able to find a measure of peace at his passing.

She turned from her reflection. For some reason, when she'd dressed for dinner she had been plagued with the knowledge that—on a night not long past—Morgan Grayson had removed every stitch of her clothing.

The peculiar fluttering sensation she'd come to associate with Morgan Grayson teased her stomach muscles. First, he would have relieved her of her gown. That wouldn't have been an easy feat, with the material of her dress heavily soaked. Next he would have pulled her drenched petticoats from her. She remembered she hadn't worn many that fate-

ful night. What had he thought when he'd encountered no
corset? Had he considered her shameless?

She wasn't, of course.

It was just that, living in the country as she had for the
past few years, she'd gotten into the habit of forgoing the
bony stays. It hadn't seemed improper to do so. After all,
most of the time her only company was Richard and the
servants. Whenever the tutor Richard employed for her
studies had instructed her, she had met him properly corsetted.

Anya smoothed her skirts. The faint rustling reminded her
that, after Morgan had removed her petticoats, she would
have been reduced to her stockings, drawers and bodice.
Then—

"Miss Anya, now that I'm feeling better, you should let
me help you dress."

At the unexpected sound of her serving maid's voice,
Anya jumped. "Oh, Mavis, you startled me."

"I'm sorry, Miss Anya. I thought you heard me come in.
I didn't mean to—"

Smiling, Anya interrupted her. "It's all right, Mavis.
Since both my gown and my corset fasten in the front, I was
able to manage."

Richard had brought Mavis Scrug into his employ three
years earlier. Everlastingly grateful, the girl continued to be
most diligent in her duties.

"I suppose Sally has also recovered, Mavis?"

"Oh, yes, and Mrs. Patterson is back, too."

Anya moved toward the door. "When did she arrive?"

"Just a bit ago. She's in the kitchen seeing what Cook has
fixed for you and your visitor."

"Visitor?"

"You know, Miss Anya. The gentleman from America."

"Oh, *him.*" Somehow the word *visitor* seemed far too
innocent to describe Morgan Grayson. Glancing about her
chamber, Anya frowned. Her trunk was open and articles
of clothing were strewn about. "I'm sorry to leave you to
such disorder, Mavis. See what you can do with it."

"Yes, Miss Anya."

Anya encountered Honora Patterson coming down the hall from the dining room. The older woman's narrow face seemed pinched with the pain of her advancing rheumatism.

"Good evening, Miss Anya. Cook has done us well tonight."

"Doesn't she always?" Patting the housekeeper's arm, Anya guided the woman toward the stairs. "I can manage now, Honora. The trip from your daughter's home is a long one, and I'm sure you're tired. Have Mavis and Sally help you unpack. Tomorrow will be soon enough for you to resume your labors."

The lines marking the housekeeper's face softened. "Why, thank you. Everything is in order in the kitchens, and I've checked to see that your guest has everything he needs."

"Then there's no reason for you to remain up. Good night, Honora."

"Sleep well, Miss Anya."

Anya took a moment to make certain her hair was neatly tucked into her braided coronet before she entered the dining room. As she'd expected, Honora had seen that the table was formally set. Two place settings, at opposite ends of the great mahogany table, faced each other.

It occurred to Anya that with half the staff still at Richard's London house, Benson would be serving tonight. She sighed. It was going to be a long evening. Edgar was much better at handling the intricacies of serving. Which was why Merrawynn had taken him with her entourage to London months ago.

Merrawynn... Anya had put off thinking about their ugly confrontation for as long as she could. Recalling the bitter scene, she realized that Morgan had softened the blow of her sister's selfish treachery.

"I hope that frown hasn't anything to do with the quality of tonight's meal."

At the sound of Morgan's deep voice, Anya spun around. Seeing him standing before her in a coat and trousers of dark gray made her forget for a moment that she was angry with him. His white shirt and dark waistcoat emphasized the width of his shoulders and the strength of his manly physique. All he needed was a top hat to polish off his image of a gentleman.

"The frown has nothing to do with Cook's efforts."

"Surely it isn't because of the weather. I know for a fact that Englishmen never expect the climate to be anything but nasty in the fall." The curve of his lips cushioned the aspersion on her country's weather.

"I suppose that the sun always shines, the birds always sing and the flowers always bloom in America."

He laughed. "I'm not an expert on the rest of my country. But the sun usually does shine in Texas. The flowers will bloom after you plant them."

"And the birds?"

"Hawks, crows and quail are the most common," he answered.

"Are the streets paved with gold?"

A sober expression claimed Morgan's features. "Not lately."

Was he remembering his nation's recent war? Anya tried to imagine what it would be like to see one's homeland torn apart with savage battles. In the papers, she'd read that it had been brother against brother, father against son. All at once she found herself curious to know what the war had been like for Morgan. Had he been a soldier?

Before she could find a way to broach the sensitive subject, however, the side door to the dining room opened, and Benson entered bearing a covered serving platter. Without further conversation, Morgan and Anya moved to the formally set table.

Morgan gestured to the place settings, which were more than ten feet apart. "This won't do."

Benson's forehead puckered in confusion. "I beg your pardon, sir?"

"It's ridiculous for us to set with the whole table between us. Move your mistress's setting to the right of mine."

Benson set the serving tray on the sideboard, moving quickly to obey Morgan. Anya resisted the temptation to countermand Morgan's order. She didn't appreciate the American's take-charge attitude. Nor did she like the fact that she was going to be sitting so close to him.

As far as she was concerned, the greater distance separating them the better when she informed Morgan Grayson that she had no intention of remaining at Hull Manor beyond tomorrow morning. Morgan pulled out her chair for her, and she slid into it. While he took his place at the head of the table, she reached for her wineglass and took a fortifying sip.

Slanting a glance at him as she swallowed, she decided he looked entirely too satisfied with himself. His confidence irritated her. Did he really think he could just snap his fingers and she would do his bidding? She drained her glass. Ordinarily, she didn't care for the taste of alcohol—especially the foul brandy Morgan had foisted upon her the evening they'd met. But tonight's wine seemed unusually mellow.

Benson uncovered the serving platter. A wreath of carrots and potatoes circled the lamb roast. Anya's stomach growled in a most unseemly manner. She flushed and surreptitiously pressed a hand against her middle, realizing that this was her first meal today. Benson began slicing the succulent roast. Her mouth watered.

"More wine, Anya?"

"What?" In the flickering candlelight, Morgan no longer resembled the laughing companion she'd played cards with earlier in the day. Instead, a hawklike alertness sharpened his features.

He smiled. "Allow me."

Anya watched him refill her goblet with wine. Such a strong hand, connected to such a strong arm, connected to...

"Thank you." She reached for the ruby-colored liquid. What was taking Benson so long to carve the lamb? It wasn't as if he had to chase it across a field, after all.

"You're welcome."

Eyeing Morgan above the rim of her glass, Anya tried to decide what it was about the shadows playing across his features that so unnerved her. And his eyes . . . so dark, so impossibly difficult to fathom.

What were his thoughts? The thoughts that made his mouth curve upward and his gaze mesmerize hers. Setting her emptied glass on the table, she silently watched him fill it again. She became aware of a sensation of warmth bathing her skin. Goodness, had there ever been such a warm September evening in all the history of England?

"Miss Anya?"

"What?"

"Are you ready to be served?"

At first Benson's question made little sense. Then her gaze dropped to the lovely floral pattern on her empty dinner plate. "Of course."

When Benson stepped back, she wasted no time cutting a portion of the lamb. It was moist, tender and stone cold. Laying aside her fork, she quenched her thirst with a few more swallows of wine. Too bad there wasn't some way whereby they could crank up Benson, the way Cook cranked the cider press.

As long as the servant hovered at the table, Anya felt obliged to eat. When he finally left the room and closed the door behind him, she pushed away the plate and reached for her wineglass, all the while aware of Morgan's silent scrutiny.

She tried smiling at him.

He smiled back. Somehow she didn't feel that his smile was the least bit sincere. But then what could one expect from a cheater of cards?

Wanting to knock his annoying grin from his face, she glowered back at him. The corners of his mouth twitched, but he didn't return her frown. Obviously he had no idea that she was on to his sneaky schemes.

"It won't work," she announced grandly.

"What won't work, Anya?"

She glared at him. The amused tone of his voice and the familiar twinkle in his dark eyes seemed to mock her.

"Your deception."

Ever so slowly the laughter faded from his eyes. "And which deception is that?" The mildness of his question contrasted starkly with the intensity of his gaze.

"It may have escaped your notice, but I am not a person to be trifled with," she explained loftily.

"I see."

"After some reflection upon the matter, it occurred to me that the only way you could have won so many hands this afternoon was if you..." Anya found it impossible to continue under his baleful stare.

"Go on, Anya."

Silk. His voice was like silk, burning silk. She moistened her lips and looked longingly at her empty wineglass.

"Are you thirsty? Here, let me pour you more refreshment. That's it, drink your fill, Anya. Now tell me how it is that I won today at cards."

Beneath the outward softness of his words, she heard the steel. Yet she wasn't afraid. There was a pleasant buzzing in her head and the feeling that—on this night—she was invincible.

"You cheated."

He picked up his glass and drank slowly, emptying it. Then he returned it to the table. His arrogant grin was back. Full force. "Miss Delangue, I demand satisfaction."

She gaped at him. "What?"

Pushing back his chair, he stood. "You have impugned my honor, blackened my name and spoiled my meal. By the traditions of your country and mine, I can and do demand satisfaction."

"Y-you mean fight a *duel?* In this day and age?"

He nodded. "It's the only way to redeem my honor. I believe the choice of weapons is mine."

"Weapons?"

"Well, of course we'll require weapons," he drawled, his tone matter-of-fact. "What do you prefer? Pistols? Sabers? Fisticuffs?"

"Cannons! For me!" She jumped to her feet. "And you, you madman, can use a—a paper knife."

When she tried to push her way past the blackguard, he grabbed her arm and turned her to face him.

"Remove your hand, sir." Even as she said the words, Anya cringed. Couldn't she have come up with something stronger, something so quelling that Morgan Grayson would shrivel into his shiny black boots?

"The hand stays, Anya. Until you select a weapon with which to meet me on a field of honor."

"You're mocking me! No man challenges a woman to a duel."

"You mean in England?"

"Anywhere!"

"You're wrong, Anya. Men and women challenge each other all the time."

"Not with sabers or pistols or—"

"Paper knives?" His left brow arched. "Maybe not, but they use other, perhaps more lethal weapons."

Anya tried to capture and make sense of his confusing statements, but her head spun. "For you, words are weapons."

"You're armed, too, Anya—with beckoning eyes, a gracefully beckoning body and softly beckoning lips. *Are* you beckoning me?"

She stared at the strong fingers that gripped her blue sleeve. Not in a hundred years could she summon the strength necessary to break their hold.

Standing so close to him, she felt the heat of his breath upon her cheek, felt the heat from his hard body radiating toward her and felt an answering heat rise within her.

"What do you want?" she asked softly, tremulously.

"Satisfaction."

"In the form of a—a duel?"

"In the form of a kiss."

His constraining hand softened its hold while his other arm came around her. Bemused, she tipped her face to him. All she saw was his mouth—holding a smile—descending toward her. She stood transfixed.

Her feelings toward the man who brushed his lips gently against hers were evenly divided between wanting to flee his presence, slap his face or...or discover how it felt to be well and truly kissed.

Suddenly it seemed very important that she concentrate carefully on what was happening. In the years to come, she would want an exact memory of this moment. Exact...

His mouth was strangely soft. And kind. She especially liked how he rubbed it against her lips. Back and forth, with so gentle a friction that she found the contact somehow insufficient for her needs.

Her hands seemed to rise of their own accord to encircle his neck. The hair she encountered above his collar was longish and silken. She found herself leaning into him. He was so satisfyingly substantial. Like a mountain.

She had grown accustomed meeting eye-to-eye the few men with whom she dealt. In tilting her face to meet Morgan's, she felt feminine and dainty for the first time in her life.

A lot of things about the American were nice. Like his scent. Traces of tobacco mingled with tangy soap, hair tonic and...and something else she couldn't quite identify. Something essentially masculine. And he tasted... He tasted of the wine she'd drunk at dinner. Heady, sweet and faintly dangerous.

She could feel his hands at her waist, anchoring her against him. At some subtle pressure from him, her lips parted and the tip of his tongue slowly entered her mouth. Her eyelids flew open in astonishment at his bold intimacy. It had never occurred to her that a man might do such a thing to a woman.

He raised his head and stared down at her darkly. Incredibly, he was still smiling. However, it was as if twin torches had been lit in his eyes.

"I didn't cheat, Anya."

For the first time she became aware of the quick, shallow breaths she was taking. "It makes no difference."

With a gentleness she hadn't expected him capable of, he stroked her cheek. "Doesn't it?"

"I cannot remain with you at Hull Manor."

"Why not?" he inquired with a husky whisper that turned her knees to vanilla custard.

"It just isn't done."

His hands fell away from her, and at their absence, she felt bereft.

"That's a cowardly answer, Anya. Somehow I expected better from you."

"Cowardly or not, in England an unmarried woman will be compromised if she remains alone with a man."

"Without a chaperon, you mean."

"I'm glad you understand. I will be leaving in the morning for my brother's home."

"Won't that be a bit like locking the stable door after the horse has bolted?"

She didn't like the way he was looking at her, as if he possessed some crucial bit of information she lacked. "What do you mean?"

"I mean that we were alone for a week before Merrawynn arrived."

"That didn't count—I was ill."

"One of my fondest memories of my time in England, and it doesn't count?"

She felt her cheeks flood with a heated burst of color. How could she have forgotten what a cad he was?

"And," he continued, "there is tonight. You and I alone—not considering the ten or so servants decorating the premises. Surely, your reputation has already been besmirched by such wild and wanton behavior."

"Are you ridiculing the conventions of my country?"

"Conventions? Anya Delangue, there's not one conventional thing about you. Don't forget I met you riding a renegade stallion—astride—through a raging thunderstorm. Name one other woman in all England who would have performed such a reckless act!"

When she didn't offer him a name, he continued. "And what well-bred English miss would spend an afternoon gambling her favors in a game of five-card stud?"

Anya shook her head, wondering how she'd gotten into such a predicament.

"Don't come prattling to me about convention." He waved a lean finger beneath her nose. "You haven't a conventional bone in your delightfully formed body."

She backed away from him, casting about her swirling thoughts for an effective rebuttal.

"Face it, Anya. You ride, play cards and hold your liquor more like a Southern gentleman than an English-woman."

"How dare you insult me!"

He laughed. "Depends on your point of view, I suppose. I thought I was complimenting you. Especially on holding your liquor. I had every intention of getting you drunk tonight."

"What?"

He shook his head. "Good Lord, who would have guessed that a slender package like you could consume four glasses of wine and still remain standing?"

Anya opened her mouth to call him a cur and hiccuped, instead.

This time only his dark eyes laughed at her. "And you kiss like a—"

"Southern gentleman?" she demanded furiously.

His sudden spurt of laughter bounced off the dining-room walls.

Ooh, how she hated the sound of his unrestrained amusement at her expense. He was worse than a cur; he was a lout!

"Are you going to hit me?" he asked, looking pointedly at the clenched fists she held next to her sides. From his wide smile, she surmised the prospect didn't strike terror in him.

She drew herself to her full height, which she'd always considered sufficient to daunt anyone, and tried looking down her nose at him. He did not appear at all chastised.

"You certainly deserve to be hit, but I don't doubt you would hesitate to strike me back."

"I might be tempted to administer an object lesson to your charming backside."

Anya's mouth fell open. She couldn't believe he had actually mentioned that part of her person. Unthinkingly, she moved her hands to shield the aforethreatened anatomy. At her protective gesture, her breasts jutted upwards.

"On second thought," he continued, "I don't suppose I'd ever do anything to mar your lovely skin."

"You—you shouldn't say such things to me."

"You're right, of course. I'm being a bear tonight. You have to realize, though, that no man approves of being called a cheat, especially by his fiancée."

"I'm not your fiancée," she whispered shakily.

He reached around her and snagged her right hand. "Since my first fiancée jilted me, I haven't cared overmuch for that particular title. But somehow, applying it to you isn't all that unpleasant."

"If you treated your former prospective bride in the same mocking manner you've shown me, it's no wonder she jilted you." As soon as the words left her mouth, Anya wanted to call them back.

The trouble in dealing with a man like Morgan Grayson was that one assumed he had a hide as thick as a pachyderm's and was therefore immune to any insult. By the sudden paleness of his taut features, Anya realized this was not the case. She had hurt him.

His hand relaxed its hold on hers. Moved by guilt, she grasped his wrist. "I—I'm sorry, Morgan. I didn't mean to be unkind."

Did he still hold a place in his heart for his past love? Was that why her thoughtless taunt had wounded him? At the possibility of his still harboring an affection for the woman, Anya experienced a surge of disappointment.

"Don't pity me, Anya. I recovered from Collette's disaffection years ago."

Anya heard the regret in his voice and released his hand. "Good night, Morgan." She turned and took several steps from him.

"Anya, about the chaperon..."

Midway across the room she paused.

"Is there someone from the village who might fill that role?"

Slowly, she pivoted. "I—I suppose."

"And do you also suppose that Richard's last request deserves more than a hasty rejection?"

"His—his last request?"

"For us to get to know each other. You need to learn that I'm from a different continent, not a different world."

"But, Morgan, surely you can see from the brief time we've spent together that we do not suit."

A reckless grin slashed his face. "Who says so?"

"But—but we *argue*—continually."

His eyes sparkled with amusement. Only this time the amusement didn't offend. She had the feeling he was laughing at himself.

"Damned if we don't. But we *kiss* like crashing bolts of lightning."

She remembered the kiss. Goodness, how she remembered the kiss. "Uh, yes. It was...nice."

"Nice! It was pure fire. Think about it, Anya. A lifetime of kisses like that."

"A lifetime of quarreling," she countered, feeling the ridiculous urge to giggle.

He moved toward her, and she retreated.

"Give us four weeks, Anya. The four weeks I *fairly* won. Let's see if Richard's matchmaking was on target. You can get the damned chaperon, too."

"If—if I did invite, say, Lady Hester, to visit, it wouldn't mean that I had promised to—to actually marry you."

Morgan was a man who'd learned to consolidate his victories. "I will hold you to nothing."

"I—I don't think we ought to kiss again."

"Why not?"

"I don't think it's healthy," she returned seriously.

"Not *healthy?*"

Feeling strangely disconnected from her body, Anya nodded. "I don't know about you, but I felt most peculiar."

"Peculiar?"

"I could scarcely catch my breath. It was as if my fever had returned. My heart was pounding at an alarmingly fast pace. And my knees ... simply vanished. No, I don't think this kissing business is at all healthy."

Morgan brushed his hand over his mouth. "You know, Anya, I think maybe the wine you drank is catching up with you."

"Oh. I didn't think of that."

Again he touched her cheek with his forefinger and lightly stroked her skin. "Didn't you?"

She smiled crookedly. "I suppose you're right. It must have been the wine. If kissing caused such distress, then people wouldn't keep doing it, would they?"

Smiling, he lowered his hand to her arm. "Let me help you up the stairs, Anya."

She wrinkled her forehead as she followed his lead, trying to recall something of significance she needed to tell him. When she remembered, she looked up at him earnestly. "Mavis will help me undress."

He sighed heavily. "Tonight she will."

Chapter Six

The following morning, Morgan mounted the roan he'd bought when he'd arrived in London. Champion had earned a day of leisure. Instead of battling the high-strung stallion, Morgan would be better served to channel his energies on subduing a particularly high-strung Englishwoman.

He headed in the direction he'd seen Anya ride and smiled grimly, trying not to take her flight personally. It had not escaped his notice that the women he planned on taking to wife had a distressing tendency to bolt. First Collette, now Anya.

Collette... How many nights had he and the hot-blooded Creole woman spent in torrid lovemaking? Too many to count. She'd been insatiable and so had he. Being young and inexperienced, he'd mistakenly believed their heated coupling had something to do with love.

Since then, he'd learned that love was a mirage—like those he'd seen on sweltering days in the barren Texas plains. A thirsting man might think he saw a shimmering lake in the distance. But no matter how doggedly he pursued it, the mirage remained beyond his reach. And if he tried to drink from the enticing illusion, he came away with a mouthful of dust. No matter how thirsty a man might be, he'd be a fool to keep choking down dust.

Still, Morgan had every intention of hanging on to his English filly—once he'd caught up with her. Not for the first time, he wondered how his father had managed to marry three women when he, Morgan, was having the damnedest difficulty securing one. His late father had been widowed twice and produced sons with each union.

With a scowl, Morgan realized he didn't envy his father. After going through all this trouble to get a wife the first time, he certainly had no desire to repeat the tedious process.

He spurred the roan. One thing was certain, the sea voyage back to America was going to be more pleasurable than the one coming over. From what he'd seen of his prospective bride's temperament, she had a good portion of hot-bloodedness herself.

Morgan intended on helping himself to another heady sampling of that passion when he caught up with her today. He figured he deserved a reward for chasing her across the English countryside.

A smart man took his pleasures when and where he found them.

Anya leaned forward and patted Lady Lore. "It's been a while, hasn't it, girl?"

In the weeks she'd tended Richard, Anya hadn't had an opportunity to ride. Looking about, she savored the surprisingly mild morning. Again, she was reminded of how much she enjoyed being outdoors. The air was crisp—the sun shining, the birds singing....

The memory of last night's conversation with Morgan Grayson intruded upon her enjoyment. It was because of him that she was riding to Lady Hester's neighboring estate to ask the older woman to act as chaperon until the duration of her bargain with Morgan Grayson had been met—a bargain Anya felt as if she'd made with the devil himself.

A satisfied smile teased her lips. It wasn't often one got the better of the devil. Wait until the American laid eyes upon Lady Hester. A giggle bubbled to life, catching Anya by surprise. It astonished her how much she was looking forward to besting her would-be groom.

There was no doubt in her mind that after spending only a fortnight in Lady Hester's company, Morgan Grayson would rescind his offer of matrimony and speedily depart to America—where he belonged and Anya most certainly did not.

She reined in Lady Lore. It had been awhile since she'd ridden sidesaddle. Anya adjusted her skirts. It wouldn't do, however, to pay Lady Hester a visit in Anya's usual mode of tearing about the neighborhood.

Thoughtfully, she nibbled her lower lip. Over the past few years, she had had more than one unfortunate altercation with the older woman. Of course, Anya had been younger and hadn't yet learned to curb her tongue. Anya now considered herself a mature woman of great decorum. Hadn't she been handling Richard's servants for years?

Anya envisioned no difficulty in securing Lady Hester's assistance. The only crucial part of her plan was to speak privately with the woman and explain how essential it was that Richard's nephew be kept in his place, and a very narrow place it would be. Anya was never to be left alone with the American. He was to be made to feel most uncomfortable at all times. Anya had already spoken to Cook, and the meals would become less appetizing. All in all, it shouldn't be that difficult to send the man on his way.

Most vital was Anya's intention to never again be kissed by Morgan. That she didn't hold up very well to his kissing was a sad and lamentable fact.

The unwelcome memory of how it felt to be held and kissed by Morgan Grayson slithered into her thoughts. She closed her eyes. It had to have been the wine that had caused the rioting sensations she'd experienced last night. It couldn't have been the man. Her eyes snapped open. Good grief, in the space of a day, he had her tippling and gaming and . . . and comporting herself like a libertine.

She dug her heels into Lady Lore's plump sides. Though she was made of stern stuff, Anya suspected prolonged proximity with the American might very well result in her becoming quite dissolute. It was a risk she wasn't willing to take—not if she expected to become a governess. Everyone knew a governess must be beyond reproach. Nodding to herself with renewed satisfaction, Anya decided that seeking Lady Hester's aid had been a stroke of genius.

The sound of approaching hoofbeats didn't unduly alarm Anya. Though this was a lightly populated area, it was not that unusual to encounter a fellow traveler. The lane that led to Lady Hester's country estate was around the next bend. Rolling hills studded with large rocks and occasional trees whose leaves had gone to red and gold provided reassuringly familiar surroundings.

It was only when the rate of speed with which the horseman was closing in on her registered that Anya pulled Lady Lore to a stop and glanced over her shoulder. It sounded as if she were about to be trampled.

At the sight of Morgan Grayson barreling down upon her as if he were being pursued by the devil himself, Anya's breath locked in her throat. She had the wild impulse to flee. Only by exercising the most rigid determination did she hold her ground.

As he drew up beside her, Anya's gaze was drawn to the odd-looking hat he wore. It was tan and had an unusually large crown. Under it's wide brim, she had a clear view only of his grim-lipped mouth. Beneath her properly corsetted ribs, her heart pounded. She had the horrible suspicion the American must have guessed what she was up to.

She smiled with what she hoped was innocent cheerfulness. "Good morning, Mr. Grayson."

"Morgan," he corrected, his voice gritty.

Lady Lore sidestepped the stallion's nudging interest. Anya swallowed. She knew just how her mount felt.

"Morgan," she repeated firmly.

"So, where are you headed?" he asked.

Expertly, she reined the skittish horse, noticing there was no good-morning for *her*. "To visit Lady Hester."

Since Anya was accustomed to doing as she pleased, explaining her actions to Richard's nephew rankled. She supposed that a woman with a husband had need of such explanations. Until this moment, she hadn't previously considered the matter.

The tension seemed to leave the American, and she wondered what he'd thought she'd been about. Keeping her smile intact—at this point her cheeks were beginning to ache—Anya pointed down the lane. "Her house is quite close, Mr. Gra—Morgan. With your leave, I'll continue on my way."

"Not so fast."

Not so fast? She was virtually at a standstill. "Was there something else?"

"I'd like to make Lady Hester's acquaintance."

Anya's smile faltered. "W-what?"

Beneath the tan rim, his lips curved. "Under the circumstances, it would be the neighborly thing to do."

"The—the circumstances?"

"Richard's choosing a foreigner for your husband might alarm the woman."

"He didn't choose you for my husband," Anya corrected hastily. "He merely wanted to see if we suited."

Morgan studied her silently for a moment. "He had more than that in mind, Anya."

She raised her chin. "Nevertheless, the choice is mine."

"And mine."

It was a stalemate. If she continued to protest, Morgan might realize that she was about to sabotage the agreement he had wrung from her. She ducked her head. It was almost impossible to choke back the angry words she wanted to hurl.

Slowly, she looked off into the distance. There was no help for it. Morgan Grayson would meet Lady Hester ahead of schedule.

"As you wish," Anya said quietly.

Morgan suspected that no description on Anya's part could have prepared him for Lady Hester. Less than five feet tall and weighing all of ninety pounds, she should have seemed slight and frail. But with her strangely fashioned silver turban and rustling maroon taffeta gown, the older woman generated a most commanding presence.

One strand of gray hair fell artfully across Lady Hester's lined forehead. Her jeweled hands rested upon an ornately carved ivory walking stick that he guessed was purely decorative, and her powdered face intensified a pair of shrewd blue eyes he would be leery of meeting across a poker table.

Morgan shifted, uncomfortable with both the flimsy, spindly-legged chair that supported him and Lady Hester's suspicious blue gaze. He wasn't used to going out of his way to charm older women. Usually they took great pains to charm him, trotting out their eligible granddaughters and great-nieces. They fussed over him with dainty glasses of sherry, tittering periodically.

His gaze ran up and down the tiny woman. She returned the favor, and Morgan felt as if he were a prize bull being driven through the auction ring. For the first time in his adult life, he felt his cheeks color. One thing was clear, the woman didn't have a titter in her.

The lag in the conversation did nothing to make him feel more at ease. After dispensing cookies that she referred to as biscuits, weak tea and condolences for Richard's death, the older woman had lapsed into silence.

Morgan glared at Anya. Seated upon the settee, she seemed perfectly content. His gaze narrowed. In fact, she looked damned pleased with herself. Impatiently, he set the eggshell-thin teacup on the ebony table near his elbow. The sound of a clock ticking torturously grated upon his composure. And Lady Hester continued to stare into his soul.

"So, Mr. Grayson, how long are you planning to remain in England?"

He jumped at the unexpected question. "Not long."

She raised a quizzing glass. "Are you being vague for a purpose, Mr. Grayson?"

It struck him that leading a charge across a Union battle-field had been less nerve-racking than being interviewed by Lady Hester. "Not at all, ma'am."

He glanced at Anya. Her soft lips were twitching in what he deduced was barely concealed amusement at his being treated as though he were a twelve-year-old boy. His gaze lingered upon that tantalizing mouth.

"You didn't answer my question, Mr. Grayson," the woman observed imperiously.

Morgan returned his attention to the miniature dragon lady. He forced himself to smile. He'd never been put into the position of charming a more unfriendly female, but desperate situations called for desperate actions. And the fact was, he wanted desperately to get Anya Delangue and her softly beckoning mouth alone. Soon.

"I know I will be in the neighborhood for at least a month. After that…" He smiled warmly, leaning toward the older woman. "As much as your lovely country appeals to me, I will be returning to America."

"Indeed?"

"As soon as I settle Richard's holdings and marry Anya, I'll be on my way."

"Marry *Anya?*" Lady Hester's voice scaled upward.

Anya watched Morgan's slowly widening grin and wanted to cheer. *Go ahead, say something vulgar, say something appallingly… American, and we'll never be alone again.*

The way Anya saw it, Lady Hester was seconds away from ordering her butler to escort Morgan Grayson from her sitting room. And if the woman did agree to act as chaperon, Anya was certain she and Morgan Grayson would *never* be alone together.

Her plan was working even better with Morgan as an accomplice. With every word he spoke, the man was digging his own grave.

"It was Richard's final wish," Morgan continued quietly. "And that's why Anya and I have come to visit you today, ma'am."

The matron's eyes fairly bulged. "As I am not the vicar, Mr. Grayson, I fail to see how I may be of service."

Anya almost crowed. It was obvious the woman would not allow herself to be cajoled by any man—let alone an impertinent American. *You're wasting your time trying to charm old starch-in-the-drawers Hester.*

Morgan chuckled softly and tipped his head, smiling in what Anya reluctantly admitted *was* an engaging manner. "Before we need the services of a minister, we're in dire need of a chaperon."

"Dire?" Lady Hester inquired ominously.

He nodded. "I don't think Anya can restrain herself much longer without some outside help."

After that singularly shocking and vulgar observation, Morgan Grayson compounded his unpardonable behavior by winking lazily at the eldest daughter of the fourth Duke of Winterburry.

Anya was both outraged and delighted. She decided then and there that she needed to be alone at least one more time with Morgan so she could slap his arrogantly handsome face. Surely she was entitled.

Her avid gaze whipped to Lady Hester. The older woman's lips quivered. Anya knew a horribly monstrous setdown was about to be unleashed.

Go ahead, Lady Hester. Wish the barbarian to perdition—or Texas. Either place will do.

A strange gurgle emerged from the older woman, a scratchy, creaking kind of cough. It took a moment for Anya to realize the sound she heard was...laughter. Rusty to be sure, but laughter, nevertheless.

"Sir, you are a scoundrel."

Morgan leaned back in his chair and grinned unrepentantly. "Does that mean you'll join us at Hull Manor?"

Lady Hester stamped her cane. "Of course I shall join you, Mr. Grayson. After all, I must see that Anya... contains herself."

Another spasm of creaking laughter shook the older woman, and Anya glared indignantly. As far as she was concerned, Lady Hester had proven a sad disappointment on all counts. The matron was a traitor not only to their sex, but to their country, as well. Tittering in the face of an enemy invasion... If she'd been in the military, the woman would have been court-martialed.

As Lady Lore galloped from Lady Hester's estate, Anya did not look back. Morgan Grayson might or might not be following. She didn't care. The blackguard could bloody well drop off the face of the earth.

Anger, hot and fierce, nipped at her heels. Her brilliant scheme to enlist Lady Hester's aid had been ruined beyond redemption—all because of the odious American. It infuriated her that at every turn Richard's nephew seemed to block her avenues of escape.

Anya leaned forward into the wind. The worst of it was that she was getting a treasured wish granted. For years, she had wanted to marry and have children. A perverted fate, however, had cast Morgan Grayson as the prospective bridegroom and father of her unborn children.

Aaugh! For the first time in her life, she wanted to throw a tantrum—to smash a vase, or knock over a pitcher, or slap a particular male cheek.

When she reached her destination, Anya fairly sprang from her horse. Before her, the sea rolled in gray waves toward a sandy cove below. She tethered Lady Lore to the reinforced railing that had been installed years earlier and began to pace. Her boots clicked against the crumbling stone terrace that Roman soldiers had constructed centuries before.

At this very moment, Lady Hester was packing her trunks for her visit to Hull Manor. Anya groaned. A fly trapped in a spider's web had more of a chance for escape than she did.

She stopped pacing and rested her gloved hands against the railing. The dull roar of the sea reached out to Anya, reminding her that she would have to cross such an ocean to reach America. She shivered.

The sound of thundering hooves joined that of the restless waves. Anya didn't look away from the churning mass of water. Why should she? She knew who it was—

Strong hands gripped and spun her around. Until her hand flew out, Anya hadn't realized she truly was going to slap the American.

Her leather glove muffled the sound. Morgan said nothing. His hat hid his eyes. He stepped forward and jerked her to him. His tight-lipped mouth came down hard on her own.

With the wind and the sea ringing in her ears, she struggled futilely. Morgan's breathing, hot and fast, scalded her senses. At some point, she surrendered. Fighting both him and her own sudden longing took more energy than she possessed.

She relaxed against him, letting her head fall back limply. She could see his eyes now. They glittered. A faint patch of redness marred his lean cheek. Slowly, he lessened the pressure of his mouth against hers.

"Don't hit, Anya. It brings out the beast in me."

His voice, low and ominously mild, chilled her. She decided the beast in Morgan Grayson lay dangerously close to the surface.

"You deserved it," she pointed out severely.

He tipped his head. "Does that mean that when you deserve to be hit, I may oblige myself?"

"Certainly not." His hold loosened, and she stepped quickly back. "Besides, I've done nothing—"

"Get the hell away from that railing."

His face drained of color, and Anya realized with a start that Morgan Grayson was afraid. Discovering a little of the beast within herself, she took a skipping step closer to the edge of the cliff. He might not know it, but though the terrace was crumbling, the railing behind it was kept in excellent condition.

"Why, Mr. Grayson, are you uncomfortable with heights?" she mocked softly.

He didn't come closer. "Anya, I'm warning you..."

That was it! The big, tall, hulking American must be terrified of high places. Anya laughed giddily and recklessly hoisted herself upon the low fence. Morgan whipped off his hat, and she saw beads of perspiration dot his brow.

"You're going to kill yourself," he growled.

Exhilarated, Anya laughed. "Then you'll have to find another bride. That shouldn't be too difficult for—"

He moved so fast she didn't have time to prepare herself. One moment she was sitting atop the world and the next he had her flattened against the stone terrace. His large body was sprawled across her, pushing the air from her lungs.

"If you *ever* do anything like that again—" He broke off.

Dry-mouthed, Anya stared into his darkened gaze, where violence seemed to simmer. She realized she'd pushed him too far. She had no idea what Morgan would do next.

"You feel good, Anya."

Numbly, she tried to make sense of his words. His mood seemed to have jumped from murderous to... passionate.

The day grew still. Her gaze skittered to where his lips hovered above hers.

Morgan's hands moved exploringly across her riding habit. "All soft and womanly..."

She moistened her lips, aware of a dozen sensations at once. His leg lay between hers. Her hips were pinned by his. His chest rested intimately against her breasts. And his mouth lowered...

This kiss was as different from his earlier one as a spring rain from a summer storm. Slowly, carefully, he continued to caress her. She felt as if someone had arranged a pile of kindling within her and Morgan had come to set it ablaze. Heat bathed her skin.

His lips moved to her throat and the high collar of her blouse. "So many buttons..."

"It's very strong, you know."

He chuckled darkly. "What is, Anya?"

"The—the railing. Richard always insisted it be properly maintained. There's even a gate and steps leading down to—"

"Hush, Anya." He pushed aside her jacket and his hand closed over her breast.

A trembling explosion seemed to go off within her. A fever raged and... and she found herself squirming beneath him. She choked back a moan. How long was he going to punish her?

Slowly, he rubbed his gloved hand over the soft material of her blouse. Back and forth. One breast and then the other.

"It feels good, doesn't it, Anya?"

It did feel good. It also felt dangerous and exciting and... forbidden. She never wanted him to stop.

Contrarily, his hand paused. "This will feel good, too."

His fingertips contracted over the tip of her breast, squeezing gently. Anya sucked in her breath. Her gaze darted to his. He was watching her reaction to his bold touch. Tiny pinpricks of sensation shot through her.

The hardened ridge that lay against her hips moved against her. She was helpless not to pattern her movements to his.

His hand moved to her other breast, and he repeated his wickedly provocative stroking. Anya felt as if a giant spring were being tightened within her.

He bent his face into the crook of her neck. "You smell so damned good."

She closed her eyes. All she wanted was to lose herself to the strangely beckoning sensations he invoked.

His mouth moved over hers again. This time his tongue plunged deeply. She shuddered against him. Coaxingly, he lured her tongue into his mouth. Her arms twined about his neck.

He tasted faintly of tobacco. Their mouths seemed to drink from each other. The weight of him, the thrust of his tongue and his hips seemed to draw her toward a precipice higher than any she'd known. She arched toward him, knowing intuitively that whatever was building inside her had to have a resolution.

He tore his lips from hers. "Enough."

Enough? Not nearly.

She whispered a protest when his wonderful weight disappeared abruptly and she was jerked onto unsteady legs.

She battled the urge to loop her arms around his waist and rest her head against his chest.

Instead, she pushed the hair back from her face. Riotous gulls and dazzling sunlight plummeted her back to an awareness of her surroundings. Heat crawled to her cheeks. She had lain with the American. She was going to the fiery gates of hell.

"You look like you're going to swoon," he said in his relaxed drawl.

With dawning horror, Anya suspected he might be right. Her too-tight corset prevented her from catching her breath. Spots swam before her eyes.

"It's these wretched stays...."

Instantly Morgan was at her side. "Take them off."

"What?"

"They're an abomination." He peeled the jacket from her shoulders. "I thought you had more sense."

She slapped at his hands. "Stop that!"

He removed the jacket and progressed to her blouse. To her chagrin, she found herself standing outside in broad daylight in nothing but her—

He wrestled her from her corset and her hands sprang up to cover her cotton chemise.

"There, now you've got some color."

Of course she did. She was brick red! "You—you—"

While she sputtered, he poked her arms back through the sleeves in her blouse, rebuttoned it and slipped her riding jacket back on.

The sight of her white embroidered stays in Morgan Grayson's strong hands was profoundly embarrassing. With nary an apology, he tossed the corset over the cliff and into the sea below.

Speechless, Anya realized that Richard's nephew was a madman. Though it did feel wonderful to breathe unimpeded without the hateful stays...

"That was the only corset I had," she observed as a forlorn kind of eulogy.

"Good."

She pivoted toward him. "You don't understand. What am I going to do when Lady Hester arrives?"

"Breathe."

"Ooh." As a scathing retort, Anya admitted it lacked a certain vitality. Her gaze fell upon the American's oddly shaped hat. During their scuffle, it had fallen to the ground. Without hesitation, she snatched it up.

Morgan held out his hand, obviously expecting her to return it. Foolish man.

"Now, Anya . . ."

She looked toward the sea. Her stays, his hat. It seemed a fair enough exchange.

"Don't you dare—"

She sent it sailing skyward.

Morgan swore shockingly. Anya felt gloriously vindicated.

"That was my hat, you little hellion!"

She nodded cheerfully.

"I paid good money for that Stetson at Foster Dunlap's Mercantile."

"I daresay if my corset were purchased at . . . at Foster Dunlap's Mercantile, good money would be spent for it, also."

She saw a grudging respect grow in Morgan's hard gaze.

"I daresay it would, if you could find someone crazy enough to buy it."

She glanced toward Lady Lore. It did seem as if now was a prudent time to withdraw from the battlefield. Before she could take a step toward her mount, however, Morgan anticipated her action.

Wide-eyed, she watched him stalk to the mare and begin unsaddling her. "What are you doing?"

"Saving your reckless neck, Miss Delangue."

In short order he had the saddle free. To her astonishment, he carried it to the railing, clearly intent on tossing it into the sea.

"Wait! You can't throw that away."

"Watch me."

"But it will be ruined, and it's a very costly saddle."

He paused and stared at her with flinty eyes. "Say good-bye to it, Anya. You won't be using it again."

With those words, he tossed it over the cliff. Had losing his precious Stetson made the man daft? He turned to her. She watched his approach warily, wondering if she were the next item to be sacrificed to the water.

He pointed a long, hard finger at her. "You are never to ride sidesaddle again."

"W-what?"

"I don't know what fool came up with the notion that women should ride a horse sideways, but I will not see you risk your reckless neck doing so again. Do you understand?"

She nodded. Privately, she'd always thought it unfair that women had to sit perched so awkwardly on the backs of their mounts.

It didn't escape her notice that two possessions of hers were gone, while Morgan had lost only his hat. Fairness, it appeared, was difficult to attain between men and women.

He went back to Lady Lore and untied her. "I assume she knows the way back to the stable?"

Anya nodded again. It seemed the only physical gesture of which she were presently capable.

A loud slap on Lady Lore's rump sent her on her way. At the sound, Anya flinched. It took little imagination to visualize Morgan Grayson applying the same hand to her backside. The man was menacingly unpredictable.

"Am I to walk back to the manor? Is that more of your punishment?" she asked shakily.

His eyebrows rose. "*More* punishment? I'm the one still carrying the sting of your slap."

She flushed. Surely, he'd hardly felt a sting at all.

Understanding dawned in his eyes. "Did you think my kissing you was punishment, Anya?"

She refused to nod for a third time. "To me, it seemed so."

"But you liked it," he countered softly. "Punishment isn't supposed to feel good."

"You are not a gentleman—Southern or otherwise."

Tiny lines crinkled about his dark eyes. "You're right."

Had she thought her words would wound him? "At this point," Anya remarked coolly, "I see no reason to pursue Richard's demented plan to see us wed."

Against his sudden smile, his teeth gleamed white. "Then I've got my work cut out for me."

"Aren't there any women in Texas for you to marry?"

He grabbed the roan's reins. "Not many," he admitted mildly.

"Since you've stated you don't need such a large share of Richard's estate, why don't you return to American and—"

Obviously not listening to her, he mounted. She shied back instinctively from the horse's shuffling hooves. It was going to be a long walk home.

"Anya."

"What?" she snapped angrily, without looking at him.

"You talk too much."

With that wholly fallacious accusation, Morgan Grayson reached down and swept her into his arms. She shrieked in protest and tried to extricate herself. The roan reared.

"Keep squirming and you'll end up on your adorable bottom."

She stopped moving at once. "Must you be so crude?"

"Yes."

The next moments passed with Morgan adjusting her position in front of him. He arranged her skirts, shifted her bottom so it rested shamelessly against him and generally took numerous liberties with her person.

"You may take the reins, Anya."

His low voice vibrated in her ear. "The devil take you, sir."

"Take the reins," he repeated softly, implacably. On second thought, Anya liked the idea of controlling the horse. She accepted the reins.

"I want my hands free," Morgan added.

Anya sat stiffly, her brief moment of calm shattered by Morgan's words. His hands rested firmly at her waist. They rode that way for some distance, neither of them breaking the unnatural silence that had sprung up between them.

Gradually, she became aware that Morgan's hands had inched higher, moving steadily toward her breasts. The steady movement of the horse beneath her seemed to fuel an aching longing deep inside her.

Finally, after the anticipation of him doing so had practically driven her mad, Morgan's palms closed over her breasts. She released her pent up breath and relaxed against him. His hands worked a slow and slumberous magic as they caressed her intimately.

"Relax, honey."

Relax? *Honey?*

Time passed and he did other things besides touch her. He whispered husky words about her supposed beauty and desirability. He told her that during the voyage back to America he would teach her games far more pleasurable than poker.

And as he spoke, as he petted her, she thought about what it would feel like to be held by Morgan Grayson all through the night.

When they finally reached the manor house, she required his assistance to dismount. Even then, her legs failed to support her, and she required the assistance of his arm. In the light of the pleasure she'd received, her weakness did not seem so terrible a thing.

Errant images arrowed through her thoughts. Morgan Grayson's horse thundering toward her. For the first time in memory, Lady Hester laughing aloud. A corset, Stetson, and English saddle sailing into the sea. Morgan's mouth closing on hers. Morgan's hands stroking her.

Morgan . . .

All the images merged and became one—his.

Chapter Seven

Clearly, Lady Hester was not amused. As the final, disastrous course of Cook's barely edible dinner was cleared away, Anya knew she'd made a serious error in not informing the older woman of her scheme to drive Morgan from Hull Manor with his stomach crying for mercy.

Since Lady Hester had arrived with her trunks and entourage of servants just moments before dinner, however, Anya hadn't found an opportunity to inform her that a tray would be sent to her chamber, a tray with an assortment of dishes that did justice to Cook's talents in the kitchens.

"Harrumph."

Anya's gaze swung to the frowning matron, and she sensed she'd sunk even lower in the woman's estimation. "Ah, shall we retire to the drawing room, Lady Hester?"

Once they escaped Morgan's company, Anya would explain the situation to the older woman. Anya only hoped her words would not further antagonize the matron. Lady Hester looked decidedly gray around the edges—due, no doubt, to Cook's inspired boiling of the roast.

"Perhaps another time, Anya. I believe I shall retire to my chambers."

Morgan stood at once to help the older woman from her chair. Anya gritted her teeth. For the past couple of hours, he had been a perfect gentleman. It was enough to give a person indigestion—without the benefit of Cook's slimy carrots.

Anya pushed back her chair without Morgan's assistance and stood, planning to join Lady Hester. Before Anya made it three steps in matron's direction, however, a strong hand closed around her arm.

"Where do you think you're going?"

"To bed," Anya snapped without thinking, staring after her chaperon's retreating back. "If you would be so kind as to let me pass?"

He shook his head. "We need to talk."

Every time he said that, Anya found herself in deep trouble. "There's no way to stop you, I suppose," she observed ungraciously.

A grin streaked his bronzed features. "No way on this earth," he agreed cheerfully.

Anya pulled her arm free. "Then get on with it, man."

He glanced at the remains that were being cleared from the table. "Not here. I don't want any reminders of the hell I just endured."

There was no malice in his tone and that seemed to make his blasphemy all the more jarring. She flushed. "I suppose you are referring to dinner?"

"At Satan's table, you might get away with calling that sh—garbage food," he observed most genially. Nevertheless, his hand had again attached itself to her arm. "Come along, Anya."

"Where?" she asked suspiciously.

"It's a mild night—the terrace will do."

In short order Anya found herself outside with Morgan Grayson. Except for the weak light coming from the lower windows, darkness engulfed them. Morgan was right. It was a mild night. Still, she shivered.

"Here, take my jacket."

Before she could utter a protest, Morgan draped his coat across her shoulders. The garment seemed imbued with his warmth, his scent. "Th-thank you."

"If you didn't choke on tonight's dinner, you shouldn't choke on a simple thank you, Anya." He pushed his hands into his trouser pockets and stared up at the night sky. "By the way, that wasn't a kind thing to do to a man who's recently returned from war."

"What wasn't?" she asked with feigned innocence.

"Sabotaging supper." He turned to her. "Though in all honesty I do admire your resourcefulness. After all, if the way to a man's heart is through his stomach, then it follows that poisoning him should dampen his ardor."

"You're exaggerating," she said quickly, uncomfortable with Morgan's reference to war. Thinking of him hungry and in danger distressed her more than she cared to admit. "Perhaps the roast was a trifle—"

"Like overcooked boot leather?" Morgan interrupted whimsically.

She shoved her hands into the jacket he'd lent her. "Cook just had an off night."

"Does that happen often?"

"No." Anya sighed, certain she would order no more disastrous meals prepared to torture the American. Even though she knew she was being overimaginative, she couldn't dismiss the image of Morgan facing an enemy charge with his stomach empty. "I'm sure Cook's next efforts will be more palatable."

"I'm relieved to hear that."

His ironic tone didn't escape her notice. "Was that all you wished to discuss?" she inquired hopefully, wanting to end this interlude with Morgan. Something about being alone with him in the darkness made her uneasy.

"There is another subject we need to discuss, Anya," he began quietly. "I owe you an apology."

Nothing he could have said would have surprised her more. She hadn't thought the American capable of an apology.

"This afternoon I took an unfair advantage," he continued. "I used my superior size to...to impose my will over you."

There was just enough light from the house for her to see that Morgan Grayson was not comfortable with his admission of wrongdoing. His hands were shoved into his pockets, and a frown marked his sharply chiseled features.

She swallowed. She really hadn't thought the man possessed enough sensitivity to admit to being wrong—about anything.

"It was most...unseemly," she felt compelled to point out.

"Now that's an English understatement if I've ever heard one."

"Uh...well...if you will assure me that it won't happen again, I suppose—"

"But I can't do that, Anya," he interrupted softly.

She wrinkled her brow. "Why not?"

"You know how it is with men. We often have good intentions, but in the heat of the moment, those intentions...fade."

Anya sighed. She didn't know at all how it was with men. "Then your apology doesn't appear to be worth much."

"I lost my temper. I was...rough with you. I will see *that* doesn't happen again."

"But the kissing and touching will?" she demanded, becoming incensed.

"For the next forty years or so."

"Only if we wed, and I don't think—"

"Anya." Her name emerged as a gruff command.

"What?"

"Don't you like me at all?"

She gaped at him. Her assessment of him possessing a degree of sensitivity vanished. "I don't wish to be rude, but..."

Her words dwindled to nonexistence. She discovered it was no easy matter to look into a man's smoldering eyes and tell him he was disliked.

He rested his hands upon her shoulders, and she became conscious of the weight of his coat. A gentle breeze made his white shirt billow lightly about his hard frame. She wondered if he was cold.

"You're prejudiced, Anya."

"I beg your pardon?"

"In the war, I saw ample evidence of what prejudice does to people. When you look at someone, you don't really see them. You only see your own mind's biases."

"Indeed?"

He squeezed her shoulders. "Now don't get on your English high horse. I'm being honest with you. Because I'm American, you seem to think that makes me some kind of... barbarian. If an Englishman had held and kissed you today, or for that matter, if an Englishman were proposing to you, you'd be inclined to accept his offer."

"Any Englishman? Is that what you think?"

"I'm young, I'm strong, I have property and I'm willing to protect and take care of you, Anya. What more could you want?"

With a sinking heart, Anya recognized some truth to his observation. He had overlooked one vital point, however. She wanted affection. Since it was obvious the American was incapable of giving it to her, she supposed she was looking for excuses to be free of him. Of course, there was no way to explain that to him. She knew instinctively he wouldn't understand. Worse yet, he would probably mock her.

"Would you consider settling in England?" Until the question emerged, she hadn't realized she was going to ask it.

"I've a ranch waiting for me in Texas," he answered evenly.

She massaged her forehead. "That's clear enough."

He bent down and brushed his lips against the spot she'd rubbed. She stiffened.

"Don't be alarmed, I am capable of controlling my bestial urges—upon occasion."

With that, he pulled her against him and began dropping light kisses upon her upturned face. The moist heat from his mouth as it touched her skin felt sweetly comforting, yet a dull ache began to grow within her.

"This isn't proper," she whispered shakily.

"We've already had this conversation," he muttered, his lips silencing her protest.

Surely, for a just few moments, there could be no harm in partaking of Morgan's gentle ministrations. Her arms reached upward, and she felt his coat slip from her shoulders. It didn't matter. There was enough of Morgan to keep her warm against the night chill.

Oh, the man was a splendid kisser. Minutes passed with him cradling her in his embrace and taking no undue liberties. She told herself she wasn't disappointed.

She lied.

At some point she became aware of a weight pressing insistently against her hips. She wondered about it, as it seemed to make her want to draw even closer to him. She pressed herself against the hardness.

He groaned. "Ah, Anya, you are a temptress, do you know that?"

The next thing she knew, he was setting her back from him and staring at her with a somewhat sheepish expression. She hadn't thought him a likely candidate for sheepishness. Wolfishness, perhaps, but never—

He retrieved his fallen coat and slipped it back over her shoulders. "But you already know what you do to me, don't you?"

She pressed her hands to her flushed cheeks. It was what he was doing to *her* that held her attention.

"I would like to marry you within the week, Anya," he announced baldly.

"What?"

"I don't know how much longer I can control myself around you."

"How much *longer?*" she choked on the word. As far as she could tell he hadn't controlled himself from the first moment they met.

"It's a dangerous combination, Anya. My desire to bed you and your willingness to let me."

Her mouth fell open. "Why you . . . you . . . you—"

"You're sputtering, darling. Not that I would mind anticipating our wedding vows. Laying naked next to you would—"

"Stop! You go too far!"

"Not nearly as far as I intend. So what do you say, my improper English lady, will you let me have my way with you tonight? If we marry quickly, there should be no embarrassments."

"Embarrassments?" she asked, fascinated despite herself.

"As in bundles of joy. *Babies*, Anya."

"B-babies?"

"One, at any rate."

"I—I hadn't thought of that." Good Lord, what would she do if Morgan had already gotten her with child? She didn't know precisely how a man went about doing that, but she did know it had something to do with a man and woman lying together in the same bed on their wedding night. She and Morgan had lain together on the ground. Could that produce a baby, even though they weren't married?

"You look like you're going to faint again. I know you're not wearing a corset, so what's the problem? Does having my child terrify you that much?"

She licked her suddenly dry lips. "Do you think I'm already... already expecting?"

For once, it was the American who lost his color. *"What?"*

"Do you think we made a baby this afternoon?"

"Today?"

"Ooh, I shall never forgive you for this, Morgan. You should have exercised more discipline."

He stepped back, mumbling something indiscernible under his breath.

She stalked him. "Say something I can understand."

"Uh, Anya, just how long have you been isolated in this place?"

"What has that to do with anything?"

He shrugged, his eyes glinting oddly. "From your point of view, I imagine nothing."

"Well, do you?" she persisted.

"Do I what?"

"Do you think we made a baby!" she shouted in exasperation.

A shuttered expression claimed his features. "There's always the possibility...."

His words struck her like pellets of frozen rain. "But I thought it only counted if we were married," she wailed.

"Hmm, I can see where you might get that idea."

"This is all your fault! What am I to do now?"

"Marry me?"

"That seems rather drastic."

"So is having a child out of wedlock."

"This is all your fault," she repeated numbly.

He moved toward her. "I accept full responsibility."

"Well, that's something, I suppose."

"Never fear, Anya. Our unborn child will have both mother and father."

"None of this would have happened if you'd kept your hands to yourself," she muttered glumly.

He chuckled softly. "What can I say? You're right."

She drew his coat tighter about her. "The debate as to whether or not I shall marry you seems to be at an end."

"Thank God."

"And I suppose the sooner the better."

"Definitely."

"I will speak with Lady Hester in the morning to see how we shall proceed. I would like to be wed in the small chapel on my brother's estate."

"I'm agreeable to that."

"Well, then, good night."

"Good night, little Anya."

His endearment was a lingering caress she carried into slumber.

* * *

They lay intertwined in postsexual languor. This was the first time Merrawynn had lain with a man other than Richard. Though she'd flirted and promised, she'd always denied her would-be lovers their final conquest. But Boyd Williams had wooed her more fervently than her other admirers, and she had at last succumbed to his long-term pursuit.

If she experienced a twinge of disappointment at the final outcome, she suppressed it. It seemed so strange and unexpected to find herself missing Richard's loving tenderness. Why did she feel so hollow inside, almost as if she wished to weep? Now, when it was too late to matter, was it her fate to discover just how rare and remarkable Richard had been?

Boyd's mouth traced a leisurely course against her bare shoulder. "You taste delicious."

Resolutely, she suppressed the alien emotions roiling inside her. "Thank you."

He raised his head. "Have I cheered your spirits, then?"

Merrawynn felt as if he'd thrown a glass of wine into her face. With a quick movement, she drew back. "I had almost forgotten about Morgan Grayson. Why did you have to remind me?"

Boyd relaxed against the tangled sheets. "I am going to have to improve my timing."

Stretching out beside him, Merrawynn stared broodingly at the ceiling. "I hate feeling helpless."

"There is nothing helpless about you, my love." Idly, he ran his fingers across her arm. "Perhaps now that we've had our amusement, we can devise a solution to your problem."

"There is no solution. Anya is going to marry that beast, and I am going to be left penniless."

Boyd Williams knew that thirty thousand pounds per annum was not penniless, but he, too, liked to live well. Fate had dealt him a minor title with no wealth attached to sustain his relationship with Merrawynn.

He had been counting upon her to provide the tangible assets in their forthcoming union. His marriage to a beautiful and rich widow would be the culmination of his life-long labors. It appeared, however, that more effort must be expended for him to achieve his goal.

"Ah, my love, there are always solutions. What is most often in short supply is the courage and determination to implement those solutions. For instance, your sister and this Morgan Grayson might never marry. Sometimes, after all the plans are made and all the arrangements settled upon, fate steps in and destroys the anticipated outcome."

"Fate?"

"What is fate but another set of opposing circumstances rushing directly across the path of our intentions? The only thing certain is that your sister is presently unmarried. If she should have an accident . . ."

"No!" Merrawynn jerked back from Boyd's lingering touch. "Nothing must happen to Anya. I couldn't live with that on my conscience."

"I wasn't thinking of anything permanent. Just a minor accident to delay their marriage."

"I'm not interested in delays. Besides, Anya is my sister, and even though she is an odd duck, I will not see her harmed."

"What's so odd about her?" Boyd asked, his voice reflecting only a casual interest.

"Well, if she isn't roaming about caves or the ancient tower of our brother's manor doing heaven knows what, she's tearing about the countryside on horseback with her skirts flying."

"She doesn't sound much like you."

"She isn't."

"I wonder..." Boyd mused, rubbing his jawing. "Do you think Morgan Grayson could be persuaded to return to America without marrying your sister? Could we approach him with some contrivance against Anya?"

"Morgan Grayson is not a man to be easily duped," Merrawynn replied, recalling the American's implacable nature. "He is a cold, suspicious creature interested only in the bequest Richard left him."

"Have the banns been posted?"

"Not yet, but then a savage like the American might not bother with such niceties. He could whisk her off for an elopement."

"It seems we have precious little time, then, to shatter their romance. Could we more easily inopportune your sister against him?"

"I think not. At this point she would marry the devil himself to escape her spinsterhood."

"Then our course is clear. We must remove Morgan Grayson."

"But surely you don't mean—" She broke off and took a deep breath, suddenly alarmed by her lover's ominous words.

"Squeamishness from *you*, Merrawynn?"

She flushed. Always, she had thought herself above the ordinary scruples that bound others. It was disheartening to discover a wellspring of those very scruples lurking within her.

"Perhaps there is no way out," she said dejectedly.

Boyd drew her to him. "I have a plan that might work."

"There must be no violence," she admonished.

"Of course not," he answered smoothly. "What kind of man do you think I am?"

Merrawynn shivered.

"It's best that you let me resolve the problem," he continued. "Why fill such a beautiful head with needless details?"

Merrawynn stared deeply into her lover's eyes. "I must have your promise that—"

He pressed a forefinger to her lips. "Enough talk, my sweet. I am only a man, and lying next to your naked beauty drives all reason from me."

She wanted desperately to find comfort in the honeyed words he spoke, but as she opened herself to his possession, Merrawynn found no comfort. Nor could she hold back the tears any longer.

Anya stood before the Hull family crypt, her head bowed. The bouquet of flowers she'd brought from the conservatory provided a splash of color against the cold ground.

The morning breeze carried a shiver with it, and she drew her cloak more tightly to her. "Farewell, friend...."

She touched her gloved hand to the plaque that would soon bear Richard's name. It seemed insufficient, somehow. A man was born, he lived, he died.... She pressed her eyes shut.

"Dear Lord, keep him safe. Keep him happy...."

She wondered if Richard was with his first wife now. Probably. Anya was convinced her little brother was with their mother and father. It seemed right that in heaven families would be together. Together forever... Yes, that was how she chose to think of heaven. It was the only possibility that gave life meaning.

"Anya."

At the sound of Morgan's deep voice, she opened her eyes. He stood before her, a heavy coat draped over his broad shoulders. He extended his hand toward her. She reached for it without hesitation.

"It's too cold out here for you."

At his concerned tone, she smiled. In the five days since she'd officially agreed to marry him, Anya had learned much about her future husband. First and foremost was that he did not enjoy their cold English clime. She assumed Texas was on the warm side.

"I was paying my respects to Richard."

Morgan glanced at the roses she'd laid upon the ground, then back at her. "The way you cared for Richard when he was ill showed your respect for him, Anya."

She brushed back a tear. "I—I miss him. My father died the year before Merrawynn married Richard, and Richard became a father to me."

Sympathy filled Morgan's dark eyes. "I lost my father during the war—nothing prepares you for it."

She blinked back more tears. "I had a little brother...George. He—he died when he was only seven."

Morgan's arm came around her, and he drew her to him. "Come on, let's walk."

He led her from the crypt, toward the house. His warmth and the weight of his arm somehow dulled the edge of her grief. Still, she felt as if she needed a good cry. Perhaps in bed tonight, she would let the tears come. It wasn't her nature to weep publicly.

She wasn't surprised when they ended up in the conservatory. She remembered the last time they'd stood amidst the carefully cultivated flowers. Then, she'd considered Morgan the enemy. Now, as they sat together on a low bench that faced the windows overlooking the grounds, she thought of him as...as almost a friend.

Strange how a fortnight could change one's perspective.

"What was your father like, Anya?"

Her gaze slid to Morgan's profile. "Papa?" A smile caught her by surprise. "He was...quiet, when he was home."

"He traveled?"

"He and Mother spent a lot of time abroad—until she began expecting my younger brother, George," Anya explained softly. "It was winter when he came, and Mama never seemed to get her strength back. She died when he was just a baby."

Morgan pulled her toward him. It seemed the most natural thing in the world to rest her head against his sturdy shoulder. The tears seemed natural, too—not at all a shameful admission of weakness.

"I'm sorry, Anya."

His words and durable strength offered an elemental kind of solace. "For a time, we thought we would lose George, too. He was such a frail baby. I remember spending hours and hours with him, just rocking him—afraid to leave him

alone lest he . . . die. We found a wonderful nanny and wet
nurse, too. All of us cared for him.''

"He was a very lucky little boy."

Anya turned to Morgan curiously. "Lucky?"

He nodded. "George may have lost his mother, but he
had a loving sister to care for him. Was he always sickly?"

Anya sighed. "No, and I think that's what made it so
hard to accept his death. He outgrew his frailness and was
a—" She laughed in remembrance, turning again to Morgan and laying her hand upon his knee. "Oh, I wish you
could have met him. He was such a rascal, always into mischief, always teasing, always running to wherever he was
headed. And he used to love to tease us by putting frogs in
the most unexpected places.''

Morgan rested his hand over hers. "I would have liked to
have met him. How did he die?"

"The doctor called it the breathing sickness. It was win-
tertime." She looked inward in memory. "Strange, we almost lost him his first winter and then, seven years later, we
did lose him.''

"Would you like to name one of our sons after him?"

Anya looked into dark eyes that she would never have
believed could hold such understanding and sympathy. "I—
I don't know. Hearing his name, *saying* his name every
day. . ." She swallowed.

Morgan gathered her into his arms until she was sitting on
his lap. "Perhaps as a middle name?"

She tilted her face toward him. "I think I would like
that."

"Texas is a good place to raise sons, Anya."

"Don't you ever miss where you grew up?" she asked,
remembering the plantation in South Carolina of which he'd
spoken.

He rested his chin upon the crown of her head. "Taopath doesn't seem home to me anymore. I consider it Lavinia's and the boys'."

"Lavinia?"

"My father's widow."

"I see."

"It's strange," Morgan continued, "but when you were telling me about George, you could have almost been describing my childhood." He squeezed her. "Except I didn't have a loving older sister to care for me. I was allowed to run wild, and I did."

Anya laced her fingers between his strong ones. "I don't find that at all difficult to believe, Morgan."

He chuckled. "When my father remarried for the second time, my perfect world came crashing down around my dirty little ears. My stepmother insisted I become civilized."

"You mean, she tried to," Anya suggested, straight-faced.

Morgan leaned forward and nibbled her earlobe. "Behave, I'm telling you my life story. Try to act impressed."

She looked over her shoulder at him. "I think I am impressed," she said earnestly.

"Don't sound so surprised, then," he growled. "Anyway, less than a year after my father's marriage to his second wife, Wilma, the union was blessed with another son, Justin. And when he was old enough to hold his own with me, we fought like cats and dogs. Everything I had, he wanted. And Wilma saw that he got it." A hardness crept into Morgan's voice when he spoke of his brother.

"You mentioned something about Justin wanting to take Taopath from Lavinia and the twins."

"Despite the war, Justin came out all right. When Collette's father passed away, he left a substantial legacy to the newlyweds. Lavinia and the boys are hanging on by a shoestring. Richard's bequest is the difference between them keeping or losing the plantation."

"You aren't interested in it for yourself?"

Morgan shook his head. "When I was seventeen, I lit out for Texas, got involved with cattle ranching and liked it."

"But—but you were just a boy. How could you become a rancher at seventeen?"

"At first I worked on other spreads. When I went back to Taopath for a visit, my father offered to loan me the money to buy my own place."

"That was generous of him."

A nostalgic expression softened Morgan's features. "I think the idea of raising cattle instead of cotton appealed to him. Having slaves bothered him, but there seemed no other way to bring in the crops."

"Did he fight in the war?"

"Fought and died," Morgan answered simply. "I couldn't stay out of it, even though I don't think any man should be owned by another. I had to stand with my family."

"So you left your ranch?"

"I haven't been back there since the war." He shifted his position so that she was cradled against him. "Now you know why I'm in such a hurry to marry you and be on my way. There's one more thing you should know." Morgan's voice had taken on an edge.

"What's that?"

"My mother was killed in a fall. She was probably about your age when it happened."

"A—a fall?"

He nodded sharply. "She was standing on the second-story balcony and the railing gave way. It was a stupid, senseless accident."

Anya remembered her reckless actions several days earlier and winced. "But, Morgan, I *knew* the fencing was solid. I took no risk."

"The hell you didn't. If you'd lost your balance, you would have been gone. There's no way I could have saved you. I want your promise that you will never go back there again."

She stiffened. "But that's one of my favorite places."

"Not anymore."

"Now, Morgan—"

"Woman, I'm to be your husband. You will obey me."

Her mouth fell open. All the tender feelings she'd felt toward him in the past few minutes vanished. "I thought you didn't believe in slavery."

His eyes narrowed. "I don't believe in one man owning another. A woman is a different story."

"Now just one moment—"

He kissed her firmly. Again she found herself a prisoner of the feelings he so effortlessly invoked within her.

Minutes passed before he raised his head and stared down at her. "Give me your promise, Anya."

She gazed up at him in bemusement. "What promise?"

"That you won't go back to the cliffs."

"Come back there with me," she challenged instead. "You'll see it's not really dangerous."

"Lord, you're stubborn." He stared down at her, his eyebrows drawn together in consternation. "Why is it so important?"

"It's my special place," she answered simply. "I go there whenever I'm discouraged. The sea and the wind take away my troubles. I like to open the gate and follow the steps to a cave smugglers once used. I can be completely alone. It . . . restores me somehow."

"We won't be here that much longer, Anya."

"I know."

"I want you to promise that you'll only go there if I'm with you."

She felt as if she'd wrung a major concession from him. "I promise. . . ."

At the sound of rustling taffeta and Lady Hester's uneven step, Anya sprang from Morgan's lap. There was no doubt in Anya's mind—after the outrageous story Morgan had spun at Lady Hester's home about needing protection from her amorous pursuit—that should Lady Hester catch them in so compromising a position, the matron would hold Anya as the culpable one.

Chapter Eight

Anya smiled reassuringly at Mrs. Patterson and handed her the list of items they'd been reviewing.

"When Mr. Grayson and I quit the manor, we will not be returning," Anya explained. "I have no idea how long it will be before he is able to sell the property and the new owners take residence, but until then the house must continue to run as it always has."

With a tight smile, the housekeeper nodded and excused herself. It was obvious the woman was uneasy about the future. She wasn't the only one.

Pensively, Anya moved to a small bowl of freshly cut orchids. She inhaled their delicate scent and thought of the coming winter. For the first time in her life, she would not be spending that winter on English soil.

Texas... Anya ran her fingertip over a silken petal. Perhaps she wouldn't be alarmed by the prospect of the voyage if she had some idea of what to expect when she arrived there. And the same could be said of Morgan Grayson. Perhaps she wouldn't be so self-conscious in his presence if she knew more about her future husband.

What was needed was an opportunity to converse with the American without them shouting at each other—like the moment they had shared yesterday afternoon. If she knew more about him, his likes and dislikes, she would become more comfortable in his company.

Also, it was important that they discuss the future security of the servants. A plan must be devised whereby everything could remain as it always had been, with the estate's servants and tenant farmers assured of their continued place at the manor.

Anya felt herself fully capable of designing such a program. Unfortunately, the duty did not fall to her. Richard had left the estate to Morgan. She dropped her fingers from the fragile orchid. With a pang, she realized how much more fortunate the locals were to be depending upon Morgan Grayson's generosity rather than Merrawynn's.

Was that the reason Richard had included Morgan in his will? Because he had hoped his nephew would be more concerned about the people who'd spent their lives toiling in and around the manor house?

The more Anya thought about it, the more she became convinced that had been Richard's intent. And the crafty man had used the generous codicil to lure Morgan to England.

She squared her shoulders. Now that Richard was gone, it was up to her to make certain Morgan considered the welfare of the inhabitants of Hobb's Corner when selling the estate. As Anya saw it, she was the caretaker of their future.

A private interlude with Morgan in an atmosphere conducive both to learning more about him *and* to influencing his selection of a buyer for the estate was surely the best means of assuring the servants continued well-being. For her to accomplish both goals, however, it was imperative that Morgan be cajoled into a pleasant frame of mind.

Anya frowned. What could she possibly do to influence Morgan's mood?

Later that afternoon, as she stared up into Morgan's disapproving countenance, Anya sighed. Gauging from his bleak expression, she had a few things to learn about cajoling men.

"It will be fun, Morgan, you'll see," she repeated, trying to infuse her voice with hearty enthusiasm.

Dubiously, he eyed the large picnic basket Cook had prepared for them. "Anya, lunching with you outdoors *would* be pleasant—if it weren't such a blustery day and you didn't want to eat inside a dank and drafty cave."

Anya shifted the surprisingly heavy basket to her other hand. If Morgan were any kind of gentleman he would offer to carry it for her.

"Goodness, Morgan, there's barely a breeze, and the cave will shelter us from what little there is."

Morgan reached out and took the basket. "I vote for the conservatory."

"Vote?" she asked, noticing that he dangled the heavy basket from one finger.

He grinned. "That's right, I keep forgetting I'm in England where Queen Vicky rules the roost."

"Morgan..." Despite her protest, Anya felt an incipient giggle. Queen Vicky, indeed. "That's not very respectful. Besides, we do have Parliament, which I daresay votes as often as your Congress."

"I daresay you're right."

She drew herself up to her considerable height. "Must you mimic me?"

A wide grin split his face. "I can't seem to help myself."

Disgruntled, she realized she'd stumbled upon the secret to cajoling Morgan Grayson. It was becoming apparent that he enjoyed nothing so much as laughing at her.

Her gaze went to the great clock in the hall. "It's getting late, Morgan. And...and I am ready to leave."

When Merrawynn adopted an imperious manner, she invariably got her way. Anya hoped the same regal attitude would stand her in good stead.

"All the more reason for us to eat in the conservatory," he returned equitably.

She was on the verge of abandoning her suggestion. Perhaps picnicking in the cave was a foolish idea, after all. "Lady Hester would probably agree. I—"

The speaking of Lady Hester's name produced a startling change in Morgan's expression. His annoying grin vanished. "On the other hand, if you have your heart set upon a ride in the country and lunch at the cave, I have no wish to disappoint you."

And just like that, Anya was donning her cloak while Morgan went to fetch his coat. The ride itself was exhilarating. She didn't miss her sidesaddle one bit. A stubborn streak of pride, however, prevented her from making that admission.

Besides, it felt glorious to be riding again. She had no desire to slow their pace with conversation. Billowing white clouds gilded with silver added a dash of brightness to the gray sky. A nip of fall laced the air, but their race across the countryside warmed Anya's blood.

When they arrived at the cliffs, she was brimming with questions about Morgan's ranch in Texas. Would she be able to ride there? Did not the local women ride sidesaddle? Were there servants? Close neighbors? How big was Morgan's ranch? How large his home? Oh, yes, she had questions aplenty for the American.

When Morgan dismounted, Anya remained firmly settled upon Lady Lore. She had learned he would assist her down if she gave him the opportunity to do so. She'd also discovered she liked the feel of his strong hands around her waist, liked the way he stood close to her, liked the way her stomach fluttered as he slowly lowered her. Of late, this was as close as the American got to her. Was that why she enjoyed riding with him so much?

As he extended his hands toward her, she leaned forward. Time seemed to wrap itself about them like an unyielding cloak. It was almost as if the earth itself had stopped spinning. She looked down into eyes as dark and beckoning as a heated bedchamber at midnight. Fine lines fanned out from those somber, watchful eyes.

Her palms rested firmly upon his sturdy shoulders, and she eased herself from the saddle. His hands tightened on her waist. Everything was exactly as she remembered. The slow descent, his powerful body brushing against the material of her riding habit. The plunge of her stomach to her riding boots.

For just a moment, their faces were at eye level. His gaze seemed to...to devour her. All she had to do was tilt her lips to his....

A cloud passed in front of the sun and, in the distance, a gull screeched. The descent continued. Her boots rested upon solid ground. She let out the unsteady breath she'd been holding and thought of their return to Hull Manor, when Morgan would again assist her from her horse.

They tethered Lady Lore and the roan, and Morgan collected the basket. Even though she'd arranged this meeting specifically to talk with Morgan, Anya fell silent as she followed him through the gate and down the steps that led to the cave.

His heavy coat accentuated the width of his shoulders. In all of her imaginings of one day having a husband, she'd never envisioned someone as strong or vital as the American who'd come thundering into her life.

When they reached the mouth of the cave, Morgan paused. "I can't believe I'm really doing this."

Anya stepped around him and through the large opening. "Where's your spirit of adventure? I thought all Americans were adventurous."

Saying nothing, he took several steps inside. "What on earth... There's furniture."

"I know, isn't it exciting? I'm sure that both pirates and smugglers must have used the premises to plan their nefarious deeds and hide their booty."

"How did they get all this stuff up here?" he asked, clearly not yet in the spirit of things.

"The steps lead down to a sandy cove. It's the only place for miles that isn't strewn with rocks. They must have beached their boats there and then carried up the tables and chairs. Even at high tide, the cave is above water level."

He sat the basket on one of the low tables. "How did you find this place?"

"Richard showed it to me years ago."

Morgan looked around, obviously unimpressed. "It's cold in here."

She stepped toward a charred pile of sticks. "Let's build a fire. Deeper in the cave, there are stacks of dried wood. I had Cook include some matches in the basket. There are candles, too."

He shook his head. "As long as we're here, we might as well."

With that less-than-heartfelt observation, they set about making the cave habitable. When Morgan voiced concerns about smoke from the fire, Anya explained that there was a natural air shaft. It was only when the blanket was unfolded, the candles lit and Cook's delicious luncheon spread before them that Morgan appeared to relax.

"So, why did you go to all this trouble to get me alone, Anya?"

She choked on the piece of chicken she was chewing. Immediately, he leaned forward and thumped her soundly. Tears sprang to her eyes. The man was too strong for his own good.

"I—I'm fine—you can stop pummeling me, Morgan."

He began rubbing her back. "Sorry, guess I got carried away."

She smiled at him through watery eyes. "That's all right."

He sank back to his original position. Between them lay the picnic basket. Anya sat with her flared riding skirt tucked demurely about her while Morgan sprawled casually on his side of the blanket. Though the cave's furnishings were interesting from a historical perspective, she had no desire to sit or eat upon the grit-covered chairs and table.

Morgan cut himself a generous wedge of cheese and broke off a piece of bread. "What did you want to discuss? You're not having second thoughts about our marriage, are you?"

Second? How about third and fourth? "I've been thinking about our journey to America."

Above the flickering candlelight, his eyebrows contracted. "And?"

She took a quick, fortifying sip of wine. "It occurs to me that I might be less anxious about the trip if I knew more about you."

Her words fell into a pool of silence. She searched Morgan's features, looking for a reaction to her statement. He was wearing his indecipherable "five-card stud" expression, however.

"Why, Anya, I'm flattered."

"I rather thought you would be," she answered, pleased that her plan was working. "Merrawynn always said men like nothing better than to talk about themselves."

He coughed, and Anya couldn't resist rising to her knees to slap him on his back. And if she whacked with a trifle more forcefulness than was warranted, who could blame her?

"Anya, are you giving me a dose of my own medicine?" he inquired curiously.

She smiled unrepentantly. "Of course."

He bent forward and placed a kiss on the tip of her nose. "Do you know what I like best about you?"

Her eyes? Her smile? She stared dreamily up at him. "No..."

"Your straightforwardness."

She scooted back to her side of the blanket, knowing it was foolish to be disappointed. After all, she was the practical Delangue sister, not the pretty one.

"As for telling you about myself—" Morgan paused to reach into the basket for a shiny apple "—I've already told you my life story."

"You haven't said very much about this Texas place," she pointed out.

"Ah, I see. You're curious about where I'm taking you."

Anya nodded. In his description of his ranch, he would reveal much about himself and the kind of man he was.

"Well, my spread is located in the Rio Grande valley, near the river that bears that name. I raise longhorn steers, then drive them to market. Like I said, I haven't been there since the war, and even though I left Laredo in charge, I have the feeling it's past time for me to be getting back.''

"Laredo?"

"My best friend, foreman and head wrangler."

Anya sighed. So many of the words Morgan used made no sense to her. "How big is your ranch?"

"A hundred thousand acres."

She gasped. "That cannot be true."

"Texas is a big place, Anya. There's no way I can describe it to you."

"But—but, it must be like living on an island in the middle of the ocean. Have you no neighbors?"

"There're other ranchers like me, and there's a town, too. Big Rock Gulch."

Anya swallowed. All at once, she was leery of journeying to this . . . this foreign land. "Are you never lonely?"

"That's where you come in, Anya. You and our future children."

"How—how many children do you propose I have for you?" she asked, wondering if he thought of her solely as a brood mare.

"Five ought to do it."

"Five . . ." Actually, that was a reasonable number. Her hand went to her stomach. She tried to imagine what it would feel like to hold a newborn baby in her arms.

"The number doesn't alarm you?" he inquired softly.

She could feel the color creeping to her cheeks, and she was grateful for the cave's muted light. "Uh, well, I shall certainly be busy, shan't I?"

Very carefully, he set his glass on the blanket, taking the time necessary to properly balance it on the uneven surface. "Despite what you might think from our earlier conversations, it is not my intention to indenture you, Anya. I have a housekeeper, Maria. And I will hire additional help as we need it."

Actually, she hadn't been thinking that far ahead. "I am relieved to hear there shall be help, Morgan," she answered honestly. "But you should know that I am not afraid of hard work."

White teeth flashed. "Oh, there will be plenty of hard work to go around."

"And will I be able to ride?"

His manner became more somber. "Never alone. It's a wild, untamed country, Anya. Even those experienced with the terrain can lose their bearings. And every so often someone crawls out from under a rock, looking to stir up trouble."

She shivered, wondering again what she'd gotten herself into. "I see."

"I protect what is mine," he said simply. "As long as you follow the rules, you will remain safe."

Frowning, she reached for an apple. A long time ago, she had discovered she did not like following an excessive number of rules.

"Does your feeling of ownership extend to Hull Manor?" she asked curiously.

His eyebrows raised. Clearly, he was caught off guard by her question. "I beg your pardon?"

"Do you feel protective toward the servants and tenant farmers of Richard's estate?"

He looked around the cave, then at her. "I thought the purpose of our private luncheon was for us to learn more about each other."

"In part," she replied. "But, Morgan, it's very important that, when you sell the manor, the servants are guaranteed their positions."

In one fluid movement, he rose to his feet. "I should have known," he muttered.

She stared up at him, uneasy at the sudden darkening of his features. "Known what?"

"That like every other female on this earth, you feel obliged to manipulate the men in your life."

She laid aside the apple she had yet to taste. "I merely wanted to discuss two separate things with you. That is hardly underhanded."

He motioned to the blanket and open basket. "This entire luncheon was a contrivance to make me more amenable to your wishes for Hull Manor."

Maneuvering her skirts, Anya rose awkwardly. "It was for a good cause."

He stepped toward her. "That's not the point. I prefer the direct approach, Anya. No subterfuge. My former fiancée had a bad habit of playing up to me to get what she wanted. I didn't like it then, and I have no intention of putting up with it from you."

"I am not your *former* fiancée," Anya pointed out through gritted teeth. How dare he compare her with his first love?

His angry gaze swept over her. "Believe me, I am well aware of that."

She stiffened, hurt by the implication that she did not measure up to the woman who had jilted him. Just once, she wished she could think of something marvelously brilliant to say to the American that would cut him down to size.

But all she could do was blink back tears she would die before letting him see. "I am ready to leave."

He pushed back his coat and put his hands on his hips. "I'm not."

She flung her arm toward the picnic basket. "If you're still hungry, then eat!"

"Oh, I'm hungry, all right."

She wasn't prepared for the swift movement that brought her flush against his chest. Astonished, she looked into his glittering gaze. "W-what...?"

"I'm hungry for what only you can give me, Anya."

His mouth sought hers with a determination that brooked no refusal. Hot and searching, his tongue parted her lips. With clenched fists, she flailed at him.

How dare he! He was kissing her, but he was thinking about his lost sweetheart. Then the words he'd spoken penetrated her thoughts. He'd said he was hungry for what only *she* could give him. Anya ceased her resistance and clutched desperately to the hope that he spoke the truth.

The kiss continued—wild and sinfully erotic. At some point the pressure of Morgan's mouth gentled, and the kiss became more shockingly intimate. His arms drew her so tightly against him that she felt the pounding of his heart. His hands had slipped to her buttocks, and through her riding skirt she felt his fingers cup and press her against a familiar, hardened ridge.

She moaned and looped her arms around his neck.

"I want to make love with you."

His words were a low growl at her throat. She trembled at the heady sense of power that raced through her. In this place, at this time, Anya knew Morgan wasn't thinking of anyone but her. His strong hand moved to the front of her blouse.

"I want to touch you—all over. I want to taste you—all over."

Her knees again vanished. The buttons were loosened, and his probing fingers freed a breast from her chemise. His warm palm closed over her.

"Oh . . ."

"Feel good, honey?"

Her head jerked up. It felt wonderful. A half-dozen forbidden desires tumbled through her. Her fingers unbuttoning his shirt, her hands stroking his chest, her tongue tasting his flesh . . .

As though he'd read her thoughts, Morgan's mouth closed over her bared breast. Anya thought she would swoon. Tiny pinpricks of pleasure seemed to shoot through her. She gazed at Morgan's dark head pressed against her bosom in both wonder and fear. She threaded her fingertips through his thick pelt of hair.

"Now the other one . . ." he growled.

New pinpoints of pleasure surged and Anya bucked helplessly. The tip of his tongue worked a fiendish magic upon her senses. Her limbs felt heavy, while within her it seemed as if hot honey were being poured through her veins. Surely, his actions were improper.

"Enough," she whispered.

His head tipped up. She felt his hot gaze move across her face, then drop. "You're right."

I am? Dimly, she wondered how she could be right about this, when he disagreed with her about everything else. In an astonishingly brief expanse of time, he drew up her chemise and refastened her buttons.

"There will be no apologies, Anya."

She touched her fingertips to her heated cheeks. "Good, because I have no intention of apologizing."

A reckless grin slashed his features and he chuckled. "Damn, you're something."

It was a totally meaningless compliment, but nonetheless it cheered her. "We have resolved nothing."

He moved to the blanket and began filling it with the remnants of their lunch. "Sure we have. You know more about Texas. I have every intention of seeing Richard's servants settled securely. And caves make me hot. I'd say we accomplished a lot."

She glared down at him in exasperation. "When did you decide to take care of the servants?"

"The night Richard died. Come on, help me get this stuff loaded up. There's a storm brewing."

Surprised, she glanced beyond the mouth of the cave. There were, indeed, angry storm clouds building. She knelt beside Morgan and began shoving their unfinished lunch into the basket. It unnerved her that while she'd been totally absorbed in their confrontation, Morgan had been aware of what was happening outside.

It also disturbed her that he had argued with her methods of bringing up the matter of the servants' future when he was apparently in full accordance with her. Again, she decided he was the most contrary man she'd ever met.

The return ride to the manor house was brisk and without incident. The storm beat them home, but by only a few fat drops of rain. When they entered the house, a footman was in attendance to take their coats.

One of Morgan's statements still perplexed her. At the bottom of the great staircase, she decided to ask for a clarification. "Morgan?"

He paused and turned toward her. "Yes, my sweet."

She blushed. "Don't call me that."

He raised an eyebrow. "Why not?"

"It sounds as if you're mocking me."

One step brought him within touching distance. "Why do you say that?"

"Because 'my sweet' is what men call their sweethearts. I'm hardly that to you."

He stared at her thoughtfully. "What is it you think you are to me, Anya?"

"A convenience, of course." Anticipating an objection on his part, she raised her hand. "I'm not complaining. I understand why you require Richard's money, and it's for a worthy cause—to save the plantation for Lavinia. I would just prefer that you . . . you eschew the meaningless endearments."

"But it wasn't meaningless. You are sweet, Anya—sweet tasting."

She knew she blushed scarlet. "Oh . . ."

"Believe me, no convenience ever tasted quite so delectable."

"Shh, you shouldn't say such things."

"But, my prickly blossom, I have every intention of saying such things and *doing* such things."

Fascinated despite herself, she licked her lips. "You do?"

"I have set my mind to wooing you, Miss Delangue."

Wooing or seducing? she wondered frantically. She almost asked, but something in his eyes made her leery of his answer.

"I hardly think that's obligatory. I mean, under the circumstances."

"*Under the circumstances,* I think it's absolutely obligatory." He chose that moment to smile at her. "I believe you had a question for me?"

She nodded. "In the cave you said we'd settled three matters. The first was me learning more of Texas, the second your decision to provide for Richard's servants."

"That is correct."

"But the third thing you said didn't make any sense at all. You were right that the cave was cold and drafty today. How then could it make you hot?"

His smile tugged to one side. "Weren't you...warm?"

"Not particularly."

"Not even when I was holding you, touching you?"

An immediate blast of heat shot through her. "Was that what you meant?"

He rested his arm on the balustrade. "It could have been the lingering ghosts of pirates past, I suppose."

"What could have?" she asked, mesmerized by the wicked gleam in his eyes.

"My sudden desire to ravish you."

"Oh hush, someone might hear you. Besides, we already did that and probably made a baby, remember?"

He coughed, then cleared his throat. "Umm, yes, I seem to recall something like that."

"Well, then, how many times do you propose to keep at it?" she demanded, dismayed by his cavalier manner.

For a moment, he said nothing. "Were you thinking of setting a limit?"

She wrinkled her brow. "If we only need five children, then it stands to reason we need only to indulge five times."

He made a choking sound that evolved into another cough. "I think not, Anya."

"But then we shall have more than five children," she protested.

"You're going to have to trust me on this, Anya. Not every time a man lies with a woman produces a child. It may require many, many occasions of most diligent effort to produce our offspring." He ran a calloused fingertip across her cheek. "But, my sweet, I want to assure you it is a duty of which I shall never tire. Two, three or more times a day, I will do my utmost to ensure success."

She gaped at him in astonishment. "Two or three times a day? When will you do your ranching?"

He smiled most tenderly, and Anya's heart raced.

"There will be time for that, also. But *you* will come first."

"I think that is most generous of you, Morgan."

"You will discover I am a very generous man."

"Thank you," she said, feeling a sincere regard for the American. "I want you to know I appreciate your consideration. And I appreciate your intent to protect Richard's servants."

"My pleasure, Anya."

As she started up the stairs to her chamber, she decided the day had been a rousing success. She had accomplished her two main objectives. For all of Morgan's talk about disliking manipulative women, she had managed him quite nicely.

And she had enjoyed those passionate moments in his arms when she'd had him at her mercy, too. It was an astonishing discovery to learn that despite her nondescript appearance, she had the makings of a seductress.

All in all, she decided this had been one of the great days of her life. And just think—she had tomorrow to look forward to.

Chapter Nine

The next morning, Morgan strode purposefully toward the stables. His mood, dark and restless, called for the challenge of Champion, but he knew he would settle again for the roan. There was no way he could concentrate on the spirited stallion while he was so furious with Anya.

After barking a gruff command, he watched the stable boys scramble to saddle his mount. It was a testament to his anger that he didn't see to the task himself. With a ripple of shock, Morgan noticed his hands were shaking. He still gripped the damned note Anya had slipped under his door. He shoved the scented missive into his coat pocket and reached for the reins. "Stand back, I'll take him."

After leading the horse from the stables, Morgan wasted no time in mounting. He had a scatterbrained female to track down. Again.

Beloved, you have become everything to me....

Morgan recalled how his blood had heated when he'd read those words.

Beloved... He'd liked the sound of that, liked the thought of Anya surrendering her heart to him. He should have stopped reading right there. He hadn't, of course. Her next sentence had set a fire in his loins.

I cannot wait until we are wed to become fully yours....

Lord, he'd practically gone up in flames right there. The mental picture of Anya lying before him, her soft body naked and beckoning, was enough to drive any man out of his mind. It was the last two lines of the message that had changed passion to outraged disbelief.

I shall be waiting for you in our special place, the one place where we can truly be alone.

There was only one spot Anya could be referring to—her precious cave. Morgan understood how a lonely English girl mourning her brother's death might be captivated by a secret place replete with a history of pirates and hidden booty.

But she had defied the direct order he had given that she not go there without him. Morgan leaned forward, urging the horse to ride for all it was worth. As much as he wanted to make love to Anya, he had every intention of tearing a strip off her instead. He was going to make sure she understood that her days of doing as she damned well pleased were over. When he gave an order, she would obey it.

Morgan arrived at the crumbling stone terrace, which according to Anya had been built by Roman soldiers, and found it deserted. There was no sign that his future wife had even been there. Nor was Lady Lore in evidence. He dismounted and looked around in frustration. What the hell was going on?

It was then that he noticed the gate was ajar. He distinctly remembered closing it behind them the day before. He tethered the roan and stalked toward the steps leading to the cave. One thing was certain. Anya definitely had some explaining to do.

Morgan darted a quick glance toward a sky roiling with ominous-looking clouds. Lord, it was going to be good to get out of this windblown, damp, foggy and frequently drizzling climate. It looked as if yet another storm were about to hit Hobb's Corner. Confirming the thought, a raindrop slashed his cheek.

When he reached the cave, Morgan's patience—and he admitted there had been precious little of it to begin with—was exhausted.

"Anya!"

At this point, even if she waltzed out buck naked, she wouldn't escape the punishment he intended to mete out.

"Anya, dammit, where are you?"

There was no answer. He stepped deeper into the cave. Damnation, he disliked this place. "The game's over. Get out here. Now."

A prickling sensation at the back of his neck was all the warning he got. Instinctively, he tried to grab for his Remington 44. It wasn't there. Since his arrival in England, he hadn't worn his gun belt.

Pain exploded in his head. He went down to his knees and didn't even feel the impact. Black oblivion claimed him.

Anya sat at the table and absently nibbled a piece of toast. When was Morgan going to come downstairs? Generally, Lady Hester remained abed until noon. That made the morning meal one of the few occasions Anya and Morgan could be alone, other than when they went riding. The matron had begun to take her duties as a chaperon most seriously.

What really rankled was that it seemed to be Anya whom the older woman watched for any breach in decorum.

Hours later, Anya was still feeling at loose ends. She had spent some of the time drafting a second letter to Edward, further expounding upon her intent to wed Morgan Grayson once they arrived in Bedfordshire.

After that, Lady Hester had claimed a nearby settee and had itemized the qualities of a dutiful wife. Throughout the discourse, Anya couldn't help thinking that a loving wife had attributes suspiciously similar to those of a faithful hunting dog. She visualized herself on all fours licking her master's—Morgan's—hand. Only the image of his shocked expression offered her the encouragement required to continue with the wedding plans.

When a furious storm broke, bringing with it an early darkness, and Morgan still had failed to return, a growing uneasiness filled Anya. Where was he? He had said nothing the evening before of leaving. As she paced the library, waiting for Harry Jarvis to answer her summons, she told herself it was ridiculous to worry about a fully grown man who'd survived a war without mishap.

Still, she could not explain away her misgivings. Something was wrong. She could sense it.

Harry strode into the library. Rainwater clung to his hair and clothes. "Miss Anya, you sent for me?"

An uncanny sense of déjà vu chilled her. It had been upon a similarly stormy night that she had sent for Tom. "Did Mr. Grayson take one of the horses today?"

Harry nodded, wiping the wet from his florid face. "Aye, he did—the roan."

"Did he say where he was going or when he would return?"

"No, and none asked. In a rage, he was."

"A rage?"

"Aye, looked liked he was riding to meet the devil himself."

"Oh..." Anya tried to think. Morgan had been angry about something. What? Where had he ridden to? Hobb's Corner, London, America? She rubbed her forehead. "I suppose there's nothing to do but wait for his return."

Harry nodded, and Anya dismissed him. Moving to the hearth, she held her hands toward the fire's warmth. It was foolish to worry. When Morgan returned, he would provide a satisfactory explanation for his absence. She would see to it. After all, if a wife must account for her comings and goings, it seemed only fair that her husband do likewise.

When a night and another day had passed and Morgan still hadn't returned, Anya could no longer reason away her worry. She entered Morgan's chambers, looking for some possible clue to his whereabouts. With a will of its own, her gaze went to his wide bed. It was neatly made. The thought of Morgan's large body lying upon it gave her pause.

She wondered if she would ever join him in that bed. Would their bodies touch? Would they speak to each other? Would he kiss her as he had in the cave, with his body on top

of hers and only their bedclothes separating them? She
shivered, a strange kind of shiver that made her loins tingle.

She turned from the bed. The dresser caught her attention, and she stepped toward it. Thoughtfully, she picked up
a brown comb. If Morgan had planned on taking a trip,
wouldn't he have taken his comb? A man's shaving blade
and bar of soap lay upon the nearby washstand. She picked
up the bar and inhaled its pungent aroma. After sneezing
twice, she set it back on the stand.

A further search of his rooms informed her that his
clothes still hung in the closet. When she discovered a large,
battered trunk, she investigated its contents without com-
punction. Somewhere, Morgan must have left a clue to
where he'd gone.

The trunk yielded all kinds of intriguing items. She found
a couple pair of men's trousers made from a peculiar bluish
fabric that felt sturdy as leather. She found a pair of strange
jingling devices with sharp-edged, spinning metal disks. She
found a plaid cotton shirt and a leather waistcoat that had
seen a lot of wear. She found a carefully wrapped leather
belt that had bullets sewn into it, along with a pistol in a
cleverly designed pocket. When she lifted the belt, she was
astonished by its heaviness.

Clearly, it was meant to be worn about a man's waist, yet
she could picture no man walking about with so primitive a
weapon hanging upon his person. Was Texas so menacing
a place that men strapped pistols to themselves? Perhaps the
gun was intended for protection against the wild Indians
she'd heard about. Her gaze fell upon a scuffed pair of
brown boots whose toes were pointed. Even though the heels
had been worn down, they seemed unusually high for a man
as tall as Morgan.

In frustration, she slammed shut the trunk. She had
learned nothing from her search about where Morgan had
gone. She stood and strode back to the closet, where she
proceeded to shamelessly rifle through the clothing hung
there.

The only thing she discovered was a crumpled envelope that bore markings from America. From it, she plucked a lavishly scrawled sheet of scented paper. Vividly, she recalled the morning Merrawynn had swept into the conservatory and announced a messenger had arrived for Morgan. Anya suspected this was the letter that had been delivered.

Dearest Morgan, please forgive me. I know my marrying Justin must have hurt you terribly, and yet I was so lonely. I still miss you. I miss lying next to you, I miss the magic nights we shared. I miss all of it, Morgan, and I shall remember you most tenderly. The reason I am writing this letter is to tell you *not* to marry some prune-faced Englishwoman for her money. I know I shall be able to persuade Justin to give up his claim to Taopath. Believe me, it is only a matter of time before he relents. Please, please, do not burden yourself with a frumpy old maid who would not know how to pleasure a man if her life depended upon it. I am sending this letter in the hope you will receive it aboard ship. Your true and faithful friend, Collette.

Friend? Anya scoffed to herself as she carefully recrumpled the letter, returned it to Morgan's coat pocket and left his chambers.

That the unsavory Collette and Morgan had indulged in some most unseemly behavior was painfully obvious. To put it bluntly, the woman was a libertine. For all of a minute, Anya tried to convince herself that this…this fallen woman had seduced Morgan. Remembering the feel of Morgan's hot mouth upon her own, however, leveled that delusion. The sad and painful truth was that Anya's future husband was an irresistible lover.

He had kept the letter.

Why?

Because he still harbored an affection for Collette?

Rather than roam Hull Manor like some demented ghost, Anya decided to go for a ride. When she met up with the

American again, she was going to give him a piece of her mind. How dare he go about cavorting with disreputable women? She would inform him that such reckless behavior was now at an end. The man would learn one did not trifle with an Englishwoman's affections.

The weather had improved sufficiently that Anya and Lady Lore enjoyed a lengthy ride. Despite her promise to Morgan that she would stay away from the cliffs, Anya decided to ride by there. She needed to look at the sea. It always soothed her.

She reached the rocky bluff and dismounted. Endless sky and sea embraced her. She stepped to the railing and stared out across the horizon.

He had kept the letter....

Perhaps Morgan had no intention of returning. Only the belongings that in his hasty departure he had left behind suggested he might come back. But a person could send for things left behind....

Why would he have been so determined to get her to accept his marriage proposal if he were pining for another woman? Collette was married to Morgan's half brother. Was Morgan's love for his brother's wife so great that he had decided at the last moment to return to her? Was he planning on taking Collette to his ranch in Texas?

Dejectedly, Anya ran her gloved fingertips across the railing. She couldn't believe that Morgan's passion for her had been feigned. Nor did she believe Morgan Grayson was the kind of man who would slink away like a coward. If he had changed his mind about marrying her, he would have told her so to her face.

She drew a great breath of salty air and turned to Lady Lore. Her hands had closed about the reins when she paused. From the corner of her eye she'd glimpsed something that didn't belong, a flash of black upon the rocky path.

Curious, she walked back to the gate and leaned forward. Midway down the steps, she saw the edge of a man's boot. The blood froze in her veins. For a moment she didn't know if her trembling fingers would be able to open the gate. When the latch finally sprang free, she practically ripped the wooden gate from its hinges as she raced through it and down the steps.

Lying exposed to the elements was a battered and bloody Morgan. Tears swam in her eyes, but she ignored them. She bent her ear to Morgan's chest.

Be alive. Be alive. Be alive.

The steady beat of his heart was the sweetest sound she'd ever heard. Her hands foraged across his chest and shoulders, searching for the wound from which the blood had sprung. She found no sign of injury. Nor was there any apparent damage to his lower body. She touched his cold cheek, then gingerly rolled him to his side. She located the wound at the back of his head, where blood matted his black hair.

"Oh, Morgan," she whispered, realizing suddenly that he must have been unconscious for two days, throughout the storm, throughout the night.

She had to get him into the shelter of the cave and then go for help. It took longer than she could bear to get him inside. She removed her riding jacket and covered him. She hated leaving him, and yet she knew there was no way she could drag him up the steps and onto Lady Lore.

Her ride back to the manor house was without mercy for herself or her mount. When she arrived at the stables, she shouted for help. Immediately, Harry and a batch of junior grooms were at her side.

Out of breath, she struggled to make her words clear. "Morgan's hurt. We have to get him back to the house."

Minutes later, Harry drove a wagon toward the cave. Anya led them to where she'd dragged Morgan, then wrung her hands until they had loaded him into the back of the wagon. She climbed in next to him and tenderly cradled his head upon her lap.

When they reached the house, she yelled out instructions like a crazed general. Lady Hester appeared on the scene and immediately surmised the calamity. The matron issued her own series of commands.

"Send for Dr. Goodwin at once. Anya, run on ahead and have Morgan's bed readied for him."

Anya raced into the manor and then waited in frustration during the twenty minutes it required two hulking men to carry Morgan to his bed. And she did not appreciate being ordered from Morgan's chamber so his clothing could be removed and his body sponged. Lady Hester's insistence upon propriety at a time like this seemed quite ridiculous to Anya.

After Morgan had been draped in a nightshirt, Anya was allowed back into his room. Not waiting for the physician's arrival, Anya examined Morgan's injury. The wound had stopped bleeding. She washed away the dirt and debris from his matted hair and wrapped the area with a wide, white bandage.

Morgan was already coming around when Dr. Goodwin arrived. She couldn't make a bit of sense from the American's incoherent words, but the fact that he was no longer unconscious cheered her.

"He's suffered a severe blow to the head," the doctor announced.

"Is he going to be all right?" Anya asked.

"He'll have a ferocious headache when he awakens fully, but he'll survive."

"Stop that hammering," Morgan mumbled groggily.

Anya flew to his side and rested her fingertips upon his forehead. "Can you give him something for the pain?"

"I've some powders that will dull the worst of it." The physician reached into the bag he invariably carried. "In the next few hours, there will be moments when he'll probably sound quite lucid, then he'll drift off again. It's to be expected."

After the grim-faced doctor had dispensed his medicine, after a fussing Lady Hester had retired to her chambers, after the servants had resumed their normal duties, Anya sat alone with Morgan.

Her hand went to his limp one. A lump swelled in her throat. Seeing Morgan, a strong and powerful man in the prime of his life, lying helpless terrified her. She had lost her parents. She had lost George. She had lost Richard. She prayed to God that she wouldn't lose Morgan.

Night was coming on and, save for the fire and a lone, flickering candle, the room was shrouded in darkness. She thought of her life as it had been before Morgan had come charging into it. Tears stung her eyes. She had been so lonely, and she hadn't even realized it.

She drew closer to him, remembering the contents of Collette's letter. What had Morgan thought when he read it? Had he missed his former sweetheart; had he regretted his engagement to a . . . a frumpy Englishwoman?

For the first time in years, Anya wished fervently that she were beautiful. Except for several noteworthy exceptions, Morgan had found it dishearteningly easy to restrain himself with her. It seemed that only when she made him angry did he draw her to him.

She wondered if she was going to spend her entire married life making her husband angry so he would embrace her. Feeling that he was too far away from her still, Anya moved closer and sat next to him on the bed. Somewhere in the chamber a clock ticked. The fire crackled. Morgan's breathing remained deep and even.

Within her grew the need to lie next to Morgan Grayson. She knew it wasn't proper, of course. But need overruled propriety and she stretched out beside him. The mattress dipped slightly. She lay on her side so that she faced him. Even in deep sleep, his eyebrows were drawn together into a frown. She reached out and lightly stroked the groove bracketing his forehead.

She wasn't going to lose him. Even if she had to hold on to him as he slept, she wouldn't let Morgan Grayson get away. She'd waited too long for him. It had been at his insistence that she had accepted his proposal of marriage, and now that she'd agreed, she would make sure he kept his part of the agreement by staying alive. After all, there were five children to be brought into the world.... Her eyelids closed.

Umm ... Delicious heat rubbed against Anya. She felt herself turned, her clothing tugged at.

"I've been waiting for you, for this."

The husky murmur made her tremble. "Morgan?"

"Come, my sweet, it's time to wake up."

Drowsily, Anya opened her eyes. She saw only a darkened silhouette hovering over her. But she could feel every inch of hot, naked flesh pressed up against her own bare skin. Anya shot upright. "What's going on?"

"Shh, darling. We don't want to disturb Lady Hester."

And then his mouth covered hers. Swamped by a myriad of sensations she'd never experienced before, Anya clung to him. He was burning up and starting a similar fire within her. His tongue entered her mouth. She never thought of denying him entrance. She wrapped her arms around his neck and drew him closer.

Again she became aware of a probing hardness nudging her hips. Only this time no clothing restricted the feel of the silken shaft rubbing against her. She shuddered, holding tighter to him, lest she fly away.

A heavy leg moved between her thighs. His hand moved downward. "So hot, so sweetly hot..."

Immediately, Anya stiffened and the wispy clouds of sleep and passion cleared. "Morgan!"

"Yes, honey, that's it, call my name."

His fingers began to stroke her. She shuddered again. A tingling warmth invaded her entire body.

"Relax, this is going to feel so good."

She wanted to relax. Honestly she did. She wanted to feel good, too. But it had suddenly dawned on her that she was totally unclothed and so was Morgan. While she had kept a loving vigil, the American had awakened and taken shameful advantage of the situation.

And he appeared to be far from finished.

She tried to scoot away from his shocking caress.

"Where are you going, honey?"

To hell, fire, and damnation, she feared. "I—I have to leave. Besides, you aren't well."

He chuckled huskily. "I've never felt better."

In the darkness his other hand came out, and she felt the shocking weight of his palm upon her breast. She tried to squirm free. "It's really best that I leave, Morgan."

"The hell it is," he growled.

His mouth found hers and he instigated a kiss of such magnitude that resistance became impossible. Losing herself to the moment and the man, she entwined her tongue with his.

As if seeking entrance to her, the shaft she'd felt earlier pushed more insistently against her flesh, just as Morgan's tongue had already sought entrance to her mouth. For one reckless moment she wanted to open her thighs for him and allow him to join with her. Almost at once sanity reigned.

The powders Dr. Goodwin had provided for Morgan's headache must have caused some bizarre kind of delirium. Surely, no man would seek to do such a thing to a woman? To put himself inside her? No, it defied all logic. Clearly, Morgan was out of his mind and driving her to a like state of incoherence.

He was so much stronger than she, though. In the next few seconds he would reach his destination. Would it hurt? Or would it feel as wonderful as it did to have his tongue inside her?

"Morgan..." Her voice was a breathless whisper as she waited for him to have his way with her.

There was no response. For an endless moment he remained poised above her, an arrow waiting to be sprung from its bow. Then, with a low groan, he collapsed on top of her.

It took a moment before she realized that he had drifted back to unconsciousness. Disappointed, then outraged by that disappointment, she slithered from the bed. Fuming, she pulled her clothes back on, her gaze flicking every so often to Morgan's gloriously naked body. When she'd dislodged herself from him, he'd rolled onto his back.

Determinedly, she strode to the fireplace and ruthlessly stirred the flames. Then she lit another candle, wanting to gaze upon this thing Morgan had tried to place inside her.

A profusion of dark hair covered his chest and lower body. He was big and muscular, with strong arms and legs that were also dusted with dark hair. In a curly, dark thicket lay the softened bulge of what had almost entered her. She stared long and hard at the "thistle" meant to prick her.

The word *couple* tumbled into her chaotic thoughts. That was what men and women did when they married....

As if the pieces of a heretofore incomprehensible puzzle were slowly falling into place, Anya began to comprehend random bits of information she had gleaned through the years. Somehow seeing a naked man added a significant piece to the puzzle.

In his present softened condition, however, Anya didn't see how Morgan *could* penetrate her. Which meant that sometimes he was...rigid, and at other times he wasn't. Biting her lip, she moved closer. With a fingertip, she gingerly touched him. Immediately, she jerked her hand away. No, he wasn't rigid now. A drop of hot candle wax fell onto the sheet and Anya moved back.

Aware that she was taking shameful advantage of Morgan's unconsciousness, she placed the candlestick on a nearby table.

Thoughtfully, she pulled the blankets over his sprawled body. She wondered if he could control when he was or wasn't stiff. She wondered if it had something to do with rubbing himself against her, because whenever he did that she could feel him through their clothing. She wondered...how it would feel when he put that..."thistle" inside her.

But what she wondered about most of all as she lay in her own bed was her wedding night—when she would discover firsthand the answers to her questions.

* * *

Morgan opened his eyes. Other than a pounding head-ache, he was aware of nothing amiss. He arose to take care of his morning ablutions, comfortable with the familiar nakedness in which he always slept whenever a bed was handy.

It was only when he picked up his razor and looked into the mirror that he realized something was definitely wrong. He had a three-day growth of beard and a bandage wrapped around his head. He touched the white cloth and wondered what the hell was going on. The last thing he remembered was . . . was . . .

Well, hell. He remembered having a picnic with Anya. And then he remembered . . . Nothing. Not a damned thing. Somehow he knew Anya would have the explanation for what had happened. He couldn't remember why at the moment, but he knew he was angry with her about some-thing. . . . Something that tugged elusively at the edge of his mind, but that he couldn't quite grasp.

When the door to his chamber swung open, he looked in the mirror, expecting to see Benson entering the room. Instead, Morgan encountered a reflection of a modestly dressed Anya standing frozen in the doorway.

As he was stark naked, he wouldn't have been surprised to see her sink to the floor in a dead faint, shriek in maidenly distress or bolt from the room.

She marched forward. "What are you doing out of bed?"

Morgan's jaw fell open. "Anya, I'm naked." Perhaps she hadn't noticed?

"So you are," she agreed briskly, her cheeks scarlet, her eyes locked on his. "Get back into bed."

"Anya—"

"Don't be difficult, Morgan." With that firmly voiced stricture, she took the razor from his hand and led him to the bed. "I'll ring for Benson. He can help you shave."

Morgan found himself buried beneath several blankets. When Anya bent over him to adjust his pillows, he felt a predictable surge of desire and groaned.

Anya's cool fingertips went to his forehead. "Oh, Morgan, does it hurt?"

Her sweet scent, hinting faintly at lilacs, reached him, and he was hard pressed not to pull Anya beneath the covers, which were rapidly becoming steamy. "Like the dickens."

"I'll send for Dr. Goodwin. He has special powders to make the pain go away."

"Somehow I don't think that would help."

"Let me send for him," Anya insisted earnestly.

"Something closer to home might work."

Her brow wrinkled. "What do you mean?"

"A kiss from your soft lips would do wonders for me, Anya."

Her wide brown eyes filled with sudden comprehension. "You are feeling better, then?"

"Better than what?" he challenged softly.

"Than you were." Concern flickered in her gaze. "What happened, Morgan?"

His fingers went automatically to the bandage that encircled his pounding head. "I was hoping you would tell me."

She sat down on the edge of bed, and he marveled at her apparent ease with him. It hadn't escaped his notice that, unless he had her in his arms and was kissing her, Anya tended to scuttle nervously around him.

"Morgan, you were gone for two days. I found you at the cliffs. You must have been visiting the cave, slipped and hit your head on the steps."

"What were you doing at the cliffs?" he demanded. "I distinctly remember telling you—"

She laid her hand against his bare arm. Immediately, his anger cooled, while something else heated. "Morgan, if I hadn't ridden to the cliffs, you would probably be dead."

He saw tears glistening in her lashes and pulled her to him. "Don't cry, honey. I'm too tough to kill. Remember?"

The blankets slipped to his waist, and he held her trembling body cradled against his naked one. Several moments passed. She rubbed her pale cheek against the hair on his chest. A hot shaft of desire flared. One thing was certain, if she stayed in his arms much longer she would learn about the fundamental difference between a man and woman—and he would put that difference to the appropriate use.

Like a whisper of rustling velvet, her breath stroked his throat while her fingertips idly caressed his chest. Her hips nudged his groin. He groaned for a third time. No man was designed to take this kind of punishment—the punishment of holding an innocent woman in his arms when his body demanded release within that innocent woman's moist heat.

She tilted her trusting face toward him. "The blow you suffered to the back of your head when you fell must have made you forget what happened. Once, when George was sliding down a banister, he tumbled off and hit his head. For days he couldn't remember the accident. Then one morning it all came back to him."

Morgan cleared his throat. There was no way he could keep his hand from going to Anya's coiled braid and removing a hairpin. "I suppose you're right."

"What are you doing?"

He thought her voice was surprisingly calm, considering their intimate proximity. "I want to see your hair down."

"Oh." Her fingertips resumed their delicate caress against his chest. "You're rigid again."

At her frankness, the blood in his veins turned to fire. "So I am."

She peered up at him, her eyes owlish. "Do you wish to place that . . . rigidness inside me?"

He couldn't keep from grinning. Evidently, there were degrees of innocence. "I would like to do that very much."

The tip of her tongue moistened her lips. Morgan was in paradise. In the next few minutes he was finally going to claim the delectable Anya Delangue. He vowed he would make it as good for her as he knew it would be for him. He carefully extracted another pin from her braid.

"Do other men?"

His hand froze. "What?"

"I mean, it's not, er . . . an unnatural thing to do?"

It required some effort to keep his features neutral. "All men do it—it's perfectly normal."

"And Lady Hester's husband put this...thing inside her?"

Morgan choked. "As difficult as that might be to imagine, I'm very sure he did."

There was a lengthy pause. Anya's fingers continued their enticing dance across his chest and Morgan took heart. It wouldn't be long now. A few more kisses and—

"But this is something that should be done only between a man and wife, is it not?"

His brow beaded with sweat. He wanted her willingly, without any subsequent regrets. "I imagine that's what you've been taught...."

She peered up at him again, and he cursed those trusting eyes of hers. "It is a very intimate act, is it not?"

He sighed. "Yes."

"Would you do it with a woman who was not your wife, Morgan?"

"I would do it with you, Anya, this very minute. I would slip inside your tight channel and show you pleasures you've never dreamed of. And it wouldn't be wrong because I will soon be your husband."

"And that is what you meant about anticipating our vows?"

He took the final pin from her hair and began freeing the dark mass from its neat braid. "That is what I meant."

"Have you done this thing with other women?"

His thoughts were on the silken tresses he was fanning about her shoulders, and on the narrow row of buttons running down the front of her dress.

"Many times. There is nothing to fear. I will not hurt you. I will only—"

She shot from the bed as if she'd been blasted from a cannon. "Aha!"

He looked up at her in astonishment. Dark hair swirled about her face and her bosom heaved.

"Aha?"

"You are a libertine, Morgan Grayson. You go about placing your... your member in women from here to Texas with nary a thought about our feelings."

Morgan's body still burned for release. His member, as Anya called it, was rock hard, and he wanted nothing more than to be inside her. With his head pounding also, he was not in the most reasonable of moods.

"I don't go about placing my..." Suddenly he realized the futility of the argument. A few moments ago he had stupidly confessed to doing just that. What had he been thinking? That was just it, of course. He hadn't been thinking with his brains, he'd been thinking with his—

"Well, have you nothing to say for yourself?"

"Hell, yes, I have something to say." He sat taller in the bed. "All men do it—every chance we get. Because it feels good, Anya. Damned good. But you're not going to find out, because I'll be damned if I give you one moment of pleasure before the minister pronounces the 'I do's.'"

She drew herself up like a replica of Lady Hester. "Indeed?"

"And another thing," he continued, frustration gnawing at him. "Once we're married, you will belong to me in every sense of the word. In our bed, there will be no prattle about convention. *Anything* we do together will be acceptable. Understand?"

"What I understand, Morgan Grayson, is that were I not already possibly carrying your child, you would be the last man on this earth I would wed." She turned on her heel and stalked to the door. Abruptly, she pivoted, her waist-length hair flying out around her like an enticing velvet cloud. "Collette may not realize it, but she is better off without you."

A stunned Morgan stared after his retreating bride-to-be. What the woman didn't know about making babies could fill volumes.

He thrust aside the blankets and noticed a splotch of white on the sheet. Curiously, he touched it. Cooled candle wax...

What the hell was that doing in his bed?

As he got to his feet for the second time that morning, Morgan Grayson decided that, while he'd been unconscious, the world had gone mad.

Chapter Ten

That afternoon, Anya was more than willing to put some distance between herself and Morgan. It was extremely difficult to look at him fully dressed without remembering how he had appeared with no clothing. The size and breadth of him, the astonishing abundance of body hair and...and his "thistle" made him seem more formidable than ever.

Finding a degree of security in her bedchamber, Anya stared out her bedroom window. There he was, stalking toward the stables, no doubt in search of Harry Jarvis and an explanation about the missing roan and the hours lost from his memory. Morgan certainly had badgered her enough about the circumstances of his accident.

Anya let the curtains slip through her fingertips. He was such a stubborn man! She had insisted most forcibly that he remain in bed until Dr. Goodwin could pronounce him cured. Morgan had paid as much heed to her as he would have a gnat.

She looked around her chamber. Mavis had already tidied it for the day. The delicate figurines Richard had given her over the years caught her attention. In her haste to flee Hull Manor and Morgan Grayson, she had forgotten to pack them the ill-fated morning of her aborted escape.

She moved to the shelf that held the half-dozen glass figures and reached for her favorite, a little shepherd girl. The tiny face stared at a distant horizon while a fragile arm encircled a lamb no larger than Anya's thumb. It was difficult to picture the shepherd girl resting upon a shelf in Texas. Would the glass figure even survive the journey?

Carefully, she returned the small statue to its proper place. A large, uneven greenish rock caught her attention. George had found it in his favorite frog-catching pond and claimed a witch had cast a spell upon the King of the Frogs, changing him into the rock. George had gone on to insist that the only way the frog could reclaim his kingdom was for Anya to kiss the rock. Because she had loved her brother and would have done anything for him—save kissing a *live* frog—Anya had obliged.

Anya smiled tenderly. George had hooted with laughter at her gullibility, then run through the house, informing all within shouting distance that Anya was in love with a frog. She had chased after him, of course—all the way to the high tower. That had been the day he'd fallen off the banister and been knocked unconscious.

She turned from the shelf. A slim volume of poetry Richard had given her lay on the edge of the dresser. In that moment, it occurred to Anya that her entire lifetime's collection of treasures would take up little space in her trunk.

It also occurred to her that in the next few years she would be collecting new mementos, making new memories. For the first time since she'd agreed to marry Morgan, she experienced an onrush of excitement. All at once, she wanted to be on her way, to begin experiencing the grand adventure that awaited her.

Hull Manor belonged to her past, and she was ready to bid it farewell. It was time they were on their way to her brother Edward's house so she and Morgan could wed, and it was high time Morgan returned to his ranch.

With that thought in mind, Anya went in search of Mavis. In order for her fragile possessions to survive the voyage to America, each item would have to be carefully wrapped. She would set Mavis to the task immediately.

Several hours later, the shelf in her chamber was bare, along with several of her drawers. The room had a satisfying echo to it, and Anya felt as if she'd made some headway toward her future. Even though she hadn't yet had a response to the letters she'd sent Edward, she felt closer to returning to her childhood home and the actual day of her wedding.

As she descended the staircase to check on the evening meal, she was feeling quite pleased with herself. There was nothing she liked better than taking charge and seeing that things got done in a proper fashion.

When she glanced down the stairs and noticed a glowering Morgan staring back up at her, a portion of that pleasure ebbed. Goodness, the man looked as if he were ready to... to attack her, and she didn't mean that in the tingling, breathless manner she'd begun to look forward to.

"Morgan?"

"We need to talk, Anya."

Again? She studied his tight-lipped features and sighed. At least life would never be boring with the American. They stepped into the library. A host of memories came flooding back to her—the storm-tossed night they'd met, the morning he'd forced her to read Richard's will, the moment she'd discovered he had undressed her....

Thinking of *that* made her cheeks blaze. Then she remembered the sight of Morgan without a stitch of clothing, and her gaze jerked guiltily to his. She wondered if at odd moments he ever recalled the night he'd removed her sodden garments.

"Anya, I've spent most of the day with Harry Jarvis and Tom."

She looked at him in confusion. "Tom? The stable boy?"

"Former stable boy," Morgan corrected grimly. "Though from his present attitude, he might yet return to that position."

Anya dropped to the brocade chair that faced the desk, trying to understand why Morgan would spend his time talking with Tom. Concerned, she wondered if the blow to Morgan's head had unsettled him. "I suppose if Tom can conquer his fear of horses, he should be allowed another chance to work in the stables."

"That is my opinion, also. Tom and several other stable boys are out looking for the roan."

"The storm must have frightened it away."

"Storm?"

As she stared up at him, tears filled her eyes. "Oh, Morgan, there was a terrible rain the night you were missing. It's a miracle you survived without becoming seriously ill."

A crooked smile gentled his expression. "There's no need to cry, Anya. Obviously, I'm too tough to die."

She shivered. No one was too tough to die, and in some strange way, his words seemed to tempt fate to prove him wrong. "It was a dreadful accident, Morgan. In the future I expect you to exercise more caution."

His smile disappeared. "I'm not sure it was an accident."

"*What?*"

"Things don't add up, Anya. What was I doing there in the first place? Where's my horse? How could I have fallen? The steps are wide and solid. And even if I had slipped, I would have caught myself. In fact, the only explanation for any of it would be if I had been rollicking drunk." His dark eyes held her. "And I wasn't."

"But you must have fallen," Anya protested. "How else can you explain what happened?"

"I don't know." Morgan stood impatiently. "If only I could remember . . ."

Anya rose and moved toward him, tentatively putting her hand on his arm. "Give it time. Perhaps your memory will return."

He stared long and hard at her hand, and she wondered if she'd offended him with her gesture of compassion. Self-consciously, she began to lift her fingertips from his sleeve. Immediately, his warm palm prevented the retreat.

"And that's another thing, Anya."

Her gaze swung to his. "What?"

"Why am I so damned angry with you?"

She blinked at him in astonishment, her offense at his profanity swallowed by his unexpected question. "Are you?"

"When I woke up this morning, the only thing I was sure of was that you were somehow at the bottom of things."

She jerked her hand from his warm embrace. "I am not at the *bottom* of anything." As the full import of his words registered, she sucked in her breath. "Are you implying that *I* caused you to fall and then . . . then *left* you at the cliffs?"

Under his intense scrutiny, her back stiffened. Even though his cruel accusation made her want to weep, she would not permit a single tear to fall. How could he think her capable of such evil?

He ran a hand through his hair, then flinched as he obviously encountered his wound. "I'm not saying that at all."

Her chin angled upward. "It sounded suspiciously so to me."

The contrary man surprised her with another smile. "Lord, you do that well—your noble-Englishwoman routine."

She refused to dignify his comment with a response. Instead, she tried to understand how the accident had happened. Until Morgan had pointed out the discrepancies, she hadn't realized how peculiar the circumstances surrounding his fall were.

"You will just have to concentrate on regaining your memory."

"Since there's a chance that isn't going to happen, I'd like to ask you a couple of pertinent questions."

"I've already told you everything—"

"Just explain to me what changed a modest, shrinking, English maiden into a woman who could look at my naked body without fainting or going into hysterics."

"I have never *shrunk* in my life!" Anya's skin flamed. "And . . . uh . . . I've never been inclined toward hysterics."

He caught her hand in his and pressed a slow kiss against her palm. Startled, she jerked her eyes upward. Slumberous eyes looked down at her. Her breath quickened.

"Were you the one who undressed me and put me to bed?"

"Certainly not," she answered staunchly. "Benson took care of that."

"He was the logical one to perform the task," Morgan said agreeably.

"And so he did."

"What happened next?"

The lazy drawl of a question made her shiver. Oh, the man did know how to get to the heart of a matter.

"I—I checked on you."

"Now we're getting somewhere."

The tip of his tongue touched the sensitive flesh between her thumb and forefinger. Instead of one fire, it seemed that the room blazed with ten.

"I think what must have happened," she began courageously, if somewhat less than honestly, "was that sometime in the night you removed the nightshirt in which Benson had dressed you."

Morgan tucked her hand into his and guided her to the settee. "That sounds reasonable."

She discovered it was impossible to drag her heels with any degree of success against the Oriental rug.

"Tell me, did I do that before, after, or during the time you were checking on me?"

"Uh . . . that's difficult to say, Morgan." She smiled ingenuously, or at any rate hoped she did. "It was quite dark, as I recall."

"There would have been a candle. . . ."

"Well, yes." She sat stiffly next to him. "But I was concerned with your head, Morgan, not your . . . uh . . . I mean, the condition of the rest of you."

"Too bad. I imagine the condition of the rest of me was downright . . . interesting."

"I—I wouldn't know."

"Anya?"

She looked at him in consternation. Sometimes when he pronounced her name, he did so with nerve-tingling huskiness. This was one of those instances.

"Yes?"

"I have something of yours to return." He reached into his vest pocket. "Hold out your hand."

She did so automatically. A half-dozen hairpins dropped into her open palm. The morning's intimacy they had shared came racing back. Somehow, she found the necessary pluck to raise her gaze to his.

"Thank you."

His left eyebrow scaled upward. "Your manners never fail to amaze me. I want you to know it gratifies me that you do not find it . . . unpleasant to gaze upon my nakedness."

She could think of no sufficient reply to his husky taunt. Nervously, she curled her fingers around the pins and rose from the settee. "I didn't say that."

"There are a lot of things you haven't said, but a man learns to read between the lines." Morgan slowly unfolded himself from the small satin sofa.

With her chin held high, Anya swept gracefully from the room. Morgan stared after her. He hadn't told her everything. He hadn't told her about the stranger Tom claimed to have seen lurking about the estate.

Frustrated, Morgan glanced around the silent library. It was becoming more and more clear to him that someone had left him unconscious and exposed to the elements with the reasonable expectation he would die. The only reason he hadn't was because Anya had found him.

Several questions nagged at him. How far would Justin go to gain possession of Taopath? Would he send a man across an ocean to kill him? The smiling, fair-haired image Morgan called up of his half brother hardly seemed that of a murderer. Justin was a charmer and a schemer, not the type of man to employ an assassin.

A charmer and a schemer . . . The phrase made him think of Anya's beautiful but selfish older sister. To achieve her goals, would Merrawynn have a man murdered?

Morgan reached for the gilded paperweight on Richard's desk. The heavy piece was shaped in the form of an owl. He wished he had a portion of the creature's purported wisdom. The only thing he seemed to have going for him was the gut instinct that something dangerous and deadly was closing in on him and Anya.

He returned the unblinking owl to its place on the desk. He had reached the chilling conclusion that, if killing him could accomplish someone's aims, then doing likewise to Anya would achieve the same purpose.

A deadly anger knifed through him. At all costs, he had to protect Anya—from whatever sinister force lurked close by and from her own too-trusting nature. If someone wanted to make sure their marriage didn't take place, then she was the more vulnerable target.

His hands clenched. She belonged to him. Her warmth, her sweetness, her...tartness. All of it, from the humor and anger that periodically waged in her warm brown eyes, to her delightfully curved body, to her soft, beckoning mouth.

His father might have survived the deaths of his first two wives, but Morgan had the terrifying suspicion he would not survive Anya's death. The world would become again the lonely and cold place he'd known before she'd raced pell-mell through a raging storm and into his life.

Morgan stared broodingly at the library door. In a few minutes he would be obliged to walk through it and have a civilized dinner with Anya and Lady Hester. He didn't feel the least bit civilized. There was an animal need growing within him to confront his unknown adversary.

He thought of the pins he'd dropped into Anya's small palm. Within him, there also surged an animal heat. He wanted to claim his intended bride, to bind her to him in the most elemental fashion.

As he strode from the room, his vow to leave Anya untouched until their wedding night rang in his ears, mocking him with his own stupidity.

"Have you received word yet from your brother, Anya?" Anya looked across the table into Lady Hester's aristocratic features. "Not yet, but I imagine it won't be much longer."

The matron reached for her wine goblet. "I have begun packing for the trip. I trust you are equally prepared to leave Hull Manor."

Anya's stomach curled, and she slanted a glance at Morgan. He was staring at her. She swallowed. "Yes, I am ready to leave."

The older woman nodded approvingly. "Very good."

"We appreciate your joining us, Lady Hester," Morgan said.

The matron inclined her head toward him. "It would be extremely remiss of me not to accompany you to Bedfordshire, sir."

"Nevertheless, you have our gratitude for taking time from your own schedule to help us." With that observation, Morgan leaned forward and smiled warmly at the older woman.

Lady Hester's cheeks pinkened. If she hadn't known better, Anya would have thought the older woman was smitten with the American.

"It's a matter of duty," Lady Hester repeated, clearly flustered.

Morgan raised his wineglass. "Then permit me to toast your dedication to duty."

Anya, too, raised her glass for the toast. Lady Hester beamed. The odd thought that perhaps the matron was lonely struck Anya. As she looked at Morgan, Anya wondered if part of his kindness to Lady Hester was because he also sensed that loneliness.

In the candlelight, Morgan's profile seemed haloed in silver. Why, if she lowered her lids just so, she could almost imagine him in shining armor....

Before she could ponder the strange phenomenon, Benson entered the dining room. "Sir, Harry Jarvis would like to speak with you. He and Tom are in the library."

When Morgan pushed back his chair, Anya automatically did the same. He flicked a cool glance in her direction.

"Stay where you are, Anya. I will see to this alone."

"But—"

"Remain with Lady Hester," he growled.

Anya jumped. "Now just one moment—"

He stalked around the table and glowered down at her. Anya sank back into her chair. "But, Morgan, I want to know what's going on, too."

His hands came to rest on her shoulders, and he leaned forward to speak into her ear. "This is man's work. Understand?"

She nodded bleakly. The faithful hound had just been commanded to "stay."

Morgan straightened. "Good."

As he stalked from the room, Anya glanced at Lady Hester. The woman was cheerfully sipping her wine. Anya scowled.

"Now, my girl, it won't do you any good to pull a sour face," the woman observed with surprising mildness. "Instead of the fops currently parading about, you've found yourself a real man."

Anya flushed. More than anyone, she knew just how "real" Morgan was. "Lady Hester, I am not in the habit of being ordered about, and I should think you are not, either. I will not pretend it does not rankle."

"Pooh."

Anya's mouth fell open. Had she just heard the esteemed Lady Hester say pooh?

"Morgan Grayson is a strapping young man who will get you safely to America. And once there, he will rule his home with a firm hand." The matron peered at Anya over her glass. "Which is just what you need, young lady. You've had the run of the land for too many years as it is. I cannot imagine what Richard was about, letting you gallivant across the countryside with your skirts 'aflying."

Anya flushed. "Lots of women ride."

"On a proper saddle, they do."

Anya wondered what Lady Hester would say if she told her Morgan had thrown away not only her proper saddle, but her proper corset, as well, and that at that very moment both items were bobbing about in the sea, no doubt in danger of becoming a whale's midnight snack. She was sorely tempted to set the woman straight. What prevented her was the possibility of Lady Hester saying something to Edward. As conservative as she knew her brother to be, he just might not approve of Anya marrying a wild man like Morgan Grayson. She might be annoyed with Morgan, but Anya definitely wanted to marry him. She would not consider life worth living until she'd tamed the arrogant savage.

"Richard was not bound by convention," Anya answered simply.

"That is obvious, or he would not have married Merrawynn." The matron's narrow lips parted in what could only be termed a smile. "Now there's a beautiful young lady."

Silently, Anya agreed. The rift between herself and her sister had begun to weigh heavily upon her spirits. She hoped when they met again the hard feelings could be put behind them.

"I always thought Richard was a fool to sit pining away in this old house for so long after Beatrice died," Lady Hester continued. "Richard should have had children of his own. I had hoped your sister would see to that."

"I'm sure she did her best," Anya replied, rising. "Did you wish to retire to the drawing room?"

The matron nodded, and a hovering footman drew back her chair. "There is a matter I feel it my duty to discuss with you, Anya."

With absolutely no anticipation, Anya followed the woman into the formal drawing room. No doubt, Anya was about to receive another lecture on a bride's proper deportment.

After Lady Hester settled her maroon skirts upon the settee, she leaned forward over her cane. "Sit, girl. I'm getting a crick in my neck staring up at you."

Obediently, Anya claimed a nearby chair of green-and-gray stripes. She would have so much preferred being in the library with Morgan and Harry Jarvis.

"Now then, Anya, I have noticed that you and Mr. Grayson are spending a great deal of time alone together."

Not nearly as much as she would like, Anya thought dispiritedly. "Only during breakfast and when we ride."

"Your rides seem to take an inordinate length of time. Also, you cared for the American when he had his accident."

Anya shifted restlessly and wished the woman would get to the point. "I felt it my duty to do so."

"Harrumph." Vein-ridged hands curled around the throat of the ivory cane. "You were alone with him in his chamber. From the looks of him, I imagine Morgan Grayson is able-bodied. You play with fire, girl, when you become too familiar with a man of his . . . virility."

Anya looked at the matron in surprise. What would *she* know of a man's virility?

"You needn't stare at me like that," Lady Hester snapped. "I wasn't always old, you know. In my day, I was considered a beauty, and I was well aware of the liberties men were apt to take of willing young women."

"Oh." There was nothing more Anya could say to such a declaration. She gazed curiously at the older woman, trying to visualize her as a smooth-faced girl.

"The point is," Lady Hester continued, "men have certain appetites that can rage out of control. Do you know what I'm talking about?"

Anya nodded. As of early that morning, she had pretty much figured out what transpired between a man and woman. It still took more imagination than she possessed, however, to imagine Lady Hester and her late husband—

"I'm sure the American has kissed you?"

"Umm, I believe so."

An imperious finger pointed accusingly. "Don't shilly-shally with me. There's nothing wrong with a kiss or two, especially if they are stolen. Such acts have a way of firing a man's blood and making him anxious to pronounce his vows. You must make certain, however, that you are not swept along by the tide of his ardor. A wanting man makes a much more eager bridegroom."

"I shall endeavor to remember that," Anya said bleakly, recalling Morgan's threat, or promise, not to anticipate their marriage vows.

"Now then, as the only female currently in residence, I find myself in the role of advisor. Rest assured, I will not disappoint you."

"Pardon?"

"I realize it is customary to wait until the actual wedding night to impart certain information to the prospective bride. As the mother of four daughters, however, I have found girls do better if they're given the facts sooner. That way, they can accustom themselves to their fate."

Anya knew her face was red. Was Lady Hester actually going to discuss—

"Do you have any idea what men and women do on their wedding night, Anya?"

"Yes, I—I think so."

The woman sighed. "Somehow, I am not surprised."

Anya found it difficult to meet the woman's gaze. "I suppose there's always the possibility that I could be mistaken...."

"I shall be frank, then. Without his clothing, a husband possesses a certain object which he places within his wife."

That was definitely frank. "I see."

"The first time this happens, it is unpleasant and painful for the woman. The man apparently suffers no discomfort. The Act takes less than five minutes."

Five minutes? That didn't seem very long.

"Because The Act is generally of short duration, you will find that thinking of other matters makes it more tolerable. I found mentally drafting a menu for the next evening's meal an excellent practice. It made the process less embarrassing for both Winston and myself.''

"And that helped?'' Somehow Anya couldn't picture herself drafting menus with Morgan.

Lady Hester shrugged. "Let us say, I had a reputation for providing excellent meals at Bidington Place.''

"Was there...uh...no pleasure for you in...The Act?''

"Other than the getting of children, there is no pleasure intended for the woman.''

"The getting of children?''

"It is when a husband enters his wife that he plants his seed.''

"*Only* then?''

"Holding hands and kissing hardly does it, girl.''

A slow-burning anger began to build. Morgan, of course, must know this. He had *lied* to her when he said it was possible she already carried his child. Ooh, how he must have laughed at her gullibility!

"I see there was some merit to our having this discussion. You did not know quite everything, did you?''

"I certainly did not,'' Anya said. "I'm not so sure I'll marry him, after all.''

"Now, now, there's no need to panic. Throughout time it has been a woman's lot to endure. There's no reason you should be any different. Besides, I feel obligated to confess that several times I almost found it a tolerable experience.''

Anya knew her mouth was hanging open. Surely, she hadn't heard Lady Hester correctly.

"You needn't look so shocked. As we got older, and Winston became less demanding, I grew to enjoy the peculiar closeness one achieves upon such intimate occasions. I realize that is a novel attitude, and I suffered a measure of guilt for it. I mention it now, however, as a means of lessening your fears about the wedding night.''

"I suppose I can endure anything for five minutes,'' Anya murmured thoughtfully.

"That's the spirit! Just remember the first night is the worst. After that it never hurts again quite so much.''

"Don't you..." Anya broke off, wondering how blunt she could be with Lady Hester. She wished she were having this discussion with Merrawynn. Somehow she knew her sister could shed a great deal of light upon the subject.

"Don't I what? Speak up, girl."

"Don't you find the whole thing... *bizarre?*"

"Of course I do. Many are the times I've wondered what the Almighty was up to when he created Adam and Eve. It would have been much more civilized to settle matters with a kiss. That way a husband and wife could retain their clothing and their dignity. Believe me, had I been in charge I would have arranged matters much more fastidiously."

Anya couldn't help blushing. Goodness, if kissing got one with child, she *would* already be expecting Morgan's baby. "I appreciate your frankness," Anya said, feeling a sincere burst of warmth for the older woman. "At least now I know it is a natural thing to do."

"I need your promise, Anya."

"My promise?"

"You are not to use this knowledge until your wedding night."

"Of course I shan't," Anya said, incensed that Lady Hester thought she might do such a thing.

The older woman stamped her cane. "Be on your guard, Anya. A man a few weeks from marriage becomes quite... desperate. I'm old enough to have heard some tragic stories of young women who surrendered to their fiancé's ardor. Believe me, all respect is lost in such cases, and occasionally so is the groom."

"Now that I know the facts, there's not a chance on this green earth that I shall surrender myself to Morgan before the ceremony—or perhaps even after it."

Lady Hester cackled. There was no other word for the older woman's spate of rusty laughter. "I doubt that, my girl. Morgan Grayson is not unlike a bull, pawing the ground for what he wants."

"He can paw all he wishes, but he is going to have to ask very nicely if he expects to claim me as his bride."

"Oh, he will ask nicely, have no doubt of that. The candles will burn low, he will be close, and his voice will whisper most insistently in your ear."

Anya heard the wistful note in Lady Hester's voice and realized that, despite the five minutes of pain, the older woman looked upon her own wedding night fondly.

A shiver touched Anya's spine. She had come very close to losing Morgan. Notwithstanding his unpardonable lies to her on the subject of her already carrying his child, she knew she would not deny him on their wedding night.

And unnatural as it seemed, she was looking forward to joining with Morgan. Or perhaps more accurately, she was looking forward to lying close to him and having his arms around her. She would endure the former to experience the latter.

Chapter Eleven

In the stables, Morgan approached the roan's stall. Apparently recovered from his fear of horses, Tom held the reins, his grimy face beaming with pride.

"Like I said, he'd caught himself up in a patch of briars. It took a mite of doing, but Morty and I worked him free."

Morgan ran his hand down the animal's scarred flanks. "He's obviously had a rough time of it. Where did you find him?"

Tom inflated his chest importantly and his Adam's apple bobbed. "He were just down the road."

Harry Jarvis pushed back his cap and scratched his head. "That area had already been checked. Can't understand how we missed him."

Morgan stepped from the stall. "Take care of him, Tom."

"Yes, sir, I will."

The boy sprang immediately to his assigned task and Morgan turned to Harry. "I'd like to speak with you in private."

Together, he and the short man walked past the stalls holding Champion, Lady Lore and several other horses of noble parentage. In a small lantern-lit room overflowing with tack and well-oiled saddles, Morgan turned to Harry.

"Tom seems to have overcome his fear of horses."

Showing his yellowed, uneven teeth, the head groom smiled. "Aye, he has. All he needed was a space of time to remember how much he loved them. He'll be more careful in the future, though, about trying to jump fences.''

"Was that how he fell?"

"That's the right of it, sir. He tried to take Champion over the top of a six-foot fence."

"He's lucky he didn't break his damned neck and damage the stallion as well."

Harry shoved his hands into the pockets of his baggy, dusty breeches. "Like I said, he's smarter than he was a month ago."

"Did he tell you anything else about the man he claimed to see hanging around the estate?"

"He couldn't remember anything else, just that he were dressed like a gentleman and looked like he was watching the house. He saw him by the old smugglers' cave a few days back, too."

"I want you to alert the male servants and local farmers to be on their guard, Harry."

The man's rheumy eyes sharpened. "Be on their guard against what?"

"I'm not sure," Morgan admitted, wondering if he were overreacting to what very well might have been an accident. "Just have them keep their eyes open for anything or anyone unusual. They can report to you and you can keep me informed."

Harry rocked back and forth, jingling the coins in his pockets. "I'll spread the word."

After Harry left, Morgan glanced around the tack room. The familiar smells of leather, harness oil and horses was oddly soothing. Idly, he ran his fingers across a shiny, black English saddle. He wanted to go home, to get back to his ranch, to ride his land. And he wanted Anya riding alongside him.

In order to accomplish that in a socially acceptable manner, he was obligated to spend at least another month on English soil to satisfy the social and legal conventions required to make her his wife. He wished he lived in simpler times, maybe even pagan times, when he would have been free to simply claim and take her.

Picturing Anya's indignant round eyes should he ever resort to such tactics brought a reluctant smile. Even if they were reduced to wearing bearskins, the woman would no doubt demand a certain code of proper behavior from him. Damn, it was becoming harder and harder to resist her female charms.

An hour didn't pass without his remembering the night he'd peeled her wet garments from her soft skin. Only now that he knew the heart and mind of the woman who wore the satiny flesh, he found her even more arousing.

With first his mouth, then his touch, he wanted to explore her, then ultimately lose himself inside her. He wanted to possess every delightful inch of her. He wanted—

"Morgan Grayson?"

Morgan's gaze jerked to the doorway, where a man stood just beyond the lantern's sphere of light. "Yes?"

"Prepare to meet your Maker, sir."

The man stepped forward, and Morgan faced the barrel of a gun raised to heart level. "Who the hell are you?"

"That doesn't matter."

Morgan gauged the distance that separated him from the obviously loaded gun. "It sure as hell matters to me."

"We've never met," the man said dismissingly.

"Then tell me who sent you," Morgan suggested softly, his gaze focused on the stranger's gun hand. Right or left? Jumping the correct way would determine whether Morgan lived or died.

"I'm afraid I've little time for conversation," the man explained coldly. "I have no wish to be trapped inside a burning building."

For the first time, Morgan smelled smoke. Without warning, a hissing pop exploded close by. Morgan seized the moment to leap to his left. A deafening blast of gunfire roared through the small room. Morgan lunged at his assailant, knocking the man to the ground.

Hands closed brutally around Morgan's throat. Even as his lungs screamed for air, Morgan cheered the fact that his attacker had dropped his gun. Viciously, Morgan brought his knee up. An enraged wail and the sudden loosening of the stranger's death grip demonstrated the accuracy of Morgan's aim. He pounded his fists with savage fury, trying to concentrate his blows on his opponent's head and stomach.

Screams from panicked horses echoed sickeningly throughout the stable as the smoke thickened around him and the struggling man. The heat intensified until the labored, panting breaths Morgan sucked into his lungs blocked out all other sound.

Morgan and his attacker thrashed about the small room until they rolled up against the table. Then a hail of burning wood rained down, and the stable itself seemed to explode.

After her session with Lady Hester, Anya did not seek out the solitude of her bedchamber. She was too curious to know what Morgan and Harry Jarvis had discussed in the library. When she reached that room, however, she found it empty.

Frustrated and impatient with the conventions that insisted she be a spectator to the events affecting her own life, Anya left the library. Her restless progress through the house took her to the conservatory. She was in search of something, she didn't know what. She only knew that she needed some activity to soothe her frayed nerves.

Her conversations with Morgan had a way of both keying her up and settling her down at the same time. Had he retired to his bedchamber without bidding her good-night, or for that matter, telling her what the head groom had wanted? She clicked her teeth together, sorely tempted to go up and wake the sleeping man so she could inform him of her discontent.

What she ought to do was make up a list of what she considered a husband's proper behavior. At the onset, she decided the first item on the list would be an openness of dialogue between husband and wife. There would be no secrets—especially regarding the conception of children.

As she stepped into the fragrant room of blooming plants, she amended that. There would be no secrets kept by the husband. A wife, of course, must at different times keep her own council. For instance, it would never do for Morgan to learn she'd climbed into bed with him when he'd been unconscious.

Or inspected his uncovered person . . .

Absently, Anya moved to the tall windows that overlooked the gardens. It took a moment for her to realize that what should have been a black sky was instead lighted by a hazy, golden glow. Her eyes noted the strange phenomenon a second before she realized she smelled smoke.

Fire!

Anya flung open the glass doors and ran outside. Heat and smoke and screaming animals turned the night into a scene from hell itself.

For a moment she stood frozen, unable to move. Huge, fiery tendrils shot skyward from the stables, turning the wood crimson. Her feet moved before her mind did. She was running toward the burning building.

The horses! They had to save the horses!

A heavy arm grabbed her waist. She didn't even realize she struggled against it until a voice spoke.

"It's too late, Miss Anya."

She continued to fight the restraining arm. "But the horses—"

"Tom and I got them out."

She sagged in relief. "Thank God."

The thought of Champion and Lady Lore dying in that fiery inferno was impossible to bear. "All the horses are safe, then?"

"Aye, we got them all out."

Anya watched in fascinated horror as the great roof seemed to rise upward before crashing down into the flames.

A horrendous eruption of noise and flaming cinders rumbled through the night.

She attempted to step from Jarvis's imprisoning embrace, but his arm continued to hold her. She glanced into the head groom's sooty face and was startled to see it streaked with tears.

She patted the burly man's arm. "Oh, Harry, it's all right. We'll rebuild the stables. Morgan will see to it."

Jarvis took a great, gulping breath and closed his red-rimmed eyes. "He didn't make it out, Miss Anya."

"Who—who didn't?" she whispered.

"The gentleman from America . . ."

Anya shook her head. It couldn't be true. There was some mistake. Morgan was safe. He was . . .

The stark agony edging the groom's grim features slowly penetrated her mind. She shook her head again. No . . .

No! Suddenly she was struggling to free herself from Jarvis's unyielding hold. She had to get free. She had to get to Morgan. She had to run. . . .

At some point, she realized she was screaming. She couldn't stop. Nor could she halt her fruitless efforts to wrest herself away from the groom. She was crying, she was coughing, she was cursing. And none of it seemed to matter.

This couldn't be real. It had to be a nightmare. Morgan couldn't be in the stables. Why didn't Jarvis understand? She wanted to pound the man with her fists! To lash out at him and demand he let her go. She had to get to Morgan. Morgan would explain. Morgan would make everything right again.

Morgan . . .

"I hate to do this, Miss Anya, but there's no other way."

There was a brief moment of clarity, just before Harry Jarvis's fist connected with her jaw.

Anya tried to open her eyes, but something wet and heavy prevented the action. She continued to lay still. Thank God, it had been only a nightmare, the most terrible, horrify-

ingly vivid nightmare of her life. She swallowed a remnant
sob of terror. It had seemed so real....

Then and there, she made a vow to be kinder to Morgan,
to forget about drawing up a list of husbandly dos and
don'ts. Instead, she would concentrate on becoming the best
wife in all of Texas. And if pleasing Morgan required taking on the characteristics of a hunting hound, then so be it.

The unmistakable odor of smoke caught her attention.
Slowly, numbly, she pushed aside the wet cloth from her
forehead. She was lying on the settee in the drawing room.
Her clothes were covered with soot and ashes.

No!

She bolted upright and looked around. It had only been
a dream—oh please, God, let it have only been a terrible
dream....

A choking agony squeezed her heart. Her lips moved. No
sound emerged. Slowly, she became aware of her raw throat
and the painful throbbing along her jawline.

"We found the body. It was nothing but a charred
stump."

The voice from just outside the library door was Dr.
Goodwin's. Suddenly, a keening despair clutched Anya. The
unthinkable had happened. She wanted to close her eyes and
never open them again. She wanted to die....

Or maybe just stop. Could a person do that? Will their
heart to stop beating? Perhaps if she concentrated she
could—

"Whoever he was, he wanted me dead. Anya's in the library. I want you to examine her."

Morgan! It was Morgan's voice!

Anya sprang from the sofa and rushed to the open doorway. "Morgan..."

Blackened from head to boot and layered in ashes, he
turned to her. "Anya..."

She flew into his arms, both crying and laughing. Her
salty tears mingled with kisses that tasted of woodsmoke.
"Morgan, oh, Morgan..."

She couldn't seem to say anything else. His arms closed about her with painful strength but she didn't protest. He felt too good.

She had no idea how much time passed with her locked in his embrace as she repeatedly kissed his cheeks, forehead and lips. Desperation drove her. She had to know that this was real, that she wasn't imagining him standing here, alive and strong and vital.

"I thought you were dead...."

The words were ripped from a dark and terrible void within her.

"Hush, darling. It's all right. I'm here."

Her hands touched his arms and shoulders. She had to be sure. "But Harry said—"

"I made it out the back way."

"Oh, Morgan..." She broke off. The tears would not be denied. She was only peripherally aware of him sweeping her from her feet and carrying her up the staircase.

Lady Hester's voice rang out. "Take her to her chamber, Mr. Grayson, and I shall look after her."

"Ma'am, I appreciate the offer, but I'll be taking care of her tonight."

Anya raised her face from Morgan's shoulder. Standing at the top of the stairs, Lady Hester wore a sleeping gown of ivory silk and an expression of quiet understanding. "Look after her in *her* chamber. You may draw a chair up to her bed and stay with her until she falls asleep."

Morgan's embrace tightened. "I need to hold her. She belongs to me."

"Only the speaking of your wedding vows will grant you that privilege." Lady Hester softened her words with a smile.

"I'm not interested in proprieties. Not tonight."

The older woman placed her frail hand upon Morgan's sooty sleeve. Anya marveled at the matron's tenacity. "The proprieties are to protect Anya. If you have a care for her well-being, you will not do anything to damage her reputation."

For several moments, Morgan stood rigid, his face implacable. "You will assist her with her clothing and help her bathe?"

"Of course, I shall assist her," Lady Hester said. "While I am doing so, you will no doubt wish to avail yourself of a bath."

Later, as Anya sat in a steaming tub, she became aware of a heavy cloud of fatigue about her. It seemed as if it required a great effort to raise her arms and soap them. A screen had been set up, and she heard Lady Hester on the other side of it instructing Mavis to throw away Anya's smoky clothing.

Grateful, Anya sank deeper into the tub and closed her eyes. She wanted no reminder of this night and how frighteningly close she'd come to losing Morgan. Even now, as she remembered the pain that had knifed through her when she'd awakened in the library and heard Dr. Goodwin's grim pronouncement, a wave of nausea swept through her.

"Are you about finished, Anya?"

"I want to wash my hair."

Lady Hester stepped around the screen. "Here's a bucket of clear water to rinse with."

For reasons she didn't understand, seeing the usually stiff and imperious matron holding a steaming pail of water brought new tears. "I . . . I thank you for your help, madame."

The woman tipped her head. "Do you? I had rather thought you would have preferred Morgan's ministrations this evening."

Anya picked up the bar of soap and worked her hair up into a lather. "He came very close to dying. It is a natural thing to want to be close to him."

"Lean forward."

Anya obeyed and hot water splashed about her head and shoulders.

"Natural can get you in serious trouble, my girl."

Anya accepted the heated towel Lady Hester thrust toward her and rose from the tub, quickly wrapping herself for modesty's sake. She used the second proffered towel to dry her hair.

"Once you're settled in your own bed with your own bed covers drawn up to your chin, Morgan can remain with you for as long as he wishes. What you have to remember is that a man who finds himself engaged *and* in love can sometimes act imprudently. It falls upon the female to insist upon his good behavior."

Anya slipped the towel from her head and pulled on a silk sleeping gown. As well intentioned as Lady Hester was, Anya knew the older woman was mistaken about one thing. Morgan wasn't in love with her.

She drew back the bed covers, suppressing a sigh that somehow developed into a wide yawn. "Thank you again for your assistance."

"You are welcome, Anya."

She heard Mavis and Sally come in and remove the tub. The sweet scent of lilies reached her as cool lips touched her forehead. She realized Lady Hester had just kissed her goodnight. Her eyelids drifted shut....

"Anya..."

The wispy clouds of sleep parted. "Yes?"

"I want to lie next to you. I want to hold you."

In the darkness, she smiled. "I'm so glad."

One side of the bed dipped. Morgan's strong arms collected, then drew her to him. She nestled comfortably against him. She was awake enough to notice he was dressed. More than a little disappointed, she supposed it was for the best.

"I love you, Morgan...."

Silence greeted her announcement. It was foolish to feel sad. She knew he didn't return her love. Theirs was to be a marriage based upon the practical consideration that he needed Richard's money, and that she was tired of being a spinster.

He turned; his lips found hers. The kiss was sweet and tender and... brief. "Are you feeling better?"

She nodded, her arms twining about his neck. "This has been the worst night of my life, Morgan."

"It was damned near the last of mine."

She trembled and burrowed closer to him.

He swore softly. "Damn, honey, I'm sorry. I shouldn't have said that."

"What happened?" she asked, needing to know what had caused the fire, and who had perished in it.

In a few, quick sentences, Morgan sketched the details of what had transpired. Anya tried to understand his explanation, but it didn't make any sense. Why would someone want to kill him?

"We should leave for America as soon as possible," she observed, allowing her fingers to stroke his comfortingly wide chest.

"Why is that?"

"Well, you would be safe in America, wouldn't you?"

"That depends on who's trying to get rid of me. I have the feeling that our forthcoming marriage is somehow at the bottom of this. The quickest way to see to my safety would be for us to marry at once."

"Only Merrawynn would benefit from us not marrying, Morgan. I understand you have little reason to trust her, but I know my sister. She is not a murderess."

"Are you willing to bet my life on that?"

Anya stiffened. "Of course not, but—"

"We will leave for Bedfordshire in the morning. I want us married by the end of the week. In six days, we will be on a ship bound for America."

"But it takes *three* days to travel there and three more weeks after the posting of the banns to—"

"I'll see what I can do to shorten that."

She was wide awake now. "But—"

"I will hire a solicitor to sell the property Richard left me, with provision that the servants will be taken care of."

Morgan's voice vibrated with a determination that brooked no challenge.

"Being a woman, you probably would prefer to be married in a beautiful gown, with all the trappings," he continued. "Unfortunately, circumstances do not permit that. My only interest is in having things legal. When we get to Texas, we'll see about hiring a seamstress to sew up some new dresses for you."

"I'm not concerned about gowns, Morgan. I cannot let you go on thinking that Merrawynn had something to do with these attempts upon your life."

"Forget Merrawynn and think about yourself for a change. None of your clothes are right for the Texas climate. You'll need some bright and pretty things made of lightweight material. I don't want to see you in anything gray or brown ever again."

"But, Morgan," she protested. "I'm still in mourning for Richard."

"Do you honestly think he would want to see you draping yourself in black?"

"Well..."

"And another thing, Anya." Morgan's voice hardened again. "Harry Jarvis told me about how you tried to go into that burning building." Arms like steel bands gripped her. "If we're ever in another situation where you think I need help, or I'm in trouble, or anything of the kind, you will *not* place yourself in danger, do you understand?"

She would have nodded, but her head was pressed too tightly against his chest. "Your smufff."

"What?"

She squirmed for a breath of air. "You're smothering me."

Immediately, his hold lightened. "Swear to me, Anya."

"Sometimes I would rather swear at you," she observed.

"Anya..."

She peered up at him through the darkness. "When you say my name like that, it sounds quite ominous. Did you learn to talk that way in the military?"

He shook her gently. "I am trying to be serious."

"I know, Morgan. And I truly appreciate your concern. But you're the one who almost died. Twice. So it seems rather foolish for you to be preoccupied with my welfare."

"But—"

"I give you my promise that I will not try to run into a flaming building again, Morgan. Nor will I do anything truly reckless." She crossed her fingers on both hands. "If I should chance to see a boatload of pirates from days gone by storm ashore and drag you off at saber point I shall wave cheerfully from a safe distance."

"Anya . . ." he growled against her ear.

"And more's the pity," she continued. "I'll have you know that I recently made the decision to become an exemplary wife, a wife far superior to all others. Now, if I allow you to be carried off, you will never discover the marital harmony you would have enjoyed."

"I'm serious about—" He broke off and cupped her chin. Deliberately, he tilted her face toward him. His lips caressed hers. "Exemplary, hmm?"

The tip of her tongue outlined his mouth. "Far and above the best wife upon this or the American continent. I daresay people would have come from miles around just to observe my manner."

"Would have?"

"Well, if I permit you to be carried off by a band of rogues, I will not have the opportunity to demonstrate my remarkable wifely skills, will I?"

A palm slid to the front of her gown. "Wifely skills . . . I like the sound of that."

"I rather thought you would."

Buttons parted. She held her breath. There was the faint rustle of soft fabric, then the rasp of callused fingertips across bare flesh. Her breasts tightened and tingled. Lower, a throbbing pulse thrummed.

"I'll never tire of touching you." He bent forward, and his warm breath stroked her. "Or tasting you."

Tongue tip touched breast tip. "Oh!"

"It feels good, doesn't it?"

"Yes..."

Her fingers struggled with the buttons of his shirt. Possessed by a desire that eclipsed any sense of restraint, she buried her face in the thick mat of chest hair, inhaling his masculine scent. His freshly washed body still bore the faintest trace of smoke. The horror of almost losing him swept through her. She shuddered against him.

His hands tightened on her arms, and he pulled her against his shoulder. "Don't cry, honey."

"I—I can't help it."

He continued to embrace her, stroking her back and arms while whispering words she scarcely comprehended. The tears wouldn't be denied, and she wept helplessly. She remembered the last time she'd cried in his arms, the day she'd told him about George. Recalling his kindness and understanding in that instance seemed to spawn more tears.

Finally, with a shuddering hiccup, she was able to bring herself under control. Gently, Morgan brushed back the dampened hair from her face. "Feel better?"

She nodded and sniffled at the same time. He kissed the crown of her head and began to ease away.

"Where are you going?"

"To my own bed, Anya."

"Must you?"

"If I stay here, I won't be able to keep from making love to you."

"Uh..."

He paused on the edge of the bed. "Was there something you wanted to say?"

She rubbed her fingers along the blanket's satin border, wondering what he would do if she invited him to remain with her. "You...uh..."

Well, goodness, she couldn't seem to muster the courage to say the words.

"Anya, only a cad would take advantage of you tonight."

"Why do you say that?"

"Because you've had a major shock, and you're not quite yourself."

Then who am I? "It's that promise you made, isn't it?"

"What promise?"

"That you wouldn't . . . wouldn't take pleasure with me until we were man and wife."

"Oh, that promise."

"Well?"

"Those words may have been spoken in haste and anger, Anya, but they had merit. Tonight Lady Hester made me realize that it is unfair for me to treat you as my wife until you are legally so. Suppose I had already lain with you and gotten you with child and then been killed? Our baby would have been born a bastard. I would not be much of a man if I allowed something like that to happen."

His words reminded her of her earlier conversation with Lady Hester. Anya's face warmed. "That didn't prevent you from lying with Collette."

"That's the second time you brought up her name." Morgan moved from the bed. The next thing she knew a candle was lighted and placed on the table next to her. He drew up a nearby chair and sat in it. "Why are you so concerned about Collette?"

Anya tossed back her hair and stared at him defiantly. "I found a letter from her in one of your coat pockets."

She refused to speak a word in defense of her actions. Let him think the worst.

He sat back and negligently crossed a leg. "Snooping through pockets doesn't sound like something the most exemplary wife on two continents would do."

"I had my reasons."

"Collette and I were lovers," he said bluntly. "I was a randy young man. She was a more-than-willing bed partner. It never entered my head to deny myself what she was offering."

"She was probably quite beautiful," Anya muttered.

"Stunning." He leaned forward. "But, Anya, I'll always be eternally grateful that Collette jilted me."

"Is that so?" Anya inquired with studied disinterest.

He snuffed out the candle he'd only moments before lighted. "Yes."

Was he going to leave it at that? "No doubt she's turned to fat...."

"If so, it is Justin's concern, not mine. The point is I will never apologize for wanting or having another woman before I knew there was a stubborn and endearing female on the earth named Anya Delangue."

Endearing? "Morgan..."

"What, honey?"

"I'm glad you feel that way." She fell back against the pillow and blinked drowsily. "I like it when you call me...honey."

"Sweet little Anya..."

"Not always," she felt compelled to murmur tiredly. "I do love you, though, and I'm very glad you're still alive."

He chuckled. "Me, too. And there's even more good news."

She yawned tearily. "Is there?"

"I remember now what happened at the cave. It all came back to me when I was fighting for my life tonight."

"Then light the candle and come sit and tell me."

"That's not a good idea, Anya."

"Why not?" she snapped, feeling achy and out of sorts. If she could get Morgan to come closer, maybe she could get him to forget his infernal nobility and the ache inside her would go away. She just knew there was something Morgan could do to make her feel better.

"Because I've also remembered the night you crawled into bed with me, and I stripped us both naked. I remember the taste of your tongue, I remember your pointy little nipples hardening in my mouth, and I remember the feel of your silky moist curls against my manhood. I remember you slick and ready and rubbing yourself against me, whimpering and needing...."

Anya's entire body trembled with the heady images his words invoked.

"When we're married, Anya, I'll know how it feels to be deep inside you, thrusting until I hear you cry out in the pleasure I'm going to drown you in. I'll feel you contract around me and milk me dry. When we're *married*."

Long after Morgan had left her open-mouthed with nothing to say, Anya lay limp, her body throbbing. She was aware of the moistness between her thighs and the tautness of her breasts. With mere words, he had shaken her to the core. He had accomplished something else, too.

Whatever it took—banns, a special license or brooking Edward's disapproval—she would be Morgan's wife by the end of the week.

And then the blasted man was going to deliver everything he had promised tonight. After that, she would be more inclined to work on her wifely skills.

Chapter Twelve

"But Edward..."

"No, Merrawynn, I will not withdraw the invitation I've sent to Richard's nephew to pay us an extended visit. I will take measure of the man myself before forming any conclusions about his character. As the head of the household, I shall decide whether or not to approve of Anya's marrying an American."

Merrawynn gritted her teeth. Her brother was behaving at his most pompous and aggravatingly complacent worst. "But I've already met the man and he is wholly unsuitable for our dear sister. He is crude and vulgar and—"

"If that is the case, then do not become overwrought. I will send Richard's nephew packing. There will be no marriage. With the newfound wealth your late husband endowed Anya, she will no doubt be able to secure an *English* bridegroom."

A plain-faced, plump woman entered the drawing room. "Edward?"

"Yes, my sweet?"

Merrawynn rolled her eyes. It always amused and surprised her to see how much her brother doted on his quite unremarkable wife. Eunice had no flair, no style, nothing that Merrawynn could detect to attract any man's affections—even those of her astonishingly unimaginative brother.

"Alice told me Merrawynn had arrived," her sister-in-law said, beaming.

Merrawynn held up her fingers in an ironic wave. "Has Alice ever lied to you?"

Eunice missed the sarcasm and rushed forward. "Merrawynn, you are looking beautiful as always."

Edward's wife gave her a hug that was more than perfunctory, and Merrawynn surprised herself by returning it. Few women seemed to like Merrawynn. Except for Anya and Eunice, Merrawynn really had no close women friends.

"Thank you, Eunice." Merrawynn stepped back. "And you are looking . . . hearty."

Eunice tipped her head and laughed. "Diplomacy from *you*, Merrawynn. Now that is a first." Eunice moved to her husband and looped an arm through his. "As Edward and I are expecting our third child, I don't mind in the least looking 'hearty.'"

"Oh, dear. Another one?" Merrawynn couldn't keep the dismay from her voice, nor could she understand the happiness that radiated from Eunice's sparkling eyes. Though she hadn't been in attendance for the first two babes' arrivals, Merrawynn nevertheless had been subjected to harrowing descriptions of the events. The thought of suffering such pain was terrifying. How did other women endure it, let alone celebrate it?

Eunice's expression sobered. "Oh, Merrawynn, I'm sorry. Here I am babbling about our good tidings when you've just suffered a major loss. Please accept my condolences for Richard's passing."

Merrawynn felt the sting of unshed tears. Only recently had she begun to realize how fortunate she'd been to marry Richard. But that discovery had come too late to do her any good. She thought about the wasted years, when she'd tried to find happiness making the rounds of the Ton. Now, she was reaching the horrible suspicion that all along real happiness had been hers for the taking at Hull Manor.

"I . . . I thank you, Eunice."

"Black becomes you, Merrawynn," Edward said with noticeable coolness edging his voice.

Merrawynn glanced down at one of the several black gowns she'd recently had sewn for her. At first, she hadn't planned on going into deep mourning. As she hadn't particularly mourned Richard's passing, it had seemed both hypocritical and needlessly expensive to do so. Lately, however, the full measure of her loss had begun to weigh upon her. Never again would she be able to dash off to Hull Manor for a few weeks of tranquility and Richard's comforting presence.

Her brother's disapproving expression sharpened, and Merrawynn surmised he thought her gown too daring for a woman recently widowed. She tossed back her head. Perhaps some things had changed about her, but she would go to her grave rebelling against the ridiculous restraints within which society seemed determined to entrap her.

"I am here to discuss our sister's welfare, Edward, not current fashion. Now that Eunice is present, perhaps she will be able to convince you something must be done to protect Anya from her own foolishness."

"I think you're overreacting, Merrawynn. I've always found our sister to be a most sensible young woman."

"In the past," Merrawynn agreed. "Where the American is concerned, however, Anya is blind to her own welfare."

Eunice smiled. "It may be that Anya is in love."

"In love?" Edward demanded, clearly shocked by his wife's suggestion. "That's hardly relevant. Except for one notable exception, I have always respected Richard's judgment." Edward looked significantly over his wife's head to Merrawynn. "That Richard condoned this union is sufficient cause for me to sanction it. Also, Anya was most conservative in her description of the American. She mentioned nothing about love, only admirable sentiments about her wish to have a home and family."

"I know," Merrawynn said. "She's become caught up by the ideal of having her own home, so caught up that she cannot see the American's faults—which, believe me, are many. He's overbearing and a bully. If Anya travels to America with him, she will have no one to protect her from Grayson's cruel nature. She will be totally at his mercy.'' Merrawynn drew herself up. "I will not allow Anya to be hurt in this manner."

"As I've already stated, when Morgan Grayson arrives, I shall weigh his character most carefully."

"But he's capable of pretending to be something he's not!"

"Are you implying I cannot detect a charlatan?"

"Edward, Anya is of age to marry without your approval," Eunice pointed out.

Edward smiled complacently. "I'm sure that, as always, my sister will obey my strictures."

Merrawynn looked at her older brother and realized she would receive no real help from that quarter. She was on her own to save Anya from her folly.

"Just have a care, Edward. I do not trust a man who would cross an ocean to secure a wife."

When the disappointing interview with her brother had concluded, Merrawynn stood impatiently on the manor's wide steps, waiting for her carriage to be brought around. She would return to the London house to decide what to do next.

Now that she had severed all ties with Boyd, she felt more adrift than ever. In the past, Richard had always been in the background—patient, understanding and approving. It was as if she'd lost her anchor.

What a fool she'd been! She had allowed herself to be seduced by someone who wasn't half the man Richard was. Boyd Williams was nothing but an opportunist. She never wanted to see him again. When she'd discovered from his own drunken lips that he'd attacked the American and left him to die, she'd finally understood that she'd traded the gold of her life for the dross.

She was grateful she'd never broken her marriage vows to Richard. Though her faithfulness had been for all the wrong reasons—fear of scandal, fear of Richard's punishment, fear of . . . Oh, there had been a dozen things to fear.

Then, Boyd had shown her the passion of which she was capable. It hurt to admit it, but she had cared for Boyd, perhaps even loved him. It had been a destructive kind of love, however.

The carriage rolled into view, and Merrawynn stepped forward. She was convinced Anya felt this same kind of destructive love toward the American. No matter what Edward claimed, her brother wasn't capable of deducing the worth of a worm. It was up to Merrawynn alone to save Anya.

As the footman assisted her into the carriage, she adjusted her skirts. Fortunately, she had a plan. No man was going to take advantage of her sister. And Merrawynn needn't suffer a pang of remorse on the American's behalf, because she wasn't going to hurt him. She was merely going to . . . to misplace him, until Richard's six-month deadline had passed. If the American still wished to marry Anya after that, then he would have passed the test and earned her sister's hand.

Merrawynn sat back and smiled smugly. One day, Anya would thank her for her interference.

The day after the fire, Anya glanced briefly around the bedchamber that had been hers for the past seven years. After today, she would never again see the familiar pattern of roses papering these walls. She had memorized the shape and coloration of each flower, making a game of noting the four different directions the petals faced and counting how many had thorns.

"Anya!"

Morgan's voice boomed through her open doorway and she took one final look before joining him.

"I'm coming," she called as she barreled into the hall and ran directly into him.

His hands came around her waist and he set her from him. "You're late. I told you I wanted to make an early start on the day."

Anya looked up at him in consternation. In the hours immediately following the fire, he had been tender and solicitous. That remarkable sensitivity had not endured for long, however. "I am hardly late, Morgan. The sun is barely up."

"Don't argue. Just come along, Anya."

Exasperated, she preceded him down the stairs. Clearly, the blush was off the rose of their courtship. Sighing, she was forced to admit Morgan's "wooing" had probably been the shortest in recorded history.

"Lady Hester is overseeing the loading of our trunks," Morgan remarked from behind Anya. "The woman is a master at issuing commands."

Lady Hester wasn't the only one, Anya thought sourly. At times, Morgan Grayson could be a veritable tyrant.

He joined her at the bottom of the stairs and took her arm. She glanced at him, realizing that part of what made him appear so formidable this morning was the rough garments he'd donned. He had dressed in the clothing she'd discovered when she'd searched his bedchamber. Her gaze was drawn irresistibly to the pistol strapped to his lean hips. She swallowed. Her future husband looked for all the world like a brigand of the most fearsome ilk.

Five minutes later, when a somber-faced Morgan handed her up into the coach to sit across from Lady Hester, Anya was still marveling at the change in his appearance. There was nothing soft or gentle about his implacable bearing.

For most of the three-day journey, he would be riding the roan while Anya and Lady Hester traveled together in the coach.

As Anya looked out the small window and caught a glimpse of Morgan mounting his horse, she forced herself to adopt a cheerful manner. Despite Morgan's somber mood, a part of Anya yearned to be outside the plush vehicle and riding alongside him. She needed to assure herself that beneath Morgan's menacing exterior there still existed a playful and tender man.

She folded her hands neatly upon her lap, trying to recapture the excitement she'd felt this morning when she'd first awakened. The coach's large wheels made a half turn and for a moment the vehicle rocked backwards. Then they were on their way.

Anya closed her eyes. The Great Adventure, as she'd begun to think of it, had at last commenced. A second coach loaded with their trunks and carrying Mavis, along with two of Lady Hester's maids, followed behind.

"I hope Morgan doesn't plan to run the horses all the way to Bedfordshire," Lady Hester said.

Anya's eyes opened, and she looked across the small space that separated her from the frowning matron. She was tempted to point out that the team of four matched grays was hardly running, then thought better of it.

"We will soon settle into an even rhythm."

Lady Hester laid her cane across her skirts and leaned against the padded, velvet seat. "At least the coaches survived the fire. I would have sent for mine, rather than ride in a hired hack. After all, you never know what kind of lowlife might have ridden in it before you."

Anya hid a smile. It required more imagination than she possessed to picture Lady Hester in a hired conveyance. The woman had disclosed her aversion to taking the train, as well, maintaining that under no circumstances would she ride in a noisy, smoke-belching contraption designed by the devil himself.

"It was fortunate that the fire caused no more damage than it did," Lady Hester continued. "If a wind had been blowing, it could have carried embers from the burning building to the manor."

Both women fell into silence. Anya hadn't thought about the manor house catching fire. She'd been too busy saying prayers of gratitude that Morgan had escaped the flames unscathed. Every time she remembered waking up in the library and hearing Dr. Goodwin's grave pronouncement about a badly burned body, bile rose in her throat.

When the coach headed down the steep, twisting section of road that led to the village, Anya recalled vividly the night she'd almost run Morgan into the sea. So much had happened since then. She sighed and glanced back at Lady Hester. The older woman was dozing, her carefully coiffeured head bobbing to the rhythm of the coach.

How could anyone sleep at a time like this? A yawn caught Anya by surprise. She had been too keyed up last night to get much sleep. Instead, she had lain awake, thinking about the trip to Bedfordshire, then London, then... America. Gradually, Anya's eyelids lowered.

When her eyes jerked open, Anya wasn't certain immediately where she was. The moment she saw Lady Hester, her confusion passed. Anya tried to pinpoint what had startled her to wakefulness. The horses were slowing, changing the coach's rhythmic sway.

She looked out the window. They came to a stop at Hume Percy's Inn, and Anya realized she had slept only a few minutes.

Lady Hester stirred. "Why are we stopping?"

"I don't know...."

The door to the coach swung open, and Morgan stared grimly up at her. "Come on out, ladies."

Anya accepted his hand and stepped down. "What is wrong, Morgan?"

"A spoke in one of the wheels has snapped."

Several moments later, she and Lady Hester stood next to him and surveyed the damage. One of the beautifully carved and painted spokes had split in two. Anya looked about in dismay. They certainly hadn't made it very far before misfortune found them. She hoped the mishap wasn't an omen of things to come.

"You ladies may as well wait inside the inn while we see about having it repaired." Morgan's suggestion came from a clenched jaw. "We're not that far from the manor. No doubt Harry Jarvis will have an extra wheel. I'll send our driver to have Harry bring it."

Lady Hester turned from the broken spoke and glanced dismissively at the inn. "I have no desire to step inside that building." She gestured with an elegant jab of her cane. "You have secured accommodations for us this evening at Wilton's Inn, have you not?"

Morgan's gaze flicked impatiently to the older woman. "Unfortunately, the coach didn't break down in front of Wilton's."

"I am aware of that, sir. There's no need to become testy."

Coming from Lady Hester, the remark possessed a certain irony.

"Anya and I can ride ahead in the other coach while you see to the repair of this one," the matron announced.

The other vehicle had drawn alongside theirs and the three maids were staring wide-eyed from its windows. Morgan spared them the briefest of looks. "You'll never fit."

"I wouldn't mind staying behind and waiting with you while the wheel is replaced," Anya suggested.

"I would prefer that the maids wait behind," Lady Hester said.

Anya's gaze went to Morgan. From his grim expression, she saw Lady Hester's suggestion held no appeal. Clearly, he did not wish to be stranded in Hobb's Corner with a broken coach wheel and a gaggle of women.

"*I* would prefer the maids ride on ahead with you," Morgan countered firmly. "That way they can ready our rooms and unpack the things we'll be needing tonight."

"Very well," the matron replied. "The maids and I shall see you at Wilton's."

Soon Anya and Morgan stood alone in the small courtyard. The driver was dispatched to the manor to enlist Harry Jarvis's aid.

"I hope you don't mind that I remained," Anya ventured, providing Morgan with a golden opportunity to say that he cherished this time alone with her. She wasn't surprised, however, when he said nothing of the sort, but instead knelt before the damaged wheel and examined the splintered spoke.

"It's been deliberately cut."

It took a moment for his words to register. When they did, a chill squeezed her heart. She had thought that with Morgan's attacker dead, they were finally safe.

"Are you certain?"

He rose and none too gently took her arm, guiding her purposefully toward the inn. "I want you to wait inside."

"But—"

"No back talk," he said tersely.

When they reached the inn, he pushed open its scarred door and practically shoved her into the dimly lit taproom.

"What's wrong with you?" she demanded, taking exception to his rough handling.

"Outside, you're an open target. In here, you'll be safer."

She stared at him in exasperation. "In case it's escaped your notice, *you're* the one who keeps getting assaulted."

He touched the gun at his hips. "I can take care of myself."

She believed him. There couldn't be a man in all of England foolish enough to tangle with the armed and dangerous-looking man presently ushering her to a table.

As she sat down, she reached across the small table and rested her fingertips upon his sleeve. "Sit with me, Morgan. Hume will see to the horses."

For the first time since the fire, Morgan smiled. "I wouldn't mind a drink."

A few minutes later, after Hume had gone to tend the team of grays, Sarah Percy brought them a tray with two mugs.

"I still can't believe they don't have whiskey," Morgan grumbled as he eyed the pewter mug of ale.

Anya sipped her water. His aspersions to her country no longer offended, they merely amused. "Ale is the simple man's brew and this is a simple place, Morgan."

He tentatively sampled his drink. From his pinched expression, one would have thought he was tasting medicine. "If a barkeep in Big Rock Gulch tried to serve this swill to one of his customers, he'd be shot dead on the spot."

"The customer or the barkeep?" Anya inquired sweetly.

Morgan wiped his mouth with the back of his hand. "You sure are full of sass today."

"I've begun my Great Adventure," she explained.

He pushed his mug aside. "Your adventure appears to be at a standstill."

She wouldn't let his dour mood dampen her enthusiasm. "Perhaps the wheel breaking was an accident, after all."

"Don't fool yourself. There's still someone out there who doesn't want to see us married."

She shivered. "You're certain?"

His eyes went flat with conviction. "Positive."

"Then I'm glad I decided to stay with you."

He nodded. "I'll keep you safe, Anya."

"I was thinking more of me keeping a watchful eye over you," she returned. "After all, you're the one who keeps getting into trouble."

His eyebrows converged into a disapproving V. "*You're* going to watch over *me?*"

"You needn't take offense. Just because you're a man doesn't mean you have eyes in the back of your head. I will make certain no one sneaks up behind you."

His expression hardened. "What you will do is make certain you run at the first sign of trouble."

She gasped, incensed that he thought her such a coward. "Never!"

"When I say run, you run. When I say duck, you duck. When I say—"

"Roll over, stay and fetch, I perform the appropriate commands, correct?"

His eyes finally flashed with fire. "Yes, dammit. You do exactly what I tell you to do, when I tell you to do it. Understand?"

"I understand that you think I'm a poor-spirited simpleton of absolutely no worth."

"Anya..." His voice bordered on threatening. "In this regard, you *will* do what you're told. In the past, I've indulged your whims, but there's something at stake greater than whether or not we picnic in a cold and drafty cave."

"Will you stop harping about that cave! Besides, you enjoyed it well enough at the time."

He regarded her outburst with what she suspected was typical masculine forbearance. The line that had formed between his lowered eyebrows deepened.

"By the time we get to Texas, I'll expect you to have grown up enough so we need never have this discussion again."

"Discussion? Hah! What this has been, sir, is a diatribe of the first order. I'll have you know that I'm already grown up and—" She broke off to take a deep breath. Dealing with bullies, it seemed, required both stamina and an accommodating pair of lungs. "Transplanting me to Texas will not alter my nature one iota."

"Proving you wrong will afford me great satisfaction."

They glared at each other across the small table. She wished she could do something dramatic to show him that she wasn't a fainthearted female prone to vapors or hysterics. Since telling him so had no discernible effect, she would have to bide her time. She wondered if they made hip pistols for women in Texas. No doubt the donning of such a barbaric weapon was what had transformed Morgan into a veritable ogre.

"Anya."

Her head snapped up. "Yes?"

"I don't want to see you hurt, honey."

It was about time, she sniffed to herself. She had begun to wonder if there were any kind words left to the man. "I feel the same way about you."

He sighed and reached across the table to take her hand. "I've told you before, I'm too tough to kill. But you, my sweet, are infinitely soft and tender—when you're not tearing a stripe off me, at any rate. And I want to protect and keep you safe."

If she disregarded the insult, she could find solace in his declaration. "Morgan, there is something you should know about me."

He rubbed his thumb across her palm, and she shivered again.

"I'm listening."

"It is generally accepted by all who know me that I am an extremely sensible young woman. There is no reason for you to concern yourself about me doing something foolish."

The movement of his thumb stopped. "Like riding alone to the cliffs, or trying to run into a burning building?"

"I will do neither again," she returned evenly, wishing he would resume his subtle caress.

"Now we're getting somewhere."

His callused thumb made a slow, circular motion across her palm, and she concurred with his assessment. Strange how she could feel his touch in places other than her hand.

"I've got to remember this," he muttered gruffly.

Her eyes jerked to his. "What?"

"The way to shut you up is to touch you."

She would have taken greater exception to his bluntness, but it was difficult to argue against the truth. He shifted his position. His leg brushed against hers and she jumped.

"Relax, honey. We're in a public place. I'm hardly going to pounce on you."

Through her skirts, she felt his leg rub slowly and intimately against her. She knew she blushed to the roots of her braid. Goodness, if anyone saw what he was doing . . .

"Come sit next to me," he coaxed huskily.

She shook her head violently.

"I'll be good."

She would be a fool to believe that.

"You'll like it," he promised softly.

Well, of course, she would, but—

The door to the inn opened and a brief flash of sunlight shot through the dingy room.

"There you are, sir." On a blustery draft of wind, Harry Jarvis strode toward them.

Anya sighed regretfully. She had been on the verge of joining Morgan on his side of the table.

"Harry, you made good time." Morgan pushed back his chair and stood. "Did you bring the wheel?"

Harry shrugged apologetically. "Couldn't, sir. It was lost in the fire."

"I was afraid of that." Morgan strode toward the tap-room door. "Come with me, Harry. I want to show you something."

Anya rose.

Without looking back or slowing his stride, Morgan called over his shoulder, "Stay put, Anya. This is men's work."

She was tempted to throw his mug—with its unfinished portion of ale included—at his departing head. Fortunately, the door slammed shut before she could do so. Looking about the dim and empty room, she wondered how she was supposed to occupy herself. It simply wasn't her nature to sit around doing nothing.

From upstairs, she heard the sound of a baby's cry. Sarah Percy had stepped outside. Anya wondered if there was anyone else in the inn to answer the baby's indignant summons. Several minutes passed with the cries continuing unabated.

Anya smiled. It seemed she'd found something to occupy herself, something that definitely didn't fall into the category of men's work. It took only a moment to locate the loudly unhappy child. Lying in a cradle with his bed covers incredibly askew was Hume Percy's firstborn—a healthy son, she'd heard.

It had been years since Anya had cared for her baby brother, and she'd really been just a child herself. With its small legs kicking angrily, the squalling, red-faced babe was surprisingly intimidating.

It took several additional moments of loud crying on little Hume's part to induce her to pick him up. When she did, he quieted nicely. Charmed, Anya cuddled him closer. Her reward was a spreading wetness that seeped immediately through her dress to her skin.

Anya stared incredulously at the out-of-focus eyes looking innocently up at her. She had forgotten this aspect of babies. The babe smacked his delicate lips and turned his face against her. She realized he was groping for his next meal.

"Oh dear, we'd better find your mother, little one. I didn't bring supper with me."

Yet she didn't go immediately in search of Sarah. It was a thrilling sensation to feel that tiny mouth turned to her in need. With her own child, Anya would be able to nourish him. It was one thing to say she wanted children, but it was quite another to brush up against the unexpected reminder of how it felt to hold a squirming babe in her arms. She almost wished Morgan's seed were already planted and growing within her.

"Miss Anya, oh, I'm sorry. Did he disturb you?" Sarah Percy came rushing into the room. "I was just outside. I thought I would hear him if he cried."

In an instant, the young mother had her baby safely in her arms. Anya realized the girl had been alarmed at finding her infant being held by another.

"I think he's hungry," Anya said softly, feeling oddly bereft with her arms now empty.

"Oh, Lordy, he's wet all over you, Miss Anya," the mother cried in obvious horror at her young son's rudeness.

Anya smiled reassuringly. "No harm was done, though I would appreciate a towel."

Little Hume chose that moment to wail loudly. The harried mother jostled him in her arms. "There's a fresh one there on the dresser and a pitcher of water, too."

Anya took the towel and dampened it with the water. Then she excused herself so Sarah could take care of her child's strident needs. Anya was standing in the hallway that overlooked the taproom when Morgan came barreling inside.

He looked around the obviously empty room and bellowed. "Anya, where are you?"

"Up here," she replied calmly.

"What's wrong? Are you hurt?" He took the stairs three at a time.

"Hurt?" she asked blankly.

He was upon her, pulling back the towel. "What's wrong?"

She shook her head. "Nothing's wrong. I was just holding Sarah's baby and he wet."

Morgan dropped the towel. "Oh."

She retrieved the offending article and laid it across the banister. "What did you decide to do about the wheel?"

"Have you heard the phrase, 'desperate situations call for desperate measures?' "

Suddenly wary, she nodded.

"I sent Harry to Lady Hester's to fetch a coach. Do you think she'll object?"

"Actually, she made the suggestion herself." Anya frowned. "Wouldn't it be simpler for me to ride Lady Lore?"

"Simpler, yes," he returned. "But you will ride inside the coach."

She knew Morgan well enough to know it was pointless to try and change his stubborn mind. "When do you expect Harry to return?"

Morgan raked a hand through his hair. "Soon, I hope. I don't want us traveling after dark."

In that moment, it occurred to Anya that she and Morgan might be forced to spend the night at the inn. A tremor of excitement uncurled. Lady Hester was miles away, and Anya and Morgan were alone together. Could he be trusted to observe the proprieties with no chaperon present?

Could she?

Chapter Thirteen

That evening, Morgan shuffled the deck of well-worn cards. "Do you remember the rules, Anya?"

From across the table, her brown eyes laughed up at him. "How could I possibly forget? It was your game of stud and its wretched rules that landed me in this situation."

Anya gestured to the inn's humble surroundings, and his gaze followed the graceful flick of her arm. The familiar, merciless tightening in his groin reminded him forcefully how much he wanted to make love to the irresistible woman staring up at him.

He loved the confident way Anya moved, as if the world needed to rearrange itself to accommodate her. Her golden eyes flashed with intelligence and humor and...fire. He was ready to wrap himself in her fire. He was ready to sink inside her, to thrust and thrust again until both of them were out of their minds with desire.

She would cry out in ecstasy, he'd make sure of it, and then—

"Well, are you going to deal?"

Anya's question jolted Morgan back to his present surroundings. "Don't be so impatient."

"That's easy for you to say, Morgan, but I've never been one to accept delays." She tipped her head reflectively. "I suppose that could be considered a fault."

He shifted but found no relief. "On the contrary, that's one of the things I like about you, Anya."

She smiled wryly. "It's probably a case of you harboring the selfsame fault."

He chuckled. "You're beginning to know me."

Her nod sent flying tendrils of hair that had loosened from her neat braid. The light from a nearby oil lamp haloed the silken wisps in gold.

Small, white teeth worried her bottom lip. "Do you think Lady Hester is alarmed that we haven't joined her?"

"Probably. She seems to take her chaperoning duties quite seriously."

"When we meet up with her again, we're probably due for a reprimand," Anya said glumly.

"I'd say we can count on it."

"I'll probably get the brunt of it, Morgan. Ever since the morning you told her you needed protection from me, I seem to be the one she watches the more closely."

Her disgruntled expression amused him. "I had to say something. You were bent on turning the woman against me. If I'd have let you have your way then, you wouldn't be accompanying me to America as my future wife."

A coral blush tinged her cheeks. "At the time, it seemed the proper course of action."

"You should thank me, Anya."

Her eyes jerked to his. "For what?"

"For my willingness to woo a thorny young Englishwoman who gave me precious little encouragement."

Her gaze turned stormy. "Are you going to deal those blasted cards?"

He obliged her by laying a card facedown in front of her. "Are you feeling lucky tonight, Anya?"

"Why? Did you wish to play for money?"

"You have better coin than that."

The tip of her pink tongue darted over her lips. Morgan bit back a groan.

"What kind of wager did you have in mind?"

He would love to tell her about a dandy game he'd heard the boys talking about around the campfire. They'd called it strip poker. But if he did, she'd probably think him perverted and refuse to marry him. Once they were married, however, and he had her securely settled on his ranch, it was a pastime he hoped she would find . . . enjoyable.

His gaze lingered on her moistened lips. "Kisses," he said simply.

Her eyes rounded. "The last time we gambled, I lost thirty days to you."

He laid down two more cards. He was showing the ace of clubs, Anya the queen of diamonds. "That's right."

"If I were to lose thirty kisses . . ." Her words trailed off. "Would you be willing to wager me riding alongside you to Bedfordshire?"

"Nope."

"Nope?" Her eyebrows raised. "I haven't heard that before."

He grinned. "You'll be hearing it a lot in Texas."

"I surmise it means no."

"You surmise right."

He laid down two more cards—a second ace for him and a lowly ten of diamonds for Anya.

"Well, what will you be wagering?" she demanded.

"Kisses. Mine."

He liked the way she ruffled up, like a brown hen who'd staked its corner of the barnyard.

"We *both* can't bet the same thing."

"Sure we can. That way we'll both win."

She stared at him long and hard. "You're impossible, Morgan Grayson."

She only knew the half of it. "Men sometimes are. You'll get used to it."

Her glance dropped to the cards, then returned to him. "Do you need to contrive excuses to kiss me?"

For a moment he simply looked at her. Was that what she thought? He shook his head. There seemed little point in spelling out in succinct detail the hard time he was having restraining himself from making love to her.

"We have to pass the time somehow."

She pushed back her chair and stood. Her hands settled on her hips. Under the demure covering of her dark gown, her breasts rose, their soft fullness calling forth pleasures more elemental and satisfying than mere kissing.

"I believe I shall retire to my chamber."

"Anya . . ." There was a quaver to her voice that scored a direct hit to his heart. With a start, he realized two things. First, his cavalier manner had hurt her. Second, his future wife had sensibilities to which he would have to cater. For the first time, it occurred to him that, unlike buying a bull for his herd, acquiring an English bride—or any other, for that matter—was more than a simple business deal. It was a stunning discovery, one he should have thought of sooner.

Slowly, he stood. Had there been a time when he'd only yearned for Anya physically? Without him realizing it, he'd been seduced by a starchy scrap of a woman with round, golden eyes and a deliciously formed body. He wondered briefly what Anya would think of him casting her as a seductress.

He couldn't help smiling. No doubt, she would slap his face and give him a stouthearted lecture upon the evils of overindulging in spirits. "It is probably a good idea for you to retire for the night. I'll keep watch."

Additional color splashed Anya's cheeks as she stalked to the stairs. He watched the sassy sway of her hips and almost followed. Sanity reigned. If he went after her, they would make love. There was no way he could be alone with her in a bedroom and not touch her. But until they married, he dare not take the risk of getting her with child—not when someone was determined he would not live to see his wedding day.

Swearing softly and quite creatively, he returned to his chair. It wasn't his nature to sit passively and wait for trouble to find him. He needed a plan to draw out his attacker. The cards spread across the table mocked him, as did the foul-tasting swill in his mug. Damn, what he wouldn't give for a shot of whiskey.

He picked up the ace of spades. The beginnings of a scheme began to form. . . .

Anya glanced around the humble bedchamber Sarah Percy had prepared for her. Everything was clean. She swallowed the lump in her throat and wondered what was wrong with her. Why did she feel like crying? Had she thought that accepting Morgan's proposal of marriage would alter him? Would make him more gentle and caring?

She knew she should go to bed. It was past midnight. Instead, she moved toward the window that overlooked the small courtyard. From an outside post, a lantern hung, casting an eerie, yellowish light across the open area between the inn and the small outbuilding that stabled their horses. Morning seemed a long time off.

Through the blur of unshed tears, she remembered her excitement when she'd awakened today. She was beginning her Great Adventure. . . . Furiously, she scrubbed her eyes with the back of her hand. Great Adventure, hah!

Any woman soon to be married was entitled to a courtship by her prospective groom. But not her. Oh, no, she had the misfortune to fall in love with a wholly unsuitable barbarian from America who—

It suddenly dawned on her with perfect clarity how unfair she was being to Morgan. Just as suddenly came the memory of precisely when his manner toward her had cooled. After the fire? Or after she'd foolishly confessed her love for him?

Anya rested her forehead against the chilled pane of glass. What a fool she was. Of course, Morgan didn't want to hear any words of affection from her. He didn't love her. Good grief, until a few weeks ago, he hadn't even known of her existence. To him, their union was merely a business transaction.

How could she have forgotten even for a moment that, in order to save the plantation, he needed Richard's money?

Anya had no idea how much time she had spent staring out the window when an unexplained shifting of night shadows caught her attention. Curious, she leaned forward and watched as two darkened forms detached themselves from the thickening darkness. They moved across the courtyard, and a ripple of uneasiness stirred within her. Why would someone seek to move through the yard in the cloak of darkness?

She remembered and dismissed Morgan's admonition that she flee at the first sign of trouble. After all, if there was mischief afoot, he needed to be alerted. Since it was due to her superior eyesight that the danger had been spotted, it fell upon her to warn Morgan. Even as she continued to stare down upon the night tableau, the outline of a third silhouette followed the first two into the stables.

Without hesitation, she opened her chamber door and stepped into the hall, grateful she had not changed into her sleeping gown. A quiet knock on Morgan's door produced no response. She tapped again, louder. Silence was her only reward. What a time to find out her future husband was a sound sleeper!

She turned the doorknob, distressed to discover Morgan hadn't thought to lock himself safely in his room for the night. Didn't the blasted man possess an ounce of caution? She hoped he took better care of himself in Texas. Several steps took her to Morgan's bed. Her eyes had adjusted sufficiently to the darkened chamber for her to see his outline beneath the blankets.

"Morgan..."

There was no movement. She edged closer. "Morgan?"

Still nothing.

She pushed against a lump that logically should have been his shoulder. Instead of firm musculature, however, her fingertips sank into feather ticking. She drew back her hand, paused for a heartbeat, then jerked aside the pile of quilts.

"Morgan!"

Two pillows greeted her. She touched them, just to make sure the darkness wasn't playing tricks on her. Automatically, she went to Morgan's window and looked again into the courtyard. From the light provided by the lamppost, she saw several shadowed figures take shape. They seemed to coalesce into a swirling darkness that kicked up dust and more darkness. It took a moment to realize she was watching a fight.

Go to him....

From somewhere deep within her, Anya felt more than heard the command. Instinctively, she knew Morgan was in trouble and needed her. She spun from the window and raced to the hall, calling out as she headed for the stairs.

The door to Sarah and Hume Percy's bedchamber was flung open. Wearing a striped nightshirt and looking sleepily disoriented, Hume rubbed his eyes. "What's all the shouting about?"

"Morgan's in trouble. Hurry!"

Without waiting to see if he followed, she charged down the stairs. When she reached the inn's wide front door and saw it had been bolted for the night, she cried out in frustration. One more delay in reaching Morgan's side...

Frantically, she threw up the heavy side bar and struggled with the unfamiliar latch. Hume's arrival saved her from having to rip the door from its hinges. She reached the courtyard in time to see a large form being shoved inside a coach. It was Morgan, she just knew it. A whip cracked and the team of horses shot forward.

"Stop!" she shouted after them.

In return she received a mouthful of dust. She rounded on Hume, who stood scratching his jaw. "Do something!"

"I'll fetch the constable."

"There's no time for that! The coach will be miles away before you reach Constable Reading's place."

"Yes, it will," the young innkeeper agreed fatalistically.

She tugged on his striped sleeve. "But—but... you must ride after the coach so that doesn't happen."

He shook his arm free. "What good would that do?"

Anya's small store of patience disintegrated. "I don't know, but we can't let them ride off with Morgan."

"I'll get the constable," Hume repeated doggedly.

Anya wanted to slap his homely face. Instead, she whirled toward the stables. "Fine. You notify Constable Reading, and I'll follow the damned coach."

She didn't know if the innkeeper's horrified gasp was because of her curse or because of what she intended. In the stables, she approached the first stall she came to. There was no time to bother with the nicety of searching out one of the grays or Morgan's roan. It was a matter of first come, first take. When Hume tried to dissuade her again, Anya paid him no heed. She led a horse from the stall.

"I'll need a leg up."

He shook his head vigorously. "I won't do it, Miss Anya."

She shook her fist at him. "Oh, yes, you will, and right now. I haven't time to argue with you."

"But you need a saddle," he protested.

"Damn it, man. I need a leg up. Now give it to me."

Clearly affronted, he did as she commanded. "Get out of my way."

She didn't have to give the command twice. The man fairly jumped from the horse's dancing hooves. Only when she was in motion with the inn disappearing behind her did Anya allow herself a deep breath. Her only thought was to catch up with the coach before the road divided at Cider Turnkey.

As her mount's hooves thundered down the moonlit path, the memory of another late night ride tumbled into her thoughts. Even as she shivered, she knew the goose bumps sprinting across her skin had little to do with the evening chill. That desperate ride had been on Richard's behalf and she had failed him. Her hands clenched around the reins and she flicked the leather tips against the horse.

Ride, she almost cried. *Ride for all you're worth.*

She wished for a cloak, she wished for a pair of gloves, she wished for a speedier mount. At least no rain lashed down upon her this night. Anya leaned forward. Nothing mattered except that she catch up with the men who'd seized Morgan.

Luck was with her. She reached Cider Turnkey in time to see the coach take the eastern fork. Anya tugged on the reins. Now that she had found Morgan's kidnappers, she could maintain a slower pace. All she had to do was keep them in sight while making certain they didn't realize they were being followed. That the coach traveled at such a slow pace gave her spiteful solace. Clearly, the scoundrels had no idea their crime had already been discovered.

The passage of time had no meaning for Anya as she steadfastly kept the coach in sight. Mile after mile and hour after hour passed with her maintaining the slow, steady pace. Several times she rested her mount. At some point during the night, she stopped feeling the cold. Once she caught herself dozing and jerked to wakefulness. Dawn caught them midway to Bedfordshire. To keep from being seen, she dropped back farther from the coach.

As morning settled in, other vehicles began to clog the roadway, and she was able to narrow the gap. Every wagon she met carried passengers who stared at her askance, clearly shocked at seeing a lone woman riding with no saddle or companion. She ignored them, pulling on a cloak of invisible dignity that shielded her from their gawking stares.

At midday the coach stopped a short distance from a shabbily maintained inn. The driver remained seated in his high perch while one passenger disembarked and entered the unsavory-looking building. Tired, thirsty and hungry, Anya struggled to dismount. She could push her horse no further without water. By the light of day she had discovered the animal to be a sorry-looking nag. She led him to a trough to drink.

After a few minutes, the man who'd entered the inn returned and the coach was on its way again. Anya used a stump to regain her seat and urged the horse onward. She tried to will away the ache in her shoulders and arms. She considered it her good fortune that her bottom had become blessedly numb. Again, Anya lost track of the hours. They passed the small shire that boasted Wilton's, and she wished there was some way to alert Lady Hester about Morgan's capture. Yet Anya knew she dared not stop, for she had to keep the coach in sight.

At last, hours later, the coach stopped for a second time, and Anya almost wept in relief. Because they presently traversed an empty stretch of country road, she'd had to drop back farther than she liked. A water-filled ditch ran alongside them. She gave the horse its head and let him drink and eat the nearby stubble.

A fortuitously placed stand of chestnut trees and a bend in the road concealed her from view. Wearily, she slipped from her mount and also drank from the stream. Water fell from her cupped hands, dribbling across her dress front. Despite the surprisingly mild day, she continued to feel cold.

Her familiar surroundings offered a measure of comfort. If they continued on this road until nightfall, they would be in Bedfordshire. She remembered Morgan's accusation that Merrawynn was behind the misfortunes plaguing him. She hadn't wanted to believe him, yet it seemed unlikely that his half brother was behind this new treachery.

Anya tugged on the reins and guided the pitiful horse toward a large rock so she could remount. She wondered how Morgan was faring inside the coach. She was still slightly amazed that he had been taken. Somehow she had thought him superior in strength and cunning to anyone foolish enough to cross him. With his pistol hanging about his hips, he had seemed quite invincible.

Three men hardly seemed a sufficient force to fell him. She thought about the heroes she'd read about. Lancelot would never have allowed himself to be captured by a puny faction of three, nor would Robin Hood or even Friar Tuck, for that matter. Evidently, Texas Americans weren't particularly hardy when it came to defending themselves.

Groaning, she pulled herself onto the obliging horse. She had the feeling she should be grateful the coach traveled at so sedate a speed, otherwise the nag she'd borrowed from Hume's stable wouldn't have been able to keep up.

By the time the coach stopped again, Anya's stomach was growling, she had blisters on both hands, and her spirits had hit rock bottom. They were on her brother's property. Since she could not imagine Edward, of all people, being behind such chicanery, that left Merrawynn responsible for this cravenly act.

The coach doors were flung open before an abandoned cottage that had sat idle for some time because its former occupant, Greta Wallace, had been regarded as a witch and had reputedly performed various heinous acts beneath its sagging thatched roof. Anya slid from her horse, making sure no sign of it or herself could be seen from a thicket of brambles that ran along the eastern side of the small clearing.

She tethered the tired beast next to a stream that cut across the back of the cottage property and inched carefully forward. The coach pitched back and forth wildly upon its springs. Gruff-voiced oaths punctuated the evening air. It took all three men to drag a kicking, snarling Morgan from its interior. The men certainly had their hands full, she thought with some admiration. Morgan had them ducking and dodging his blows.

"Get 'em Harold," yelled a short, wiry man.

"You get 'em!"

"Oof!" groaned a giant of a man as he caught Morgan's foot squarely in his groin.

Sundry blows and yelps followed. Anya moved as close as she dared to the struggling men. Morgan was noticeably silent as he concentrated on defending himself against his three assailants. Oh, how she itched to jump into the melee and help him. It took all the discipline she possessed to wait until the odds were more in their favor.

"I thought you tied him up," the short man gasped, ducking one of Morgan's mighty leg thrusts.

"I thought he was still out."

For a few minutes conversation ceased. Then, as if suddenly tiring of a game, Morgan slumped to the ground. Immediately the three ruffians pounced upon him. Stricken, Anya pressed her hand to her lips, lest she cry out.

"The lady said not to hurt 'em, Dickie," one of the men pointed out, getting to his feet.

"She'd sing a different tune if she had to get 'em inside the cottage."

The three men backed away from Morgan. Through her tears, Anya saw he had been trussed up like a Christmas goose.

"Open the door, Dickie. Let's get 'em inside."

In short order, the deed was accomplished and the cottage's weathered door slammed shut. Anya crept around to the back and tried to find a window that would let her see what was going on inside. Her luck seemed to run out. There was only one window, and tall as she was, she couldn't look into it.

Sinking to the overgrown grass, she closed her eyes wearily. Now that she knew where Morgan had been taken, all she had to do was ride to her brother's estate and get help. Morgan's rescue was surely no more than a couple of hours away. Exhausted, she struggled to her feet.

"Let's kill 'em and say it were an accident."

The angry voice reached Anya through the window above her head, and the blood froze in her veins.

"I'm with Dickie. I say we kill 'em."

"That's not what the lady's paying us for," protested a third voice.

"When I get my hands on you, I'll wring all your necks."

The final voice was Morgan's. Oh, blast the foolish man. The last thing he needed was to antagonize his captors. Just this once, couldn't he show some manners?

"Shut up," someone snarled.

Silently, Anya agreed.

"The lady said we had to keep him for five months. Then she'd pay us."

"How are we going to keep him tied up for five months, Harold?"

"Well . . ."

"Can't be done."

"Dickie's right. Can't be done."

"We can try, can't we?"

"I don't like it. He'll kill us in our sleep, he will."

"We got his pistol, so he can't shoot us."

"I'll strangle you," Morgan suggested matter-of-factly.

Anya wanted to strangle *him*. How could she ride for help when she didn't dare leave him, lest he precipitate his own death?

"You want to die, mister? Then keep talking."

"Who's the lady who set this up?" Morgan continued, as if he hadn't been told to desist. "Merrawynn Hull, the Marchioness of Broderick?"

"We don't know her name. We're just helping a pretty woman out of a fix."

"How much is she paying you?" Morgan demanded.

"Fifty pounds."

"Shut up, Alvin. He don't need to know that."

"Why not?"

"'Cause it ain't smart to tell 'em too much."

"I'll pay you a hundred pounds if you'll take me to her," Morgan offered in a surprisingly cheerful voice. From listening to him no one would guess Morgan's life hung in the balance.

"Won't do us any good if they hang us for snatching you."

"Who'll know?" Morgan asked softly.

"Don't listen to him, Harold. It's a trick."

"I know that. I'm not daft."

"I still say we kill 'em and say it were an accident. The lady will still pay."

"What if she doesn't?" Morgan inquired caustically. "If you don't know who she is, how can you find her to collect what she owes you?"

"We're meeting her next Tuesday," one of the men bragged. "That's how we'll get our money."

"What if she doesn't show up?"

"She will, if she knows what's good for her."

"If you don't know how to find her, that's an empty threat."

"He's right, Dickie. I never thought of that. What if she doesn't—"

"I know her!" the man Anya recognized as Dickie roared.

"You do? How?" both his companions demanded simultaneously.

"'Cause I followed her back to the fancy place she was staying, and I asked around."

"Who is she?" both men clamored.

"That's fer me to know."

A sound like the scrape of a chair cut through the approaching night. "I want to know, Dickie."

"Me, too."

The men's voices were at once menacing and uncompromising.

"All right. All right. I'll tell you. It *is* the Marchioness of Broderick."

Anya's heart sank to her feet. Her worst nightmare had come true. Merrawynn was behind the attacks upon Morgan. A feeling of fierce betrayal cut through her. She would never forgive Merrawynn for this duplicity. Never.

Blinking back tears, she decided it was time she rode for help. She straightened, wondering how many men it would take to rescue Morgan.

"I say we kill 'em tonight. The lady will still pay. Now that we know who she is, we can make her."

"I agree with Alvin."

Tears of frustration fell. How could she ride for help? Morgan might be dead before she returned. Her hands clenched. She had to do something herself to save him.

Frantically, she looked about her, hoping to discover something she could use as a weapon. All she saw was tall, uncut grass and a few dead wild flowers. She stood and shook her head, trying to clear it. Hungry, tired and thirsty, she seemed unable to concentrate.

She took a step forward and promptly pitched over something concealed in the grass. Her knees banged painfully against the hard earth. She groped in the near darkness and came up with, of all things, a broom. She pushed it from her path and moved on. She had made it to the east side of the cottage when she stopped suddenly.

The broom had boasted a satisfyingly thick handle. If it were applied with sufficient force to a man's head . . . Smiling grimly, she returned to the rear of the cottage, then spent half an hour searching the tall grass before she found it again.

Closing her blistered palms around its fat throat, she took up a position near the only door to the cottage. Sooner or later someone was going to come out, and when he did, she was going to whack him with every bit of strength she possessed.

Her wait was a short one. Only a few minutes passed before the door creaked open. She held her breath and closed her eyes the exact instant she brought down the broom handle. A single, muffled thud dropped the man to his knees. She whacked him again and he pitched face forward into the dirt.

Flushed with victory, Anya laid aside the broom and tried to pull the man toward the deeper grass. Her work was made easier by the fact she'd knocked out the smallest of the three men.

One down, two to go.

When the door opened again, she was barely back in position.

"Harold, what's taken so long? Can't you find his pistol?"

Whoosh!

She brought down the handle again. Unfortunately, the second man was taller than the first, and she succeeded only in hitting him on the back of his broad shoulders.

"Ouch!"

The indignant howl spurred Anya to swing again and quickly.

"Oomph!"

He was still standing when she rose on tiptoe and swung the handle once more. It broke in her hands just about the time the man crumpled.

Two down, one to go.

"Alvin, what's wrong?"

The question was asked only a foot away. Anya gazed at the shattered broom handle in dismay.

"I said—"

Anya looked into the open doorway and faced the tallest and widest of Merrawynn's henchmen. Her mouth went dry.

"Well, what have we here?" he growled, stepping forward. He stumbled over the unconscious body of his cohort and snarled, "What did you do to Alvin?"

Anya wanted to run. Her feet seemed stitched to the ground, however, and she couldn't move.

The giant lunged toward her. She squeaked once and was miraculously freed from her paralysis about the time a meaty paw closed around her wrist.

Chapter Fourteen

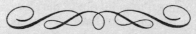

Anya looked from the broad, coarse hand manacling her arm to eyes that bulged with murderous rage. *I'm going to die,* she thought, dazed.

As if savoring that likelihood, the fiend leered at her. "Feisty, ain't you?"

She answered by kicking him in the shin. Pain shot from her slippered toes. Too late, she remembered she wasn't wearing her riding boots.

Not even a flicker of reaction shone in the giant's gaze. One moment ground by, then another.

He raised a hefty fist. Anya watched, mesmerized, expecting any second to feel it come crashing down upon her. She closed her eyes and braced herself for the end.

"Let her go, and I won't kill you."

She hardly recognized the quiet, lethal voice as belonging to Morgan. Summoning what courage she had left, Anya opened her eyes. Sure enough, there stood a somewhat-battered Morgan holding a wicked-looking knife to the giant's throat.

"Nice and easy..." Morgan growled. "Let her go and step back."

Anya found herself released so quickly she stumbled backward. "Oh, Morgan, thank God you're free."

"Shut up, darling, and fetch the rope from the cottage."

The fact that Morgan's tone remained tensely furious startled Anya. She dismissed the preposterous thought that he was angry with *her*.

Morgan ended up using all the rope to secure the largest of the ruffians who had seized him. The two that Anya had managed to knock unconscious were bound with strips of cloth supplied from her petticoats.

She was tempted to point out to the glowering and silent Morgan that he would not have had the use of said petticoats had she not ridden after him. A rudimentary sense of self-preservation, however, kept the observation behind pursed lips.

Still not speaking, Morgan took her by the arm and led her from the cottage. It was quite dark now, and she was unable to see his expression. She sensed that was to her good fortune.

"Wait here," he ordered through what sounded like clenched teeth.

Enough was enough. "Look, Morgan, I have no intention of standing out here and freezing while you—"

His hands closed around her shoulders. He shook her. "Listen to me. I have some questions to ask, and I'm not going to be particularly genteel about how I get the answers. Believe me, you don't want to be *inside* when I do."

"It seems you already have your answers," Anya said miserably, remembering that her own sister was behind Morgan's capture.

"Take my coat. It will keep you warm."

"I don't want your coat," she practically wailed.

The heavy garment fell almost immediately about her shoulders. "Damn, you're stubborn."

With that parting observation, he returned to the cottage and closed the door behind him. She didn't waste a minute before making her way to the back window. Even if she couldn't see, she would be able to hear what was going on.

From the pale light that suddenly spilled from the cottage, Anya assumed Morgan had found a candle. In the next half hour, she learned that Morgan had been right. He didn't care how he got the answers to his questions. Through browbeating, occasional blows and an abundance of profanity he induced the three men to virtually tell their life stories.

What he discovered cheered Anya somewhat. Merrawynn hadn't taken the three miscreants into her employ until a few days ago. The men knew nothing about Richard's stables burning or the accident at the cliffs.

When Morgan finished interrogating his former captors, Anya barely made it back to the front of the cottage before he stunned her by sending them on their way—in the coach, no less. His only condition for doing so was that they never show their faces in this part of the country again. Anya shook her head in disbelief. Surely, the men had earned a prolonged stay at Newgate.

The coach had scarcely pulled away before Morgan's attention became focused upon her. She experimented with a smile. His frown deepened.

"We'll spend the night in the cottage."

"What if they come back?"

"Don't you trust my judgment?"

She decided to keep her opinion to herself. "They were dreadful men, Morgan. They might not keep their word."

He tossed back his head and laughed. "They were derelicts, Anya, without a working brain among the three of them."

"They were smart enough to kidnap you," she snapped impatiently.

"Only because I let them."

Her eyes widened. "What?"

"Come inside, Anya."

She eyed him warily. The small amount of light coming from the opened doorway cast his face in a shadow. "They'll be back, Morgan, and they'll kill us in our sleep."

"They're not that stupid."

"But they might be that greedy."

"Anya, it is very insulting to have my judgment continually questioned."

"Is your vanity more important than your life?"

Instead of answering, his hand closed around her arm. Since she didn't think she'd win a tussle with him, she allowed herself to be led inside. The smell of ancient dust assaulted her.

About the time she noticed a nearby chair—the only one in the room—her legs gave out. She sank to it gratefully.

"The reason I don't think they'll be back, Anya, is because I paid them more handsomely than Merrawynn."

She bolted to her feet. "You didn't!"

"With a purse of coins they'd overlooked in my coat pocket," he continued evenly.

"But—but that's outrageous. How could you reward them for *attacking* you?"

"Had I not your welfare to consider, I wouldn't have. But as you'd thrust yourself into the middle of the situation, I had no alternative. Believe me, they will not return."

She looked around the shabby cottage for something to throw at him. Since there was nothing save the candle, table and chair, the only reasonable thing to do seemed to sit back down, which she did. "All right then, Morgan, let's have it."

"A bit of advice, Anya. Don't push."

She felt like crying. She couldn't believe how ungrateful he was. It was horrible not being appreciated—never mind that Morgan had deliberately gotten himself kidnapped and scared her nearly to death. If the tables had been turned and he had ridden all night and a day to rescue her, *she* would have been most generous in *her* gratitude.

He went to the rock fireplace that made up one wall of the cottage. "Dare we build a fire?"

"Oh, let's live recklessly."

He arched a brow. She raised her chin.

Turning, he plucked the candle from the table. "Hold this."

She did so automatically. He picked up the table and proceeded to smash it against the earthen floor. At each jarring crash, she flinched, realizing that with each whack of splintering wood, Morgan was working out his ferocious temper.

He knelt before the hearth and began arranging the broken bits of table into a pile of kindling. When he extended his hand to her, she silently presented him with the candle. In very little time, a cheery fire burned in the fireplace. He set the candle on the floor. Only a bit of smoke backed from the chimney into the cottage. She suspected that by morning the chair upon which she sat would also be sacrificed to the flames.

Sullenly, she watched Morgan move around the small room. He eyed a dusty pallet in one corner and shrugged. The next thing she knew he was dragging it toward the fire. Good, more kindling.

"Give me my coat, Anya."

Tiredly, she rose to her feet and took it off. Morgan reached for it and, to her surprise, spread it across the pallet.

He held out his hand again. Anya stared at it blankly, having no idea what more he wanted from her.

"Come along," he said softly.

Fighting back tears of weariness, she put her hand in his. He led her to the miserable-looking, makeshift bed. It seemed as if every muscle in her body had suddenly given up. She had no resistance left. Exhausted, she permitted him to draw her downward. When he stretched out beside her and opened his arms, she went willingly.

"Sleep, little warrior. I'll keep watch."

His words barely penetrated the muddle masquerading as her mind, but her body recognized the security he offered, and almost at once her eyelids dropped. Never had she been so tired. All she wanted was to rest her head upon Morgan's strong shoulder and sleep.

Sleep...

Sometime before dawn, Anya's eyes opened. Instantly, she knew where she was. The fire had burned down, and she was stretched across Morgan, her head upon his wide chest, her hand upon his middle and her leg nestled securely between his.

In all the time she had followed his abductors, she hadn't let herself think about him...dying. But now, as his arms cradled her, she thought about how easily he could have been killed. She didn't understand how Merrawynn could be party to such evil. Despite her differences with her sister, Anya had always believed, upon some level at least, that love existed between them.

But no loving sister would do what Merrawynn had done.

"Can't you sleep?"

Morgan's voice seemed to rumble directly from his chest into her ear. She tilted her face toward his. "Were you serious about letting yourself be captured?"

"I had to find out who was behind the attacks against me. It seemed the quickest way."

"You could have been killed," she said, pain piercing her words.

"I had a knife in my boot. I was armed."

"They had your pistol!"

"Before I entered the stables, I'd emptied the Remington's chambers."

"What?"

"I overheard Dickie and his friends talking about how they'd been ordered to take me prisoner without hurting me."

"But thanks to your winsome nature, they changed their minds quickly enough about that."

"To find out who'd hired them, I had to push a little."

"It seems to me you should have left them here and *we* should have ridden away in the coach."

"I wanted them as far away from us as they could get—in London, preferably. We'll ride the roan to your brother's place tomorrow. I gather it's near here."

"Fairly near," she said, yawning. Until it became absolutely necessary, she had no intention of telling Morgan she hadn't brought his horse.

"You sound tired—go back to sleep. We'll talk in the morning."

What else was there left to discuss? "Are you still upset with me for following you?"

"Lord, yes."

That settled that, she supposed bleakly. Sighing, she nestled closer. They lay in darkness with an uneasy truce stretching between them. Despite the displeasure he'd voiced, his arms came around her and he stroked her back.

She closed her eyes and pressed her face into his shoulder. In all her life, she didn't think she'd ever felt as safe as she did being held by him.

He had let himself be captured as part of a plan to find out who was behind the attacks upon him. His cold-blooded courage stunned her. Morgan Grayson was so much more complicated and courageous than she had realized.

"What are you thinking?"

She started. "How did you know I was still awake?"

His hands made a sweeping foray across her. "You're stiff."

"Oh..." She supposed he was, too, from the various blows he'd received from Dickie, Harold and Alvin. "I'm sorry, Morgan."

"That's not good enough, Anya. I told you to run at the first sign of trouble."

She pulled away. "I wasn't apologizing about *that.*"

"You mean you've done something else you need to confess?"

She thought of the pitiful nag she'd taken. "I'm sorry about your injuries," she clarified.

He shifted, taking her with him, so they lay sideways, facing each other. "I'm not hurt. I've been in better fights than that at O'Reilly's."

"Who is O'Reilly?"

"It's a place—one of the more lively saloons in Big Rock Gulch."

"Someone started a fight in a salon?" she asked incredulously.

"A sa*loon,* honey. There's a big difference."

Anya sighed. "Even so, I'm certain the hostess who invited you didn't appreciate fisticuffs on the premises."

"Sally O'Reilly isn't your typical hostess. As I recall, she's fought in her share of brawls."

"Your hostess?" Anya asked, aghast.

"More or less." He pulled her to him. "There's a lot you need to learn about Texas, honey."

"It seems there's a lot Texas needs to learn about civilized behavior."

He chuckled. Shivers skittered through her.

"I'm looking forward to seeing what happens when English meets West."

Was he? she wondered. Or was she just part and parcel of what he had to tolerate to get his hands on a large enough portion of Richard's money to help his stepmother?

In the faint glow from the fire, his features looked dark and forbidding. She twisted, trying to get comfortable. Her much-abused bottom came into contact with the unyielding earthen floor.

She groaned.

"What's wrong?"

"I'm sore."

He rose on an elbow and stared down at her. "Where?"

"Everywhere," she admitted, suppressing another groan. "And if you're going to start chastising me again about following after you, please don't. I'm thirsty and hungry and my blisters hurt."

If nothing else, perhaps she could enlist the ungrateful man's sympathy. At this point she would take whatever charity he had to offer.

There was a moment of silence. Then he sat up. "Anya, there's a part of me that wants to wring your neck for the risk you took in coming after me."

Why didn't he tell her something she didn't already know? "I did what I thought was right."

"I know you did, but I'm a man. It's my duty to look after and protect my woman."

Duty... The word rankled, reemphasizing his reasons for marrying her, reasons having nothing to do with love or affection. She found it impossible to speak past the growing lump in her throat.

He pushed back the coat that covered them. "Come with me."

His hands found her and he tugged her from the relative warmth of the pallet. When he drew her outside, she had no idea where he was taking her.

"I have no food to offer, but I noticed a small stream nearby."

A cold night breeze knifed through her clothing and she trembled. He sprinted back to the cottage, returning with his coat.

He held it up for her. "Here, put your arms through."

She did as instructed. An immediate wave of warmth that carried Morgan's scent wrapped itself around her, and his arm settled about her shoulders. She realized that since he had no vessel with which to carry a drink, he was taking her to where the water was. A sensation of inner warmth touched her heart. He was a remarkably caring man—a man who deserved to love the woman he married.

As they knelt beside the fast-moving stream, Anya tried to push back the drooping sleeves of his coat. Seeing her predicament, he eased the garment from her. She cupped her hands to carry the precious liquid to her parched throat. The icy water hit her palms and she gasped.

"What's wrong?"

"It's my blisters...."

He took her hands and held them toward the moonlight. "Poor little warrior. The night we met you'd also ridden off without your gloves."

Gently, he pressed a light kiss to each hurting palm.

"There wasn't time to fetch them," she said, her voice shaky. The pain retreated from her hands, and she discovered there was a healing magic in the brush of his lips.

He released her and laced his fingers together, dipping them into the cold channel. For a moment she stared at the strong, innately powerful hands thrust toward her. Then, sighing, she leaned forward and drank. Strangely, this seemed the most intimate act they had shared.

Moments passed. The hoot of a distant owl broke the night silence. She continued to sip from his cupped fingers. Faintly salty and utterly delicious, the water quenched her thirst.

When she'd drunk her fill, she sank back on her heels and wiped her mouth with the back of her hand. "Thank you, Morgan."

"I only wish I could as easily find food for you." He dried his hands on his shirt. "Do you have any of your petticoats left?"

She nodded, wondering why he asked.

"Tonight, we'll let the air heal your hands, but we'll wrap them before we head for your brother's place tomorrow morning."

His consideration brought fresh tears to her eyes. He helped her to her feet and dropped his coat back over her shoulders. "The moment we arrive tomorrow, I'll make sure you're fed."

She took an absent swipe at the tears that refused to be denied. Morgan's unflagging consideration really was too much. He had gone as long as she without food or drink, yet he seemed totally absorbed with her welfare.

Duty...

He led her back to the cottage and again fashioned a place for her next to him, covering them both with his heavy coat. When her bottom connected again with the floor, she tried to swallow another groan.

"Is it your hands?" he asked sympathetically.

She shook her head. There was no way she was going to discuss with him the sore and tender state of her derriere.

"What is it then?"

For the first time, she realized what an unattractive trait persistence was. "Nothing."

"Anya, if you're hurt, I want to know. Now."

"It's just a few assorted aches," she mumbled. "From the ride."

There was a prolonged space of welcome silence. She hoped he had finally let the matter drop.

"I think I've figured out the problem."

She knew she blushed, and blessed the darkness. At least she didn't have to face his knowing eyes.

Again he moved from the protection of the coat. She heard him cross the room, and sat up to stare after him.

He went to the chair and proceeded to smash it into smaller pieces. He shoved the splintered wood into the hearth and the fire flared up, flooding the room with additional light. Perplexed, she watched him walk back to the pallet.

"Lay on your stomach."

A shaft of uneasiness cut through her. "Why?"

"I'm going to give you a rubdown."

She knew she blushed crimson. He couldn't possibly mean what she thought. Could he?

"Come on, roll over."

She almost barked her refusal, but restrained herself. "I most certainly will not."

He stood above her, his hands poised on his lean hips. "Don't tell me you're shy?"

"What I am is respectable and—"

"Saddle sore, sweetheart. Be a big girl now."

"B-but..." She knew she was stuttering.

"Relax, you'll thank me when I've finished."

His hands gently but relentlessly turned her. She rested her cheek against the scratchy pallet, thinking she ought to resist somehow. No course of action came to her, however—especially when his strong fingers began to gently knead her sore shoulders and back. Methodically, his hands made slow circular motions across her aching muscles. Her entire body began to relax. She sighed in satisfaction.

"Feel good, honey?"

"Wonderful," she murmured lazily, hoping he would never stop.

Her eyelids drifted shut and she lost herself to the rhythmic stroke of his ministrations. She was almost asleep when she felt him raise her skirts and push her petticoats aside.

Her eyes shot open. "Morgan!"

"Hmm?"

"What are you—"

His hands moved to her hips. "You're going to like this, too, Anya. Trust me."

He had to be jesting!

Before she could utter another word, Morgan pulled down her pantaloons. The next sound she expected to hear was that of holy lightning ripping through the thatched roof and cooking Morgan Grayson to a crisp.

The cottage remained silent, however.

A ribbon of warmth wafted from the fire to caress her exposed flesh, flesh that only rarely saw the light of day...or night. She pressed her cheek against the scratchy pallet. Just how much light did the pitiful fire provide?

"Poor, little brave-heart...."

She felt Morgan's husky murmur against her bare skin, and her heart raced. Then she felt what seemed like—but couldn't *possibly* be—the brush of his mouth against her.

Her head whipped around as she tried to see what was going on. A firm hand pushed her shoulder against the pallet. Slowly, Morgan began to massage her abused bottom. His touch was light, the movement of his fingertips a mere caress. Within her, a welcome sense of relief uncurled. His touch wouldn't have felt so healing if blisters had formed.

It was a shocking intimacy she allowed him. If anyone were to find out, Anya would be mortified. Surely, even husbands did not perform such private acts for their wives.

And yet...

And yet, she was grateful for Morgan's ministrations and would have willingly done the same for him. Scarcely had *that* thought formed than another flush of embarrassment swept through her. Imagine rubbing Morgan's—

"Think you can sleep now?"

Sleep? She almost laughed aloud. That was the last thing on her mind. "Uh ... I think you've done enough."

As it was, she didn't know how she was going to face him by the light of day.

He drew her pantaloons back up, then stretched out next to her. More moments passed. She rolled to her side and slanted a sideways glance at him. He was staring straight at her.

"Damn ..."

She wet her lips. "What is it?"

"I should have known this wouldn't work."

Her eyes widened. Did Morgan already regret his familiarity and hold her in contempt for allowing it? "I ... uh ... understand."

Through the meager barrier of her traveling gown, she felt his palm close over her breast.

"That's what a man likes—an understanding woman."

Stunned by the unexpected contact, Anya gasped. Protest seemed beyond her.

As if memorizing the shape of her, he rotated his hand over her. "As well as a charming backside, you have beautiful breasts, Anya."

His fingers stroked until she knew he felt the outline of her hardened nipples. Pinpoints of sensation seemed to squeeze their sensitive tips. In the rest of her, heat gathered.

She moaned.

The buttons running down the front of her dress proved no hindrance to his intent to bare her to his touch. Soon a current of cool air moved across her. "Are you hurting?" He sat up and leaned over her. "I can make the hurt go away."

No longer innocent of what happened between man and woman, Anya knew what he asked of her. *Don't,* an inner voice cautioned. *He doesn't love you.* The clamoring needs of her aroused body, however, swiftly smothered the discordant protest. She was Morgan's for the taking.

In less time than she would have thought possible, he stripped away her dress and underclothing. Utterly nude before him, she braced herself for the excruciating embarrassment any well-bred woman should feel. A warming languor stole the strength from her limbs.

He looked long and hard at her, his darkened gaze moving with deliberate slowness across every inch of her. From the pinkened tips of her breasts, along her rib cage and waist, to...to the V between her thighs. His gaze seemed to linger there longest. It was as if his eyes were the sun, casting a burning heat upon the most secret part of her. She shifted and the dark curls caught and reflected the fire's light.

He groaned.

She held her breath. Even though Morgan was fully clothed, she was fiercely conscious of the part of him he would place inside her.

"You're beautiful," he said again. "All of you." He stretched forth his hand. "For a month I've remembered the look of you the night I undressed you. You've been branded into my brain—the white and the pink and the . . ." His fingers gently probed the triangle of black curls. ". . . And the dark of you."

His touch unleased a slick explosion of heat. Her hips raised. She waited for shame or embarrassment to flood through her. She waited in vain. Of their own accord, her arms raised in supplication.

He gathered her up and held her naked body against his clothed one. She rubbed herself against the surprisingly seductive feel of his faintly abrasive clothing. He groaned again.

She didn't know how much longer she could endure the aching hollowness within. His mouth feasted upon hers. Tingles, sweet and piercing, rippled through her. Tongue to tongue, he pitched her into a storm of shattering dimensions.

When it seemed she no longer even existed, his mouth dropped lower. He took the tip of her breast between his parted lips and she cried out. Fire and ice seemed to explode simultaneously. Then his fingertips returned to the throbbing place between her thighs. She bucked helplessly. Sensation roared at her from all sides.

He looked up. "Now it's my turn to brand you, Anya. Before this night is over, you'll know you're mine."

His mouth returned to her breasts. That combined with the rhythmic caress of his fingertips drove her to the brink of madness. Something fierce and dark and primitive possessed her.

She clutched his shoulders and muttered incoherently. Something... There was something waiting for her.

"Morgan?"

"Let go, honey. Just let go and—"

"Morgan!"

The something found her, bold and hot and savage in its fury. It gripped her madly, shook her like a rag doll caught in the grip of a frenzied beast, and then released her—slowly, particle by particle, until she felt as if her mind and body were one floating entity.

Awareness returned just as slowly. Morgan was raised on one elbow, a sea of sweat beading his brow. His fingertips still remained...*there*. A searing blush swept her naked skin.

He leaned forward and touched her breast with the tip of his tongue. "It's still hard." He raised his head and stared deeply into her eyes. "Are you still feeling it, honey?"

She nodded.

His finger slipped inside her. "And you're still wet."

She swallowed, a prisoner of his eyes and his touch.

"You're so tight, even against my finger...." Slowly, dizzily, he explored the inner shape of her. "Such a passionate little maiden."

His caress carried her to where she had been moments before. "Oh..."

"This time, open your eyes for me. I want to watch when it hits you."

Her gaze shot to his slumberous one. Her breath caught in her throat. He looked hot enough to catch fire. There was tension to him, a heightened sharpness about his features that suggested a rigid control. Somehow, the sight of him holding back, his dark hand against her, his clothed body, her naked one...

It took only an instant before she was twisting beneath his touch and crying out again.

"Sweet... You do that so sweetly, Anya."

"What about you?" she blurted, uncomfortably aware that she was the one out of control—and nude—while he seemed almost a spectator to what was going on.

He leaned forward and placed a kiss on her stomach, then looked up. "What about me?"

"Don't you want to... I mean..." She found it impossible to continue under his unwavering stare.

"I want to." He pulled her hand to him. "Feel how much I want to."

The hardened bulge beneath her fingertips seemed to increase the hollowness she felt. Heat and power pulsed beneath the coarse fabric.

She looked at him confusion.

"Believe me, there's no place I'd rather be than inside you, Anya." He closed his eyes briefly, then opened them. "But until we're married, I will not risk your getting pregnant."

"But—but..."

His head dipped, and again his tongue lazily sampled her breast. She squeaked.

"I'm going to make tonight something you'll never forget."

"Uh, I think it's safe to say that you've already succeeded."

"There's more," he said simply.

"More?" she inquired dubiously.

He nodded. "When I come to you on our wedding night, you'll be looking forward to it as much as I will—because you're going to know exactly what's in store for you."

She touched the dark lock of hair that had fallen across his forehead. "You're bragging."

"Texans never brag." The tip of his tongue found her navel. "We just have bigger truths than anyone else."

She smiled. "If I hadn't followed after you, you never would have had this opportunity to...instruct me."

Abruptly, his features sharpened. She regretted immediately bringing up the painful subject. When would she learn to keep her thoughts to herself?

"Anya, in my whole life, other than my father, I know of no one who would have put themselves in danger to ride after me. I want you to know that your gesture—"

He broke off, carefully pulling the coat over both of them. It shocked her that she had forgotten her nakedness, forgotten her ingrained sense of modesty even for a few minutes. How could she have changed so radically in the short time Morgan Grayson had charged into her life?

"Anya, I don't want to encourage this reckless streak you seem to possess. But I have to admit that I admire your courage. I know you're worried about the future, about adjusting to life on a ranch." He drew her to him. "Don't be. I consider it my duty to look after you. I won't let anything or anyone hurt you."

Duty...

In the darkness, lying next to his hard body, she sensed his leashed restraint. What would it take for Morgan Grayson to fall in love with her?

More to the point, could she travel all the way to America with a man who *didn't* love her? What if she discovered that all he could ever feel toward her was lust?

Her cheeks heated. There was a surprisingly strong case to be made for the physical side of marriage. She frowned. On the other hand, she was certain that without genuine affection, no union could long endure.

His strong arms drew her closer yet. It dazed her to realize she was laying naked in the arms of a man while calmly trying to organize a logical train of thought. The sound of his heartbeat, his deep even breathing, his musky scent, contrived to stir her in a way she'd never before experienced. She decided logic and reason could wait for another day. Morning wasn't that far off. And Morgan had promised to. . .

His hand moved slowly up her thigh.

Chapter Fifteen

As was its habit, the sun rose. Even though Anya's eyes remained closed, daylight sifted through her lowered eyelashes. She sensed she was alone on the pallet. At any rate, none of Morgan's solid frame pressed against her.

She lay on her side, facing where he had slept last night. Heat tingled along her skin. Not slept...not all night long. No longer did her body seem hers alone. Imprinted upon her flesh was his male scent. His husky words of praise echoed in her head, and his intimate touch warmed the blood flowing through her veins.

And, somehow, she was going to have to face him.

Last night there had been no guilt. Probably because, amid the rioting sensations whipping through her, there had been no place for guilt to hide. This morning, however, there seemed space aplenty for self-reproach to take hold and grow. She was well and truly a...a wanton. Her breathless cries of last night, her gasping pleas that Morgan join his body with hers...With vivid clarity, she recalled all he had done to her, and all she had begged him to do.

The door to the cottage opened. "Anya, where the blazes is the roan?"

In an effort to cover her exposed limbs, she pulled his coat up to her chin. "Uh, where you left him, I suppose."

"Where *I* left him?" The door closed. She heard him cross the small room. "I left him in Hobb's Corner."

"Yes..." She cleared her throat. "Yes, you did."

"Then . . ."

She was beginning to get used to the odd silence that so frequently sprang up between them. "I didn't have time to search him out," she explained, her eyes still sealed shut.

"Then what did you ride? There's nothing but an old, broken-down nag staked by the stream. . . ."

Another silence fell. It lasted the longest time. Long enough for her to wish Morgan's coat reached to her curling toes, long enough to wish she'd dressed, long enough to wish—

"Tell me you didn't, Anya."

"Didn't what?" It might be cowardly to stall this way, but look where bravery had gotten her.

"Didn't steal—"

Her eyes snapped open and she sat up. "I didn't *steal* him."

Morgan's coat fell to her waist. Immediately she felt his hungry gaze move across her bare skin. Flushing hotly, she jerked the coat back up.

Another silence. She darted a quick glance toward him. He looked as if he were in some kind of pain.

"I just . . . borrowed him," she continued, because at the moment Morgan seemed incapable of speech. "It was dark, I was in a hurry, and I took the first horse I found."

The muscles in his jaw flexed. "Get dressed. Now."

He turned on his heel and stalked to the door. Seconds later, it slammed shut with such ferocity that it flew clear off its rusted hinges and collapsed into a heap of rising dust motes.

Anya sneezed twice, then reached for her discarded clothing. Dressing took an inordinate length of time. The blisters on her palms made the process both difficult and painful. Her braided coronet had loosened, and her hair kept getting in the way. Frustrated, she decided to work it into a single plait. With her hairpins lost, however, there was no way to anchor it or secure the end.

Muttering, she glanced around the dismal cottage. Last night she'd been so enraptured by Morgan's intimate caresses she hadn't noticed the room's filthy condition. She reached for Morgan's coat and groaned. Twinges of soreness radiated from her bottom and . . . and other places that had been buffeted during the night.

She stepped over the broken door and blinked against the bright sunlight. Shivering, she slipped on the coat. There was no sign of Morgan. Her hands sank into deep pockets, where she encountered small pebbles in one and a piece of crumpled paper in the other. Absently, she withdrew the paper and smoothed its crinkled edges. Without making a conscious decision to do so, she began to read.

"Beloved . . ."

Another love letter from Collette! Anger, raw and fierce, spiraled through her. Blast the woman! Did she have nothing better to do than send shockingly improper messages to a man who wasn't her husband? It both hurt and frustrated Anya that Morgan had surely done the same things with Collette that he had done with her last night. And more, Anya reminded herself.

"No gloves, no saddle. Anya, what were you thinking?"

She spun around and shoved the letter back into the pocket. Morgan led the swaybacked beast from the thicket. Two sets of dark eyes reproached her. "I was thinking of—" She broke off and sneezed.

Morgan sighed. "Never mind."

He walked the horse about the clearing, no doubt examining it for a limp. She derived immense satisfaction that the beast managed to keep its four legs in motion with no evident flaw.

"It's obvious he can carry only one of us. You ride, Anya. I'll walk."

"I've ridden quite enough, thank you. You may ride and I shall walk."

Morgan's eyebrows lowered. "I'm only going to say this once. *I'll* wear the pants in our family."

Against her will, Anya's gaze lowered to his long legs and lean hips. "You may keep your trousers, Morgan. Believe me, I have no burning desire for them."

"Too bad," he drawled. "Now that I think about it, you'd look damned fetching in britches."

She knew she blushed. "Shall we go?"

"In a minute." He looped the reins over an accommodating branch and strode toward her. "Raise your skirts."

It was as if the day had turned to night and she were again naked in his embrace. "I will not."

"Then I will." He knelt before her and grabbed the hem of her skirt.

She batted his shoulders. "Stop that."

"Relax, honey. I'm not after your maidenly virtue, only a bit of petticoat."

She stood stock-still. It was demoralizing to admit to herself that she had precious little maidenly virtue left. Two quick rips rent the morning air.

He stood, casting a long shadow across her. "Hold out your hands."

She did so, and he swore savagely. She flinched both at his language and at the sight of her cracked and bleeding palms. It astonished her that when she'd wielded the broom handle last night, she'd felt no pain.

Morgan's jaw clenched as he gingerly bound her swollen flesh. "I'm going to strangle your sister."

"Merrawynn?"

He raked her with gleaming eyes. "Have you another?"

"No..."

"Then Merrawynn it will be." He pointed a finger at Anya. "And you can thank your lucky stars that your backside is already sore, because if it weren't, I'd paddle it."

He gripped her shoulders. "And another thing, Miss Delangue. A man likes to wake up to a sweet-tempered woman."

With that, he pulled her into his arms and kissed her soundly. It really was too much. She squirmed free.

"And how many different women have you wakened to, Mr. Grayson?"

His hands dropped from her and he stepped back. "We've already settled that."

She jerked the letter from its resting place and shook it beneath his nose. "I'm tired of finding letters from your paramours scattered from pillar to post."

He plucked the page from her wrapped hand, scanned its contents, then raised his gaze. "You read this?"

She nodded sharply.

One eyebrow arched. "All of it?"

She drew herself to her full height. "I do have scruples."

His gaze moved deliberately to the horse then back to her. "Where I come from, horse stealing is a hanging offense and reading a man's private correspondence is—"

"Is what?" she interrupted angrily. "A shooting offense?"

He had the gall to grin at her. "Read the rest of the letter, Anya."

She looked at his outstretched hand. She'd as soon pick up a snake. "I've already read one of Collette's letters. I have no desire to read another."

"This wasn't written by Collette."

"What? How many former lovers do you correspond with?"

"None. Now read the damned letter."

The exchange was reminiscent of another they had shared, the one where he had compelled her to read Richard's will. It did nothing for her peace of mind to recall she had lost that particular confrontation. She snatched the letter and began to read.

Each passing word blackened him further in her thoughts. Then she came to the signature. She knew her cheeks were scarlet.

"I did not write this, Morgan."

"I've already figured that out," he said dryly. "It's obvious from the wording, however, that Dickie, Harold and Alvin didn't, either."

"But I don't understand. What was the purpose behind it?"

"To lure me to the cave, where I could be assaulted."

"But not killed," Anya said thoughtfully.

"Not outright, but I was left to die. And when my body was found, it would look like an accident."

"That way no blame could be cast...."

"Right."

"I'm sorry, Morgan."

"That's all right." His grin returned. "Your jealousy is flattering."

"It wasn't a matter of jealousy," she corrected, lest he receive the wrong impression.

"Wasn't it?"

She shook her head emphatically. "It was a point of common decency, of...of propriety."

He nodded slowly. "I see."

"Good." She smiled back at him. "Shall we be on our way?"

"Just as soon as you give me what's in the other pocket."

She dug for the small pebbles. "I can't imagine what you need with..." Her words trailed off. The dull metal pellets contrasted against her white bandage. "What on earth?"

"Bullets," he answered succinctly. With that observation he calmly withdrew and loaded the pistol that hung about his hips.

She didn't ask if a loaded weapon were necessary. He could blast to kingdom come the next person who attacked him. Unexpectedly, her sister's image rose in her thoughts.

"Uh, Morgan..."

"Yes?"

"You wouldn't shoot Merrawynn, would you?"

He looked up from the ominous weapon he'd just loaded. "I don't think it will come to that."

"I know she's caused you nothing but trouble," Anya continued. "And she certainly needs a sound talking to, but... I don't want to see her hurt."

She told herself it was understanding she saw in Morgan's gaze.

"I feel the same way about my half brother, Justin. He's been nothing but a source of aggravation to me, but I'd hate to see him dead."

"Even after he stole your fiancée?" Anya asked softly.

"At the time, I was ready to kill him." A corner of Morgan's mouth curved upward. "Now I'm glad I restrained myself."

For fall, the day was pleasantly warm. They walked in another of their lingering silences, with Morgan leading the nag. Anya wondered what thoughts darkened Morgan's countenance. Every now and then a sharp rock cut into the thin soles of her silk slippers. She had no intention of complaining, since she'd learned long ago that complaining in and of itself never accomplished anything. She did envy him his sturdy boots, though. Perhaps in Texas, she would be able to purchase a pair for herself.

They came upon one of Edward's tenant farmers loading a cart with wheat for the grinding wheel. Morgan turned to her. "Do you want to ride in the cart?"

She eyed the half-filled wagon, then Bob Thatcher, a congenial man who'd once helped her down from an apple tree she'd had no business climbing. Bob's eyes widened in shock as he recognized her. "Good morning, Bob. It looks as if you're working hard."

"Miss Anya?"

"Yes, it is I." She smiled bleakly, wondering what gossip would be spread through Edward's estate before nightfall. Would the message be that the master's sister had fallen into madness? She groaned inwardly. Her brother did so hate gossip, especially that connected with the family name.

Bob glanced nervously at Morgan. "Do you need my help, Miss Anya?"

She shook her head and put her arm through Morgan's. "We were just . . . taking a walk."

At her inspired remark, Bob's round eyes shifted to the horse. "All three of you?"

Instead of answering, Morgan cleared his throat.

"Why, yes," she said quickly, not trusting what Morgan might say. Bob's gaze moved to her hands. "I went riding without gloves," she felt compelled to explain. "Blisters, you know."

Morgan's arm settled on her shoulders. "Come along, Anya."

She shot another what she devoutly hoped was a reassuring smile to Bob, then allowed herself to be led away. It amazed her that in the space of a few moments, her reputation could have become irrevocably tarnished. From her disheveled state, it must be obvious to Bob that she and Morgan had spent the night together.

"We'll marry at once."

She turned to Morgan. "That's hardly going to help now."

"You'll be living in Texas, Anya. Does it matter what the locals here think of you?"

Of course it mattered. She just didn't know why. They walked a short distance farther. A horseman rode into view. Anya recognized the rider as being Horace Winthrop, her brother's nearsighted bailiff. The man slowed his mount, obviously curious about the man, woman and horse walking along his employer's private country lane. It was just as obvious the bailiff had no idea who she was. Considering her rumpled appearance and the filmy spectacles perched upon his bulbous nose, Anya did not find his lack of recognition surprising.

Horace reined his mount, thereby effectively blocking her and Morgan's path. "Have you lost your way?"

"This is the road to the Delangue estate, is it not?" Morgan asked.

"Aye," Horace replied, adjusting his spectacles and craning his neck to get a clearer view of them.

And what a view he must have! Morgan with his bruised face, stubbled jaw and the weapon strapped to his hips, holding the reins to a bony horse in one hand and the arm of a wild-haired woman in the other. Casually, Anya used Morgan's shoulder to shield her face.

"Then we are not lost," Morgan returned matter-of-factly.

Horace removed his eyeglasses and wiped them against his sleeve. "Are you expected?"

"I'm Morgan Grayson and this is Anya Delangue, Sir Edward's sister."

Horace plopped his glasses back on and leaned so far forward he lost his balance and almost toppled from his horse before righting himself at the last moment.

"Miss Anya?"

She nodded miserably. It went against the grain to realize her appearance was frightful enough to knock a man off his saddle. "We suffered a slight mishap, Horace."

The man's jaw sagged. "I was headed to Greta's cottage because someone reported seeing smoke rising from her chimney, but I'll ride back to the manor and send a carriage for you."

A breeze snaked through Morgan's borrowed coat and Anya shivered, then suffered the indignity of having to wipe her nose upon one of the trailing sleeves. "We'd appreciate that, Horace."

"We'd also appreciate your being quick about it. Anya needs a hot bath."

How many times could a woman blush in one day? Apparently there was no limit to Morgan's unnerving directness.

"Thank you, Horace," she called after the retreating bailiff. He was in such a hurry, she doubted he heard her.

A short time later, the carriage arrived. To it, Morgan tethered the horse Anya had appropriated. It impressed her that even though the animal was a paltry piece of horse-flesh, its welfare was still important to Morgan.

Once inside the carriage, Morgan reached toward her, fishing about in the overlong coat sleeve until he found her hand. "It appears I'm going to make a less than favorable impression when I meet your brother."

"I fear we both are."

Morgan ran his fingers gently over her bandaged palm. "You're not afraid of him, are you?"

"Afraid of Edward?" Despite her gloomy state, Anya smiled. "My brother is not exactly the kind of man to strike fear or trepidation in anyone's heart." She nestled against

Morgan's accommodating shoulder. "What he is, however, is the most proper Englishman you will have the pleasure of meeting during your sojourn in England."

"Is that right?"

"Be prepared to be on your best behavior." She turned to Morgan and frowned. She wasn't at all convinced he had a best behavior. "Don't think you can get around him as you did Lady Hester. Edward has no sense of humor. Since he's a man, your flirtatious manner will be wasted."

Morgan's eyebrows rose. "I beg your pardon?"

"Well, it's quite obvious that you charmed Lady Hester by flirting with her and—"

"Lady *Hester?*" he all but sputtered.

"Do not pretend ignorance with me, Morgan Grayson. I saw you wink at her."

A corner of his mouth curved upward. "Oh, you saw that?"

"At the time I considered it a sneaky maneuver."

"It worked."

She sighed. "Yes, it did. But you need to understand about Edward. It has to do with our name."

"Delangue?"

"Quite so. Surely, you've noticed it isn't a proper English name at all."

"Sounds French."

"And so it is, from quite a few years back, you understand. Well, when my brother was in school, it seems the other boys teased him excessively about it. Anyway, when Edward returned home for the yuletide holidays one season, he had transformed himself into the most incredibly mannered young gentleman you would ever hope to meet. Of course, now and then he would forget himself and act quite human. But when father died, so did the old Edward."

Morgan squeezed her hand gently. "Anya?"

"Yes?"

"Don't worry. Your brother and I will get along fine."

She tried not to show her skepticism. The lean, hard American sitting next to her was as opposite from her generously paunched older brother as a man could be. "I hope so...."

The carriage drew to a stop before the manor house, and her words trailed off. The last time Anya had been home for a visit had been for the christening of Edward's second son. Morgan assisted her down, and she stood before the gracious manor where she'd grown up.

Like an irresistible force, the rock tower drew her gaze. She compelled herself to look away. Once the abandoned chamber had held a special magic for her and George. Now, it only reminded her that her brother was gone forever.

The wide doors to the manor sprang open, and a smiling Eunice rushed out. As she caught sight of Anya's disreputable state, however, the smile disappeared.

"Whatever happened to you?"

The question had scarcely passed her lips before another coach joined them on the wide lane that curved in front of the manor. Lady Hester's voice rang out clearly from inside the vehicle.

"Open this door at once." A footman jumped to obey, and Lady Hester emerged. Her gaze fell instantly upon Morgan and Anya. "It's about time you put in an appearance. I'll have you know that I've been twiddling my thumbs at Wilton's all this time, waiting for your arrival."

Even as the matron spoke, Anya saw the woman's eyes widen as she, too, took in Anya's and Morgan's rumpled state of dress.

Anya glanced at Morgan. In the face of both Eunice's and Lady Hester's shocked expressions, he seemed amazingly calm.

"We'll tell you about our... adventure later. Right now, Anya needs food, balm for her hands and a bath—in that order." He took her elbow and led her up the steps.

Both women brought up the rear. Lady Hester was the first to regain her aplomb. "Don't dawdle, Lady Eunice. You heard the man."

Several hours later, Anya looked about the bedchamber she had known as a child. Oddly, it seemed empty without Morgan's presence. How strange life was. She and Morgan had been alone together for only a night and half a day, hardly time enough for her to have grown so attached to him. Yet during that short space of time, they had been separated from the rest of the world. Somehow a powerful bond had been forged between them. Without Morgan beside her, Anya felt . . . incomplete.

Later, clean and scented, she bore no trace of the recent ordeal, other than her tender palms. Anya looked at the fresh bandages, the only outward evidence of the harrowing experience. Perhaps, if she looked into a mirror, she wouldn't notice the difference, but within her something had changed forever. She had become aware of a power, a feeling beyond herself. There had been a rush of excitement and . . . more. A connection had been made.

She felt more womanly than ever before. She also felt freer. And not only because of Morgan's impassioned lovemaking. The time they'd spent without the finer trappings of life, the trappings to which she was so accustomed, had made her realize there was a soaring kind of freedom to be found without the burden of civilization.

Was that what had drawn her to the abandoned smugglers' cave, a search for freedom? Was that why she had once enjoyed the manor's high tower, because a part of her longed to be unchained from the ordinary? She thought of her desire to become a governess and smiled wryly. It would never do. Now, being a mistress of a ranch in Texas—*that* seemed incredibly adventurous. There would be no stuffy drawing rooms, no frowning matrons—just herself, Morgan and their children building a new life for themselves.

A Great Adventure, to be sure.

Once the banns were posted, she would marry and travel to a new continent. Did it really matter that Morgan didn't love her? Couldn't she have enough love for the both of them? As the mother of his children, she might even be able to win his love. It could happen. If she believed enough . . .

There was a knock at the door, then it opened. Eunice peered inside. "Edward and Morgan have concluded their conversation, Anya. They are waiting to speak with you in the drawing room."

Anya's fingertips went automatically to her neat coronet. "I'm ready."

As she walked down the staircase with Eunice beside her, Anya thought of the times she'd run down the stairs with her braids flying. Her heart pounded. She had never really thought she would be walking calmly down the wide staircase to discuss arranging a wedding for herself. Had Morgan behaved himself and made a favorable impression upon her brother? In the final analysis, it didn't matter. She was of age and could marry without Edward's approval. Still—

"I wish I could tell you not to be nervous, Anya. But I honestly don't know what the state of affairs is between your fiancé and Edward. Several times, I heard raised voices."

Eunice delivered her dampening assessment as they stood outside the closed doors to the drawing room.

Anya moistened her lips. "It will be all right."

Not at all certain she spoke the truth, she opened the doors and stepped inside.

Edward directed a frowning gaze toward her. "Good. You're here."

Since the last time she'd seen him, her brother's paunch had widened and his hairline had receded. Morgan stood next to him, also wearing a forbidding expression. Despite their shared sober countenances, the contrast between the two men couldn't have been greater. Edward's coat and trousers were of the finest fabrics. There were rings on his smooth hands and a precisely tied cravat about his jowled neck.

Even though Morgan was freshly shaved and bathed, he had dressed in roughly textured trousers and a simple cotton shirt. Slung low about his hips, his pistol was still in marked evidence. Lean and fit, her fiancé resembled a circling hawk.

The moment she entered the room, Morgan moved toward her. "You look revived."

At his approving smile, her stomach lurched. He always made her so conscious of her femininity. "I'm quite recovered, thank you."

He brushed his fingertips against the pale material of her sleeve. "I've never seen you in yellow before. The color becomes you."

Another blush came to call. "Eunice lent me one of her gowns."

"I doubt I shall ever fit into it again," her sister-in-law said regretfully.

Anya's brother harrumphed. "We have more urgent matters to discuss than the color of Anya's gown."

"Of course we do, Edward," Eunice said smoothly. "But it's been a long time since we last saw your sister and in the interim she's grown into a beautiful young woman."

Beautiful? *Young?* At four and twenty, Anya considered herself very mature. As for being beautiful, that was probably politeness or nearsightedness on Eunice's part.

A look of impatience crossed her brother's features. "Fine. Fine. Anya is young and beautiful and ruined. Does that make you happier?"

Unperturbed, Eunice smiled. "Yes, dear, it does. Shall we be seated? I'll ring for tea."

Somehow seeing a rough-and-tumble Morgan cross the dainty drawing room sparked a feeling of lightheartedness within Anya. It was almost as if a knight had burst forth from the pages of King Arthur's court, ready to do battle on her behalf.

Morgan joined her on the settee. "Anya's reputation would not have been compromised if she'd done as she'd been told and stayed put."

Her tender feelings vanished. "I saved your ungrateful life!"

He captured one of her bandaged hands. "Considering I survived a war on my own, I would have managed."

"Oh! I—"

"Desist, Anya," Edward interrupted unceremoniously. "Morgan Grayson has the right of it. We had a long discussion on the subject of your foolhardy escapade, and both of us are of the same mind. You need your wings clipped."

Anya tried to jerk her hand free. Morgan patted it affectionately, then had the audacity to wink at her. At once, she understood what he had done—used the same tactics with her brother as he had with Lady Hester. He had made allies of potential antagonists by focusing upon *her* unconventional behavior. His underhanded methods wrung a reluctant smile from her. It seemed her knight wore tarnished armor.

"The sooner the marriage takes place, the better," Edward continued. "First thing tomorrow, Morgan, you can ride to the registry office and secure a special license. When you return, the Reverend Dingby will marry you at the family chapel."

"What about the banns?" Morgan asked.

"The special license will dispense with the need. We will post an announcement in the papers after the ceremony takes place."

Morgan nodded. "That's fine with me."

So cut and dried. So much a matter of business.

The maid arrived with the tea and cakes. Eunice gestured to the low oval table before them. "Leave the tray, Lottie. I'll pour."

Morgan's large hands dwarfed the delicate cup Eunice handed him. Anya accepted a cup and sipped slowly, her earlier euphoria ebbing in the face of Edward's and Morgan's casual dispensing of the most important event in her life.

"Ah, there you are."

At Lady Hester's greeting, Morgan and Edward rose. "Madame, please join us," her brother urged.

The matron marched into the room and accepted the chair Edward offered. "Tea. Good." She set aside her cane and, sitting straight-backed, allowed a cup to be poured for her. "Now, then, where are we on the wedding arrangements?"

* * *

The following morning, Anya stood on the front steps of the manor house and politely bade Morgan farewell. Eunice and Edward stood next to her. She wished she and Morgan could have this moment alone.

A damp chill pervaded the morning air and a mist hung over the courtyard. Morgan wore his greatcoat with the wool collar turned up. She wanted his arms around her, as they'd been last night. She wanted his mouth on hers and—

He drew her hand to his lips. His warm breath against her knuckles chased away the chill.

"I see you've dispensed with your bandages."

"Since my hands are almost healed, I didn't think I needed to wrap them." Such trivial words to express what she wanted to say.

I love you.

Return quickly.

A carriage pulled up. Anya tried not to resent the fact that their wedding was being postponed for two more days because Morgan had been summoned by Richard's solicitor in London to settle the estate.

When Morgan turned to leave, an invisible cord seemed to pull Anya toward him. "Morgan . . ."

Stopping, he looked back at her. "Yes?"

"You'll take care, won't you?"

A familiar look of mischief flickered in his dark eyes. "I always take care, Anya."

His cocky words drew a reluctant smile. "So I've noticed."

He stood, midway between the carriage and herself. She knew this was one of those frozen moments out of time she had read about in novels. And even though Anya had no memento of it, she would remember forever the look of Morgan standing before her—tall, virile, undaunted. That would be the image of him she would always hold in her heart—even when he was old and stooped.

"Ah, hell . . ."

It took a second for his words to register. That was all the time he needed to cross the distance separating them and pull her into his arms. His hard mouth found hers and unleased a wild summer storm. The hard heat from his body magically transformed the month to August. He was so solid, so...strong.

She kissed him back—the way he'd taught her. Her hands circled his neck, drawing him even closer. When she became aware of the softening pressure of his lips, she countered by deepening her part of the kiss.

His mouth ranged to her forehead, cheeks and the tip of her nose. "Passionate little warrior..."

Only she heard his husky endearment.

"Believe me, I'll hurry back, Anya."

She let go of him reluctantly, thinking it was the hardest thing she'd ever done. He got into the carriage that would take him to the train station, and an unreasonable anger stirred. Why couldn't she go with him? Why did custom dictate she wait behind? Ooh, if she were in charge of things, the world would be a different place indeed.

"Anya..."

She looked over her shoulder at Eunice. "What?"

"Morgan will return the day after tomorrow."

"So?"

"Uh, I think you'll be more comfortable if you wait for him inside."

"Oh..." Anya looked around the deserted courtyard and shivered. As she turned to go inside, she kept her gaze from Edward. Why go out of her way to encounter what she knew would be a disapproving glance?

Later that afternoon, Anya stood on a footstool in Eunice's bedchamber while Mary, a local seamstress, knelt before her.

"A flounce will do it," Mary pronounced with obvious satisfaction. "And it won't take no time at all to put it on."

Anya looked at Eunice in surprise. "I never noticed how tall you were."

Her sister-in-law shrugged. "I've never felt particularly tall. Actually, I think I'm of average height."

With a start, Anya realized Eunice was right. "I suppose that because Merrawynn is so petite, I've felt like a giant next to her."

Eunice's gray eyes filled with sympathy. "Poor Merrawynn."

"Poor Merrawynn?" Anya wasn't certain she'd heard correctly.

"Why, yes. I've always felt sorry for her being so short. As lovely as she is, she'll never be able to wear the kind of gowns you can."

"What do you mean?"

"Well, anything truly dramatic would overpower Merrawynn. With her pale coloring, she can't wear very vivid colors, nor any heavy pieces of jewelry."

At Mary's nod, Anya stepped from the stool and moved behind the dressing screen where the seamstress assisted her from the white gown. As she pulled on a silky pink wrap— also lent to her by Eunice—she thought about her sister-in-law's comments.

Feeling sorry for Merrawynn took some getting used to, especially since Anya was furious with her sister. "Thank you again, Eunice, for lending me your wedding gown and veil."

"And corset," Eunice added, her eyes twinkling. "Did you really think you could get away without one?"

Anya flushed. "It wasn't exactly my idea."

"Whyever not? They're odious, hateful things and I go without whenever I'm at home."

"Really?"

Eunice laughed. "Oh, Anya, quite a few women do. We just keep it a closely guarded secret."

"But—but I never knew that."

"That's because you grew up without a mother to teach you these things." At her words, Eunice looked stricken. "Oh, I didn't mean to bring up something painful...."

"It's all right. It doesn't bother me to talk about it."

"Oh, Anya, you've had a hard life, what with losing your parents and George, and Richard dying...." Eunice hugged her. "I'm so glad you found Morgan Grayson. It's time you had some happiness. And being married to a man who's madly in love with you is the best thing of all."

"Oh, he doesn't love me," Anya felt constrained to point out. "It's a marriage of convenience."

Eunice laughed. "You can't expect me to believe that! I saw the kiss you exchanged this morning when Morgan left."

"Oh, that..." Anya gestured with her arm. "That was strictly passion."

"What?"

Anya nodded sadly. "Merrawynn explained it all to me years ago—except I really was too young to understand what she was talking about. About how men desire women but don't really love—not the way we read about in books."

"Morgan *loves* you, Anya. If you're too blind to see it, that is your problem. But never believe that men are unable to give and receive love. They are quite capable of experiencing deep sensitivity. Finding the right woman is the most important event that can happen to a man."

"Perhaps," Anya conceded.

Eunice sighed. "I'm feeling a bit tired. I'm going to rest for a while... and perhaps have a cherry tart."

"You do that."

Anya stared after Eunice's departing back. Thoughtfully, she slipped off the wrap and reached for her gown. Instead of comforting her, Eunice's words stirred up old ghosts for Anya. If Morgan were capable of falling in love and he hadn't yet done so with her, then... it was unfair to insist he go through with the wedding. Anya finished buttoning the front of her dress. She refused to feel guilty about not being noble enough to let Morgan go. *No* woman was that noble.

An hour after her nap, Eunice returned to Anya's bedchamber carrying a shimmering veil across her arm. A vague memory stirred—of another veil, of another time. Wispy netting trailed downward and outward into a cascade of billowing white. The satin crown narrowed to a V from which a single, teardrop pearl hung suspended.

"It's beautiful," Anya breathed, her voice reverent.

Eunice fluffed the delicate folds. "Mother was determined that—at least upon the occasion of my marriage—I would be beautiful."

Anya's gaze darted to her sister-in-law. "You *were* beautiful."

"Yes, on that day I was." Eunice smiled ruefully. "How could anyone help but be radiant when draped in satin and pearls? You know, I believe that's when Edward first began to love me—when he saw me in my wedding finery."

"I'm sure you're right," Anya said quickly. "Thank you so much for lending me these—"

"You've already thanked me. Here, stoop down a bit and let me slip this over your head."

Anya complied.

"Your braid is in the way. Hurry and unfasten it."

"If I do, there will be hair flying every which way. You have no idea how wild—"

"Anya, I know for a fact that you are four and twenty. And I've never seen you wear your hair in anything but a coronet."

"It's tidier that way."

"And spinsterish. In case you haven't noticed, you're getting married, not joining a nunnery. Now let down your hair."

Anya did as she was instructed, and with her free hand, Eunice ran her fingers through the unloosened braids. "What I see is lovely, dark hair, and it's a shame to hide it. We'll have Maude dress it for the ceremony. We'll also have her instruct Mavis, so she can style your hair when you're in America. As lovely as it is, it will have to be cut. There," Eunice pronounced at last. "Look into the mirror."

Anya moved to the mirror that hung above the dresser. For a moment she couldn't speak. The reflection that stared back at her was not that of a gawky girl. In fact, with her hair feathered about her face and the veil swirling about her head and shoulders ... Even to her own perfect vision, she was quite lovely. No longer did her eyebrows seem so heavy, nor her nose so prominent. All the features of her face combined together in a wholly pleasing manner.

"Do you suppose anyone would think it odd if I wore the veil every day?"

Eunice shook her head. "Oh, Anya, you don't need the veil to make you beautiful." Her image joined Anya's in the mirror. "Compare our features. I truly am unremarkable—"

Anya opened her mouth to protest.

"No, don't try and make me feel better by spouting nonsense. I have two chins and my eyes are too close together. My lips are thin and my nose turns up. But, Anya, I *like* the way I look. It suits me. And even if your lashes were not quite so thick or your eyes quite so wide or your mouth quite so full, it would still be important for you to like yourself. It just so happens, however, that you *are* truly lovely. And I think you need to know that."

Anya turned and hugged her sister-in-law. "No wonder Edward loves you so."

Eunice's gray eyes sparkled mischievously. "Now, there's a handsome figure of a man, don't you agree?"

Anya blinked. "Uh, my brother?"

Eunice nodded vigorously. "The first time I saw him, he quite took my breath away."

Edward? "I ... I agree. My brother is quite ... an ... eyeful."

Eunice giggled. "Oh, Anya, you are priceless. I'm going to miss you. Perhaps I will be able to talk your brother into taking us to visit you and Morgan in America."

"You would be most welcome."

Mary stepped into the chamber. "Lady Eunice, Sir Edward wants you to join him in the library. There's a visitor waiting for you."

"All right, Mary. Tell him I'll be right down." Eunice's brow puckered. "I wonder who's come to call unannounced?"

Left alone, Anya adjusted the crown of the veil. She liked the way the pearl fell against her forehead, reminding her of a picture she'd once seen of a Far Eastern princess. When Morgan saw her in the gown and veil, would he think she was beautiful?

"Hello, Anya."

At the sound of Merrawynn's voice, Anya's gaze jerked to the chamber doorway where her sister stood garbed in an elegant black gown. Unable to force any words beyond the anger and hurt that choked her, Anya stared numbly at Merrawynn.

Chapter Sixteen

"Eunice said she was lending you her veil." Her sister closed the door and leaned against it. "You do more for it than she ever did."

Tears burned the back of Anya's eyes. "I don't want to talk to you, I don't want to look at you. Please . . . leave."

Merrawynn flinched but stood her ground. "I'll leave—after I've convinced you not to marry the American."

Her sister's callous words unloosed the strange paralysis that had gripped Anya. Yet despite the fury raging through her, she carefully removed the veil and laid it across the bed. She was determined that, after this day, she would never speak to her sister again. It was important she let Merrawynn know precisely what she thought of her.

"You'll never talk me out of marrying Morgan."

Her sister stepped forward and raised her hands imploringly. "Just listen to me. That's all I ask."

"All you ask?" Anya demanded, her voice shaking. "You try to kill Morgan upon three separate occasions and you think you have the right to ask anything of me?"

Merrawynn's bright blue eyes filled with tears. "I had no part of that. You must believe me."

"Liar! The men you hired to kidnap Morgan told us everything—and they named you, Merrawynn. They *named* you."

Her sister put a beseeching hand on Anya's arm. "They were only to capture and hold him, not kill him."

Anya jerked her arm from Merrawynn's touch. "So they said. They weren't the kind of men to balk at murdering an uncooperative hostage, however."

"It's hard to hire decent criminals," Merrawynn said apologetically. "But believe me, I did try. You should have seen the scoundrels I refused to entrust with the American's life."

Anya almost wept in frustration. "You don't seem to understand what you've done."

"I was concerned only with your welfare. You cannot hate me for that."

"*My* welfare?" Anya asked bitterly. "For once in your life, Merrawynn, be honest with yourself. Your only interest in whom I marry is based on what it means to you financially."

"That's not true!"

Anya's hands curled into fists. "It all comes down to Richard's inheritance and the difference in pounds per annum to you."

Her sister shook her head vehemently. "Not this time. I was thinking only of you, Anya."

Anya laughed hollowly. "You never think of anyone save yourself."

"Maybe that's how it's been in the past, but—"

"Not the past. Now. Today." Anya stepped forward. "Morgan almost died. Can't you grasp that? He almost *died.*"

"At the cliffs," Merrawynn agreed quickly. "But when Boyd told me about the man he'd hired to kill Morgan, I cut Boyd from my life."

"Then who held a gun on Morgan and set the stables ablaze?"

"I...I don't know." Merrawynn's eyebrows drew together in confusion. "I didn't even know there had been a fire. After Boyd told me about the attempt on Morgan's life at the cliffs, I told him I never wanted to speak to him again. That's when I set about to solve the problem myself."

"Well, someone set fire to the stables."

Merrawynn's eyes widened. "You cannot believe it was
I!"

"If not, it must have been this Boyd person you've mentioned."

"You don't know Boyd. He might hire someone else to
commit such an act, but he wouldn't do it directly."

"Well, Merrawynn, apparently your friend decided to
take matters into his own hands. It doesn't matter at this
point, I suppose. He perished in the fire."

The color left her sister's face and she swayed, reaching
out to the dresser for support. "Boyd is dead?"

A surge of sympathy rose in Anya. She fought against it.
"If he'd had his way, it would have been Morgan who was
killed."

Her sister slowly crossed the room and sank to the bed.
Probably not even aware she did so, she caressed the shimmering veil next to her. "There was a time when I thought I
loved him, when I thought he loved me."

Merrawynn's huddled form struck a responsive cord
within Anya. Again, she tamped down any feelings of tenderness.

"I surmise Boyd was your lover?"

Her sister's head snapped up, and she brushed back the
falling tears. "Only after Richard's death. I never betrayed
my marriage vows."

"Considering the small amount of time you spent with
Richard, you had ample opportunity to conduct an affair."

The pale hand stilled. "I'm not proud of my behavior,
Anya. Looking back on my life, I see I've made some terrible mistakes. That's why I'm here now, to keep you from
making the same kind of mistakes. Why can't you understand?"

"There's always the matter of Richard's estate."

Merrawynn's lips thinned. "Damn the money. This is
about something more important—your happiness."

Anya looked into her sister's face and for the first time felt
a stirring of doubt. She couldn't remember Merrawynn ever

being so insistent about being believed. "And what is this terrible mistake from which you must save me?"

"From marrying a man you do not love," she answered simply.

"But I love Morgan."

Her sister stared at her solemnly. "Do you? Do you really?"

"I do."

Merrawynn rose from the bed. "And does he love you?"

Anya flushed. "Perhaps not now, but—"

"In life there is only now. Believe me, I've learned the hard way that there are no guarantees. Life is too short to spend it living in the future. For years, I kept thinking that when Richard died I would have everything I needed to be happy. And there was Boyd, courting me, wooing me, for all the wrong reasons.

"I talked myself into believing I could never love Richard. I talked myself into believing I did love Boyd. And all of it was a lie. Happiness was there for the taking, but I never saw it. I wasted my life wishing for something I didn't realize I already possessed—Richard's love."

"My love will be enough for both Morgan and me," Anya said stubbornly, wishing her sister would let the subject drop.

"How can it be, when your chief appeal to the American is the wealth Richard has made available to him should you wed? You deserve better than that! Even homely Eunice deserves better than that."

"But Edward didn't love her when they married," Anya pointed out, clutching at straws.

"He respected her. He admired her. She was exactly what he wanted in a wife. For our brother, those attributes constituted love."

"I'm sure Morgan feels those selfsame sentiments toward me."

Merrawynn reached out and grasped Anya's hands. "I pray you are right."

"It will all work out. You'll see."

Her sister studied her with obvious concern. "Then you're determined to go through the ceremony? No matter what?"

Anya nodded abruptly.

"I . . . I do not trust him to love and care for you as you deserve, Anya. He is not worthy of you."

"No matter how you feel, Merrawynn, the choice is mine." Anya squeezed her sister's cold hands. "And I want your promise that you won't interfere again between myself and Morgan."

"But—"

"But nothing." She let go of Merrawynn. "I don't know if I'm ever going to be able to forgive you for the pain you've already caused Morgan. If you try again to prevent our wedding from taking place, I . . . I shall never see or speak to you again."

"Everything I did was for your benefit," Merrawynn repeated woodenly.

"And yours. There is no way to separate the fact that if Morgan and I don't marry, you increase your share of Richard's estate."

Her sister shook her head tiredly. "It's no use, is it? You'll always believe me to be the selfish girl you grew up with."

"I . . . I love you, Merrawynn. But I won't let you run or ruin my life. If you require more funds to live comfortably, perhaps Morgan will—"

"Never mind, Anya. Don't go to Morgan on my behalf. Richard did leave me comfortably settled. As he had no heir, save a foreigner, I am content with the title of Marchioness and Richard's bequest."

As much as she wanted to believe her sister, Anya found it impossible to do so. For too long, Anya had lived with a self-centered and greedy Merrawynn. It would take years for Anya to trust the "new" sister standing before her. Feeling guilty for her skepticism, Anya cast about for something noncommittal but reassuring to say. Her gaze fell upon the veil.

"Will you stay for the ceremony?"

Merrawynn laughed ruefully. "Edward will have my skin if I'm not in attendance." She glanced down at her finely textured black gown. "I'm in mourning. Will that cast a pall over the occasion?"

"Morgan is very impatient ... to return to Texas."

A wistful expression claimed Merrawynn's delicate features. "Richard was also a very unusual man, was he not? Despite the gossip, he married a woman young enough to be his granddaughter...."

"A very beautiful young woman," Anya added softly.

"A very *ambitious* woman," Merrawynn corrected. "It's so strange.... I thought I knew exactly what I wanted and what I needed to do to get it." She sighed. "Ever since I was born, Mama taught me that I must marry and marry well. I think Papa was a disappointment to her. She seemed to think she married below her station.

"Perhaps that's why they spent so much time on the continent. That way Mama could impress strangers with her importance. And that's why she probably gave us such peculiar names, to make us seem unique. You should have heard what she wanted to name George, until Papa put his foot down."

"She doted on you," Anya observed quietly.

"And Edward, also."

"After she had both of you, she really didn't need more children, did she?"

Merrawynn smiled sadly. "Oh, poppet, it hasn't been a very good life for you, has it? Mama scarcely noticed your existence, Papa was always off in his own world, and Edward was a well and proper bore. And I ... I was concerned only with myself."

"At least you were never boring."

"I take that as a compliment." Merrawynn moved toward Anya and enfolded her in a tight hug, then stepped back. "You were never boring, either. I remember you and George playing in the high tower, dashing hither and thither to thwart imaginary pirates and spending hours in the library looking through Papa's nature books." Her sister paused, staring at Anya intently. "You know, I loved him, too."

Anya looked into Merrawynn's wide blue eyes, eyes that were filled with pain, and realized she had never considered what George's death had meant to her sister.

"Sometimes, he would slip into my room at night and leave a present for me. I still have several tucked away in my jewel box."

In that moment, Anya felt a kinship with her sister she hadn't experienced in years, perhaps ever. "I've saved a couple of things, too."

"I have this grotesque piece of what I'm certain is the tip of old Dolly's tail," Merrawynn continued, obviously lost in the past. "George claimed it was the tip of a leprechaun's beard."

The quick rush of tears caught Anya by surprise. "He was very special, wasn't he?"

Merrawynn nodded. "I . . . I think I'll retire to my chamber and freshen up."

Anya noticed her sister surreptitiously brush away new tears. "I shall see you later, then."

"Count on it, dear sister."

Morgan stared out the train window and, for the first time since coming to England, began to doubt both himself and his mission. It was impossible not to contrast the lush beauty of the farmlands flicking by to the rugged and primitive terrain to which he would be transplanting Anya.

How would she react to summer days when the temperature climbed to the century mark? Would she find any beauty in the stark plains and desert hills that made up his ranch? And what about Big Rock Gulch? How could that pitiful little town compare with London?

She had resisted him at every turn, but he had waged a major campaign to win her. By using her innocence, her untouched passion and her sense of honor, he had finally gotten her to agree to marry him. For the first time Morgan wondered if he was being fair to her.

Anya was everything he could have hoped for in a wife and mother to his children. But what was he to her? She'd called him a beast.... He shifted in the hard leather seat. In the civilized atmosphere of London society, he certainly qualified as that. But in the do-or-die environment of Texas, beastly qualities kept a man alive.

The train's whistle sounded, and Morgan felt the train lurch as the engineer applied shrieking brakes. A platform emerged from the thinning morning fog, revealing a thatched cottage and a grove of chestnut trees. One thing was certain—once she stepped foot in Texas, Anya would never again see another quaint scene like the one unfolding before him.

In a way it would be like going from the future to past. He couldn't help wondering how his bride would adapt to living as her countrymen had, say... fifty to a hundred years ago.

The train slowed, then stopped. A fashionably dressed young lady with a plump matron in tow came down the narrow aisle toward him. The coach car was crowded, and the only empty bench was the one across from him. With obvious reluctance the older woman motioned to the younger one to take the seat next to the window. The matron settled her ample frame in the aisle seat as the train began its swaying motion.

Morgan's gaze drifted over the young lady. She was startlingly lovely, with a pale English complexion and delicate mouth. Her eyes were wide and blue and... sparkling with interest. A brief glance at the rest of her revealed her to be charmingly curved.

Morgan looked away from her smiling face. He didn't experience even a flicker of interest. That discovery caught him off guard. Had he become so entranced by the thorny, stubborn and headstrong Anya Delangue that he was no longer attracted by anyone else? It was a sobering thought.

Obviously a one-woman man, Morgan realized he was different from his father. He thought of Collette and smiled grimly. Thank God he'd been given a second chance to find the right woman. Anya Delangue... Proud and starchy in her high-necked gowns and English drawing rooms. Anya Delangue... Soft and passionate and...eager in an abandoned cottage. He'd take her both ways. For a lifetime. And she would damned well adjust to life on a Texas ranch.

In one blinding moment of comprehension Morgan realized he could not live without his English thorn.

"Now, Frederick, don't pull at your Aunt Anya's skirts," Eunice instructed her two-year-old son from across the drawing room.

Despite the fact that a full day had passed since the confrontation with her sister, Anya's emotions were still raw and close to the surface. As she stared at Eunice's sons, Anya tried to smile past the rising lump in her throat. Herbert Delangue was a dark-eyed, slender boy who bore an uncanny resemblance to George. Herbert's younger brother, Frederick, was a chubby, golden-haired two-year-old with round eyes and an equally round tummy. The duo reminded Anya of two frolicsome puppies.

"He's all right, Eunice. I don't mind a few creases in my gown." Anya knelt to stare directly into the lad's eyes. "I'm very pleased to see you again, Frederick."

At once, the boy stuck his thumb into his mouth and scampered back to his mother. "He's so unpredictable," Eunice said, gathering him onto her lap. "Sometimes he's bold as brass and sometimes he's fiercely shy."

Anya heard the love in her sister-in-law's voice. It was late afternoon and the nanny had brought the boys, freshly bathed and dressed in proper little suits, for their mother's inspection. There was no question they met with her approval. "Are you hoping for a daughter this time?"

"Boy or girl—it doesn't matter as long as it arrives healthy."

"Do all small children drool so?" Merrawynn asked, wrinkling her nose.

Eunice laughed. "I'm afraid so. It has to do with cutting teeth. Frederick's getting the last of his."

Merrawynn nibbled on an almond biscuit. "Thank goodness for that."

Anya stared at her sister with a mixture of affection and exasperation. She wondered if Merrawynn would ever change, if there was a man somewhere who could teach her what true love was all about. Had Richard been younger, perhaps he could have been the one. As Anya stared at her beautiful sister, she almost pitied her. There was so much of life and the reason for living that Merrawynn still failed to comprehend.

Anya's gaze returned to the boys. The nanny had returned to take them upstairs for their dinner. Eunice rose awkwardly from her chair. "I think I'll take a nap before the evening meal."

Anya and Merrawynn stared after their sister-in-law.

"How many do you suppose she intends to have?" Merrawynn asked in horrified fascination.

"Five is a good number, don't you think?"

"Five!" Her sister shuddered. "I would strangle any man who did such a thing to me."

Anya couldn't help smiling at Merrawynn's offended expression. "I'm looking forward to having children."

"You would." Her sister yawned. "I think I'll rest before dinner."

"I'm going to take a walk."

"It's raining."

Anya looked out the drawing-room windows to the darkening sky. "It's at times like this that I miss the conservatory."

"An expensive piece of nonsense, if you ask me."

Anya shrugged. "I'll see you at dinner."

Left to her own devices, Anya wandered through the house she'd known since childhood. She considered braving the rain for a brisk walk through the gardens and decided against it. There was a chill in the air that seemed to seep into the manor itself.

Instead, she went to her room. There were some books she'd left behind when she'd gone to Hobb's Corner, volumes she'd decided to take to America with her. From Morgan's descriptions of his homeland, she suspected there was no nearby place to purchase reading materials.

It was a pleasurable way to spend an hour. The small fireplace in her room had been stoked, and she felt cozy and snug while thunder and lightning vied for supremacy over the approaching night. After the books had been packed away, her gaze fell upon the ungainly green rock, George's King of the Frogs, sitting on her dresser.

She went to it and cupped its heavy weight in her hands. Her thoughts went to Herbert and Frederick. She wondered if they would ever find and explore the high tower. Somehow she could see them there in a few years, playing their own games of adventure. With a start she realized it had been almost eight years since she'd last stepped inside the old chamber.

Not bothering to analyze her actions, she hugged the King of the Frogs to her while reaching for several long matches from the mantle. She tucked them into her skirt pocket and headed for the tower. Before she could travel to America, she had one more goodbye to bid. She took the back staircase and her familiar route through the kitchens. Succulent smells of dinner wafted through the air and her stomach growled. She snatched a raisin tart, expecting Cook to chastise her. But the times had changed and a new cook reigned over the kitchens. Evidently, he didn't consider it his place to chide her for filching a trifling tart.

She quickly demolished the pastry and took a narrow hall to the oldest section of the manor, passing a thin-furred calico cat as she went. The cat had no business being inside the house. Its mousing definitely should have been conducted outside. Probably Herbert had smuggled the animal into the house. She decided to keep the boy's secret, and continued walking.

She passed several small storage rooms and took an even narrower hall to a seldom-used stairway that led downward. She struggled to open a heavy door, which admitted her to a tiny, closed-off courtyard. The storm found her

there, and she hurried across the ivy-choked flagstone. She
remembered well how she and George would feel at this
point, as if they had magically moved into the past.

A rock wall shielded her from the worst of the rain. Exhilarated, she reached for the heavy latch of a weathered
door, the door that led to the high tower.

A noise from behind made her jerk around. She saw
nothing through the growing darkness and supposed the cat
had followed her. Driven now by a sense of urgency she
didn't understand, she hurried up the steep stone steps that
led to the private bower. The staircase curved sharply, re-
quiring one to literally wind his way upward to the high
chamber.

At last, one final door separated her from her destination. It was locked, of course, but Anya wasn't disappointed. She knew the key would be exactly where she had
left it eight years ago. There was enough light and her
memory was good enough for Anya to locate the key on her
first try. It lay beneath an ancient pot sitting next to the
door.

It took only a moment for her to fit the key into the lock
and push aside the last barrier. Despite the meager illumination that poured from a high window chiseled in the stone
wall, the room was dark. Purposefully, she moved toward
a table she remembered being in the center of the room. She
sat the King of the Frogs upon the table and reached into the
folds of her gown for the matches she'd brought. The candles were where she'd left them, and in short order a yellowish light spilled through the room.

Her curious gaze probed the darkened, dusty corners. It
was the same. Smaller than she remembered and definitely
dirtier, but basically the same. A secret place shut off from
the rest of the manor, where one could imagine he had been
cast into an earlier century. Here and there she saw mementos of games she and George had left—a couple of sticks
they'd pretended were swords, a few faded pillows they'd
sneaked into their special, private place, some trinkets
they'd won at a fair and pretended were priceless gems.

She looked around the small room and sighed heavily. If she closed her eyes, Anya could almost hear George's laughter—and her own, mingled with his. Her gaze fell upon the King of the Frogs. Smiling past her tears, she looked around the chamber. Where should she leave him? In a place of honor, surely. Atop the table in the center of the room, where he could watch over things until another generation of young explorers came calling?

Anya picked up the rock. When she squinted just so, it did resemble a haughty frog who might have boasted a royal ancestry. She kissed it lightly, then sat it on the table.

"Merrawynn was right," a male voice observed. "You are an odd duck."

Anya whirled around. Beyond the small perimeter of light cast by the candle stood a darkened form. "Who are you? What do you want?"

"Why, I've come to congratulate the *bride....*" he said, drawing out the final word until it sounded obscene.

Anya's hand rose to her heart. "I asked you who you are. I expect an answer."

"Allow me to introduce myself," he said with a mocking bow. "Boyd Williams, at your service, madame."

Anya's stomach lurched. "B-Boyd Williams?"

He stepped into the light, his lips twisting into a stiff smile. "I see my name means something to you."

"You're the one who tried to kill Morgan."

His dark brows rose in distaste. "*Tried* being the pivotal word, I'm afraid. Hard man to kill, your fiancé."

Feeling light-headed, Anya sagged against the table. Boyd Williams's manner of dress was that of a gentleman. He was tall, well-formed and smoothly handsome. A wave of revulsion cut through her. Somehow those attributes made him all the more menacing.

She licked her dry lips. "What are you doing here?"

"Since your bridegroom is so damnably difficult to dispatch, I've decided to— Please accept my heartfelt apology for this, Miss Delangue, but I find myself in the embarrassing position of having to kill you."

That he could pronounce such words in his calm, cultured voice terrified her. "You're mad."

"No," he countered almost gently. "Not mad, just desperate. You're standing between me and what I want. Believe me, if I had a choice I would not hurt such a comely woman. It goes against my grain to destroy beauty in any form."

He moved toward her and Anya cursed the table that blocked her retreat. "W-what good will my death do you?"

"As Merrawynn's husband—"

"She won't marry you," Anya interrupted hastily. "She's furious with you for trying to kill Morgan."

"I will apologize for that."

"And you think she'll accept your apology?" Anya asked on a thread of hysteria.

"She'll be grieving your death. I'll comfort her, tell her how keenly I regret her pain. I know you love your sister. Rest assured I will help her recover from her grief."

"She thinks you're dead," Anya said frantically.

He paused. "What?"

"She thinks you burned to death in the fire that destroyed the stables."

"Does she?" He smiled at the news. "Then she will be relieved to find out that is not the case."

"No," Anya countered. "She's not mourning you. She could never love a murderer."

"But I won't be a murderer," he replied patiently. "Your death will be a horrible accident. Morgan will still live. What cause will she have to reproach me?"

"The man you hired to kill Morgan—"

"I'm truly sorry for that. In my desperation to protect Merrawynn from Richard's demented will, I lost my senses. Ashamed, I went away for a time. But I couldn't live without Merrawynn, so I returned to ask her forgiveness. Imagine my shock and dismay to learn her sister had broken her neck in a tragic fall."

Anya shivered. "She won't take you back. My death will accomplish nothing."

"Of course it will. Merrawynn will be heartbroken, and I will be there to comfort her." His eyes gleamed with satisfaction. "Trust me, Anya. I know how to comfort a woman. My embrace, the caress of my hand against her flesh, my mouth upon hers... She will turn to me and I will bring her happiness."

"Who died in the fire?" Anya asked, casting about for a weapon to use against him. Oh, how she wished she had Morgan's pistol, or even a broom handle.

"His name is unimportant. Suffice it to say, he was no match for the American."

"You don't sound—"

"Shh, Anya. You have all the answers you need. It's time to accept your fate and make your peace with God."

The table's edge dug into her hip. "It will never work. Merrawynn won't take you back."

"Don't worry about your sister. I'll take care of her. Just close your eyes, Anya. I'll make this quick, almost painless."

She shoved against his chest. He gripped both her wrists in his. "Don't fight me. I'm going to snap your neck. It shouldn't hurt much. I'm a strong man."

He raised the hands manacling her wrists as if to assure her. "I don't think you'll experience more than a twinge of discomfort. A quick twist and it will be over."

"Then what?" Anya asked, almost hypnotized by his reasonable tone.

"Then I'll push you down the stairs. Everyone will assume the fall broke your neck. I'm going to rip your hem. It will look as if your toe became caught in the rent and you tripped. I've thought of everything. No one will doubt it wasn't a tragic accident."

Fascinated despite herself, Anya realized he *had* thought of everything. He'd thought of everything, that is, but the fact she would not go tamely to her own death. No matter what, it would *not* appear an accident. She'd see to that.

"And you'll be united with dear little George," Boyd said softly.

That this beast should know, let alone speak her brother's name, spurred Anya to action. She kicked out viciously against his shin. Unlike the giant, Dickie, Boyd proved eminently hurtable.

His shout of outrage cheered her immensely. She followed that attack by sinking her teeth into the flesh of his right hand. Yelping, he let her go and stepped back. It was obvious he'd been unprepared for her defensive action.

"You bitch!"

He lunged for her, but she'd already made it around the table. Without hesitation, he shoved the barrier aside, pitching the lighted candle and the table's other contents onto the stone floor. Anya tried to dart past him. He grabbed her elbow and spun her around. She kicked out again, but her skirts had twisted and she was unable to deliver a powerful enough blow to hurt him.

His other hand clamped on hers, and he jerked her to him. Her frantic struggles succeeded only in toppling both of them to the floor. He fell hard on top of her, knocking the breath from her lungs. She lay dazed beneath him and felt his strong fingers close around her neck. She tried to claw his face but couldn't reach him.

Faint-headed, she dropped her hands, one falling painfully against something hard. She needed air desperately, but his powerful grip denied her the precious element. Spots swam before her eyes. He jerked her upward and she felt him reposition his hands. Just as he'd threatened, he was going to snap her neck.

With her last vestige of strength, Anya closed her hand around what she realized was the King of the Frogs. She smashed it viciously against Boyd's head. The sickening thud of rock striking flesh made her stomach heave. Boyd fell backward, his stranglehold loosening. She wrested herself from beneath him and scrambled away on all fours, trying to find the doorway. The pervasive darkness hemmed in about her, however, and she feared she'd lost her bearings.

Her groping fingers found the wooden door frame, and she sobbed in relief. Still crawling, she reached the landing, then stood. Her throat was raw and she swayed dangerously. With trembling hands, she braced herself against the rock wall.

Anya heard the storm raging outside. At the moment, the crashing thunder represented a beckoning freedom from the terror that engulfed her. But before she could descend into the storm-tossed night, there was a sudden jerk against her skirts.

No...

"There's no escape, Anya."

She resisted the traitorous pull of her skirts as Boyd used them to reel her to him. A heavy hand fell upon her shoulder. She screamed.

"No one will hear you," he rasped, his voice shallow and breathless. "It's time to die...."

She dove at his face with her nails. Boyd's growl of pain roared through the stone stairwell. The rest of their struggle took place in silence. Suddenly, she felt him lift her. She clung to him, her feet dangling over the nothingness of the stairway below. A sickening sensation of helplessness raced through her.

Her only thought was to keep herself from plummeting down the treacherous stone steps to her death. His hands gripped her shoulders and he peeled her away as if she were a loathsome leech. Then he shoved her from him. Frantically, she twisted to the side, falling hard against the upper landing and perilously close to the edge of the first step.

Afraid to move, she lay still. Her heart hammered in her ears, as did Boyd's gasping breaths. Feeling bruised and battered, she tried to inch back from the stairs and the drop below. Boyd towered above her. She could see nothing save the shadowed shape of him as he moved slowly toward her.

She choked back the sobs that threatened to render her helpless and struggled to rise. She had two choices—to return to the chamber, or to try and make it down the stairs. Neither offered a likely prospect of survival, but the cham-

ber had no other exit. The staircase did. Before the thought
was formed, she tried to dart past him.

She made it to the second step before hard fingers closed
about her shoulder and spun her around sharply. She cried
out in despair. Was there to be no end to the nightmare?
With the last bit of strength she possessed, she kicked at
him.

"Damn you," she wept, knowing there was no hope of
rescue. No one knew she had come to the chamber. She was
on her own to save herself, and it appeared she was woe-
fully unprepared for the task.

Boyd jerked her back so viciously her head snapped. She
wondered if he'd already succeeded in breaking her neck.
"Damn you, bitch."

She strained against him. "Help me.... Somebody help
me...."

Anya knew her pleas were useless, but something welled
up inside her and demanded she call out. Perhaps she was
calling to the Almighty himself to intervene on her behalf.
Dazed, all but paralyzed with terror, she was little more than
a quivering animal, panting out the last moments of her life.

"I'll help you," Boyd snarled, his hands converging on
her throat. "All the way to purgatory."

"Anya!"

Dimly, she thought she heard her name being shouted
above the rumble of thunder. Anya's breath caught in her
burning throat. Morgan? Surely, it was only the wind and
her terror causing her to imagine she heard him.

Boyd's fingers tightened their death grip. "It's almost
over, Anya."

"Anya!"

Morgan's voice—and it *was* Morgan's—grew louder.

"Morgan..." His name was little more than a gurgle.
Somewhere she found the strength to raise her hands and
again use her nails to score Boyd's face.

He yelped but didn't release her. Still, for a precious moment, sweet dank air rushed into her lungs. "Morgan..."

To her own ears, the cry sounded despairingly faint. Morgan would never hear her above the wind and the thunder. Anya tried to claw at Boyd's face again, but he held her back, addressing himself to the grisly accomplishment of her murder. She felt her windpipe being sealed off.

A terrifying darkness gathered at the edges of her mind. Her lungs clamored for another sweet breath of air while her arms and hands lost their strength and hung uselessly at her sides. Death, close and unmerciful, opened its jaws.

She would never see Morgan again.

She would never know if he would have grown to love her.

She would never see Texas....

She found herself falling, tumbling into a dark, cold void. Once there, the pain ceased. She was in the smuggler's cave.... From a distance, she saw a light at the far end of it. Someone called her name.

George? A long-ago memory surfaced. She recognized the voice as her brother's. Smiling, she drifted toward the light, toward a cushioning warmth and sense of profound peacefulness. She understood now. Morgan would find someone else to love.... It was over. She began moving faster through the cave. The light grew brighter, more beckoning. She was almost there, where George waited. She knew it. She was no longer afraid.

"Anya! Damn you, don't you dare die."

The words lashed at her, stopping her flight with jarring abruptness. For a timeless moment, she was poised between the darkness and the light.

Anya, go back.... Again, she was certain she heard George's voice. Instinctively, she tried to bridge the final distance that separated them.

"Anya, breathe...."

It's not your time....

"Oh, God, don't let her die. Don't let her die...."

She couldn't move. Not forward. Not backward. Then, suddenly, it was as if she were a cork being popped from a bottle. With dizzying speed, she was pulled back through the

cave, away from the light. A force greater than any she'd
known swept her into a thickening blackness.

She coughed. Pain snatched at her, making her raw throat
burn and her entire body ache. Had she been trampled by a
team of horses, she could not have felt worse.

"Anya . . ."

She opened her eyes and found herself cradled against a
broad, unyielding chest. As if she were a small child, she felt
herself being rocked slowly.

"Morgan?"

He stilled. In the darkness, his features remained invisible, yet she sensed a rock-hard tension thrumming through
him. She had only a moment to accustom herself to that
tension before he swept her into his arms and stood.

A wave of dizziness rushed through her. "Boyd . . ."

She spoke his name as both a question and a warning.
What had happened to her attacker?

Morgan let her slide against him, still supporting her with
one strong arm. "The man who assaulted you?"

She nodded weakly.

"He's at the bottom of the stairs."

Morbidly, her eyes were drawn downward from the landing where she and Morgan stood. Because the narrow staircase curved, she could see nothing. "Is he . . . dead?"

"No, Anya. I'm not dead. Nor do I intend to be."

In horror, she watched Boyd step into view and point a
pistol at her and Morgan.

Morgan shifted subtly, exposing himself more fully to the
drawn weapon, while easing her behind him. "Whatever
you planned, it's not going to work. Why don't you—"

"Skulk away? Like a cur with its tail between its legs?"
Boyd sneered. "I've come too far and worked too hard to
give up now."

"Who are you?" Morgan inquired almost conversation-
ally.

Even as Anya marveled at his control, she tried to move
so that each of them shared an equal portion of exposure to
the pistol Boyd held. Morgan's arm tightened, and she

found herself pinned to his side, unable to move. Not once did he take his gaze from the man holding the gun.

"Boyd Williams, at your service. Merrawynn's future husband."

"Don't listen to him, Morgan," Anya said quickly. "Merrawynn has no part in this."

"Not directly," Boyd admitted. "There's no need for her to know the precise chain of events leading to our union." He raised the pistol's barrel. "Now which of you wishes to die first? It makes no difference to me."

"You're a fiend," Anya said, swallowing back a sob.

"No, I'm just determined to have what I've worked a lifetime to achieve. I have no desire to hurt anyone. Believe me, if there were a way to let you live, I would. I'm not a bad man."

Suddenly, without warning, Morgan shoved her roughly to the floor. His body crashed down upon hers. An explosion rocked the stairway.

Chapter Seventeen

The silence was more deafening than the explosion had been. With Morgan's unyielding body stretched across her, Anya lay motionless, waiting for a cry of pain from a wounded Morgan, or for another burst of gunfire. The waiting continued, until she thought she'd go mad with the uncertainty of not knowing what had happened.

"Morgan?" Her voice was a scant whisper.

"I'm all right." He eased his weight from her. "Are you?"

"Yes..." She sat up. "What—"

"I really had no choice, did I?"

At the sound of Merrawynn's low-voiced question, Anya and Morgan looked down the staircase. Below them stood Merrawynn, her eyes wide with shock. She held a pistol.

Morgan rose quickly and descended the stairs. "You're right, Merrawynn, you had no choice."

Gently, he pried the gun from Merrawynn's shaking fingers. Then he bent over Boyd's lifeless body. Numbly, Anya joined her sister. Without realizing quite how it happened, Anya was embracing the quietly sobbing Merrawynn.

She stared over her sister's bowed head. "Is he..."

Morgan straightened. Fired at point-blank range, the bullet from Merrawynn's gun had entered Boyd's back and then ripped a hole the size of a fist when it had exited his chest. "He's dead," Morgan pronounced grimly.

"He deserved to die," Anya said, tightening her arms about her weeping sister.

Morgan examined the gun he'd taken from Merrawynn. It was his Remington. He looked at Anya's sister with grudging respect. It took guts to shoot a man up close. "Let's get out of here."

Anya and Morgan left the tower, supporting Merrawynn between them. Lightning lashed out, filling the night with silvery shafts of momentary brightness. Thunder followed. Anya remembered when she'd first met Morgan. Then, he'd been a menacing stranger. Tonight he'd been her savior— along with Merrawynn.

Anya looked at Morgan's grimly cast features. "It's over, isn't it? We're finally safe."

He reached around her sister and squeezed Anya's shoulder. "Yes, honey. We're finally safe."

Only absently was Anya aware of the turns she and Morgan made as they progressed through the manor's back corridors. She had no idea how much time passed before he came to a sudden halt.

"Damn, I'll never find my way through this maze."

Anya stumbled to a stop and glanced around. "We're headed in the right direction. I'm amazed you found your way to me in the first place."

"When I returned and couldn't find you, Merrawynn gave me directions to the tower. She said I'd probably find you there. I can't count the number of wrong turns I took." He looked down at her sister. "I guess Merrawynn sensed something was wrong and followed me."

Merrawynn raised her head. "It was the strangest thing. I went to Morgan's room so that when he returned from the tower we could talk, and saw the pistol and... It was almost as if I heard a voice telling me you needed help."

"I'm glad you listened," Anya said, looking around the dimly lit hall and shivering. "You saved our lives."

They resumed walking and soon reached the main house. Animated voices came from the drawing room.

"I suppose we should inform Edward that there's a dead man in the tower," Merrawynn said tiredly.

"I suppose we must," Anya agreed.

They stepped into the room, where Edward appeared to be in the middle of one of his hunting stories. Eunice and Lady Hester looked toward the doorway as if hoping for an interruption.

"What on earth happened to you?" Eunice asked, taking in the trio's disarray.

"It's a long story," Morgan answered as they assisted Merrawynn to a sofa.

"We were attacked in the tower," Anya explained, sitting next to her sister and patting her hand. "Merrawynn saved our lives."

"Attacked?"

"Was anyone hurt?"

"*Merrawynn* saved you?" The last question was from Edward. He shook his head in disbelief. "I'd better send for the constable."

Morgan knelt before the settee, his attention focused exclusively upon Anya. "If you're going to send for anyone, make it a doctor for Anya. Edward, fetch her a brandy."

"Sherry would be better," Lady Hester pronounced.

"Brandy," Morgan repeated, his voice gruff.

"I'm fine," Anya protested. "It's Merrawynn who needs—"

Morgan held the glass of brandy in front of Anya. "You almost died tonight. Drink the damned brandy."

Merrawynn nodded. "He's right, Anya. You're the one who needs attention."

Shaking her head, Anya accepted the proffered glass. Indelibly etched in her memory was the fateful night she and Morgan had met. In Richard's library, he had resorted to brandy as a remedy for her chills. Over the rim of the wide glass, her gaze locked with his. Did he, too, remember?

"Drink up, Anya," he instructed huskily.

Recalling her last experience with the strong beverage, she tipped back the glass and drank its contents in one prolonged gulp. No medicine had ever tasted so vile. She shuddered. "I'll never become accustomed to it."

"Well, I should hope not," Lady Hester said.

"Quite so," Edward concurred.

"You develop a taste for it," Merrawynn mused.

"Forget the brandy," Eunice snapped impatiently. "Tell us what happened in the tower."

Edward moved to the ancient swords crossed above the fireplace. "If there's a madman loose on the estate, we need to protect ourselves."

At the thought of her brother wielding such a weapon, Anya felt an incipient threat of hysteria and pressed a hand to her mouth.

"He's dead," Merrawynn said softly. "I killed him with Morgan's gun.

A pool of shocked silence descended upon the room.

Anya looked into Morgan's watchful gaze. Her throat stung and she ached through and through, but she was alive. She knew now what she had to do. Tears welled and she brushed them back. She had survived the worst of it. She wouldn't break down now.

"Both Anya and Merrawynn need hot baths and changes of clothing," Lady Hester, ever practical, said briskly.

At once, Eunice and Lady Hester moved to assist them. Morgan and Edward stood back from the cluster of women.

Anya looked at Morgan and caught his unguarded expression of irritation. In that moment it became obvious to her that he considered her his responsibility. Reluctantly, Anya remembered the truth she'd accepted when she'd hovered between this life and the next—that without her holding him back, Morgan would be free to fall in love with a woman of his choosing.

"Don't glower, Morgan," Lady Hester admonished. "Soon enough Anya will be your wife and there will be none to interfere."

Anya flushed, then pushed herself from the settee. "Actually, there isn't going to be a wedding."

Her statement created a greater stretch of silence than Merrawynn's announcement had.

"What?"

"You're overwrought."

"Surely, you don't mean that."

"Oh, but I do," Anya said firmly, forcing herself to meet Morgan's enigmatic stare. From his remote expression, it was impossible to determine his thoughts. Nor did he say anything to reveal his feelings.

Anya felt as if she'd tweaked a dragon's tail. On wobbly legs, she crossed the room, then paused at the doorway and looked over her shoulder. "Good night."

In a single group, the other women rose and surged toward Anya, chatting noisily about nothing at all, leaving Edward and Morgan alone in the drawing room. No doubt they had manly tasks to attend to, like disposing of the body in the tower.

Merrawynn's arm came about Anya's shoulders. "Are you cold?"

Colder than I've ever been before, Anya thought, taking comfort from the contact with her sister. "I'm just tired and sore."

In her chamber a short time later, Anya still shivered. The bath had felt wonderful. So did the fresh nightgown she wore. But despite the heavy weight of the blankets that covered her, she didn't think she'd ever be warm again. She found it impossible to hold back her tears.

Why was it so hard to do the right thing? Marrying Morgan would have been so easy. But if she had done so, she would be denying him the opportunity to share his life with a woman he could truly love. And Anya was convinced Morgan had a great capacity to love, surely as great as his capacity for honor and duty.

Duty... How she despised that hateful word.

The indecipherable look on Morgan's face when she'd rejected him troubled her. What had he felt? Had he *felt* anything?

She brushed away more tears. Other than knowing she had done the right thing, being noble carried no reward. As she reflected upon the scene in the drawing room, it seemed to Anya that Morgan hadn't been particularly disturbed that they would not be marrying. One scowl. Was that as shallow as his feelings for her had been? One piddling, insignificant drawing together of his dark eyebrows... Actually, it hadn't been truly a scowl, only a frown.

She turned on her side and groaned. Battling Boyd had exacted a heavy toll. It was the invisible aches, however, that claimed the major portion of her thoughts. What was she going to do now? Being a governess no longer held any appeal. Even though she liked children, she decided she didn't possess the even temperament required for such a position.

New tears threatened. Perhaps she shouldn't have fought off Boyd so energetically. Without Morgan, there really seemed little point in living. As that cravenly thought registered, Anya stiffened. What a cowardly sentiment—to prefer death to life. She sat up and pushed back the blankets. She was made of sterner stuff than that!

Anya pulled on the wrap that lay across the foot of the bed. These last few weeks with Morgan in her life had taught her enough about herself to realize she was no coward. Determinedly, she shoved on a pair of slippers. She needed to speak with her former fiancé.

The house was silent. She padded quietly down the hall to his chamber. Since it was likely he would return to America tomorrow, she wanted one last conversation with him. It was important he understand why she was refusing to wed him.

She paused, wondering precisely what she would say to him. Sighing, she continued on her way. The words would come as needed. The important thing was that they converse openly about their feelings. Perhaps she needed to hear from his own lips that he would never love her and that she had made the correct decision. Whatever force drew her along the darkened corridor to his room, Anya knew she was doing the right thing in listening to it.

Outside Morgan's closed door, she paused again. With trembling hands, she secured the wrap's sash, then knocked tentatively.

The door opened. A shirtless Morgan towered above her. She swallowed a startled gasp and tried not to stare at his powerful male chest. The task proved beyond her as her gaze was drawn irresistibly to the thick, dark mat of hair covering his upper torso. She licked her suddenly dry lips.

"Hello, Anya."

His voice was low and husky. She shivered and fought valiantly against the mad impulse to throw herself into his arms and beg him to love her. To compensate for her deplorable spinelessness, Anya squared her shoulders. She would never beg.

"Hello, Morgan."

"You shouldn't be here," he said neutrally.

She didn't know what she'd expected from him. Disappointment, perhaps, or even anger. Unprepared for the controlled calm of Morgan's mood, she felt her face grow hot. It hurt that breaking off their marriage left Morgan seemingly unshaken while she was virtually unhinged—which only proved she'd made the right decision, she supposed. That knowledge offered precious little comfort, however.

"I ... We need to talk."

"After the harrowing experience you had tonight, you need to rest," he countered softly.

"I—I wanted to explain," she persisted.

His eyebrows rose. "Explain?"

"About why I can't marry you," she elaborated.

He astonished her by smiling. "We can have this conversation tomorrow, after you've had a good night's sleep."

She studied him dubiously. "You're being very understanding."

"I haven't had a lot of experience with overwrought women, but I'm trying to adapt."

Her eyes narrowed. She couldn't have heard him correctly. "Overwrought?"

He nodded. "A man tried to kill you tonight, and you're still reeling from the aftermath."

Anya sighed in exasperation. "That isn't it at all."

Morgan's smile was so understanding she wanted to weep. He took her arm. "The hall is no place for this discussion. Come inside and we'll . . . talk."

Beyond his naked shoulder, the bedchamber loomed, darkly beckoning. Her gaze dropped to the lean fingers wrapped around her arm. She blinked, then glanced down the hallway. "Perhaps it *would* be best if we had this conversation in your chamber."

He stepped aside and opened the door wider. "Come in, Anya."

She took three steps into his room and heard the door shut behind her. The back of her neck tingled, as did the tips of her breasts. She drew another shaky breath and turned.

He leaned against the door. The firelight from the hearth provided the room's only illumination. Clearly, he had been about to go to bed. He wore his peculiar, roughly textured blue trousers. The top metal button was not secured. Dark hair peaked provocatively from the unfastened closure. She brushed her hand across her forehead.

"Anya?"

"Yes?"

"Would you like a drink?"

His casual posture didn't change. Yet he had seemingly drawn closer. His face remained in the shadows, and she would have given anything to be able to read his expression.

"You keep spirits in your room?"

"It's more convenient that way," he answered, easing from his relaxed position. "When I was in London, I found some good Irish whiskey. Have you ever drunk it?"

"Not that I remember."

He stepped toward a valise next to the bed. "You would recall the experience."

The bottle he withdrew from the bag was almost full. He removed the cork and raised the bottle to his lips. The gesture seemed inordinately primitive. The fine hairs on the nape of her neck raised. Something about Morgan's controlled politeness alerted her to the fact that he wasn't as relaxed as he appeared.

"Here, try it." He thrust the container of whiskey toward her. When she failed to accept it, his features tightened subtly. "I suppose a fine lady like you wouldn't want to drink without a glass—is that the problem?"

"I—I'm not thirsty."

"I am," he returned quietly. "I'm burning up with thirst."

"I don't require anything, Morgan."

"That's right, you're here only to tell me why you won't marry me, aren't you?"

She nodded mutely.

"I'm waiting with bated breath, Anya."

"It's because of you," she answered simply.

His eyes glowed with unnatural heat. "That's direct enough."

"It's just that I've thought over everything very carefully, and I realize that, under the circumstances, it wouldn't be fair for me to marry you."

"Would you care to enlighten me about these circumstances?" In the stillness of the room his voice was a mere murmur.

Reluctant to bare her feelings, she fidgeted. She'd already told him once that she loved him. His silence following that declaration had been most telling. She would like to leave herself a remnant of pride with which to clothe herself when she left his chamber. "Being a man, I'm not certain you would understand."

Muttering, he set the bottle of whiskey aside. "My patience is running thin, Anya. Since I *am* a man, and not inclined to regret the fact, I'd appreciate your telling me what the hell is going on in that beautiful head of yours."

Tears stung her eyes and she raised her palm to cut off his meaningless compliment. "Please don't."

"Don't?" His voice roughened and he moved closer. "Don't what? Don't call you beautiful? Don't refuse to leave your life without an argument? Don't...touch you?"

He raised his hand slowly and brushed his knuckles against her cheek. Her knees weakened, but she met his stare head-on. "Yes...I mean, no."

He leaned toward her. "I'm waiting."

She knew now that seeking out his company had been a grievous mistake. Why hadn't she thought twice before barging into his chamber? Abruptly, it occurred to her that Morgan was not an easy man to banish from one's life. "If...if you laugh, I shall never forgive you."

With his forefinger, he raised her chin. "Trust me, laughing is the last thing I'm likely to do."

"I won't marry you because...because it would be unfair to you."

"'Under the circumstances,'" he mocked softly.

"You don't...love me." It was a stark whisper, torn from the depths of her.

The silence between them deepened so profoundly that her ears rang with the weight of it. Beneath his dark eyebrows, his eyes narrowed. "But you do love me—at least you've told me so."

At his cruel jab, she went numb inside. "Yes. I said that."

His lips touched hers lightly. She swayed toward him. "When I left for London, you bid me as loving and tender a farewell as any man has ever received. I carried the memory of it all the way there and back."

"Oh..."

His hand cupped her elbow. "Come sit with me, Anya, and we'll have our...talk."

Uneasily, she eyed the bed to which he led her. "I really don't think—"

"Humor me. I'm trying my hand at being...sympathetic. It doesn't seem to come naturally to me."

"But—but—"

"Sit with me," he urged huskily.

Feeling self-conscious and wondering how on earth she'd come to be sitting upon Morgan's bed with him, Anya drew her wrap more closely about her. When he sat beside her, the mattress dipped significantly. She slid inexorably closer to him.

Since their confrontation with Boyd Williams, Morgan had bathed. Anya's gaze drifted to his stern profile. For the first time, she noticed a faint sheen of moisture covering his dark hair. He had even shaved. Devoid of its earlier stubble, his square jaw seemed oddly beckoning. She sighed and folded her hands in her lap. No, Morgan was not easily banished—not from her thoughts or from her heart.

She moistened her lips and sat stiffly so she wouldn't roll closer to him. "I wanted to make certain you understood why there would be no wedding."

An emotion she couldn't put a name to flickered briefly in his dark eyes before his expression became shuttered.

"As a matter of fact, I am curious about your change of heart."

"It has nothing to do with me being overwrought," she hastened to explain.

"No?"

"No," she repeated emphatically.

He brushed her hair back from her face. His hand stilled. "The bastard bruised your throat."

Anya heard the suppressed violence in Morgan's tone and shuddered. She knew that if Merrawynn had not killed Boyd Williams, Morgan would have. "The bruises will fade."

"Have I ever told you what beautiful hair you have?"

Morgan's voice cracked, and Anya sensed the Herculean effort it took for him to speak calmly.

She shook her head. "I don't believe so."

"So thick, so silky," he continued, gathering her waist-length hair into both hands. "Hair as soft and luxurious as yours fills a man's head with ideas."

"What—" She cleared her throat. "What kind of ideas?"

He looked deeply into her eyes. Her heart began to pound.

"Bedchamber ideas..." He pressed his face into the dark mass, inhaled, then looked up. "I love the way you smell. Like lavender."

"It's the soap I use. It—"

"...Reminds me of an English garden, all neatly laid out with delicate flowers and fragrances to tempt the senses."

"Indeed?" Her voice startled her by wobbling.

"Indeed," he concurred, letting her hair slip through his fingertips. "You remind me of a garden, Anya."

"I—I do?"

"Um-hmm..." He bent forward and brushed his lips against her cheek.

She shivered, bracing herself against his chest with one hand so she wouldn't tip forward. As it was, she was practically on his lap.

His gaze dropped to the hand anchoring her. He smiled. "You're not nervous, are you?"

She stared at the splayed fingers that pressed against the dark hair swirling across his broad chest. "Why, no, of course not. It's just that I came here to explain why I can't—"

"Good," he interrupted. "There's no reason for you to be nervous. In fact..." His fingers trailed across the satin lapel of her wrap. "I want you to relax. After everything we've been through, you know you can trust me, don't you?"

Did she trust him? "Well, now that you mention it, I—"

"I trust you, Anya."

Her thoughts splintered into nothingness. Suddenly she was fiercely conscious of the night closing in about them, aware of the uneven rhythm of Morgan's breathing, aware of the steady throb of his heartbeat beneath her fingers.

His head lowered and his mouth touched the corner of hers. She sat utterly still.

"You're so quiet. . . ." He shifted his position and leaned over her. His lips claimed hers, exerting sufficient pressure to push her back, back. . . . The mattress cushioned her descent. Somehow her hands came to rest upon his shoulders.

As natural as a sparrow taking to the sky, their kiss took flight. Anya sighed and opened her mouth to the sweet invasion of his tongue. Beneath her fingertips, Morgan's skin burned as if he were on fire.

On fire . . . That was how she felt. A slumberous, melting kind of fire that seeped into all the forbidden places of her body. She felt his hands tugging at the flimsy wrap and it parted before him. In the next few moments both it and her sleeping gown disappeared.

It was so strange. She knew she was naked, of course. She knew Morgan was removing his trousers. She knew that soon no barrier would exist between her flesh and his. Yet that knowledge rang no warning bells.

"Oh, Morgan."

"Such pretty breasts. . ." A callused fingertip stroked her. "Such pretty nipples . . ." The tip of his tongue tasted her. "You are a garden."

His hand ranged lower. She shifted beneath him. "What are you doing to me?"

"Everything." With heavy-lidded eyes, he caressed her. "Everything a man does to the woman he loves."

Not certain she'd heard him correctly, Anya tensed.

He continued to stroke her, his gaze locked upon hers. "I can't believe you didn't know. But if you need the words, you can have them, Anya. I love you, and I probably have since the night you stood in the driving rain and demanded

I loan you my horse." His gaze grew darker still. "All that I have is yours. You are mine."

His finger slipped inside her. "I want you ready for me."

Her heart pounded so that she thought it might burst from her chest. "If... if we do this thing—"

He smiled. "Rest assured we *are* doing it. Now."

Slowly, with agonizing gentleness, he began to use his hands and mouth together to tantalize her flesh. The blood flowing through her veins heated. Her breath came faster. She shivered and burned and... wanted. The tension inside her heightened until Anya thought she would shatter. His fingertips, damp and gently stroking, caressed the most private part of her. His tongue lathed her nipples. His hot breath rippled across her skin. His murmurs, husky and primitive, went to the very core of her.

She twisted, trying to draw closer to him. It was as if he had become a wild flame sent to thaw the frozen pond she'd been in all the years she'd waited for him. Her hands pulled the flame closer. She wanted him inside her. She sensed that her urgency and soft moans were driving him to the same feverish heights that drew her.

She opened her thighs to him. Never had she felt so vulnerable. Never had she felt so connected to her own body. She stared into Morgan's face. Intense concentration stamped his features. He was both stranger and lover, both the source of her agony and her deliverance. She clung to him, instinctively arching her hips. The pain of wanting had become almost unbearable. No matter what the future held, in this moment she would die without Morgan.

"Oh, Anya..." He began to enter her slowly. "I've waited forever for this."

"Forever..."

The blunt pressure of his penetration paused momentarily. He stared deeply into her eyes. "Forget the pain, darling. But remember always, I love you."

He completed their union swiftly, in one full stroke that sealed them completely. She was helpless not to cry out. His gaze still held hers—hot, scalding, possessive....

She anchored her bottom lip between her teeth. Lady Hester had been right. It *was* painful for a man and woman to join. Anya tried to think about dinner menus and failed utterly. She was conscious only of the pain between her legs and Morgan's powerful body locked with her own.

"I love you, Anya...."

She squeezed her eyelids shut, not wanting him to see her tears. "I...I love you, too, Morgan."

"Look at me."

Reluctantly, she raised her gaze.

"Oh, darling, it will get better, I promise you."

She smiled bravely and was proud of herself. It wouldn't do for Morgan to discover how horribly disappointed she was by the whole affair. Somewhere along the line she'd come to expect a bit of magic. There had certainly been magic aplenty in the cottage they'd shared a few nights ago. But tonight there was nothing save—

His lips closed around her nipple. A shimmering ripple quivered in her loins. She sucked in her breath. He drew back and she wanted to protest the separation. She liked his mouth on her—

His fingers explored the juncture of her thighs with his rigid length still embedded inside her. Amazingly, that touch caused her breasts to tighten and burn while another current of tingling pleasure swept through her. Slowly, rhythmically, he continued to rub her. Beneath the delightful friction, she twisted, straining.

From their time together in the cottage, Anya knew there was more than the building, endless yearning gathering within her. His mouth came down upon hers and he used his shaft to stroke her deeply.... The memory of pain blurred and she became aware only of the pleasure—an incandescent kind of pleasure that made the particles of her body tighten as if in preparation for a springing leap.

Faster... She moved against Morgan in a frenzied burst of desperation. Somewhere she knew the release awaited....

It happened suddenly, without warning. A kind of shattering storm that swept her up into its swirling vortex. Like before...but different. Better... She clung to Morgan as he rode out the last of the tumult.

She hadn't realized her eyes had been closed until she opened them and saw Morgan's glittering gaze.

"You're mine, Anya. I'm never going to let you go."

His words thrilled her. She comprehended that, without their love for each other, the intimate act they'd just shared would have been meaningless.

"That is fortunate, Morgan."

He tipped his head. "Fortunate?"

Anya smiled softly and brushed her fingertips through his hair. "Now that you've confessed your love for me, Morgan Grayson, I have no intention of letting you return to America without me."

"You'll like Texas, darling. I'll see to it."

The determination in his voice touched her. "You make it sound as if you'll change things if I don't approve."

"I will."

Her smile widened. "I daresay that would be a challenge, even for a brash and cocky American."

A grin swept his features. "I daresay you're right." He rocked against her and she felt the swelling hardness of his renewed desire. "But, honey, as an adopted Texan, I feel more than up to the challenge."

Anya's arms gathered about his neck and she pulled him closer. Their kiss was long and deep. Then Morgan began to move inside her again. She smiled to herself. It was clear that she would never be able to plan her dinner menus during these wondrous moments with Morgan. When he held her in his arms, there would be only him.

Only him...

"I love you, Anya."

Misty-eyed, she lost herself to the pounding cadence of his fierce ardor.

Later, feeling both substantially depleted and strangely invigorated, she rested her cheek against the beating rhythm of his heart. Lazily, she trailed her fingertips across the dark hair matting his chest. She decided that belonging to Morgan Grayson was a bit like having a dragon on a leash, though she supposed he would never truly be bound by any tether. He was much too stubborn and independent. Anya sighed. A man like Morgan probably wouldn't spend much time speaking tender words. And surely a sensible woman such as herself had no need of such endearments.

Yet, when he'd told her that he loved her...

She sighed again.

"Anya?"

"Hmm?"

"I've got something for you."

She rubbed her cheek against his chest. "So soon?"

He chuckled. "Think lofty thoughts, dear heart."

Dear heart... Now that rang with a certain degree of tenderness, did it not?

"I bought it for you in London," he said, slipping from the bed.

She sat up and held the blanket to her. At the sight of Morgan padding magnificently naked across the bedchamber, Anya brushed the hair from her eyes. Would she ever tire of looking at him?

He removed something wrapped in tissues from the valise and returned to bed. "I saw it in a London shop window and knew you were meant to have it."

Curious, Anya began peeling away the folds of paper. The glass figure she uncovered brought an immediate lump to her throat. It was a porcelain of a young lad holding a green frog. Too moved by Morgan's thoughtfulness to speak, she simply stared at the figure through a growing blur of tears.

"I hoped you would like it...." His words trailed off.

She brought the small statue to her chest. "Oh, Morgan."

Her gaze jerked to his and she was startled to realize that Morgan Grayson was unsure of himself. She smiled secretly. A dragon with sensibilities . . .

"I love your gift, darling. I love your thoughtfulness. I love . . . you."

Her words seemed to loosen Morgan from his unnatural stillness. His arms came around her. "Damned straight you do, and today you're going to marry me."

She shook her head. "You mean tomorrow."

"I mean today, woman. The sun is up." His lips brushed her throat. "And so am I."

The statue was wedged between them. "Morgan, if you're serious about us being wed today, then—"

"I am," he said with a low growl.

"We should start getting ready."

His arms relaxed their hold and Anya scooted away, pushing back the bed covers and slipping from the bed.

"Then let's be quick about it."

Shaking the hair from her face, she placed the figure he'd given her on the table. "Morgan—"

Before she could finish her statement, he was out of bed with his arms around her. "Damn, you have a beautiful body."

Her skin flamed. How could she have forgotten her nudity? "Th-thank you."

The contact of his hair-roughened flesh brushing against her produced a satisfying series of tremors that diverted her embarrassment. She allowed herself to be turned into his embrace. Standing in the middle of the bedchamber without a stitch of clothing while being held by a nude male . . . Somehow none of it seemed quite real.

Morgan smiled down at her. "Such a mannerly maiden."

"Mannerly, perhaps," she said dryly. "But maiden no more."

"When you came into my room last night, it was a fore
gone conclusion we would make love, Anya."

"Was it?"

He nodded. "I wanted you in the worst way."

"Yet you didn't protest my calling off the wedding."

"I told you I was being considerate."

She smiled. "Is that what you call it?"

"Yep."

"Yep? I surmise that means—"

"Yes."

"Shall I be hearing that a lot in Texas?"

He drew her boldly against him. "Depends on how you
play your cards, honey."

She stood on tiptoe and put her arms around his neck.
"You should know I *never* bluff, and I have no intention of
folding."

His lips held a familiar smile as his head lowered. "Then
I'd say we're in for a long game...."

* * * * *

◈ Harlequin®

JANELLE TAYLOR

Valley of Fire

HARLEQUIN IS PROUD TO PRESENT *VALLEY OF FIRE* **BY JANELLE TAYLOR—AUTHOR OF TWENTY-TWO BOOKS, INCLUDING SIX** *NEW YORK TIMES* **BESTSELLERS**

VALLEY OF FIRE—the warm and passionate story of Kathy Alexander, a famous romance author, and Steven Winngate, entrepreneur and owner of the magazine that intended to expose the real Kathy "Brandy" Alexander to her fans.

Don't miss VALLEY OF FIRE, available in May.

Following the success of WITH THIS RING, Harlequin cordially invites you to enjoy the romance of the wedding season with

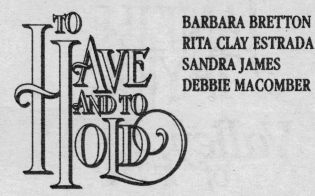

BARBARA BRETTON
RITA CLAY ESTRADA
SANDRA JAMES
DEBBIE MACOMBER

A collection of romantic stories that celebrate the joy, excitement, and mishaps of planning that special day by these four award-winning Harlequin authors.

Available in April at your favorite Harlequin retail outlets.